DIFFERENT DESERTS, SAME STARS

DIFFERENT DESERTS, SAME STARS

A Persian Gulf War Adventure

JAKE JOYCE

All attempts have been made to retain historic verisimilitude in this work of military fiction. Because of the short time frame of the Desert Storm conflict (100 hours instead of several years), in this story the Highway of Death section was moved up out of actual time sequence for dramatic effect. It is the sincere hope of the author that this will not put off the historically astute reader.

This novel is a work of fiction. All names, characters, places, and incidents are the product of the author's imagination, or if real are used fictitiously. Any similarity to persons living or dead is coincidental and was not intended by the author.

Print ISBN: 978-0-9983058-4-4
E-Book ISBN: 978-0-9908419-4-4

Published and printed in the United States of America by the Write Place, Inc.
For more information, please contact:

the Write Place, Inc.
809 W. 8th Street, Suite 2
Pella, Iowa 50219
www.thewriteplace.biz

Cover and interior design by Michelle Stam, the Write Place, Inc.
Cover artwork by Wendy Joyce.

Copies of this book may be ordered online at Amazon and BarnesandNoble.com.

View other Write Place titles at www.thewriteplace.biz.

CONTENTS

ACKNOWLEDGMENTS

The author would like to thank Wendy Joyce and John (Tiny) McTaggert for the cover art, Nikki Belcher for her typing skills, Frank Kresen for proofreading the draft, Don Flowers for editing the work, Joe Cothern for his advice on military aviation, Dewayne Knott for his contribution to the burning oil well sections, and Hannah Crawford for the final proofreading and preparation for the publication of this work. It would have been possible to create this work without their help, but the book would not be nearly as good as it is. All of your help is greatly appreciated.

Chapter 1

DESERT SUNRISE

A pair of bronze, weathered hands twisted a handful of dried grass into a little tawny knot and tossed it atop the seemingly lifeless ashes of last evening's campfire. The sun's first light glowed behind a distant hill, standing in front of a charcoal-black horizon. Another day was struggling to begin in the New Mexican desert. Bright stars still twinkled in the clear sky of the moonless night. It was very quiet; even the birds were not yet singing. The coyotes howled good morning to each other in the distance to see who was still alive after another evening of canine mischief.

The old Indian kneeled down and blew his breath, until, as if by magic, the dried grass knot burst into a tiny golden flame. The gnarled old fingers then began to carefully place small kindling sticks over the growing flames, which soon began to consume the bone-dry desert wood. Gray wisps of smoke rose upward toward the night sky that was about to give its place to the day. Next, larger sticks of firewood, broken and stacked the night before, were gently set on the glowing campfire.

As the hungry flames grew and began to consume the fuel, the wood crackled and sputtered while beginning to light the early-morning darkness in the roofless stone shelter. The young man lying on the other side of the fire began to awaken.

Something is wrong, he thought. *It is not like Grandfather to be up so early before the morning sun.*

"Grandfather, is everything all right?" he asked sleepily in their south-western native language, known by few but spoken by them. All was quiet except the hissing and popping of the fire. "Is it your heart?" he inquired of his grandfather with a note of urgency in his voice.

"My heart is troubled, but it will not require a visit to the Outsiders' medicine house," he answered truthfully in their ancient tongue.

The grandson curled up in his woolen blanket and listened intently to his grandfather. He waited with anticipation as Grandfather put more wood on the fire and poured water from an earthenware jar into his favorite old cooking pot. While waiting for the fire to burn down into a bed of hot coals upon which to make breakfast, the old man spoke again.

"I could not sleep because I had a terrible dream about you. You were a soldier in the Outsiders' army. You were wearing unfamiliar tan and brown spotted clothing. It was not like the green army clothes you have worn. Enemies surrounded you on a strange battlefield, with sand colored differently than this desert sand. There were flames shooting from holes in the earth. Black smoke blocked the sun and made night out of day. The sand was burning so hot that it was on fire. There were explosions and fires that lit the sky. There were dead and wounded soldiers with strange uniforms everywhere. Some were screaming in anger, and some were crying out for help in a tongue I did not understand. All their words were lost in the roar of the fire. It screamed like a beast in the darkness. I dreamed you were in a place the Outsiders call Hell."

The young man quickly sat up and listened to the father of his father tell him of his visions. He knew Grandfather's dreams were powerful, but he could not possibly know about the military and those kinds of things. He sat in shocked silence for a while and thought about what he had just heard.

"Grandfather, it was only a bad dream. There is no such place as you have described," the young man said reassuringly, but not convincingly. "You are worried about my going into the army, and you had a nightmare." The old one was silent, but no look of relief came over his life-worn face. Then he stated with true, heartfelt concern, "Please, stay here and continue the old ways, as our people have always done. We have lived here longer than anyone can remember. We use the rain, the grass, and the animals of the earth to feed and clothe us."

As they warmed themselves by the fire, the sun rose a little higher on the horizon as it spread a tangerine-colored backdrop across the morning side of the American Southwestern sky. The first birds began to whistle and chirp their morning songs. As he spoke, Grandfather pointed toward the flock of sheep and goats nibbling the dew-laden grasses and herbs on the nearby red sands. They were silhouetted in front of the horizon as the sky slowly mellowed into an iridescent peach color. The reddish-orange and white-striped sandstone mesas in the distance accented the view with their massive presence.

"This is how we have lived for as much of always as we have known. Since the time before our people came here," he added emphatically.

"Grandfather, the way of life of our people is changing. Already there are too many of us to live by the old ways. There are too many animals, too many people, and not enough land left to us by the Outsiders to live as our ancestors did. We must forget the things of the past and learn the things of the future."

The old one again did not speak. After a minute or so of silence he stated slowly, as was his way, to his eighteen-year-old grandson, "Our way is here and in touch with the earth at each moment. It has always been this way. Never forget the things of the past, for they grow into the things of the future." He stirred and poked at the fire with a long, thin stick between phrases. "Last year's seed becomes next year's crop."

Young One, which was his first name translated into English, did not want to argue with the old man, both out of respect for him and because he seldom won. This was his last stay with his grandfather in the herd camp before going off to war.

He listened in silence but was not sure what his grandfather meant about their people coming there. Was it the old legend about how the Indians had walked over the great water far to the north when it was conveniently frozen? The Outsiders believed that barefoot people with their feet frozen and bleeding left the comforts of their home fires to walk more miles than all the known villages combined could count. This had brought a smile of disbelief over the old man's face when his grandson told him that he had heard it at school.

"It was just the Outsiders' craziness," Grandfather would laughingly say. Or did Grandfather mean the old stories of their people coming up from the earth like ants, not descending from the sky, as others believed?

"I do not want to see you in a war party so many days from our home," Grandfather continued, speaking his thoughts.

"It's not a war party. I am in the Army Reserve and have been called up for active duty in the Persian Gulf. I am going to learn about computers and technology. I can bring these things back to help our people."

Grandfather knew his grandson's heart was pure and true to the spirits. But the birth of new ways is often the death of old ones. He threw more sticks on the fire, and the hungry flames eagerly licked at the hissing and popping wood. He was frightened and sad. His grandson, whom he had raised since his parents' death, was going to a horrible place and would not listen to him. The son of his dead son was drawn as the moth to the bright light of the flame by the things of the outside world. Of all the youths in the pueblo, Young One was without question the best. He was strong, generous, and kind. He had a brave heart, but was not foolhardy. His medicine was strong, and he had a gentle warrior's spirit guiding him along the path of his life. Many thoughts ran through Young One's head as his methodical mind processed the words of the father of his father. There was much silence between statements, as had always been their way. Each one carefully thought about what the other had just said, as well as his own next words, which were carefully judged before being tossed upon the weighing scales of the other's measure. Grandfather had planted many seeds of wisdom in the young man's mind, and they would grow or fail, depending upon the seasons of his life.

"I do not want you going into battle so far away." Grandfather did not know where the Persian Gulf was, but he felt it was too far away to fight there. He especially did not want his grandson to fight over the underground wells where the rolling ponies drank. With his ancient foresight, Grandfather knew what was about to happen in the Persian Gulf.

"Today, the young listen to the songs of others. They do not respect the ways that have allowed us to live here since time began. If there is trouble so far away, who will sing the ancient songs for you?"

"The songs are no use in battle today. The army has missiles, tanks, helicopters, bombs, and machine guns that make so much noise the songs will be blocked out," his grandson said almost defiantly. Grandfather said nothing for what seemed a long while. Then he spoke again.

"Nothing that humans can make can block out the songs that come from the heart," he answered, both patiently as well as with some annoyance

7

in his voice. But he saw a look in his grandson's eyes that told him that Young One was unconvinced. Internally, his grandson's attitude quietly outraged him, but he would not allow it to show, for it was not time for action in this matter. Action should come only when the time is correct for such things. Then it should be swift and certain. That had always been their way of doing things. He knew that later that afternoon his grandson would be picked up by his sergeant and taken to a new life on the other side of the world. The wise, old one did not want to have an argument and send his grandson into the Outsiders' war camp with cross words between them. His grandson had misspoken about their beliefs and would now have to live through the words, to see if they were true or not. He would find his own punishment or reward as it will come along the trail to the future he must walk.

"Son of my son," Grandfather said, still speaking in their old Pueblo tongue, "if you have given your word to be in their war party, so be it. You must die before breaking the vow your mouth has spoken. I will give you my counsel." Again, the old one was silent, as if he were recalling something from the past. When he finally spoke, it was with such quiet intensity that it was more frightful than any angry, screaming person could be.

"In the other eyes in my head, I have seen your tomorrows. You will cross the great waters in a smoking sky wagon." His grandson sat in silence and took in every word.

"There will be many warriors from many lands in your camp. Make your people proud," was Grandfather's short message on the subject. He had spoken his words and would say no more. Again, that which is not said is often the more powerful message.

Young One was not sure what Grandfather meant by this strange talk. Did he mean the modern, culturally diverse army, or was this more of his dreams again? But he knew better than to discount the old man's visions. Many times, the old one had foreseen the future, and his dreams had come true. This troubled Young One because Grandfather had a powerful spirit inside of him. "You will start your journey on the path of a warrior when you climb the long, iron steps." Young One did not know what it meant, but he remembered the words.

In silence, Grandfather put an old, dented metal pot full of water on top of a pile of glowing wood coals. Innumerable juniper and cedar wood fires had blackened the outside of the cooking pot. When its water came to a boil, he threw a handful of coarse ground coffee into it. When it had reboiled for a minute, he took it from the fire to allow the coffee to steep. After several minutes, he dropped a quarter of a tin cup of cold water into the brew to cause the grounds to settle. Then they each drank a cup of camp coffee out of old metal cups from the trading post.

They had a breakfast of camp bread wrapped around sticks and baked next to the fire until it was golden brown. It was only flour and water with a sprinkle of earth salt from the sacred dried lake to the south. When the delicious bread was baked, pieces were dipped into melted sheep fat as if it were butter. It was an acquired taste, but one their palates had long ago embraced. It was washed down with several more cups of camp coffee. Grandfather's two dogs each received several large pieces of stick bread dripping with sheep fat. The world was good that morning to the hard-working canines.

>―――×―――>←

After their breakfast and fire talk, they began the long walk back to the pueblo together, with Grandfather's flock of sheep and goats. The dogs kept all the other four-leggers together and moving in the direction that the two-leggers chose. They were going to Grandmother's house on the edge of the main pueblo, and it was several hours' slow walk with the herd. On the way, they talked for much of the time, allowing the herd animals to graze upon choice spots of verdant vegetation. They'd had good rain that year, and the grass was plentiful. After the sheep were put away in their wooden pen, Young One went inside Grandmother's house and spent time with his grandmother and his aunties. Among their people, the women built the houses and inherited them from their mothers. If a woman wished to divorce her husband, she merely threw out his belongings. In cases of acrimonious marital dissolution, the unfortunate husband's belongings would sometimes be burned. If the husband wanted to divorce, he simply took his things and left. Young One remembered hearing a story of an old man who wanted to leave his wife. Each time he left his house, he would wear several sets of clothing, one on top of the other. In no time, he had all his belongings removed from his former home, so his wife could not burn them.

The first time Young One went away from his family was for basic training and advanced individual training in the army. His relatives were sad because the army made him cut his beautiful long, black hair. They screamed and laughed together when they saw him four months later. He looked funny with a short, cropped haircut. He was a handsome young man, with bronzed skin and a fine face. All the time he spent running through the hills with Grandfather and doing chores in the garden had given him a good, youthful physique. His grandmother knew the reservation was growing smaller and that opportunity for the youthful ones was limited. She understood the irony of the fact that he would have to go into the world of others to find himself.

After their midday meal, Grandfather and Young One went outside to tend their waffle gardens in the shade behind their stone and adobe house on the edge of the pueblo. The waffle beds were square holes about three feet across and two feet deep. Each was dug into the hard-packed clay and backfilled with a mixture of manure, sand, and red clay, all mixed up together into a fine planting soil. Grandfather's garden had twelve waffle holes and was considered large. Around each was a small adobe berm that kept in the water when it rained or when it was carried from the nearby stream in earthen jars made by Grandmother.

The gardens got their names because, from a distance, they resembled a large waffle in the earth. Grandfather's plantings were surrounded by a fence made of sticks. They were the ideal way of planting in an area where, in the spring, the fierce west winds would blow away the fine soil. The stick fence served to slow the wind like a snow fence. It also kept stray animals out of the garden. It rained infrequently, but when it did it was often quite violent. Any conventional garden would be washed away or blown away by the harsh, dry winds that were sure to precede them. But these plantings were protected by the stick fence from the wind, and by the adobe berms from being washed away. This manner of gardening had been practiced for thousands of years in the southwest.

Each year, new manure was placed in them to replenish their fertility. In olden times, the herders carried baskets of the precious stuff on their backs for miles to their gardens. Then the horse-drawn wagon replaced foot travel. For Grandfather's garden, the pickup truck was used to bring sheep and goat manure to the gardens from distant pens. When a new house was made and when the young started their own waffle gardens, they would be given fine soil from the parent garden to begin their own. Thus, the garden was never lost, just continued.

Grandfather also had a flock of turkeys that were the descendants of birds left by the Spanish hundreds of years before. They had been in their family ever since. Their manure was added to the waffle gardens to fertilize and condition the soil.

Grandfather grew chilies, as his people had done before there were Mexicans. Along with his chilies, he also grew the three sisters—beans, corn, and squash. He also grew medicinal and ceremonial herbs in his garden. He was a living example of how his tribe had lived for thousands of years. Their house was similar to a simple museum, and it was used by the ceremonial dancers for religious purposes because of its old-style architecture. There was no electricity or telephone affixed to the structure. This old man was admired and praised by many for his adherence to the old ways, yet was silently mocked by others, who had already been made crazy by the Outsiders' ways.

Grandfather did not dislike the Outsiders, but he did not like or understand the notion of corporate ownership or profit or governments. He did not like money and lamented the day his people started using it instead of the time-honored practice of bartering. He also thought it was a bad idea to have pockets in trousers because people did not feel rich without money in them. Grandfather particularly did not like blue jeans.

Some time before, Grandmother bought him a pair from the trading post. After his wife had proudly presented him with these "pants of progress," he caught part of his anatomy in the metal zipper. Young One never saw him wear jeans again. Instead, he wore baggy peon pants of rough-spun yucca plant fibers. In their culture, the men were the weavers and spinners, and he made excellent things from the past, the old way. They resembled tan karate pants. They were extremely durable and protected the legs from the many thorns and spines in the desert. In the summer, he wore sandals woven from tough desert fibers. In the winter, he wore sheepskin boots with homespun woolen leggings that went up to the knee to protect against snow and ice.

His waist was girdled with a woolen sash that served as a belt. He carried a large, homemade sheath knife stuck in his waist sash. He always wore the headband of his clan, so everyone would know which of the people he came from. He dressed very much like his ancestors had for thousands of years. Seeing him was like looking into the past. In addition to weaving, Grandfather would also trade wool from his sheep in the pueblo. The finest wool he kept for himself to weave. His skills with the loom were well known in the pueblo. The herders all had primitive looms out in their camps, and, while the sheep grazed, the men would spin wool into yarn and dye it with boiled berries, leaves, bark, or roots of plants. Then, they would weave the colorful yarn into beautiful and functional woolen items. Each clan of the pueblo had its own design that distinguished their kind from others.

Along with his homespun native footwear, he did wear sneakers from time to time. He had an old pair of canvas flat-bottom sneakers that were popular in the 1960s. He called these his "running moccasins." They were so old they had outlasted the company that made them. They were sewn together with so many shades of tough thread and twine, and had so many leather soles inside to cover the many holes, he could hardly get them on his feet. Grandfather was not so much a purist as he was a practicalist. To see this leathery-faced old Indian man with homespun, loose-fitting clothing, a colored clan headband, and old sneakers was truly an incongruous sight. He also had a large, black cowboy hat that he wore on special occasions.

Grandfather used to laugh with his younger relatives when they would say he had an "Indian three-piece suit," consisting of shirt, pants, and hat. He did not get angry, both because of his general good-natured ways and because he really did not understand the source of their amusement upon translation. Their kidding was good-natured because he was a clan leader with well-known mystical powers. Grandfather told Young One to be careful of those who kid others all the time. He knew that kidding someone was just telling the truth with a smile for a shield.

The conversation in the waffle garden was soon interrupted by a honk of an automobile horn from the dirt road next to his house. Young One looked over the stick fence to see his sergeant from the Reserve Center. "Hurry up, Private. We have two more guys to pick up on the way to the airport."

Young One grabbed his duffel bag, which he set next to the front door after saying his good-byes. Grandmother gave him a lunch of fresh-baked, beehive-oven bread and roasted sheep chunks. Several roasted red chili peppers completed the simple meal. When he and Grandfather parted, Grandfather repeated to Young One, "Your life will change, son of my son, when you climb the great iron steps." His family waved goodbye to their son going off to fight in a war halfway around the earth. They were still waving long after the military vehicle disappeared over the dusty road in the horizon. They all said their prayers for his safe return...

Chapter 2

ON THE WAY TO WAR

The sergeant from the Reserve Center drove Young One on the first leg of his long journey to war. No one was allowed to take their privately owned vehicle to the airport, as long-term parking was not authorized. To eliminate this problem, several sergeants had been tasked with picking up and dropping off the soldiers at the airport in military vehicles.

These troops were not expected to be back soon anyway. They had been called up for a minimum of ninety days active duty. Young One was being called up upon emergency mobilization orders. They would be over there for the duration of hostilities. Everyone knew that their length of active-duty service could be extended with a mere stroke of the pen. They were not going off to training for a weekend or a couple of weeks. They did not know it at the time, but they were going to war, and some of their number would not return. The sergeant's job was also to make sure the privates and specialists got to their flights and were not sidetracked to somewhere else. There is a lot of distraction in the world for young men away from home with money in their pockets.

Young One looked at the landscape as they sped through the desert in an army sedan. The gnarled pinyon pines looked like giant bonsai trees protruding from the red-and-white-striped sandstone cliffs. Along the way, they stopped and picked up two other men. One was a Navajo mechanic, and the other guy was an Anglo radio operator. Young One shared his lunch with the mechanic, but the radio operator would not touch it. Roasted mutton is an acquired taste, but, when wrapped inside homemade bread, it is quite good. A frequent bite of chili pepper added zest to their repast.

Three hours later, they were in the civilian airport at Albuquerque and ready to board a plane to Newark, New Jersey. They were told to ask for the military aid station when they landed, from where they would be taken to the processing center in Fort Dix. The sergeant bid them goodbye and good luck. He waited to leave until their plane took off. He had orders to make sure they were finally gone before starting the long drive back through the desert.

This was not Young One's first flight. He had been on a plane twice before. His first flight was when he went away for his initial boot camp and infantry training. The two months of infantry school that followed made basic training look like a cakewalk. It was boot camp, part two. It was harder and meaner than everybody's basic training. His second plane flight was when he had come back from training only two weeks earlier.

He never imagined he would be called up to action so soon, or that there was even going to be armed conflict. The eighteen-year-old Pueblo Indian loved flying in what Grandfather called a "smoking sky wagon" nonetheless. He felt like he was inside a burning arrow streaking through the sky. The plane was like a shiny silver eagle soaring above the clouds. He had often seen aircraft sailing overhead on his reservation. But now he had the chance to see the earth from the air looking down. On this flight, a kindly older woman gave him her window seat, as he seemed so fascinated with everything. With his child-like nature, he was amazed to see what the tops of the clouds looked like.

Shortly after returning from Infantry School, he remarked to his grandfather (with a proud attitude) that he had seen the tops of the clouds. Grandfather sat quietly for a while and then asked, "What did the tops of the clouds look like, son of my son?"

Young One thought for a second and then said, "They looked like from the bottom up, except the other way around, Grandfather," he answered truthfully. Grandfather began to laugh, and when Young One realized what he had said, he began to laugh as well. Then he realized that the smoke looked the same from both sides of the campfire. The Indian boy growing into a man had a warm smile of remembrance as he recalled the incident in his mind. He missed his grandfather and home already as he was streaking toward his destiny.

It was dark as the plane swooped in for a landing. As the great silver bird carrying Young One on his way to war descended from the clouds, the lights on the ground looked like sparkling electric jewels in the distance. They got larger and larger as the plane approached its destination. Another sergeant met them at the airport and, after securing their bags, drove them in an army van to the barracks. It was after 2300 hours when they arrived at the processing center.

They were issued bedding for their bunks and given stale sandwiches, as the mess hall was closed for the night. It was almost 0100 hours when they finally sacked out. The wake-up at 0530 was brutal. They had fifteen minutes to "shit, shower, and shave." They were then marched to the mess hall, where the smell of morning cooking grease filled the air. The aroma of buttery eggs, greasy bacon, and sausage commingled with the scent of hot coffee. Long lines of soldiers made their way through the serving lines and then to the tables.

It was August, and it was hot. Someone had left the mess hall door open. The mess sergeant came up and hollered, "Close that damn door. Don't let my flies out."

No one was allowed to talk in the mess hall. You waited, they filled your tray, and you found a place to sit. You ate, you emptied your tray, you left, and then you found a place to shit. It was real simple. All of this was, of course, supposed to be done with your mouth shut except when filling it with food. This was not a restaurant back on the block. If the sergeants caught someone talking, the offender was immediately ordered to dump his tray and leave the building. Over in one of the corners some guys were sitting and obliviously talking low under their breaths.

The mess sergeant stalked over to them and told the three guys to "dump your trays and leave."

Two of the soldiers got up and reluctantly obeyed. One was stuffing food in his mouth like John Belushi from the *Animal House* on the way to the trash can. The third guy sat there and kept eating. The sergeant screamed at him, "Didn't you hear me, son? I said, for talking in my mess hall, you have to dump your tray and leave."

All eyes in the quiet room were focused on the little guy still sitting there. The soldier, with a strong New York accent, looked up innocently from his table and said, "I wasn't talking, Sarge. Honest, I wasn't even listening."

The old mess sergeant looked at him for a second. He knew this guy had been speaking. Then he started laughing. The kid had a good line of shit. The sergeant walked away and let him finish his meal. Everyone who heard the guy laughed. This was the first time Young One saw Private First

Class Bernard Feinstein. Young One did not know it at the time, but they would be in the same squad over there.

Reservists from mechanized infantry units, especially from the arid southwest, were activated, in the belief that they were already acclimatized for the desert. Then some military geniuses put them into air-conditioned barracks in New Jersey for a week. They then mixed these guys with men from all over the country.

It did not make any sense. Maybe they were hoping that desert acclimatization was catching. The reserve unit Young One was assigned to was a composition of folks assembled from all over the country. Older soldiers called these "Shake-and-Bake Battalions" because they were assembled quickly for the present conflict, not from older units with war history.

Because of military commitments elsewhere in the world, moving major military units could have jeopardized national security. Thus, in mid-August of 1990, reservists were called up to fill in the front line. Much has been written of the exploits of the Persian Gulf War involving the big, high-profile, active-duty army units. The story of some of the unsung heroes of the Persian Gulf War needs retelling. These were common citizens who, with a patriotic bent and an adventurous nature, went to war. They were willing to give their lives for their country, but their officers would not let them. These sons—and later daughters—of America were a mixture of well-trained veterans and inexperienced recent high school graduates.

Later that day, they received all their inoculations against diseases endemic to the Persian Gulf. They got shots for diseases with names most of them couldn't pronounce. Shots for yellow fever, hepatitis, meningitis, typhoid fever, tetanus, botulinum toxoid, and many more were administered. The outbound troops walked down rows of medics with air guns who blasted them with vaccines. Getting a pneumatic shot was kind of like getting punched in the arm by someone wearing a ring. It didn't hurt that much, unless you flinched, and then the pneumatic high-pressure air could cut like a knife. It was best to stand still. Their arms were so sore that, for the next two days, the Persian Gulf destinees could hardly move them. To cure this, a concerned sergeant had them do push-ups while issuing insulting comments concerning their manhood to toughen them up. Army medicine was still full of cruel cures.

They even got the deadly anthrax bacteria vaccine. They were told they would get the rest of their anthrax shots "in country," when they got there. This would consist of three doses two weeks apart; then they would be given booster shots at six months, one year from the first shot, and the last a full year after that one. It sounded as if they were going to be over there an awful long time. The shots produced a red nodule at the injection site. The medics called the eruption "anthrax acne" because of its likeness to a small boil on the skin. It itched like hell, but you weren't supposed to scratch it. They also got screening for HIV. None of them wanted to hear that they couldn't go because they had that. It was the old good news/bad news thing. "You are not going to war, but you are going to die anyway." A couple of guys got pulled for failing a drug test.

They also requalified on their weapons and went on long, hot marches to toughen them up. They took physical training and ran every morning. They were issued two sets each of desert-camouflaged uniforms and boots. They made out their wills by signing mass-produced forms, directing what should happen to their limited belongings in life should they become part of the dearly departed. They elected beneficiaries for their GI insurance policies. Someone back home would win the $200,000 lottery if they "bought the farm."

They were familiarized with basic Arab customs and taught how to don and doff the chemical protective gear. It was the first time American soldiers had worn chemical protective clothing in anticipation of hostilities since World War I. This was going to be a different war. They met their new buddies and some of their sergeants and officers. It was a busy week. The sergeants scared the guys with classes on terrorism and weapons of mass destruction. Both were common to the Iraqis. They really psyched them up about what to expect when they arrived in the war zone. The nuclear, biological, and chemical warfare stuff was called NBC. Up till that time everybody called it "No Body Cares." When they started hearing what Saddam could hit them with, they started caring right away.

>━━✕━━✕━━✕━━<

On the night before they were to ship out, several of his buddies— or, more correctly, barracks acquaintances—wanted Young One to go drinking with them at the enlisted men's club. He didn't want to go, and, after taunting him, one of the black guys said, "Ah, come on, you know what they say about Indians and firewater." In his offensive way, he was trying to be funny. Young One was not offended, as he had seen it for himself in real life. In reality, the only Indian the black guy had ever seen was on television. There is bigotry in all kinds of people. Somebody is always trying to put someone else down. The big-mouthed black's name was Simms, and he was to be in their squad in Saudi.

"Chief, you know there is no booze allowed in Saudi Arabia." It was the most factual statement the guy ever said, but the racial overtones were obvious. Young One had never tasted an alcoholic beverage. How could he explain that alcohol had changed his life forever shortly after his birth? His mother and father had both been killed in a single-vehicle, drunk-driving accident when he was four months old. His grandparents, who lived by the old ways on the reservation, had raised him. His was a harder life than most children his age had, but it was fulfilling. But this matter was also none of this other guy's business, so he said nothing about it.

The guys destined for hangovers departed and left him alone in the barracks. With their departure, the large room became strangely quiet. The buzz of a fluorescent light was the only sound to be heard. There was usually the din of human conversation, someone playing music, locker doors slamming or someone roughhousing in the place. Now, it was almost silent. Young One had plenty of time to be with his thoughts, and he actually preferred to be alone.

Because of his quiet nature, he was one of the people in the army known as "ghosts." These are guys who are always there, but no one ever seems to see them. Almost like the quiet kid who sits in the back of the classroom, he is there and he is not, as no one really notices him. When someone gets picked out for work details, it is usually some wise guy with a big mouth, not the ghosts, who is put to work. You see them, but you don't. The only other guy who did not go out was a private from North Carolina named Porter. He was reading his Bible at the other end of the barracks. He was a deeply religious Christian who kept to himself. At least he was also a quiet person, and Young One appreciated that. They, too, would be in the same squad in the Arabian sands.

Private First Class Young One Asabathithez lay on his bunk and looked at his uniform with his new *nom de guerre* sewn over his right breast pocket. It was carefully draped over a coat hanger that was hanging on his gray metal wall locker. It was colored like the fawn print that Grandfather had dreamed about. There were four shades of brown, ranging from tan to medium brown. There were also little white-and-black-outlined spots, made to resemble pebbles or small rocks. It really did look like a deer fawn's coat. It troubled him that Grandfather's dream was coming true. Then he remembered when he first had to write his name. The Bureau of Indian Affairs schoolteacher helped him to write out his name by sounding it.

His native tongue had never been written down and was strictly an oral one. His last name meant literally "People of the Coyote Clan." In English, what it meant in his native tongue was twenty-two letters long, all run together. Now it was abbreviated to twelve letters long, but it did not mean anything. No one could pronounce it, including him, because it was not really his name. Because his name started with A and ended with Z and had so many letters in between, they called him "Private Alphabet." People said his name looked like every letter of the English alphabet all stuck together. The Outsiders had now even taken his name. He lay on his bunk and questioned himself in his mind. His thoughts were in the words of his people in their ancient language. It was the one he spoke exclusively until six years of age. Then he had to learn English to go to school because the law required it. But he thought in his first language, as does everyone. That made him automatically a truer member of his people than those who thought in English. No matter how many languages you learn to read and write, you will always think only in your first language. Words in other languages have to be translated in the mind. It was the mental translation that hampered his efforts to get into a technical field in the army. He was very bright, but his comprehension of the English language was not good.

As he lay on his bunk, he also thought, *Should I have tried to be sociable and have gone out to drink with them? Should I try to be something I do not want to be, just because someone else wants me to be that person?* He answered himself firmly in his mind, *No.* Then he remembered the words of his grandfather, spoken years before. His mind drifted off to the past, where his memory was speaking to him...

><><><

Young One had once asked his grandfather why he did not drink from the brown bottle like many others around him did. Many men from the pueblo used to come to the herd camps to drink their booze. It was forbidden on the reservation, but many snuck the stuff in anyway, having purchased it from the stores posted just across the reservation line. Way up in the hills was a safe place to drink. No tribal police and no wives ever came way up there. Young One had seen plenty of booze but never touched it himself.

"When I was a younger man, I, too, was lured away from the old ways by the Outsiders' poison," Grandfather answered truthfully.

"Why did you not continue drinking alcohol?" he asked the father of his dead father.

He remembered his grandfather answering slowly:

"Many changes of the seasons ago, when I was not much older than you are now, I saw something that turned my heart. There was a celebration of the harvest, and our people were brought together to sing praise to the Creator for so much bounty. There were women, children, sheep, goats, horses, and dogs. The women cooked and sang songs and told stories. Young men raced on foot and with horses. The old men smoked and told stories and laughed. These were easy hours in hard lives. There were steaming bowls of corn and squash and chili soup. There were haunches of deer, elk, antelope, and mutton for all to eat. It was a very festive time of plenty before the coming desert winter. The girls giggled in youthful, innocent delight. There were so many of our people there that they had broken up into different groups.

"One of the other bands invited me to their camp, and there was liquor there. The brown-glass bottle was passed around, and we all took mouthfuls of the stuff. Everyone was pretending they liked the taste of the burning liquid. There were two brothers from the Fox Clan. After feeling the effects of the brown bottle water, they began to disagree about something insignificant. But to them, it was important. A fight soon began. The younger brother was pushed into the fire. He grabbed a knife used to cut the melons from a blanket near the fire. Without thinking, he plunged the knife deep into his older brother's chest.

"When he saw what he had done in his anger, he was very sorry, but it was too late. His older brother died in his arms telling him, 'It is all right.' He was forgiven. Their mother wailed beside them both with grief. She died of a broken heart two winters later. She had no one to bring her firewood and food. Because that night, she lost two sons. One went to the graveyard, the other to the tribal prison. Since that day, the poison from the brown bottle has not touched my lips," his grandfather explained with tears welling in his eyes. He finally added, "Where there is drink, there is no happiness."

Young One knew that his own father had been a disappointment to Grandfather. He had fallen into outside ways. He did not respect the ancient songs and stories of his people. He took to drink and was killed when he ran his pickup truck into a large boulder alongside a lonely stretch of road off the reservation. He also killed his wife, Young One's mother, that night.

He remembered his grandfather once speaking of his parents' deaths: "They died alone with no one to sing ghost songs to help their spirits to the other side." He thought his dead son still walked the lonely hills and chaparral desert, trying to find his way to the other side.

"Sometimes I can hear their cries in the night wind," his grieving grandfather once confided to Young One.

"His spirit is lost and cannot find his way back to the center of the earth. He died of drink, and his spirit is still intoxicated and cannot find his way to peace." He said these words with tears of concern flooding his wise and weary eyes. These native people did not fully accept the Outsiders' version of Genesis, with life coming from the skies. They believed that all human life sprang from the center of the earth and that humans should look not to heaven, but to the center of the earth for return and eternal peace.

Young One had his own stories about alcohol. A few months before, he went with several friends to the "Arroyo Lounge," a canyon where pickup trucks full of booze and young American Natives congregate for purposes of refreshment. He drank only soft drink, while most of the others consumed hard drink. After a while, two young men, who had obviously harbored ill will towards each other, began to argue. It ended up with one going to the hospital with a smashed skull and the other going to the tribal jail for assault. During the altercation, one of the participants temporarily disappeared and returned with a lever-action rifle, which he swung by the barrel like a baseball bat. Its wooden stock scored a single hit that night, deep into the left side of his drinking buddy's head. It took seventy stitches to close the wound and caused a concussion. The guy was in the hospital for a week. The tribal police asked, "Why did you hit him in the head with the rifle?"

He answered truthfully, "Because I could not find the bullets."

That was the insanity of alcohol, and the reason Young One did not drink as well. Soon his thoughts went to other things as his mind floated off to sleep.

>‒‒×‒‒×‒‒<

He was awakened after midnight by the returning revelers. They returned the temporarily peaceful barracks room back to its normally noisy condition. At 0530 hours they were awakened again to begin their trip to war. One guy was barfing in the latrine. It was Simms, and he was as sick as a dog. A lot of the troops were in rough shape that morning. Some of them had gotten tattoos and body piercings. Some of them had met prostitutes in town and got something else. Even the brothers looked like they had lost some of their color painting the town the evening before.

After their morning allotment of greasy food, their company was ordered to report to their barracks, to clean it thoroughly and stand ready for inspection. After an inspection was conducted and the discrepancies corrected, they were allowed to go to war.

Their gear was loaded on trucks, and they were transported to Dover Air Force Base in Delaware. The soldiers were loaded onto buses and driven for four hours to the base. An air force enlisted guard in a black beret with an M-16 rifle presented a snappy salute as the convoy entered the base.

All the other soldiers were milling around and were not sure what to do. They hung around for a while, each experiencing his own private anticipations of what was to be. A sergeant first class named Evans, whom they had never seen before, soon interrupted their reveries of future glory or mortal destiny. "All right troops. Quit your grab-assing and fall in over here with your gear. Everything has to be inspected before you board the aircraft. Line up straight, and don't cluster-fuck me."

They were taken to a large hangar where their gear was searched for contraband. Before they started, an amnesty box was passed around. The crusty old sergeant explained that they could put anything in it with impunity. After the offer of amnesty, they would be charged with violation of a direct order under the Uniform Code of Military Justice. Several embarrassed soldiers turned in adult magazines and bottles of booze.

One guy had a bottle of vodka wrapped up to look like cookies from home. When the sergeants saw this in the amnesty box, they laughed. They opened up the booze, and everyone was allowed to fill their canteen cups with a taste of the liquid. The master sergeant said, "You had better enjoy this, because it's going to be a heap of Sundays before you get another drink." It was not even noon yet. But free booze is free booze. Young One sipped water from his canteen so as not to appear unfriendly, while the others toasted themselves to war with contraband firewater. The sergeant was telling them the truth. For most of them, it was the last drink of alcohol they would taste for a long time. For others, it would be the last drink forever.

All of their military gear and personal stuff was thoroughly looked through by the military police. Each soldier spread his poncho out on the concrete floor, and everything they were taking overseas was dumped onto it. The military police went through everything, looking for contraband. No personal weapons, no pornography and no intoxicants of any sort were allowed. No muscle books, swimsuit editions of magazines, or profane music was to be brought with them. Many religious items were also prohibited. Bibles were banned, but medallions, crosses, and other religious jewelry could be possessed, but must be kept concealed inside clothing. They did not want to offend the intolerant culture of the Saudi Arabians. Porter had his Bible taped to the middle of his back, and it went undiscovered when he was frisked.

All around them were the largest aircraft Young One had ever seen. They were waiting on the apron of the runway for a couple of hours. There was still plenty of "hurry up and wait" in the modern army, as there had always been.

Young One looked at the guys all dressed in their desert-camouflage uniforms.

They were like the clothing in his grandfather's dream. They were slated to go aboard an Air Force C-5A Galaxy. It was a huge aircraft. As Young One saw the long, metal stairway going up three stories being brought up to the aircraft to load them in the top compartment, he shuddered because it reminded him of what Grandfather told him at their last parting. These were Grandfather's iron steps.

It was the longest steel stairway any of them had ever seen before. Young One had a strange feeling as he approached it in a moving line of soldiers. He knew his life would change the moment he climbed it with the other soldiers. It did. Although what happened took only a fraction of a second, it seemed like a long time as he raised his foot to step upon the stairs. He felt something churn deep inside of him as he climbed the stairway to his future fate. More of Grandfather's dreams were coming true. A chill ran up his spine as he realized it.

Young One continued to feel frightened as he took step after step in file with his peers into the large aircraft. For the next nine hours, they sailed backwards, as the seats, with crash safety in mind, faced towards the rear of the bird, just the opposite of a commercial airliner. But there were no windows except two small portholes mid-center. They flew over the Atlantic Ocean without knowing it was there. Once in flight, they were given a boxed lunch. Later they got dinner, also boxed up.

They landed at Ramstein Air Force Base in Germany in total darkness. They were instructed to "disembark the aircraft." Sitting in a grassy strip between runways, they awaited their next aircraft that would take them to Saudi Arabia. After a while, three noisy four-engine, propeller-driven aircraft rolled up and turned in front of them. They were C-130 Hercules. The rear belly of the plane opened up and swallowed the men and their desert equipment as they entered through ramps in the back. The aircraft was buttoned up, and they took their places. The soldiers on their way to Saudi Arabia sat sideways on what looked like large, plastic patio-furniture benches. The air force load master briefed them on emergency exit procedures as though he had said the words a thousand times before. In fact, he had said it only hundreds of times before. Young One and his buddies felt like pieces of cargo. It was just another mission for the crew of the aircraft, but the soldiers they were transporting were on their way to war...

Chapter 3

HOTEL HELL

The troops were jerked from their dreams by the rapid deceleration of the large aircraft as it touched down. The forest-green camouflaged air force plane came to a screeching halt on the hot tarmac runway. The black rubber tires smoked as they were braked upon the stove-hot pavement, which had been baked by the relentless Saudi Arabian sun. It had been another long flight. They had traveled nine hours in the noisy, windowless jet, and five more in this plane. No one knew what to expect when they landed. There was great concern about terrorist attack.

They had been issued rifles, pistols, and live ammunition during the flight. They would receive their heavy stuff—grenades, machine guns, anti-tank rockets, *et cetera*—in country. They loaded their twenty-round magazines and were instructed to place them in their ammo pouches. No man was to place a box magazine full of live ammunition into his rifle and place a live round in the chamber under any circumstances unless ordered to do so. This was to prevent some knucklehead from accidentally shooting his buddy in the ass or popping a hole in the aircraft while in flight.

They slept with their unloaded rifles, but were ready to load them at a moment's notice. Once they were issued live ammunition, everyone knew this was the "real deal." They also carried their chemical protective gear, ready to put it on at any time. No one knew what was going to happen when they arrived in Saudi Arabia. For all they knew, they might have to come out shooting.

The Hercules aircraft taxied over to the apron near some cream-colored metal hangars. The four whining engines were, one by one, shut down. A minute or so later, the vacuum seal on the aircraft's rear ramp gave a loud, hissing noise. It sounded like the opening up of a giant can of coffee. Slowly, the metal drawbridge to destiny opened for the sleepy soldiers, while the cargo bay was flooded with eye-welding Arabian sunshine. The sunlit silhouette of the air force crew chief could be seen speaking to someone over a headset and microphone.

At first they were kept on the plane because the air force load master thought the hot air was from a nearby aircraft's exhaust, but the other plane's engines had been shut down. No, it was just the Arabian sun heating up the apron. He turned and gave a knowing nod to the company's first sergeant, known army-wide as "Top." He, in turn, gave the word to the company commander, who ordered him to, "Assemble the troops."

"On your feet. Unass this aircraft," was the sergeant's laconic command. The jet-lagged soldiers literally obeyed blindly. They began to straggle down the ramp, squinting and shading their eyes from the cruel sun. This was the X-Generation's war, commanded by the Pepsi Generation, then grown up. They stepped into it with all the confidence of cattle coming down the ramp to the slaughter yard.

There was no bravado, no joking, just filing out into the blinding light. They put their rucksacks on their backs, slung their rifles over their shoulders, and stepped forward into the Persian Gulf conflict. They were the "boots on the ground" the media spoke of. They carried everything they owned in the world in two bags. One was a military rucksack in which they carried their field gear. Their duffel bags, in which they carried their personal effects, were crew-loaded onto flight pallets. They would retrieve that gear later. No one dawdled, as the fear of an ass-chewing quickened their steps.

The hot desert air hit them in the face like walking into a blast furnace. At altitude, the aircraft interior had been chilly, and the rapid change in temperature was quite noticeable. It was one o'clock in the afternoon, the hottest time of the day, and it was the middle of August, the hottest time of the year.

They were in the giant sandbox. It was over 120 degrees Fahrenheit at that moment. It was strange for the medics to see soldiers simultaneously sweating and shivering without having malaria. The bright sunlight blinded them. Everyone who had sunglasses put them on. The rest pulled down their shaded, desert goggles. Once outside the aircraft, they formed several scraggly lines on the asphalt. Their squad leaders inspected the soldiers, informing them to "button that button" and "put your helmet on straight"—the usual shit they've been saying since helmets and buttons were invented.

All around them, aircraft were taking off and landing on the busy runway. They were in the middle of one of the largest airlifts ever conducted. Cargo vehicles of every sort hurried about the busy airport ferrying supplies, equipment, ammunition, and food. Air force maintenance vehicles swarmed around the parked aircraft, readying them for their next flight. The take-offs and landings were almost non-stop. Their duffel bags were unloaded from several plastic pallets. The nylon cargo nets that had held them for the flight were untied. Every bag was alike except for the name of its owner, which was stenciled on the side.

A detail was ordered to distribute the bags to the respective soldiers. Each had his name read by the sergeant, and they retrieved them one at a time. Everything they had in their possession was in those bags. They slung their bags over their shoulders and route-stepped over to one of the metal aircraft hangars. It was so hot in the sun that some paratroopers from the 82nd Airborne outside of the hangar were frying eggs on the fender of their truck as a stunt.

As Young One's platoon route-step marched by them, one of the soldiers asked mockingly, "Hey, any of you guys want breakfast?"

His companions laughed heartily, but none of the new arrivals found amusement in the heat. It was a good demonstration for them, however, concerning the power of the sun. If the air is 110 degrees Fahrenheit, the sand can be 140 degrees, so no bare feet could touch the ground without burning. Metal objects got even hotter. To touch any metallic object would burn your skin because they got as hot as skillets in the searing sun. It was one of the lessons they learned being there. No one was chilly any longer. It was so hot they stood at parade rest with beads of sweat running down the cracks of their asses.

"Welcome to the Kingdom of Saudi Arabia," said a desert camo-covered colonel they had never seen before. After some reassuring bullshit delivered in fine familiar military style, with a tone and pitch somewhere between a preacher and a football coach, they were given a briefing on customs, especially the do's and don'ts in that ancient land. They soon learned there were a lot more don'ts than there were do's in the Saudi area of operations.

While they were listening to the officer speak, there was suddenly a loud BOOM outside. Everybody hit the deck, thinking it was a terrorist attack. The colonel just stood there smiling, and told them, "As you were, men. It is just an over-inflated tire exploding in the sun. They come in from the States or Germany that way, and the sun heats and blows them up. Just one of the things you'll have to get used to over here."

Everybody got up and mocked the others for appearing to believe it was a bomb and for being afraid when it happened. Anybody who was faking it should have been in Hollywood working as a stunt man, because they all "got down" very realistically.

After the colonel's welcome speech, they were loaded into military cattle cars for transit to their temporary barracks. These were modified tractor-trailers, which were not much different from their namesakes. The troops stood up in them like cattle. It was hot and hard to breathe the air, heated by both the baking sun and everyone else's warm, expired breath. After a twenty-minute journey through the desert on a brand new asphalt road as smooth as a billiard table, they arrived at their new home. The arriving troops soon found themselves billeted in a huge warehouse, which could sleep hundreds of troops in bunk beds three high. It was one of many large, corrugated-metal buildings planted together in the desert sand.

They looked like something that construction equipment is stored in back in the states. Until recently, they held cargo from the airport. Inside each were rows of bunk beds stretching to the other wall a long way off. Each building held an entire battalion-sized element. Over the doorway, some GI with a sense of humor had erected a sign reading "Hotel Hell." There was no air conditioning, as this was an acclimatizing barracks. Two huge fans set at opposite ends of the building circulated hot air throughout the structure. It was essentially a "repo-depot" or a place of assembly before moving the men and their replacements up to the front. All hours of the day and night more guys would arrive. They would turn on the lights and slam lockers and talk shit until someone screamed for them to, "shut the fuck-up." With planes arriving every hour of the day and night, it was a continuous process. No one got much sleep in Hotel Hell.

The warehouses that became their barracks buildings were surrounded with large concrete dividers like those seen along the highway. Each road leading up had a maze of concrete and earth barriers to force a vehicle driving through to turn right or left, thus slowing them down. Some barriers were pieces of concrete pipe filled with sand. They prevented vehicles full of fanatics from driving straight into the barracks like they did in Lebanon. Around the building were hardened concrete emplacements for the guards. These were further reinforced with several layers of olive drab sandbags. Everywhere guards with locked and loaded machine guns watched every movement. There was even a 20-mm antiaircraft heavy machine gun aimed at the circuitous road in front of them. It could chew a tractor-trailer into metal shards. Technically, it was against the Geneva Convention to shoot such weapons at thin-skinned vehicles, but Switzerland was a long way from there.

Security was real tight for fear of terrorism. Rumor had it that there were up to 10,000 terrorists in Saudi Arabia, waiting for the secret signal to attack. Young One wondered how anybody knew how many of them there were if they were so secret. Every time they saw a Bedouin on the horizon, there was a desire to shoot them just in case they were terrorists or spies. They could have been both or neither, so there were strict standing orders not to shoot civilians. Saddam had promised "a line of American bodies with a beginning but with no end." Now they were beginning to arrive, and there seemed to be no end in sight. And all of them were still alive and well. They would find out if Saddam would keep his word or not.

The troops had been sent to Saudi Arabia in a transit company. They were every military occupational specialty needed. Now, they were separated out into combat squads. The infantry were in the 11 series: 11-bravos were foot soldiers, 11-charlies were the mortar men, and so forth. Each type of soldier in the series was identified by what he did. Each day, more and more new guys were arriving. The many empty bunks were soon filling up.

They even had women on the other side of them in the warehouse. They were told to stay strictly away from them. As soon as they were up to fighting strength and most of their gear had arrived, they would be moved up to the front line. The barracks would be spit-shined and the process repeated over and over until the front line was filled with fellows such as themselves. In the meantime, they would be held as a crash reserve to serve as replacements to the elite troops already on the line, should the "balloon go up."

The troops were required to take pyridostigmine bromide, or "PB pills," in case of nerve gas attack. The side effects were severe diarrhea. It was hard to drink enough water in the desert while having the shits. Quite a battle took place in their intestines as these two competing forces fought for dominance. As usual, there were insufficient latrine facilities, and as the troops from the support units were of mixed gender, anyone with sisters could tell you who hogged the bathrooms. Everyone was awaiting orders to proceed somewhere else, but right then they were all there together looking for a place to crap.

>—※—※—<

It was outside of Hotel Hell later that afternoon that they met their platoon non-commissioned officer, or NCO. They already had a partially "fleshed-out" platoon, and new guys were arriving hourly. They stood at attention in the afternoon sun.

"Good afternoon, people. My name is Sergeant First Class Virgil Franklin, and I am your platoon sergeant. For the duration of armed hostilities, I will be your mamma and your daddy. Any problems you have, you should come to me first. Go somewhere without informing me, and I make that little problem of yours go away. I will perform this magic by giving you a bigger problem to worry about. We have a chain of command here, and should you jump it, I will make you the missing link. Do I make myself clear?"

"Yes, sergeant," the entire platoon shouted at once.

Standing to his side was a young Mexican-American lieutenant who was introduced by Sergeant Franklin.

"This is your platoon leader Lieutenant Ramirez. He is our boss, including mine. But don't forget I run this platoon on a day-to-day basis. His job is to look good, sign the paperwork, and go to jail if I fuck up. Remember this, people; he's not going there alone. Do I make myself clear?"

"Yes, sergeant," they responded in almost unison.

"Does anyone have any questions?"

"Sarge, will we be able to go to church on Sundays?" The look on the sergeant's face froze the other soldiers into shocked silence.

"Who asked that question?" inquired Franklin, with sarcastic disbelief in his voice.

"I did, sergeant," replied Porter, the real religious guy from North Carolina.

"Son, pull your head out of your ass and take a good look around. Do you see any churches around here?"

"No, sergeant."

"Troop, take a good look at that vehicle over there," Sergeant Franklin said while motioning with his hand at a military ambulance parked near them with a large red cross on a white background painted on its side.

"For the duration of hostilities, the closest you will come to the Lord may be a ride in that thing," he said, referring to the emergency vehicle. Everybody started laughing, and the guy sat down in embarrassed silence.

"Any other dumb questions?" he asked of the other men in his platoon.

No one had any questions, dumb or otherwise. Franklin finished his talk with, "Always remember this, men. In this world, there are no dumb questions. Just dumb people asking things. Squad leaders, take charge of your people."

This was classic Franklin. Another time, somebody asked him some dumb shit to which he responded, "It is just a case of mind over matter, son. I don't mind and you don't matter. Got that, troop? Move out." He was not being disrespectful to the young man. He was merely "getting his mind right."

Another time, Franklin was heard screaming at some private from another squad, "If you are looking for sympathy, just look between shit and syphilis in the dictionary because there is none of it here, son." Everyone learned early on to stay away from Franklin with their problems.

Second Lieutenant Alfredo Ramirez was the most squared-away, clean-cut soldier anyone had ever seen. His haircut was whitewall, and his uniform was always clean and sharply pressed. This is not to say he was a slacker who never got dirty. No, just the opposite. He was a real leader, or at least tried hard to be that way. He did everything his people had to do. He had been accepted for ROTC in college and, because of his extraordinary zeal and his attention to detail in performing his duties, had been given a Reserve commission. He volunteered for duty in the Persian Gulf to pay back the United States for how good his second-generation family had it in America.

Technically, Ramirez, as the platoon leader, was in charge of everyone on paper. But it was really the platoon sergeant who ran the show. A young lieutenant cannot operate without the support of his sergeant, the "backbone of the army." Ramirez was a "shave tail," not much older than the privates in his command. Although he was a commissioned officer and outranked Franklin, he was actually lower than a private was to the sergeants. But the difference was that everyone had to salute him.

Young One looked around at the other guys in his infantry squad. They were certainly a cross section of American youth. Along with himself, an American Native from the Land of Enchantment, there was Sergeant Eliot, a thin white guy from Wisconsin. He was their squad leader. There was John Walters, a specialist fourth class or a "spec-four," who was the assistant squad leader. He was from California. There was Feinstein, a wise-guy Jewish kid from New York. There was Simms, a black atheist from Kansas City; Turner, a black agnostic from Texas; Porter, a white born-again Christian from North Carolina; McHugh, a Catholic from Pennsylvania; and Jones, who was a new-age vegetarian from Vermont. Finally, there was Samuella—he was from American Samoa. Nobody knew what he was. This group of ten culturally diverse guys made up first squad. Their squad, along with three others not noteworthy enough to mention, formed their infantry platoon over there. Sergeant Franklin was a middle-aged man with short-cropped graying hair. Back in Tennessee, he owned a paint store, went to church and lodge meetings, and was leader of his kid's Boy Scout troop. He was a real solid citizen. He joined the Reserve not for the pay, not for patriotism, and not for the travel. He joined for the chance to get away from the wife and kids for a weekend a month to play soldier, drink beer, and play cards. It was a great release. Now, he was playing soldier for real again.

He had served in Vietnam, but that was almost eighteen years earlier. He was assigned to the last eight months of Nam, retreating in anticipation of cessation of hostilities. He was there during the fall of Saigon. An army going backwards takes a terrible ass-kicking because the rear is definitely exposed to the enemy. It's doubtful that he really thought he would go to war again in this lifetime, but there he was. When he got his notice calling him up for duty in the Gulf, he was elated. This was the chance of his life, to go to Saudi and shoot a couple of "dune-goons."

"After all, they aren't Christians," he was once heard saying.

Back home, he worked hard and had a good, middle-class life. He could sell you any kind of paint, varnish, shellac, brushes, rollers, and any other paraphernalia particular to the surface-coating industry. For a long time, he hoped for some action to break up the quiet boredom of his reasonably successful civilian existence. Now he had it—a chance for adventure and excitement. He was going to really do it, as they say. This was his chance to reaffirm his manhood through the rite of passage of war. There would be no middle-aged men muttering new-age chants sitting in some wigwam beating their tom-toms for him. No siree, Bob. Those Ay-rabs had better watch out. We're going to kick some Eye-raky ass real soon.

Their three platoons, along with the heavy-weapons section and the headquarters component, formed their company. They trained or went on work detail from sunup to beyond sundown because there was no air conditioning in the warehouse. They suffered terrible jet lag. They just went in at night and collapsed on their bunks. The brass trained the GIs hard and kept them busy to keep trouble down. The last thing anyone wanted was to piss off the prudish Saudis. For three days, this continued. They were confined to their barracks and were not allowed on pass to go into the city. They were issued sunglasses, lip balm, sunscreen, insect repellant, and desert-colored camouflage makeup kits. Then, on the fourth day in country, their unit—along with many like theirs—was scheduled to be moved up to the front line, along the Kuwaiti border...

Chapter 4

BUTTS IN THE GIANT ASHTRAY

Early the next morning, their company went forward in a convoy of Humvees, two-and-a-half-ton and five-ton trucks, along with an assortment of civilian buses and rented trucks and vans. They were escorted to their new home by a truck full of Saudi Arabian paratroopers. The officers and senior NCOs went forward in the Humvees. The enlisted men rode in chartered metro buses still decorated with Arabic advertisements for Western goods.

The fat Saudi driver turned on the air conditioning, and their box with wheels was immediately transformed into a temporary temperate climate moving a mile a minute through the scorching desert. So much for desert acclimatization. The Saudi driver was not supposed to have done it, but they were far away from his supervisors, and no one complained. It was a job he would do every day for months to come, and, being a local, he did not need acclimatization. In his defense, it really did feel good to escape the incessant heat of the Saudi summer, if only for a while. They would pay later for that short vacation in the cool clime.

Anything with wheels was used to get them to the front line in the beginning of Desert Shield. During World War I, French soldiers were transported to the front lines in chartered Parisian taxis. Most guys were catching some Zs and those who remained awake looked out of the windows at mile after mile of visual monotony flashing by as they sped past. Young One enjoyed looking at the desert.

Periodically, a Bedouin with a flock of goats or an occasional camel could be seen. Young One was so interested in seeing new things that he stayed awake for the entire ride. It excited his spirit. They drove past sand dunes, rocky plains, and plenty of flat, shrub-covered sand. After a five-hour road ride, they turned off the paved roads and drove out into the desert on a sandy trail.

One of the buses got stuck in the sand, and the third platoon had to dig and push it out and then march the rest of the way, while the four-wheel-drive vehicles went forward unimpeded. The heavy-weapons platoon got to ride to camp with their equipment. They drove by laughing and waving at them. The drivers of the other buses refused to go forward for fear of also getting stuck in the sand. The men were dropped off in the middle of nowhere. The grunts had to hoof it into camp the rest of the way. They shouldered their packs and rifles, and their boots beat the sand. Their duffel bags were on the trucks waiting for them in camp, wherever that was.

As they disembarked from the bus, the hot air hit them like the breath of a dragon. The chilled meat their bodies were composed of was going to pay for the few hours of cool air they enjoyed. The rapid change in temperature was a source of immediate suffering to them. They marched through the parched sands like something out of a Foreign Legion movie. It crunched under their feet because no one had stepped there for thousands of years. From high in the summer sky, the skin-searing sun stared with its one unblinking eye.

The reservists had no idea where they were going or how long they would be there. Their marching column followed vehicles' tire tracks in the sand. One platoon was split up to provide flank security while the rest of them marched in step, calling military cadence. The company guidon was held proudly overhead. Its silver spearhead gleamed in the sun with polished pride. Only a stray camel watched the human caravan from a distance with curiosity. He just kept chewing and nodding his head as if he knew what was in store for the newcomers to his desert. Their several-mile hike through the desert terminated as they marched up to their vehicles, parked in a circle. The vehicles were formed up like a modern wagon train in the middle of the desert.

Everyone thought it was a rest break or something just until they could march to a better location. Then they realized that this lonely, forsaken place was to be their home for some time to come. There was absolutely nothing there except a long line of wooden surveyor's stakes stuck in the ground. The wooden stakes had little orange, plastic streamers attached to them. They hung lifeless in the hot, motionless air. There were letters or numbers or something written on them in Arabic with an indelible marking pen. They must have meant something to somebody, because it was there that they stopped. It was their new address in Saudi Arabia.

Surprisingly, no one said anything. A seemingly endless expanse of sand and scrub vegetation unfolded before their eyes. Another of Grandfather's visions was coming true. This was deep desert with very little vegetation. Young One's home desert at least had chaparral and sagebrush, creosote and mesquite bushes. Here, however, nature was harsher, and life had a harder time struggling to continue its existence.

The tan-colored, sun-roasted sands were just as Grandfather described them from his dream. There were no trees, no rock outcroppings, and no sand dunes. It was just a wide, flat place in the middle of the desert. There was nothing there but them and things that crept and crawled. There also were biting, stinging, and blood-sucking creatures that slithered, ran, and flew.

Before the gaze of the coalition soldiers was the largest expanse of open space anyone, including Young One, had ever seen. It was much like being on the sea with its unobstructed vista, only the natural curvature of the earth terminated their view at the horizon in any direction around them. The desert just seemed to disappear under the cloudless, turquoise-blue sky. There were no mountains, or hills, or valleys; there was nothing. Sticking out from the sand were occasional patches of sparse vegetation. Arid botanical life forms worked hard to hold on to what they had won in the struggle against nature.

Usually GIs complain about almost everything. If soldiers aren't complaining, they are either satisfied or just recognize the hopelessness of the situation. But there was nothing satisfying about this place. There was no joking, no grumbling or grab-assing around. They were in silent shock when they saw their area of operations.

So much open space gave them agoraphobia, the morbid fear of open spaces. Simms was especially affected by the fact that there was no place to hide. This is especially important, because anywhere out there, an Iraqi in a hidee hole with a sniper rifle could get some loved one back home a new house. It seemed that danger could be found everywhere in the three-sixty compass degrees all around them. There was no safe wall to put your back against. Trouble could come from anywhere. No one was really afraid yet, but they knew they had anxious futures.

The soldiers who grew up in the city, with its close conveniences, suffered greatly from culture shock. City dwellers have long joked about country folks living in the sticks, but in this part of the desert, there weren't even sticks. The tallest thing was the low-growing *arfaj* bush, which never reached over two-and-a-half-feet tall in the best of places for them. Most were less than six inches tall. Even those hardy desert shrubs had a difficult time making a living there.

The troops knew that if they were overrun or cut off, they would be dead in days from want of life's necessities, or driven over by Iraqi tank treads. They could never march back to the coast without dying of thirst, and there were not enough vehicles for all of them to ride out in. There were not enough helicopters to fly them out, either. Only the dead and wounded qualified for a chopper ride out of a combat zone. If the Iraqis attacked, the reservists knew they would have to stand and fight and die to the man, as there was no place for them to run to, and no one wanted to be an Iraqi POW.

The reservists all knew that if the Iraqis invaded Saudi Arabia, as was their stated intention, they would be dead, or worse, captured and wishing they were dead. The Iraqis reportedly still had Iranian POWs, even though their war with them had been over for two years. Saddam had taken foreign persons from Kuwait and from inside Iraq and made them human shields around sensitive military targets. He also kept them for old-fashioned slave labor, in great Middle Eastern tradition.

The reserve soldiers took up defensive positions on the border in anticipation of hostilities, but would have been killed as quickly as the Kuwaitis had been when Saddam overran them several weeks prior. They knew that however brave and determined they might be, they were outnumbered and out-gunned exponentially. They could count on air superiority, which gave them an advantage. But if it weren't for these patriots, the Kingdom of Saudi Arabia and its vast oil riches would have been the next prize in the madman's march to mayhem. But even Saddam wasn't crazy enough to drive over a bloodied American flag. He would keep his prize, what he called, "the nineteenth province of Iraq," and wait it out. He would watch and see what the rest of the world would do.

Far off over the horizon in almost every direction, the drums of war were beating. The bugles were blown, and troops were mustered from around the world. It takes a lot of time to send armies and their necessary paraphernalia halfway around the Earth. Meanwhile, a massive air and sealift of war materials and personnel was underway. It was the greatest airlift since the Berlin Wall went up. The outside world promised it would come to the defense of Kuwait, and help was coming. No one thought it would take seven months to get the entire cast on the stage. Their battalion had no heavy equipment and no combat engineers to operate it. They carried a mere three days' worth of food and water with them. They unpacked the trucks that immediately went back for more supplies. It was upsetting for the troops to see their only way out leave without them.

They had to dig in with entrenching tools and picks and shovels. Half the company dug in and prepared the area, while the other half was on guard duty, forever watching. When they were not digging foxholes or filling sandbags, some soldiers went on convoy duty, ferrying military construction supplies, food, and water. Over the next couple of days, corrugated metal, crooked two-by-fours, and sandbags arrived in a mix of military and chartered civilian trucks. These materials were for the construction of their company headquarters and defensive positions. They did not have barbed wire or landmines with which to protect themselves.

In the beginning, there were so few coalition soldiers that their company of 120 men guarded five kilometers of territory across the front. Each of three platoons had over a kilometer and a half to cover. This was for two reasons. First, there were not enough soldiers in country to adequately man a battle line. Secondly, they were deliberately spread out along the border to prevent presenting an attractive, bunched-up target to minimize the threat of weapons of mass casualties.

From the first day on the line in the sand, the infantry dug in. They used their folding entrenching tools, called "E-tools." They were little better than beach shovels to excavate sand. They filled sandbags incessantly. The top layer of the ground was crusted sand that varied in depth from a few inches to several feet deep. Every time a soldier would shovel it, half of it would blow in the wind and fall back in his meager excavation. Each shovel-full had to be frustratingly removed several times. Under the sand was hardpan clay that had been pressed by great pressure when it was an ancient sea bed. It proved to be hard digging. A couple of feet under that was a layer of gypsum-like clay the Arabs called *gatch*. It was extremely tough digging. It was like trying to chop through several feet of wallboard buried under the sand.

They set up sandbagged machine-gun and anti-tank weapon emplacements every couple of hundred meters. In between these were individual foxholes, continuously occupied by riflemen. In reality, they were nothing more than listening and observation posts—not combat positions. Hence, they did not set up a base camp, as there were not enough of them for that. They were needed badly to secure the border. Each company had a fortified bunker that served as its headquarters. The troops called it the head shed, and this sandbagged shelter was the center of activity for the soldiers.

Heavily armed Humvees drove up and down until their wheels had hard-packed a country road out of the trackless sand. Their unit did not have the newer Bradley fighting vehicles. The reservists also had no tank or artillery support. These things were still on the way. The 82nd Airborne had light, air-transportable tanks, but they were no match for the large Soviet T-62 and T-72 main battle tanks. Besides, they were guarding the airports and would not be of help to them. The marine expeditionary force had armor attached to it but was assigned to guard the coast, which at the time was the likeliest attack route. Their armor was too far away to help the thin line of army reservists stretched out in the sands if serious trouble fell upon them.

That left the Reserve, stretched out far to the west along the boot heel of Kuwait. If the Iraqis were to sneak attack (for which they were famous), running over their area would also be an easy route to Riyadh. The hard ground was excellent terrain for armored vehicle movement. The troops used to laughingly call themselves "Iraqi speed bumps." They knew that they could not stop the Iraqis, just slow down their onslaught to the Saudi capital. Top brass estimated Iraq could have taken Saudi Arabia in six days, with a tremendous loss to front-line troops. Young One and his companions would number among the future loss should such an invasion take place.

Everyone knew they could not hold the line at their strength at the time. If the Iraqis released chemical weapons, they would have cooked in their protective suits. They used to call their chemical protective suits "roasting bags" because, in the hot sun, heat stress would kill as quickly as the gas they were designed to protect against. Fortunately, no enemy gas attack occurred, but they were ready for it if it did. At least they thought they were. The rubber on their gas masks soon became dry rotten, and the chemical-protective garments developed cracks in them from the heat. This fact was not reassuring to the troops. It really was lucky for them that the Iraqis did not release chemical or biological weapons.

Just across the border were hundreds of thousands of Iraqi troops, 12,000 tanks and 800 artillery pieces capable of lobbing either high-explosive or chemical shells at them. They were dug in and determined. Had the Iraqis pressed their advantage then, they could have taken Saudi Arabia with little difficulty. Saddam was content with his prize for the meantime. He would wait and see what the world would do. But the world did not know what he would do. This weighed on the minds of the troops, and they soldiered in earnest because of it. At any moment, they could be overrun, and they all knew it.

The American army hadn't had to worry about air attack since World War II. The brass knew Saddam had a lot of Soviet MiGs and attack helicopters with which he could come strafing and bombing at any minute, so air security was a concern. Infantry commanders assumed that the air force flyboys would always be there on top. Fortunately, a situation occurred that the troops were not aware of that helped them immensely. The air force sent a larger number of fast attack jets than were expected. These required large ground crews to maintain, fuel, arm, and control them. The air force took priority over the army for air troop movements. So it took longer for new army troops to get in because they were given a lesser priority than the air force ground crews for available air transport. This meant there were fewer new ground troops, but the air coverage was excellent. The front line stayed sparsely populated for some time. But that was okay, as long as the U.S. jets kept screaming overhead. Whenever a jet screamed by like silver rocket, as in an air show back home, the troops would cheer.

They were billeted in old-fashioned, two-man canvas tents called shelter-halves. They slept on rubber pads and on heavy-duty inflatable air mattresses that the GIs called "rubber ladies." In the daytime, the old canvas tents were too warm to sleep in, so they slept in the dugout defensive emplacements. Their tents stunk from the sun baking out the waterproofing compounds that permeated the fabric of their cloth homes. Some guys rolled up the sides of their tents to provide ventilation and protection from the sunlight. But the snakes and spiders, also desiring to escape the blazing sun, had the same idea.

To keep the dangerous vermin down, the guys spread diesel fuel all over the place. It kept down the dust and the critters, but it stunk and gave them more headaches than it prevented. Many guys took to filling empty ration boxes with sand to pile atop one another to fabricate a makeshift bed. At least it kept them up off the ground and away from the creeping, crawling creatures that shared their encampment with them.

To the casual observer, it appeared that nothing lived out there in the searing sands. Most guys looked and saw nothing, but the desert was not devoid of life. There were jackals, foxes, vultures, desert rats, and wild camels, goats, and sheep wandering around their sparse encampment. Some of the guys said they did not see anything alive out there; however, they did not know how many creatures might have seen them. There are many living things in the desert that live nocturnal lives. Nature instinctively understands that mad dogs and Englishmen thing about the sun.

They had to contend with poisonous snakes, as well as large, long-legged spiders that the soldiers called camel tarantulas. There were also large, venomous scorpions; big, black wasps; and, of course, shit flies aplenty. But the worst pests of all were the sandflies. They bit and caused painful, itching bites that the men called "Baghdad boils." Worse than the mere annoyance, they carried and transmitted the deadly leishmaniasis organism.

While putting up with the heat, the sand, and the vermin, day and night alike, they "kept eyes out and ready" on the large open space between themselves and the Iraqis. The troops were spread out pretty thinly and had all the comforts of nomads. Trucks or helicopters brought everything they needed to them. They were permanently camped out on the front lines. It was hard for the guys who pulled nighttime guard duty. It was too hot and often too noisy to sleep in the day. The guards had to be checked continuously to make sure they stayed awake.

The reservists knew that they would have a hard time defending themselves, because they were "teeth to tail heavy," meaning that they were unsupported combat troops. The teeth referred to the fighting troops. The tail referred to the large entourage of REMFs that keep the fighting troops supplied and going—cooks, clerks, medical staff, transport troops, military police, supply folks, etc. In Vietnam, it was a ratio of 8:1 tail to teeth. In other words, it took eight support troops to keep one fighting infantryman going. The reservists did not have this numerical advantage. If the enemy came charging over the hill, they would soon shoot up, shit out, or piss away their limited supplies and be overrun. Unsupported troops are casualties in modern warfare.

><--><--><

Their butts were literally stuck in the biggest ashtray on earth. Geographically speaking, the great sands in that part of the world are divided into the Arabian Desert and the Syrian Desert. On the ground, one would have a difficult time telling which is which, or where one begins and the other ends. In the desert, from sunup to sundown and in between each day, there is sand. The desert can range from verdant oasis, to barren, lifeless rock, to shifting sand dunes. The sand can be as fine as flour or as coarse as cobbles, depending upon how fast the wind is blowing.

The shifting Arabian sands have successfully resisted the ambitions for advancement of Alexander the Great, the Caesars, the Crusaders, the roving hordes of the great khans, and the popes. Even the Turks, whose empire once stretched from Spain in the west to Poland in the north, managed merely to straddle the Arabian Peninsula.

There are really only three seasons in the Arabian Desert: rain, mud, and dust, with the latter season lasting immeasurably longer than the other two. When Young One arrived in late August, it was still dust season in the place the Arabs called the Ad Dibdibah Plain. It was located halfway up the boot heel of Kuwait.

The border that separated Kuwait from Saudi Arabia was ill-defined, and there were no clear landmarks such as mountains or rivers that normally delineate nations' boundaries. Only a surveyor could actually find where one country ended and another began, if he or she did not become lost. No one had ever fought for the open sand before except Arabs on camels. Until now, it had not been worth anything to anyone in particular.

There were just long stretches of nothingness as far as the eye could see. The coalition drew a line in the sand across this vast wasteland. "Do not cross over it!" was the message for Baghdad. Actually, there were two lines in the sand. Saddam also drew a line that his troops were to defend with "their last breath." The GIs called the Iraqi front line "Smuggler's Berm." An officer said it one time, and the name just sort of stuck.

The front lines of the Persian Gulf War were not like those of World War I, where at times the warring participants could hear the enemy's voice or have him in rifle sights. The coalition forward line was about thirty miles from where everyone estimated the Iraqi border to be. The Iraqi front line was set back ten miles on their side of where they assumed the border to be. That kept the opposing forces about forty miles apart from each other. This was out of artillery range, but still within theater-range missile capability.

Iraqi artillery could shoot over twenty-five miles, and the coalition didn't want casualties before it was time—and then, they wanted them to be enemy casualties. Iraq had huge 155-mm howitzers that they bought from South Africa. These howitzers could outshoot by several miles any cannon the coalition had. Military intelligence also told of Saddam's attempt to make a super gun that could hurl a shell almost a hundred miles. The troops knew about Saddam's Soviet Scud missiles that could go hundreds of miles. These could be loaded with a variety of conventional as well as unconventional warheads. There was also a great concern that the Soviets would come to Saddam's defense, and that could have started Armageddon.

The coalition forces could not afford to allow the Iraqis to use their limited-range weapons to good effect. To minimize this threat, all the large coalition units were kept well to the rear as they were forming up. The front line was held by the reservists and paratroopers, who were out there all alone.

The large American and European divisions were still months away, and when they came, they would be staged far to the rear, south of the Tapline Road. It takes a long time to move an army halfway around the world with all the necessities of life. Saddam was betting that they couldn't do it, or couldn't afford to do it. He was wrong to begin with, and he was soon going to be wrong again.

The area between the coalition and the Iraqis was full of landmines, booby traps and snipers. Both Iraq and the coalition forces had observation and listening posts out beyond the front line. Armed roving patrols from both sides completed the perilous puzzle. Everyone stayed out of No Man's Land, unless they had serious business there.

The Iraqi forces across the border were simply called the "IFs." Some of the classier GIs called them "Indigo Foxtrots," using radio lettering. Some guys referred to the Iraqis as "Abdul and Habib." Other soldiers called them "Homers" from the satirical cartoon show that had just begun back home on TV. It was the Persian Gulf version of the Nam era "Gomer." Feinstein referred to the Iraqis as "Omar Simpsons." Whatever they called them, there were plenty of them across the border.

In addition to enabling U.S. petroleum addiction and its codependent steel and rubber industries, one of the Americans' goals was to protect the sacred places in Saudi Arabia. Mecca and Medina would have fallen into profane hands. Since the words of the last prophet were first spoken, the holy places had been kept safe in Saudi Arabia. If Saddam took Saudi Arabia, he would have all the oil and, even more important, control of the real wealth, the wellspring of the Islamic faith. But when Saddam appeared to threaten the holy sites of all Islam, he galvanized the whole Arab world against him. This caused the military forces of his neighbors to march upon him.

The Butchers of Babylon made several major errors, the greatest of which was to poise their army ready to attack and conquer Saudi Arabia. Not that anyone really cared about rich chauvinists dressed in bedclothes with tablecloths on their heads, but it was they who controlled how much the motorist paid at the gas pump. Therefore, Saudi Arabia was important to the rest of the world. Instead of finding allies, Saddam made more enemies. The best he could do was to tell more lies and pull strings to keep heads in his government nodding approvingly. As soon as they stopped, Saddam would get one final nod from their heads with a bullet.

Like a necklace of outposts with the elite troops as elegant beads, hooked together with the camo-dyed macaroni of the inexperienced reservists, they were strung across the ill-defined border between the Kingdoms of Kuwait and Saudi Arabia. As strange as it seems, it was all that was needed.

Even with new guys arriving every day, there were less than 50,000 of them. Across the border, there were a half million battle-hardened Iraqi veterans in uniform. The coalition was outnumbered ten to one. Everyone had been psyched out by the threat of nuclear, chemical or biological warfare—the so-called weapons of mass destruction that the Iraqis had.

Some of the troops were going through mild alcohol withdrawal, as the Arabian sun distilled the last of the ethyl alcohol from their sweating, dry-docked bodies. There is a simple reason that the Arabs do not drink alcohol. If one were to fall asleep dead drunk in a hot tent, one might never wake up. That is how the infidel would be found—dead drunk. The air was as dry as the atmosphere in a baker's oven. Sunburn prevention and heat stress recognition had been stressed in their training. Nobody needed to ask why. It was like being in a sauna bath all the time. It hit 125 degrees Fahrenheit in the daytime and dropped only to the mid-90s at night. It was almost like living in Hell.

Young One, along with his platoon, attended classes on desert survival, tactics, and war maneuvers. They learned about snipers, landmines, sappers, and night stalkers. They slowly became acclimated to fight in one of the most inhospitable places on earth.

The reservists continued to dig protective holes and fill sandbags incessantly. It was exhausting work in the hot sun. Some guys lost count after personally filling and placing ten thousand bags. They dug out from sandstorms. They ate space-age combat rations and shit them away; they drank water and pissed it down a plastic tube with a funnel on it. The fecal matter they collected in fifty-five gallon drums was taken out and burned with diesel fuel and gasoline.

It stunk terribly if you were downwind of it when it was being burned. The weirdest thing was that the Saudi *Mutawa,* or "morals police," would come around to witness the procedure. It seemed that they did not want pork-laden infidel shit contaminating their sacred soil. They especially did not want Jewish soldiers' shit on their sands, whether they ate pork or not. They would show up periodically and look around for religious infractions. Nobody wanted to mess around with them because their criminal justice system allowed tortured confessions, amputations, beatings, whippings, and beheadings. It was even illegal to have a Bible in the Kingdom. Porter kept his hidden because he would be in serious trouble if it were discovered, and Franklin did not report him or make him give it up...

Chapter 5

THE MAGIC BOX

Young One did not like being an infantryman. It was not what he expected when he enlisted in the Army Reserve. He wanted to learn the new ways of technology, not pound the ground and hunt other men. He wanted to learn about computers and aircraft and all the technological wonders. His life, like the lives of many of the other native people, had been torn apart since birth. They had the desire to learn the old ways, but were attracted to the things from outside their world. The members of Young One's generation were the crossovers, hybrids of primitive and advanced learning. They knew many more things than did their parents or grandparents. But what value did they bring if the things they learned displaced their culture?

Many of Young One's contemporaries back on the rez smoked dope, drank booze, and listened to heavy metal music for satanic messages. They wore cowboy clothes and abandoned their native dress. Worse, they ridiculed those who remained native and bullied and assaulted the traditionalists at will. It was the first time the Red Sands Pueblo people had become enemies of their own kind. This had never happened in their history. Sure, there were disputes over land, over water, over love affairs gone bad, and the same myriad of reasons neighbors miff each other, but this was different. There was a cultural struggle brewing among them—the old versus the new.

Many of these mistaken youth were rejects from Pueblo religious groups. Some were never even deemed worthy to invite to join in the first place. There was wholesale rejection of the old ways, and Young One, for all his goodness, was also caught up in it. He was different, however. He wanted to learn the new ways to help his people. The Outsiders had caused many problems, but they also could have many solutions to the problems.

The sacred places were littered with broken brown glass and used plastic bags and condoms. Gangs from as far away as Los Angeles were sending representatives to the rez to expand their turf. Fancy cars rolled down the dusty streets playing music that made the pueblo inhabitants think an earthquake was occurring. These Outsiders were not only accepted into their lands, but were eagerly greeted.

Young One remembered the time he was helping his grandfather hoe and weed the waffle garden. It was a task he had always enjoyed since he was a boy. It gave him great peace of mind to work in the garden. It was his last afternoon in the pueblo with Grandfather before being called up to active duty in the Persian Gulf. Grandfather had seen much of this happening. He knew that the youth were not bad, merely driven crazy by the outside influences. He also saw his grandson's attraction to things from outside their lands.

"You are going to become a warrior now. You have matured to manhood. If there is anything you need to know, I will answer now." Young One was surprised and honored that the old one would treat him like an equal. He was becoming a man. Grandfather was normally very quiet and spoke only when necessary. But when he did, he meant every word.

"Grandfather, why don't you like television and computers?"

The old one laid down his hoe and was silent for a while, as was his way, and then burst forth with a monologue as if it were a question he had been asked before, or he had long before thought out for himself.

"Our people have always tried to live in harmony with the Outsiders. We have taken things from their culture into ours. From the Spanish Conquistadors, we got the sheep and goats. From our old Indian enemies, we got the horse, and from the wagon train, we got the gun. From each kind of Outsider, we took what their culture offered and adapted it into our own. In that way, the small nibbled on what the large left behind. But since the television came to our people, they have taken us into their culture. Now the large is swallowing up the small. Many of our people complain about what the Outsiders took from us—our best lands, the water holes, and the sacred places. But worse than what they took is what they have given to us."

Although he could not speak or understand English, he understood the hypnotic effect of the invisible messages that flew through the air. He occasionally saw the moving-light box, and he didn't care for it.

Their traditional way of life did not condone photography, or even drawings of people. Grandfather regarded the moving-light box as a malevolent influence, not only on his people but on the Outsiders as well. He felt these influences captured the spirits of the people and made graven images of them. He felt they lied and deceived the people about the true nature of life. He did not like the peoples' images on the flickering screen. From the limited amount of it he had seen, there was entirely too much human misconduct in it for the young or even the elders to witness.

"The people in the magic box make believe. They do things they would not think of doing in real life. The evil magic box has them doing bad things in public for money. The Outsiders wonder why their villages are not safe. It is because the magic box has taught their children to be bad. It has trained young and old alike to do wrongful things."

They sat in silence for several minutes so Young One could digest the chosen words of his oldest living ancestor.

"The Outsiders' magic box also causes a thirst in the hearts of the people worse than salt in their mouths. It causes the people to want things they do not need and, cannot afford to buy. At one time, our people made everything they needed from the desert. Mother Earth fed us, clothed us and provided things to defend ourselves with. Today, all sorts of things must be purchased from the trading posts. The people are trading the old for the new, thinking they are winning, but they are losing the barter. Life in the desert camps gives freedom. Life in the town gives servitude to the ways of the Outsiders.

"The hunger for things they cannot afford to buy brings bad cravings into the hearts of the people. It creates too much want in their minds. Too many of the things of desire from the outside must be bought, not grown or made by hand. It is not good for their spirits. But this is not the worst of it. The craving it causes in the minds of the people looking at it causes them to sell their way of life as well, to buy the things they see. The desire for new things has lured the women away from their homes for no good purpose other than to make money to pay for things they do not need. The home fires go untended, and the children are forced to raise themselves. The magic box has become their teacher in the Outsiders' tongue. The people are hypnotized and made crazy by its flickering lights."

Again, there was silence, and Young One thought Grandfather was done, but he had just begun to talk. This was something that had troubled him for some time.

"But worse than all of these things, the magic box has replaced our traditional way of life. For time as long as anyone can remember, our people have sat around the campfires. The fire was the center of learning and entertainment. Our people have always looked into the fire and told stories, and sang songs, and cooked and ate, and mated, and slept and dreamed in front of its flickering lights. The fire lit the dark places, kept us warm, cooked our food, and kept the wild animals away. Around the fire, the tales of our people were told and retold and handed from generation to generation, from mouth to ear, for time beyond remembering. It made us a people with culture and homes and a way of life fit for the desert." He was silent for a while, and then he continued in his way of speaking.

"Another bad thing about the magic box is that it must have Outsiders' lightning for its fuel. For always our people have followed the streams and rivers through the *arroyos* and hills, following the animals in their search for water and grass. Now our people follow the lightning ropes next to the rolling pony paths."

"We cannot make that kind of lightning. We do not know how to catch it from the sky. So now the homes of our people must follow the trees they are hooked to. In days past, there were small bands or clans of our people living in different parts of our lands. They lived in small groups so they could live from the meager gifts of life the desert offered. No enemy could approach unnoticed, because no matter what direction they came from, someone was sure to see them and light warning smoke fires or beat alarm drums. Our people live closer together than ever before in our history. Like animals living in over-crowded conditions, we are more susceptible to disease. In one way, we have more than ever before. In another way, our people have less than they have ever had, even when they were poor.

"The old pueblos farther from the main village are empty and silent except for the whistling of the wind. No one tends the fire hearths or guards the secrets hidden in the floors of their ancestral homes. No sounds of laughter or sorrow can be heard in the abandoned stone and adobe structures. Only the howling of the desert winds carry songs there, where the people before them had lived. The spirits of the ancestors are unsettled because they cannot see how their children are doing so far away from their old homes. Today no one lives in the outer lands of our reservations, and soon the Outsiders will claim these lands as well." Young One was amazed how this simple old man with a different way of looking at life could see what so many others could not. He really did like talking to Grandfather, because it was like visiting someone in the past.

"Our people have always lived within the circle of life. The turning of the sun and moon, the changing of the seasons, the circle of time itself has guided our kind through life. The electric firebox brings the ways of the Outsiders, who have already lost their culture, into our lives. They are guests you invite in once, and it is difficult to say goodbye to them. Soon, the spirits of the people will be put under a spell by the flickering light that comes through their eyes to their hearts, and they will be lost. That is why I do not have a television set," Grandfather answered both proudly and apologetically. Young One never heard him speak of the matter again.

About the subject of computers, Grandfather didn't know what they were. When Young One explained to him what computers were, Grandfather thought they sounded like just a fancy magic box. Young One knew that the songs of his tribe and stories of the Red Earth Pueblo natives were being told before the printing press, indeed before the scribes of Mesopotamia touched cuneiform stick to wet clay. The tales from the old days, when his people were famous for their mystical skills and wizardry, fascinated Young One. Grandfather used to admonish him about believing in magic. He used to say, "There is no such thing as magic, but there is mysticism." The difference, he explained, is that magic is something that cannot ever happen in reality. Mysticism is harnessing and using the forces of nature under human direction.

"Magic is used by deceivers to fool the unwary. It is the misguided belief of the believer that gives it strength, not something in and of itself," he explained in their ancient language.

Young One knew Grandfather was right. Too many of the old ways were being lost because the young were listening to rock and roll or country and western music. "These are the songs and stories of others. The young are not learning their own culture and it is dying as surely as if the Outsiders had killed us outright. The songs of the Crow Clan were lost. None of their sons bothered to learn them, and they went from the earth when the old ones passed. All the peoples of the earth are feeling this loss of cultural identity. They feel for the loss of the past, but have gone too far in progress to turn back. That is why the tourists come here to see what they have lost. But we are only a generation behind them."

After Grandfather spoke, Young One continued pulling weeds from the garden. He remembered a troubling incident from when he was younger. He had his own story about television that had a profound effect on the rest of his life. He was having a fine time at his relative's house. There was plenty of food and drink. The children ran into and out of the house in youthful revelry. The older ones were drinking beer while watching the football game on the television. Their team was the Broncos, not only because it was an animal's name and the team did not use Indian names, but also Denver was the closest city with a football team.

Young One loved and respected Grandfather and his ways dearly, but the lure of electronic entertainment was too much for him to resist. Every chance he could, he would go to his modern cousin's house to watch television and play video games. Soon he was well-versed in the various cultures of cartoons, sports, and movies. The electronic magic was a powerful drawing force upon his adolescent mind. He also listened to the songs on the radio, but he preferred television.

He had seen both older black-and-white television shows as well as movies. He also saw newer color programs and came to an erroneous conclusion. It seemed like a simple thing, but it changed the direction of his young life. The particular delusion that took residence in his then thirteen-year-old mind was that once the world was merely black and white, like in the older television shows. Then suddenly one day, everyone woke up and the whole world had amazingly turned Technicolor. This was a mental delusion that grew in his mind and was to shape his future destiny. It was one more way that the Outsiders deceived these simple people without realizing it. Young One wondered what it had been like to sleep one night in a black-and-white world and to wake up to a brilliantly colored world.

His mother's third younger brother was his favorite uncle. He was in his early twenties and was learning the modern ways. He had a pickup truck, wore cowboy clothes, and had a machine to wash them in. He was the worldliest person Young One knew. He had always wondered about this seemingly miraculous event and felt he could confide in his older, wiser relative. During a commercial, while watching the football game, he became bold enough to ask a confidential question. This was a mistake, but he didn't realize it at the time. As the elders had whooped and hollered in delight as the Outsiders threw a ball on the field, he thought this was a good time to get an honest answer.

"What was it like the day the world turned color?" he innocently asked his favorite uncle.

"What?" was his incredulous response. Young One repeated his youthful inquiry, with explanation, and this time his uncle understood. His uncle was immediately brought back a thousand miles and hundreds of years into their past speaking to this simple child, who was ignorant of the ways of the world. Then his uncle did something that hurt Young One right down to the fabric of his very being—he laughed at him. He had been drinking beer and was not as sensitive to his nephew as he should have been. He burst out in a guffaw of derisive laughter.

"Did you hear that? Ask them," his uncle said, motioning with his head toward the other adults in the room. Young One was confused, but made his request a third time. It was greeted with howls of laughter from everyone in the room. To be laughed at by elders was a great embarrassment to an Indian. But the more they watched the Outsiders' magic box, the more like them they became.

"Foolish boy. You have been too long in the herd camps with Grandfather."

His cousin also laughed, "You do not understand modern things." He said this half to put his younger cousin down, and half so the adults did not think he was as stupid as Young One in these matters.

"You foolish goat boy," he said.

Young One went outside and cried real tears, as he was so hurt by their laughter that hit his heart like so many fists. He could do so much more than his chubby cousin could ever imagine, but he could not show him what he really knew.

From that time on, he resolved to learn as much as he could about the Outsiders' technology. His spirit was pulled apart by the competing forces within him as each world vied for his attention. Never again would he be laughed at because of his ignorance of outside things. He craved to learn everything modern. He worked hard to perfect his broken English, but he always had an accent most Outsiders could detect, though they couldn't quite place where it came from. His speech was marked with the southwestern accent particular to his people.

Every free moment, when he was not helping Grandfather or working at his job in a trading post, he spent learning modern things. He was interested in computers, airplanes and pickup trucks. He would learn the technology of the Outsiders to help his people. He wanted to be an Outsider. He wore his long hair under a cowboy hat, wore Outsiders' clothing and spoke their language, even though he could speak the native tongue better than most older Indians could on the pueblo. He particularly liked country and western music. These Outsider singers had money, fame, women, and everything they wanted. He even dreamed of being a famous musician, but realized he couldn't play the guitar. As he grew older, he spent less and less time with Grandfather in the herd camps and in his studies of the past ways. The halfhearted effort he made was enough to complete his religious tasks, but the powerful spirit within him was not satisfied with the effort he had expended. Further and further his body and mind drifted from the center of his universe. This is not to say that he abandoned his father's father, because he knew that one day, the light in the old one's eyes would cloud over and be snuffed out like the spent embers of a campfire. He did not want to lose touch with the old one this way. His heart was good, and he avoided most of the bad Outsider influence. Because of his austere upbringing, his inner spirit was stronger than many around him. This was to prove both a blessing and a curse later in his life.

He began to abandon the ways of the old for the ways of the new. These were the things of the future. But his limitations with the English language hampered his progress toward technology. On his army entrance exams, he topped the chart on abstract reasoning and mathematics. But he did not do that well in the English proficiency tests. Although he could speak English pretty well, he still had trouble reading and writing it. He was informed that his scores were not sufficient to give him technical training. He was sent to the infantry. He became a "grunt."

Young One could not help admiring the determined, hard-working old man who gave everything to life and expected little in return. He still went to the herd camps as much as he could to help the old man. And although he listened with great attention and respect to Grandfather's stories and advice, the old man knew all his words of wisdom were not taking hold in Young One's mind. No more than one could scatter fine corn seeds on rocks and expect a good crop could all the kernels of wisdom the old one placed in Young One's mind take root at that time. Grandfather only hoped that many of his thoughts would be put into the seed jars of his grandson's mind for future growth. Many of Grandfather's words of wisdom were coming true, and many of the kernels of knowledge that he placed in the mind of the son of his son were not being wasted...

Chapter 6

WITHERING HEATS

The relentless Arabian sun burned their flesh and faded the camo color away from their uniforms while they were wearing them. They greased themselves with sunscreen, smeared on with the fingertips from an olive drab-colored can that looked as if it could have had shoe polish in it. They painted their lips with lip balm. The dust stuck to the greasy stuff like metal filings to a magnet. You could not stay in the sun, ever. It would cook you. Anything metal lying in the sun would soon become as hot as if it were in a furnace. It could burn flesh. Their black M-16 rifles, designed for the jungle, were too hot to touch without gloved hands. Saudi Arabia always wins the contest for the hottest place on earth. During the daytime, if you stayed in the shade, if there was a breeze, and if you moved slowly, it was bearable.

It was so hot that they would cook in their chemical protective clothing and respirator, called MOPP gear. It stood for mission-oriented protective posture, and was in essence an olive drab or sage green-colored, heavy charcoal-impregnated suit with a full-face air purifying respirator, gloves, and booties, all designed to ward off chemical warfare agents from contact with the skin. In the summer sun, the chemical protective suits could kill almost as fast as the chemical agent they were designed to protect against. If an enemy fired a chemical shell at noon, by sundown an entire army could be slow-roasted in their green rotisserie bags. The desert heat would do all the work.

In addition to the heat-stress issue, the charcoal suits were a real problem to wear. They were supposed to protect the troops from getting "slimed" with chemical agents. The problem was that when a person sweated, the charcoal would rub off and cover the body of the individual. The troops called them "Kingsford suits," in reference to the popular brand of backyard barbecue fuel.

No one went out in the bright sunlight. It could kill you. It was like sticking your head in an oven. The only time the climate was actually nice was in the early morning, and then again as the late afternoon turned into early evening. The desert sunrises and sunsets were spectacular to see. For a brief period, the bright colors of the sun itself lit the drab desert. They were the most beautiful sights over there. Young One loved watching the change from light to dark in the Arabian Desert. He made it a point to observe the daily changing of the guard between the sun and the moon. The troops were usually too tired from working all night, or conversely, from working all day, to appreciate the few nice times there were.

In the nighttime, it was cooler, but also scarier, because that was when the animals and the terrorists came out. That time of the year, the night got less hot, but not really cool. But at least the sun was not shining. It got real dark there, as they exercised light security to keep the enemy from knowing their exact position. The open desert of the daytime seemed to close in on a person in the darkness, especially when there was no moon. Once in a while, the glow of a cigarette would spark the darkness. That was all the light there was. If there was a sniper out there, he could have shot a lot of guys catching a smoke just after the sergeant of the guard drove by. They were actually spread out too far for light discipline to be effective.

You could really see the stars at night. The dark desert makes the best planetarium that there is. Young One loved looking at the stars. They were just like the ones back home, halfway around the world. *At least the two deserts have the same stars*, Young One thought.

Each reservist secretly longed for and, at the same time dreaded, enemy contact. The constant "hurry up and wait" of the army had not changed, only gotten worse. One moved quicker and waited longer in the age of modern warfare. The worst thing was that nothing ever seemed to happen. Each day seemed to blend into its predecessor and meld into a new tomorrow with monotonous regularity. For weeks their lives were the same, the weather was the same, and their duties were the same. It was the old story of "same shit, different day." But any soldier will tell you that this is still preferable to lots of different shit hitting you in the same day. It can pile up too quickly that way.

Everyone wondered about war with Iraq and if it would really happen. Was this to be just another peacekeeping mission? They knew, as did everyone about this time, that Saddam was not going to attack them as they first had feared. What they did not know was that several months from then, they would attack him. The original shock of going to a potential war zone was wearing off. The longer they waited, the less likely they were to be overrun by the overwhelming Iraqi force across the Kuwaiti border. Instead, coalition newcomers were overrunning them. There were people constantly running around in strange military vehicles. No one knew whether to shoot them, wave at them, or salute them. A lot of folks liked to see what the front line looked like. It was not what some of them expected.

The time they spent over there was not pleasant, but looking back, it was not as unpleasant as it could have been. Some of the troops would rather have been back in Hotel Hell or some other building, because it was more similar to wherever they came from than bivouacking in the barren sand. Young One found life better in the field than in the large building surrounded with a maze of concrete barriers and razor wire to minimize the likelihood of a terrorist attack. He felt he was more of a target in the warehouse than he did in a field emplacement. Several months later, when the Scud missile hit the barracks in Dhahran, he was very glad to have been in the open desert, rather than in a metal death box.

Once on the front line, life became more familiar to Young One. He liked the desert air, the vast expanse of sand, and the open sky overhead. Just as Grandfather had predicted in his dream, the sand was strangely colored and different than the red earth back at home. He remembered the smoking sky wagon, the iron steps, and now the odd-colored sand. He wondered if Grandfather's vision of burning sands and screaming soldiers would also come true. This troubled him terribly.

Next to the air they breathed, water was the most essential life commodity for the troops deployed in the Saudi summer. They had to drink up to five gallons a day when they arrived there because they sweat so much. The weird thing was that the air was so dry that perspiration seldom developed. The heat just sucked the water out of the troops without waiting for it to bead up on their skin. When they first got there, their officers had them work and train in the full sun to toughen them up. Working in the hot sun in the heavy battle dress uniform and leather boots took the sweat out of them, as a sauna bath does. Anything that the sun could see, it would heat up. Everybody had wicked sunburns and cracked lips from the excessive solar radiation and the dry air. The sun was so bright that even the black and Hispanic soldiers got terribly sunburned. Although the Arabian sun was an equal-opportunity scorcher, those of European heritage with pale complexions suffered most.

After several days, many soldiers developed "prickly heat," which is a skin rash caused by the sweat glands becoming clogged and inflamed by too much perspiration. Some guys with severe acne also suffered horribly from their skin conditions. The rough uniforms kept rubbing the moist skin off their zits. This extreme irritation was very discomforting, and a couple of guys had to be given antibiotics for skin infections. Just about everyone experienced heat exhaustion from working in the sun. The gung ho were the first to go, but even lazy Walters got it, or he pretended to, in order to get out of a work detail.

Even Young One was not immune to the insidious effects of the heat. After a session of very strenuous digging and filling sandbags, he began to feel ill. His stomach muscles cramped and became as rigid as a board. His hands cramped in the shape of the shovel handle and seemed to "freeze" in place. Next he felt the clammy skin, the flushed complexion, the nausea, the weakness, and the overwhelming urge to vomit. He sat down, and his skin began to dry and get hot. Sergeant Eliot, recognizing what was happening, took him for medical treatment immediately. This trooper was slipping from heat exhaustion into heat stroke.

To help alleviate the effects of heat stress, they had several 55-gallon barrels of rusty water in which they dunked soldiers suspected of developing heat-related illness. The medics had a portable generator and a freezer to keep their heat-sensitive medications fresh. They also produced ice, which they dumped into the water to cool it in order to treat heat stress, or to apply to sprains and muscle aches as a cold compress.

The first time Young One hit the ice-cold water, he thought his heart would stop beating. He went in uniform and all. The medic also poured cold water over his head to rapidly cool him down. It was as if he were a member of the polar bear club but in the withering heat. Young One could hardly catch his breath. He was taken out and allowed to slowly dry, and he began to feel better. They had caught it in time. He was given cold water to drink to cool down his internal organs. They all quickly learned the harsh lessons of the Arabian sun and how deadly the scorching desert can be. After losing several men to heat stress, they lightened up a bit. But by then, most of the hand-dug field fortifications had been completed.

After two weeks, most guys had cut back to three gallons a day, as the forced daylight labor slackened. They slowly learned to live more like desert natives. One had to stay out of the sun during the hottest part of the day. They also learned to work slowly during the day. Most of their body water was lost as sweat, some in the exhaled breath, and a little in the urine. If you did not drink enough water, your urine would turn the color of tea. That meant your kidneys were not working properly. That's why so much water was needed every day, to flush out the kidneys and to regulate temperature. Also, if a guy did not drink enough water, the food in his intestines would dry up and turn to cement in his entrails. Then a medic in the rear area would have to pull out the plug with a pair of stainless steel pliers.

⋊—⋊—⋊

Ice was the most precious commodity in the Saudi summer. Walters figured out a way to get a steady supply of the stuff from the medics, who kept a freezer for medical emergencies that was run by a gasoline generator. Walters filled a sock with a bar of soap and tied a knot in it like a knight's small battle mace from medieval times. He would swing it and strike some part of his body to produce a visible and painful bruise. He would make up some story for the medics about how he had injured himself in the line of duty, and they would give him some ice in a plastic bag to use as a compress. He had a leg injury, an elbow accident, and once he even hit himself in the head to produce a discernible welt. He got ice for a week with that one. Rather than use it for its intended purpose, he used it for cool drinks.

Soon, other guys started catching on and began doing it themselves. Their medics wised up, and ice availability was severely restricted. The frozen treasure chest was locked to them. Walters, however, discovered a new source. One time when there was a layover at the Al Jubayl port facility, Walters found the mother lode for his ice project. There were some sailors stationed there who had something to do with facilitating cargoes through the port. They were set up in some nice barracks that resembled an inexpensive motel back in the states.

There were two sailors trying to carry a heavy desk up some stairs. Always the helpful sort (at least he was always helping himself to something), Walters volunteered to assist them with their load. This was where the navy petty officers were quartered. The squids treated him to a cold pop for helping them. They had a television room, pop and junk food machines, and the unbelievable luxury —an automatic ice machine, just like in a hotel back in the states. Walters had discovered the golden goose for frozen diamonds. The sailors liked hearing his stories from the trenches on the front line.

Walters had a good line of bullshit, but he was one of those guys who could go either way in life. He would either end up on a chain gang or on the board of a major corporation because of his lack of moral values. Walters learned their names and asked them if they would mind if he took some ice back to the poor soldiers on the front line. They said of course, and even drove him in a naval vehicle to a civilian store where he purchased a large, Styrofoam-type cooler. He took it back and filled it completely with the frozen gems as if it were a treasure box. He hid it in the vehicle, and soon he had a thriving business.

It was amazing how much some guys would give for their creature comforts. Any of the ice that made it back was quickly bartered away, much of it to Feinstein, who delighted in its possession. Any of the cold water melted from the ice that was left over, Walters would mix with powdered beverage mix from the MREs and trade that as well. He would trade ice for cigarettes that he would sell for cash to the Arab truck drivers, who paid premium prices for American smokes. After a while, Walters had in his possession all sorts of contraband, and he created a thriving black market along the front line. Everyone knew he was doing it but looked the other way, because they were his customers.

If you want to hear about something crazy, this is it. They had a tractor-trailer full of sparkling mineral water. They brought it forward in one of the first trucks. The first week they were there, the only water available was bottled mineral water in quart containers procured in country from a civilian source. They were told that fresh water would get trucked to them the next day. It was three days before the water trucks finally found them. No kidding, the guys took baths and shaved in sparkling mineral water because there was no other water available.

They wished they had it later when they had to drink the rusty, chlorine-tasting stuff from the water tankers and canvas water bags. The day before, that stuff had been seawater with fish reproducing in it, and the next day, it was going to be urinated down a funneled tube into the sand. Some thought it was starting to change right in the tank, as it was just as warm and stank as bad sometimes. It was desalinated and heavily chlorinated, and they poured it into anything that could carry it to the front. They even had water delivered in a contracted cement truck that had been modified to haul water.

They used their Nazi-style, Kevlar composite helmet liners as a basin to wash and shave in. They were not as good as the old steel pots of Nam days for cooking, washing, or shaving in. But the old steel helmets were unfortunately obsolete, as most modern bullets could go through one quicker than a diamond drill bit through an aluminum pie pan. Their uniforms were heavy and not suited for the climate. They were the heavy-cloth, six-color patterns that were designed for the Desert Warfare Center in the high desert in California. It was cooler there, and the terrain was a different color. They were told that they would get new uniforms with the three-color print and made of a lighter fabric weight at a later date. They finally got them around Christmas, when it was too cool to wear them. The army never changes.

They were allowed a quick shower once a week, and they were not guaranteed what day it would be. There were a lot of guys to shower, and water had to be trucked a long way to their position. When their time came, the troops were trucked a few kilometers a squad at a time to take a quick Tarzan shower. It was so named because the troops screamed like the dude in the cheetah-skin jock strap in the old black-and-white movies.

All the water was trucked in, and, if delivered in the day, it was scalding from the microwave-strength sun, or it was merely warm if it was delivered during the night. Often it was rusty and full of chlorine. Sometimes it smelled like fuel, as that had been the tank's last cargo. They used this for wash and shaving water, but not for potable water. The troops had to wash quickly, as any soap left on the body would cause a terrible itch and discomfort the rest of the week. Drinking water was always delivered in a potable water tank, but wash water could be brought in on anything smoking with wheels. Before enough tankers arrived, they would line the beds of pickup trucks with plastic and fill them half full of water and drive them for hours back to the company area sloshing all the way. They had usually lost half of it from sudden stops by the time they got back to camp.

Communal showers had been set up for the soldiers. There were two plywood boxes set up as shower stalls. Each soldier got a quick dowsing, moved to the next box, and then soaped up. When ready, his soap was quickly washed off to make room for the next soapy soldier behind him. A lot of folks could wash with just a little water. Trucks ran constantly to keep them supplied with the fluid of life itself.

It doesn't sound like much, but it removed the body effluvia and gave these comfort-deprived individuals a chance to be in a water environment for just a while. It was really physically and emotionally exciting after a week's worth of sweat salt, grease, and shit was removed. But it was short-lived. After the dowsing, the water stopped and "NEXT" was called. To Young One, the feeling was exhilarating. Everyone seemed to be in a good mood for a short period of time after their shower.

Sergeant Eliot came up to Private Johnny McHugh from Scranton, Pennsylvania, and asked, "Feel better now?"

"Yeah, I feel like a new piece of shit, Sarge."

Eliot walked away laughing and shaking his head, knowing exactly what he meant. There was an exhilaration that came from being temporarily cleansed.

Jones, the new-age vegetarian from Vermont, said he could "feel his aura shining through," once the insulating filth was washed away by the shower. No one knew where it was shining from. Simms provided an answer: "Maybe out of his ass."

Their uniforms got sticky and stiff with body funk. They also had a chance to wash their clothes at the shower point. Some guys would put on their uniforms, and wash them first. They would lather them up like their own bodies and then rinse them off. This usually cost a five-dollar tip for the civilian driver for the extra shower, but it was worth it. They would then put on their clean uniform and take their wash back to hang up to dry. There was laundry service available, but sometimes you did not get all your clothes back or got someone else's stuff instead. The laundry service sucked, so mostly they hand-washed their uniforms and allowed them to drip-dry while wearing them, or they hung them from the tent ropes to dry in the breeze.

After their showers, they could usually be seen washing their socks or underwear, as no one wanted to get someone else's under garments back from the laundry. They would sit around and swap rumors and talk like regular wash women. Clothing dried very quickly there, with air like that from a blast furnace, but everything was as stiff as rawhide. A wash towel would dry so stiff that it could almost be used for sandpaper.

Some guys used the rusty water from the emergency immersion barrels to wash their uniforms, which developed a telltale, rust-brown color after a while. They had to hang their wet uniforms inside out to prevent them from getting sun-bleached like a dress in a downtown store window. It only slowed down the process, as any time they were in the sun, it bleached the color from their equipment and uniforms.

One time, while they were waiting their turn to take their showers, a dusty, beat-up looking Humvee pulled up with some Special Forces guys in it. There were four of them. Each was rough looking and dirty. They walked up to the guys and asked, "Do you mind if we take a shower? We're kind of in a hurry for a debriefing back at our headquarters and haven't had one for three weeks."

"No, go ahead," they said. They let them cut into the line. They came out cleaner and somehow more human looking. One of the Special Forces sergeants, an E-7, was drying and putting on a clean uniform. He had all kinds of patches and badges sewn on his uniform: master jump wings, combat infantryman, scuba diver, pathfinder, ranger, and Special Forces. This sergeant had certainly been around the army, but he did not look so scary after cleaning himself up.

Feiny was hanging around near him and asked him, "Are you a Green Beret?"

"No son. This is a green beret," he said pointing to his green war beanie. "I'm a Special Forces soldier."

Feiny should have let it go at that, but he had to ask one more question. "Is it true that you guys can kill a man five hundred ways?"

The hard sergeant said nothing at first, then looked him straight in the eyes and said, "Pick a number, motherfucker," and continued shaving.

Feiny did not know whether to shit or wind his watch when he heard that, but was smart enough to keep his big mouth shut. Everybody got a good laugh over it, and no one wanted to tangle with those guys. It was great to have Feiny get his balls busted by someone else. Usually, he was the one operating the verbal nutcracker. One of the other "snake eaters" brought over a small cardboard box with various Iraqi insignia and medals in it. They passed it around and allowed the guys to have some of the souvenirs in thanks for letting them cut in.

Then Jones just had to ask the question. "Where did you get this stuff?"

"From some guys who didn't need it any longer," said the sergeant.

They rode away still laughing over such a funny joke. The war had not officially begun yet, but the special ops folks were getting plenty of action engaged in covert activities in No Man's Land and behind Iraqi lines. Nobody but them ever heard of it, and they were not talking. The reservists were glad that they were out there, patrolling the barren sands for trouble. They could at least provide advance warning of enemy attack.

>―――✕―――✕―――✕―

Guard duty sucked. It was military monotony at its worst. While standing guard, Young One was thinking about a class on border security they had received a few days before. They had been given a demonstration about how important it is to stay alert on perimeter guard duty. One of their training classes was about terrorism and enemy night infiltration. The platoon was assembled, and they were about to watch a wicked play unfold before their eyes in the theater of war. Everybody squatted or sat on the sandy ground by a mock perimeter set up for training purposes. It was just starting to get dark. It was the middle of the twilight hour, that transition time between daylight and nighttime, when even shadows disappear.

They were told to watch as a scenario was enacted before them. There was a simulated minefield with a barbed-wire perimeter set up. There was a guard post, and there were two soldiers on guard duty. One guy was standing, keeping watch. His buddy appeared to be sleeping. For a long time, nothing happened. No one could see anything. None of the guys knew what to expect. The sergeant giving the demonstration just kept saying, "Be quiet and watch."

The other sergeant spoke, "It's night. The stars are shining. You are pulling perimeter guard duty. Some of you would rather be back in your fart sack making love to your inflatable air mattress. You are listening to a civilian radio you are not supposed to have; you are enjoying your favorite tune on the Armed Forces Radio. The sergeant of the guard just checked the posts and won't be back for a while. But you are not taking any chances of being heard, so you are listening with headphones. No one will ever know. It's hot, and the sand is blowing in your eyes. It's dark and you're dreaming of a taste of Mom's apple pie or some sweet sugar britches back home. That is when Habib gets you."

There appeared to be some movement in the dark sand. Suddenly, an Arab jumped up from hiding in the dark and took a knife and slashed with the speed of a magician at the guard's throat. He had crawled twenty meters in plain sight of them, and no one saw him. He next dispatched the sleeping soldier, likewise with the prowess of a prestidigitator.

"No one will hear you die because he slit your throat below the voice box. You cannot scream through it. Your carotid arteries on both sides of your sorry neck are squirting blood like water guns.

"Gentlemen, let me remind you of just one thing. This man, just like a half million of his friends across the sand, is here to kill you and your buddies. He does not need a Scud missile, or a Warsaw Pact tactical vehicle. We are in their backyard, and these folks have been killing each other for thousands of years before the firearm was invented. Do not think that they have forgotten how to do it the old-fashioned way.

"Not everyone in this country loves you. You have just seen a demonstration of how a determined enemy can penetrate even the securest of areas. He can creep up in day or night like a ninja and cut your balls off. Your buddy, who is supposed to be watching your ass, is taking a nap while you look out for the sergeants. He will not feel a thing, because he will be next.

"The enemy crawled right through the minefield in front of you. How did he do that? This is his third night visiting your position. Each time, he probed your position for landmines and marked them with little stones that no one but him noticed. Last night he clipped through the barbed wire and nobody noticed. The guard these jokers relieved was busy reading a paperback book he snuck in. Each night he creeps a little closer, marking his path, until he is through the defenses. And next, he will be through with you."

This got everyone's full attention. This guy had just crawled up, while everyone was watching, like a slow moving bush, and took out a guard in half a heartbeat. He did not make a sound.

Then Sergeant Franklin spoke. "Let's thank Sergeant Zabirah of the Saudi Special Forces for this demonstration of perimeter penetration. And let us also thank Master Sergeant Mel Broom of the 5th Special Forces Group for his narration of this graphic event. Let's give them both a hand."

The Arabian sergeant stood there in his camouflaged suit with a broad smile on his face. He still held the large knife in his hand. It could have been dripping blood. The men applauded half-heartedly, as they were not sure whether what they had just seen was good or not. Each secretly promised himself not to allow that to happen to him. But as the old adage goes, "Vows made in the fury of the storm are soon forgotten in the peace of the calm."

✂— ✂— ✂—

The sergeant of the guard drove by in a dusty cloud and, seeing that they were awake, waved and kept on going in a cloud of dust. He was part of the roving patrol, as well as the boss for the day of all the front line guards. A lot of the other guys wished something would happen to break the boredom. Young One and Walters were on guard duty together. As he stood there behind his machine gun, Walters felt something almost imperceptible touch his leg. He felt it again and looked down to see a large, hairy spider on his leg. It was what the soldiers called a camel tarantula. They were large, ground-dwelling spiders that inhabited the area.

"Holy shit!" he exclaimed in a startled voice. The large-fanged spider jumped off his leg and scurried to a corner of the two-man defensive position.

"Look at the legs on that dude."

"Quick, hit it with your helmet." A few clumsy bashes with their helmets failed to exterminate the fist-sized pest. Instead, it ran up behind one of the corrugated metal sheets that shored up the hole in the sand.

"Missed the muthaw," said Walters, as he kicked at the metal sheeting in a vain attempt to kill the swift spider.

"Did you see the ass on that thing? It looked like a hairy glove with fangs on it."

"Do you think they bite?" Young One asked.

"No man. The teeth are just for decoration. What the fuck do you think they're for? A medic told me about a guy that got bit on the hand by one of those things over in the 106th. It hurt so bad, he had to chop off his own hand with an E-tool to make it feel better."

"I do not believe that," said Young One, who did not want to anger or engage in argument with him.

"No, dude, he said it was true. He said they came for him in a helicopter ambulance and took his hand back to a hospital in Dhahran to sew it back on. It was green when they picked it up and so fuckin' rotten a couple of hours later that they had to throw it away to keep the emergency room from stinking."

"I do not believe that," said Young One again after carefully considering the facts.

"No, it's true. Why would he lie about a thing like that?"

Then they went back to swatting sandflies and wondering who would gain an advantage from making up such a story...

Chapter 7

SUDDEN SANDSTORM

Young One was on guard duty with Jones in one of the dugout machine-gun emplacements on the front line. It was already particularly warm that day, and it was not even noon. It was still the first week of September, and the sun was blazing like a giant welding torch in the powder blue, cloudless sky. The sun was baking the corrugated metal roof right through the layer of sandbags atop it.

Jones was slumped over the machine gun and not particularly paying attention, trying to stay awake on guard duty in the heat. It would be three days before their next scheduled shower. The dry, elevated temperature sapped the strength of the soldiers. They had been in country three weeks already. It was a hot, windless day. Usually there was some sort of breeze, however slight, but that day the weather was dead calm. If the devil were to take a vacation from Hell, he would not have found the climate of their bivouac area inclement whatsoever.

Guard duty was decidedly better than filling sandbags or digging foxholes. Young One was looking through the binoculars. It was a large, tripod-mounted unit. He was peering across a great space of emptiness. Through the binoculars, the soldiers could see for miles. In reality, the binoculars merely gave them a closer look at nothing. Every so often they would see a camel or a jackal in the distance, but usually there was nothing to be seen in the daytime. At night, with the starlight scopes, it was a different story. Everything could be seen in its magnified light, very much like a green-and-white movie.

All sorts of things moved in the cooler desert night, confident of their concealment in the darkness. The coalition positions were reconnoitered nightly by all sorts of wildlife, using nocturnal stealth skills. Most of the men were completely unaware that wild, living things had been there, so close to their encampment. The soldiers with the starlight night scopes could see some of them. The infrared scopes could spot all wildlife a long way off. Young One loved watching the wildlife in the night. Even though it was harder to sleep in the daytime, nighttime guard duty was the best, he thought.

The strong sunlight in the daytime could cause cataracts to form in the eyes. Neither the camo-colored boonie hats nor the Kevlar helmets provided shade for the eyes. Therefore, it was necessary for the troops to wear sunglasses or tinted sand goggles with appropriate ultra-violet radiation lenses at all times during the day. If a soldier lost his lenses, he could lose his sight as a result. Sunburned eyeballs were not a good thing. In addition to the constant sunlight, the windblown sand was also unpleasant to the eyes. The fine sand had the opposite effect of a mirage. Instead of allowing a soldier to see what was not there, it caused him not to see what was there. Both were bad for sentries on guard duty.

The constant waiting for nothing to happen was beginning to grate on their nerves. Staring into the sunlight hour after hour had an almost hypnotic effect on the soldiers, even through their goggles. It was easy to sleep standing up with the dark goggles on because they hid the closed eyelids. If one had something to lean on, it was possible to sleep standing up. It was very dangerous, and the sergeants had to be on the lookout for that. Most of the time, they would drive by in a Hummer and wave at the guards, and if they waved back, they usually kept on going. Sometimes they would blow the horn to get the guard's attention. If that did not work and they had to get out of the vehicle, there would be hell to pay.

It was really eerie when the wind did not blow. The only way to describe the silence in the windless desert is deafening. The mind likes noise and, in its absence, will create it artificially. The human ear needs external stimulation. That is why isolation confinement in prisons is a particularly harsh punishment. Having a hidden battery transistor radio helped eliminate the wearisome silence. Also, talking helped to pass the time. If there was not someone to talk to, a soldier could listen to the Armed Forces Radio Network and hear all the politically acceptable tunes from back home.

Many soldiers had secret portable radios but kept them hidden. They turned them off when the sergeants came by to inspect them. Batteries were both expensive and hard to come by, so they were saved for special programs. The sergeants even listened to Armed Forces Radio themselves in the Humvees. Some fellows secreted paperback books to read while on guard duty during the daytime. Mostly the sergeants looked the other way as long as a guy was awake and alert. Walters used to read them even at night with a flashlight. He was not only next to useless, but he could be very dangerous to be around. He was always up to something.

Young One and Jones each took turns scanning the horizon for evidence of enemy approach or any other movement. The wind was perceptibly swirling the sands, in a hypnotic, wavelike movement, very much like moving water. The undulating sands had a mesmerizing effect upon humans. The old desert has always been a conjurer. Her worst sleight-of-hand feats are the mirages she creates with light and heat. She can play tricks with the eyes of mortals.

Her mirages are legendary and are accomplished without smoke or mirrors. One of the worst mirages is the appearance of rain on the horizon. A thirsty, dying individual would march toward it, only to find no water. When it is extremely hot in the desert, the rain evaporates from the oven-like air before it hits the ground. It is a cruel trick to play on the thirsty. It really is raining, but only in the dry air. The heat can also create shimmering appearances that, in the distance, resemble pools of life-giving water.

Mirages are one of the desert's cruelest deceits. Hot, sunny days were the worst for mirages. Sometimes it was better to only periodically glance at their coverage area, because continuous staring can bring on the mirage effect. In one of their desert survival classes, a sergeant told them, with perfect military diction, "Mirages are illusory optical phenomena caused by the refraction of light through heated air." They did not know what it meant, but it sounded good to them.

Young One also remembered hearing, "As a human being dies of thirst, the eyeball loses pressure as water loss depletes the body of its most precious resource, its stored water. This causes further visual disturbances that make the mirage appear more real to the unfortunate. It can really play tricks with sight." Back in the moment, Jones said, "Look out there. Doesn't it look like a pool of water?"

"Yes, but it is not," Young One retorted. The sandflies were buzzing and biting as usual. His hand batted them away almost like the instinctive tail of a horse that unconsciously swats at flying pests. They were a constant annoyance during the long wait. Jones reached back and swatted one on the back of his neck. He looked at the palm of his hand; there was a spot of his own blood from the ruptured insect.

"Damn, it got me!" Jones exclaimed in exasperation.

"You better worry about getting a Baghdad boil."

"Don't remind me."

"Remember what they told us," said Young One.

They remembered another desert survival class they had been given when they were still in Hotel Hell, by some preventive medicine specialists who told them about the diseases in the area. Of all the pests they had to contend with, the sandflies were the worst. Not only could these winged pets of the devil annoy with bites that itched far beyond their tiny size, they could carry the deadly leishmaniasis protozoa.

This tiny protozoan lives a complex life cycle between desert rodents, jackals, dogs, and humans. The sandflies pick up the parasite from feeding upon the infected and give it to the uninfected through their insidious bite. There is no vaccine to prevent it. The only way to prevent the disease is by not getting bitten. That was next to impossible for the soldiers. The miserable little beasts were everywhere. They were worse at night, but they would still pester humans in the daytime, if shade was available, as in their roofed foxholes.

It could take up to two years to know if they had the disease. Some GIs carried the disease home in their blood without knowing it. Leishmaniasis could cause disfiguring scars and could eat away the face or other body parts.

The good news was that if a human survived it, they were permanently immune. The bad news was that no one wanted it even once. The "bug juice" repellent that was issued to the troops was good for mosquitoes, but it was cologne for the sandflies. If one swatted a sandfly, the miniscule creatures inhabiting its infected body fluids could bore right through intact skin and cause disease in human beings, without even a bite. These winged vermin made desert life a pestiferous hell.

Another problem that the soldiers faced was breathing microbe-laden dust suspended in the air. There were many respiratory hazards created by so much excavation of the desert soil. Dust blew on the breeze even with very little wind. Stuff could "hatch out" in their lungs and cause horrible disease. Many soldiers wore paper, industrial-style facemasks to filter out some of the dangerous dust. When they took the masks off, everywhere the mask covered was not sunburned. It was really strange to see that, especially on the white guys. From their nose to their chin and around their mouths was pale, and everywhere else was reddened by solar exposure. It really looked comical, but no one there thought it was funny. It was a tough adjustment for the pale skins.

✕ ✕ ✕

The wind is the breath of the desert. There were times when the wind never blew, and there were times when the wind blew with seemingly incessant ferocity. The desert winds were slowly sandblasting their equipment little by little, and the sands of time would carry away the bits. As the Arab song goes, "The dust of the bones of the martyrs is in the air," and eventually the greatest assemblage of military machines in the world's history would join it. Every day the coalition forces sat, delicate optical devices, machinery, and equipment of every type was scoured, plugged, clogged, and dusted inside and out with a fine coating of the desert itself. Computers were filled with the destructive powder and would not operate. The gritty sand, as fine as talcum powder, seemed to get everywhere.

Mother Nature has always been a finicky housekeeper in the desert. She is constantly rearranging things, moving them, and replacing them.

She may form a sand dune, come back a short time later, and it is gone. Sand is almost like a living thing in the desert, moving upon the wind. Granules of sand are in constant motion, and sand is continuously being created as the wind blasts the rocks into minute bits of the gritty stuff. The large particles become small, and the small become many.

The desert creates dunes at her pleasure, and, almost as a naughty child, she blows them down with fury. In the past century, British archaeologists reported seeing a huge sand dune in the Arabian Desert created after a very large storm. It was, by report, over seven hundred feet high. When they returned a few years later, they could find no trace of it. Please bear in mind that these were sober scientists and engineers with mapping and surveying skills. The giant dune had simply vanished, like a massive mirage. Its sand had been redistributed throughout the desert, carried upon the winds of subsequent storms.

This is how the desert reclaims her building materials. It is one reason people can become disoriented and lost in the desert; the landmarks change so often through the "shifting sands of time," as the desert poets say. The shifting sands have buried whole, lost cities. Even native Arabs sometimes get lost and die in the desert. No one is really welcome in the desert. The ones who live there are temporarily tolerated.

The winds blow the sand to the Gulf, and the storms bring it back up to the beach to be blown away one more time in an endless cycle of ebb and flow, of give and take. The wind and the sand sing together, ranging in sound from an almost imperceptible tinkling, as grains of salt hitting a dinner plate, to that reminiscent of a howling, whistling freight train during the infrequent sandstorms. During the morning, the wind can be negligible, but by late afternoon, the sun-generated winds can scream at seventy-five miles per hour.

There are reports of people going mad after days of listening to the incessant screaming wind, causing them to hide in some temporary shelter. They have reported hearing the wails of the dead and their grieving relatives in the howling, screeching air. To one with an already guilty conscience and a superstitious nature, the voices on the wind could prove enough to send him over the edge. Old Bedouin law allowed a man to kill his wife and children out of mercy after five days of sandstorms.

The worst of the desert sandstorms is called the *shamal*. This creates huge walls of swirling winds. It is the hurricane of the desert, It is the mother of all sandstorms. During World War II, the Germans fighting in Africa under Rommel suffered a major logistical defeat when a large ammunition dump near Tobruk blew up in North Africa in 1942. A *shamal* produced sufficient storm-generated electricity to spark an explosion that destroyed both their ammunition and their hopes for victory. The Desert Fox suffered a stinging slap from the hand of Mother Nature. When a *shamal* blows, visibility becomes zero, and humans must gasp for air as hurricane-like gusts of sandy wind fill eyes, nose, throat, and lungs. Makeshift masks serve as poor filters. The dust seems to find its way into everything.

Pilots tell of dust storms miles high in the sky. They say it is comparable to flying into a wall of sand that can suffocate jet engines and sandblast the props off a propeller-driven aircraft. It was wise aviation to avoid them.

Several times, the soldiers' encampment was besieged by sandstorms. The storms blew down shithouses, tents, and camo netting. It was scary because the wind could blow a tent pole like a spear or the pegs like daggers as it ripped them from the ground. Sandstorms always left behind work in their wake and always seemed to change things. Everything had to be put back up or dug out again. They usually averaged a sandstorm per week during their first few months there, but this one in particular was by far the worst they encountered.

Young One and Jones were supposed to have been relieved by the sergeant of the guard shortly, but Mother Nature had other ideas. It was a *shamal*, and climatologists say it was one of the worst sandstorms in recorded history. At first, everything was in its usual state of meteorological monotony. That day, the air became unusually still. It was a particularly hot early afternoon. Even the seemingly incessant motion of the roasted sands had stopped. Then the wind began to blow ever so imperceptibly.

The wind always moves in the desert, but had not really blown very hard since they started pulling their guard duty. There had been an eerie calm to the climate. Very slowly, the wind began to pick up in velocity. Then it began to come in puffy gusts. Wind, then stillness, then more wind, then more stillness. Finally the wind came. Its continuous force at first caused the grains of sand to dance upon the earth. Young One watched the grains of sand start to bounce on the ground as they were moved by the winds. It was a strange sight. Climatologists call the phenomenon "saltation," but Young One or Jones did not know that. Then the soldiers could feel the winds pick up and grow stronger and stronger.

In the distance, dust devils danced like whirling dervishes in the wicked wind. It was a fascinating, as well as frightening, show. The sand was being picked up upon the swift breeze and transported downwind. Young One and Jones pulled down their sand goggles from their Kevlar helmets and rolled down their sleeves. All of a sudden Young One cried aloud, "Look at that!" as he pointed toward a wall of sand a mile high coming upon them. It was an absolutely frightening atmospheric apparition that bore down upon them. They watched in helpless awe as the fury of the storm fell upon them.

The wind howled ferociously and drowned the screams of those who experienced the fierce storm. It roiled in the sky with inexorable force toward them. The wall of sand in the sky engulfed their positions with frightening force. Guys were blown down trying to run for their shelters. Tents were ripped out by their ropes, with stakes and poles going along for the ride. After the wind picked up and carried away the sand, it started on the gravel next.

Sand, dust, dried vegetation, and even small living things were drawn up into the swirling winds. Lightning strikes hit the sand and cooked it to glass. Some soldiers got hit with scorpions that were flying through the air like frogs in a hurricane. Turner caught one right in the face, and he got a bad sting on his cheek. His screams of pain were not heard through the howling winds.

Jones and Young One ducked down into their two-man foxhole as pea-sized projectiles were hurled with the force of buckshot. A sergeant in another platoon set out on foot to check on his guys. He got beat up by the gravel. The lenses of his sand goggles were even cracked by the force of the stone projectiles hurled by the wild wind. Any part of the body not covered with a flak jacket or helmet got severely pelted with the flying missiles. It was like a thousand guys shooting slingshots at you continuously.

Slowly, their foxhole was filling in. They had to keep shoveling out sand, similar to bailing a sinking boat, to keep their foxholes from completely filling up. They could not see anything and had trouble catching their breath as the sandstorm raged.

Simms was with Sergeant Eliot in one of the guard Humvees, going up and down the line checking the guard, when the sandstorm hit. The storm blew so furiously that they could not see over the hood of the vehicle. The windshield wipers did not work to remove the gritty stuff, and headlights only reflected the light from the dust back into their eyes. Visibility was so poor that they pulled off to the side of the road just as the engine sputtered to a halt and waited for the storm to blow over. They felt as if they were in a tan, choking snowstorm. Their radio was reduced to static by the electricity in the air. They could not call for help or report their whereabouts. The gusts of wind were all coming from the same direction, and the sand blasted the sides of the trucks all night. Gravel blasted spider-web-shaped holes in the windows.

The winds howled for all day and for most of the night. Just as suddenly as it started, it was over. When the wind finally died down the next morning, entire sides of vehicles that had been exposed to the wind had been sandblasted down to bare metal. It frosted the windows on one side like those in bathrooms. One side of the vehicle was camo painted, and the other side was shiny, silver metal. The camo side of the vehicle was piled high with sand like a snowdrift. The fierce Arabian winds had not only removed the paint, but had actually pitted metal on the other side of the sturdy military vehicles.

After the storm was over, several guys had to be evacuated to the rear to remove sand grit from their eyes. A flying tent pole speared a guy in another platoon, and a sergeant checking on the troops got whacked in the face with a metal tent stake still attached to the tent as it sailed past him in the fierce winds. They thought he might lose an eye from that. Their radio mast had snapped off, and they were out of communication with everyone. Turner got three days in a military hospital and got to sleep in a bed with clean sheets, eat real chow, and watch television in Arabic.

They had to dig out with their helmets and with entrenching tools when the storm died down. Next, they had to begin setting up their encampments again. They were trapped in their holes like frightened rabbits in their warrens. It was a lot easier digging out the second time; the sand was loose and easy to shovel. There was a lot of complaining with each shovel of sand they dug. Sand dunes formed by the storm now surrounded them. They had to dig cuts through the dunes to open the roads so they could get the supply trucks through.

When the soldiers who had been on convoy duty arrived back after the winds died down, they thought they were in the wrong place. Everything they knew was gone. Every landmark previously familiar to them had been obliterated by the winds and the sand. All the bushes and sparse vegetation were buried alive in a shroud of sand. It was like a snowfall that never melted. It was as if they had been transported to a different place. The entire landscape had changed as if by evil magic. Tents and camo netting had been torn down by the fury of the storm. It would have been a good time for the Iraqis to attack, but now it was too late. They, too, had been blasted by the sandstorm and were in no condition to attack.

The scariest thing was that they were cut off from everyone except by foot. Their vehicles sank up to their axles in the loose sands. Water was again strictly rationed until resupply trucks arrived. It was a week before everything was close to normal again...

Chapter 8

THE LAST SECRET PLACE

If one were to ask soldiers from different times and places in the world to describe their war experiences, invariably they would be remembered as: hard physical labor, long periods of anxious boredom, and short bursts of exhilaration or terror. Needless to say, it is boredom that so often marks the moment in a soldier's life. Walking or sitting guard duty gives one plenty of time to think and daydream. Often Young One's thoughts were of his family, his grandfather, and of the Last Secret Place...

In the eyes of his mind, he was ten years old again and was walking with Grandfather and his mother's brother along with the herd. It was June, and the Outsiders' school had given them the summer off. They had journeyed farther to the south and the west than was usual for them. They were far beyond the earth salt ponds where they went occasionally to get their cooking salt.

Young One silently thought it was strange, as there was plenty of grass for the animals closer to the pueblo. Instead, they were walking two days from home. And there seemed to be a quicker way in a straight line to where they were going. But Young One was not sure, for he did not really know where he was. It was a part of their lands he had never ventured to before that day. They left his mother's first brother with the herd, and

Young One and his grandfather set out alone, continuing their long walk. It was getting hot, and they were traveling in the full noon sun. Usually, they would relax in the shade when the summer sun blazed across the empty pale-blue sky. But there was to be no midday rest for them that day.

One of the young herd dogs tried to accompany them, but was turned back three times by Grandfather brandishing a stick and scolding the dog. Young One laughed loudly as he saw the old man chasing the nimble young dog. He never caught it, but the dog finally got the message and ran back to stay with the herd, as it had been instructed.

"She is young and doesn't realize she has to stay with the herd. She wants to walk and to play with you," said Young One as he smiled.

"This is not the time for play," Grandfather replied with a serious look upon his face.

Then, Grandfather did something quite curious. He bent down and carefully cut a branch of sagebrush. Going back to the plant, one could not tell where it came from as he had hidden it so well. He hid the fresh-cut whiteness the slash mark on the stump of the growing limb by rubbing dirt on it. He then used the branch to brush away their tracks in the soft sand. In a few hours' time, the gentle wind would erase even these fleeting remembrances of human passage from the red sands.

"Why are we walking in the sun? It is so hot, Grandfather."

"So witches cannot follow us. They want to learn our secrets and use them against us." Among their beliefs were those of the existence of sorcerers and other evildoers. They are collectively called witches, and they cannot come into the sun. Sunlight is painful to their unnatural skin. The sun will cook them in the black clothes they wear to sneak around in the night. Or so they believe.

"We came with the herd so our travel to this place would be explained in case we were watched. We rub away our tracks to make sure we are not followed."

Young One and Grandfather took turns erasing their footsteps with the branch. Whenever they walked on hard stones, they took great care not to disturb the pebbles lying around. They also did not step on grass lying over rocks, which could give away their passing. The grass juice would leave a stain that a good tracker would notice. As an additional precaution, they walked through the pathless sagebrush stands, changing direction from time to time.

From a high place, they rested in the scant shade of a pinyon pine tree. Grandfather also observed the sand closely, looking for the tracks of others. There were none. There were pinyon nuts on the ground, and Young One started to pick some up to eat. Grandfather told him to put them back. A tracker could follow them, not by noticing where the nuts had been removed, but the spit-out shells would be a dead giveaway to even a poor tracker. They stopped periodically both to rest and to watch the trail behind them to make sure that no one was following.

For hours they kept walking south, toward a strange-looking mesa in the distance. They made a zigzag trail where there was none. The desert sun burned its way through the cloudless sky overhead, scorching the hot, red sands under their feet. They walked in the direction as if they were going around the mesa; then they cut back toward it. Grandfather explained that this was done in case they were being followed. Once they reached the giant stone outcropping, they slaked their thirst from a spring that emanated from it as if by magic. But it wasn't magic, merely the laws of hydrology, fluid dynamics, and gravity. These things are some of the medicine of the earth. A large bull snake slithered away at their approach and took up shelter at the base of a nearby flat rock.

"From now on, we must be very careful," whispered Grandfather. Young One nodded approvingly, not exactly knowing why.

"Where are we going, Grandfather?"

"You will see, son of my son."

As they stalked through the sagebrush, along the base of the ancient mesa, Grandfather showed Young One how to walk with twisting motions from one side to the other, so as not to break the branches and give a tracker indication they had passed that way. The branches went with their movement, and then sprang back into place. Young One learned a lot of useful tricks from his grandfather.

They worked their way through cracks and crevices in the side of the red and white-banded sandstone, past ancient stone hoodoos and spires, whose age was that of the earth itself. They eventually found themselves walking through a crevice in the stone wall that seemed like a dead end. Grandfather pulled a living bush aside to reveal another narrow path hidden behind it. They carefully erased their tracks before continuing. They scampered through the opening and were soon walking on an ancient, hidden trail. As they walked down the path that resembled a long, roofless hallway, ten-year-old Young One had the distinct feeling that someone or something was watching them. But he could see no one. At any moment, someone from above could hurl large stones upon their heads, and no one would ever know what happened to them.

They walked up the old trail, still carefully erasing their tracks until they came to some old ruins. They took turns rubbing their tracks away while continuing to watch to make sure no one was following them. It was a dwelling of the ancient ones. In front of them were the crumbling remains of an old settlement, abandoned tens of centuries before. The dilapidated stone walls of the ruins were all that was left of the people who had built them.

No one knows what happened to those people. Perhaps disease, famine, drought, enemy attack, or all of these things may have caused the ancient ones no longer to be a people of the present. The Outsiders wonder where they went. The Red Earth Pueblo people know where they are—inside them, still carried in their loins. For they are the true descendants of the lost people of the Southwest desert. The old pueblo may be abandoned and its inhabitants scattered, but their blood is carried undiluted in the veins of some of these modern Indians. Young One wandered around the old, abandoned place. Ruins of former settlements were a common sight on the reservation. Many pueblo people gave up their traditional way of life to live in the main village or among the Outsiders. But these ruins were different. They were much older than any other that Young One had ever seen. He was stepping around, looking at the old place, taking in its sights, its echoing sounds, and experiencing its scent of antiquity.

Suddenly, Young One felt someone grab him by the arm and pull him back. He almost jumped out of his skin. Startled, he turned around to see an Indian even older than Grandfather. He just appeared there like a ghost. He spoke patiently in their words, "Be careful, it is not safe." As he said these words in their almost-forgotten language, he pointed to a hole in the floor where Young One could have fallen through. "There are many pitfalls here. Walk with me. Be careful of your step." Young One obeyed the old man instinctively.

Grandfather seemed pleased to see the old one. They greeted each other in their custom, and he introduced Young One to the man. His old face was furrowed and cracked by time. And although he was old, he was still as nimble as a youth. He was dressed entirely in the ancient clothing of their people. He was attired in homespun pants woven of tough desert fibers. His shirt was held to his waist with an antelope leather belt. From his left side hung a large metal knife. His belt was adorned with silver artwork called *conchos*. Young One thought he was a ghost from the past, but he was not.

Grandfather explained that he would be Young One's teacher, as the old one had been his own teacher many years before. He was living here with his grandsons and students, away from the eyes and the thoughts of others who were not aware of this place. Those who were aware of his existence did not speak of him, ever. He was one of the oldest of their people. Not even students spoke of him to each other. No one knew his name, or if they did, they did not speak it. It was as if he existed, and yet did not.

Grandfather explained, "He wears the robes of time that causes forgetfulness. Few people even think of him, but he thinks of them always."

It was one of Grandfather's riddles in their language. No one had seen or heard of the old teacher for so long, that most assumed he was long part of the earth. They were wrong.

They followed the old one through the dusty, empty rooms as if time itself had forgotten them. They went into one of the stone rooms carved into the sandstone cliff. There was a hole in the floor, with a wooden ladder extending down into a hand-hewn chamber beneath. It was an old kiva, a sacred place of worship for the ancient ones. Since time for them began, it had been a holy place. But it had been long forgotten by others.

They descended the rickety, cedar wood ladder into the sacred place. The old one lit a small oil lamp fueled by sheep fat. Its wick was a short strand of braided goat hair. Its tiny flame illuminated the holy place with flickering firelight. This was where the secret rites of the people who came before were conducted. We call them the Anasazi today.

They walked to the center of the floor, where the old one brushed away the dust to find a stone slab which he pulled up to reveal another hidden tunnel. The tiny lamp lit the walls of the hand-carved excavation. It was so small that they had to crawl on hands and knees to reach the other end. It was their protection. A few determined warriors could hold off an entire army forced to crawl one by one.

With a whispered voice, Young One asked Grandfather, "What is this place?"

"It is called the Last Secret Place," he explained in their ancient tongue. "This is the doorway to the last place the Outsiders have not found. It is in a hidden place." Then they had to ascend another rickety wooden ladder. It was a large pine log with notches chopped in it to climb up and down. Below was a limb-or hip-shattering fall to the unwary of mind or the less nimble of limb. The tunnel formed a natural chimney, so if an enemy tried to climb in, the defenders could build a fire, and the smoke and heat would block their entrance and smother them.

In their own way, Young One's ancestors had used flame throwers and chemical warfare thousands of years before they were "invented" by the Outsiders. They knew which bushes and leaves to throw on the fire to make toxic smoke to repel their enemies.

This tunnel was the only way in and out of the large mesa. They continued crawling upon all fours for about one hundred feet; then, one by one, they emerged into a narrow crevice in the rock wall of a blind canyon. They followed a dirt path through the crack in the middle of the mesas. There was a steep overhang of rock about 250 feet above them that allowed a stream of light to pierce the dimness of the place. Hidden from observation from above were more cliff dwellings. They had been carved into the face of the mesa thousands of years before. The place was completely hidden from outside observation.

The Last Secret Place didn't seem to exist, but there it was. It existed as a narrow valley with a series of cliff dwellings on its northern side, where most of the light shone throughout the year. Only at noon was it really light there, and then for a short period of time. During the winter months when the sun was low on the horizon, it was very dim and gloomy.

Grandfather spoke. "This is the great hidden village. It doesn't exist on the paper pictures the Outsiders travel with." (By this, Grandfather meant maps.) "Because of this, the Outsiders have never found this hidden place." Even satellite telemetry, about which they knew nothing, showed it was only a big rock in the trackless southwest desert. It had never been charted or otherwise noted on any cartographers' sheets.

"We have kept it hidden for as long as we have had time. Our old enemies, the Commanches, Apaches, or Navajos, have never found this place, although their songs speak of searching for it. Once, the songs told of Outsiders with horses, hair on their faces and iron hats who came to find this place."

"What is this place used for, Grandfather?"

"It is a place where the ancient skills are taught by the old to the young, from mouth to ear. It is a place where the ways of the past are remembered from father to son."

"Why is it hidden?"

"The old songs say it was not always hidden. Once, this was a well-known place. Then, very long ago, Outsiders came from the south with iron hats and horses. They were looking for a lost city of gold. Some traders from another tribe told them about our people and that we had secret cities in the desert. The Outsiders with guns thought that there were villages full of hidden gold. But they did not realize that the real things of value come from the heart, not from a pouch.

"One time, they almost found this place. They tortured villagers, and, under fear and pain, they told what they knew. They tried to force their way in here. There was a battle, and not one of the invaders made it out alive to tell others. There was not a trace of the invaders ever to be found. All of the Outsiders were killed, and their horses were eaten and their bones burned."

Some time later, Grandfather showed him a stone room full of weapons and armor, from rawhide shields with bullet holes in them, to conquistador helmets that had been crushed with large stones. There were piles of ancient weapons lying rusted in the room. There were also war clubs and spears with shafts so brittle with time that they would crumble in the hands of the holder. There were rusted guns old enough to be in a museum. Neither the Outsider soldiers nor visitors had seen the hidden place. "It is here, and it is not." Young One knew what Grandfather meant.

"Did they find the gold, Grandfather?"

"There was no gold, son of my son. We have no hidden wealth except our great spirits. All that we have is worn on special occasions as adornment. Our jewelry is made of silver and turquoise. There are no hidden fortunes among our people. What we have is for all to see, but they did not believe their eyes and thought there was more."

Looking about the place, one could see that, in times of emergency, about a hundred people could live there, if provided with sufficient provisions. There was a natural spring that flowed all year long except in the driest of years. But there was only the old one and his three grandsons, and an older boy about twelve years old. Young One knew from their dress and headbands that they were from the Cougar Clan. They are the most secretive of all the Pueblo people. Like the animal they are named after who lies hidden in the rocks, they guard the hidden place and keep it safe. Young One belonged to the Coyote Clan, which has long been allied with the Cougar Clan.

For the next six years, when others thought Young One was in the herd camps with Grandfather, he was studying with the old one and the three sons of his first and third daughters. After taking several vows of silence, the boys were allowed to learn the old ways. However, if the vows were broken, they could suffer physical punishment, including mutilation, banishment from the pueblo, death, and even loss of their very spirits.

Some of the things he learned there were ancient survival skills such as hunting and tracking. He learned how to chip arrowheads and carve his own bow out of cedar wood. Young One also learned about weaving, pottery making, cord making from tough desert fibers, and how to travel using the sun and stars. He learned to fight with a war club or a spear, and how to wrestle Indian style. He also underwent spiritual training, to develop his inner self. That was what the witches wanted most of all to learn.

As the Oldest Elder explained to him, "All the people of the earth have mystical power. But only those who listen to their hearts can feel it." Young One's spiritual training taught him to strengthen his warrior's spirit. As he learned, a warrior's real strength lies not in the limbs, but in the mind.

Grandfather once told him, "The mind is what connects the body and spirit on the earth. It is a little of each, and it is neither." It was just another of his riddles.

Young One learned all of his people's ancient hunting skills. He particularly liked throwing the *atl-atl*, which was a javelin hurled with the aid of a detachable throwing stick. It could be thrown much farther than a regular spear and with greater accuracy because of the throwing stick.

The javelin shafts had detachable points that made them the "repeater rifle" of their day. One shaft could hurl many points. It was like carrying ten spears, which would be impossible in the combat of their day, because of their weight and bulk. If shot into an animal, it would eventually lose the shaft while the pointed tip would remain in the wound. The hunter would retrieve the shaft and take a new point from a pouch and affix it to the shaft and have a renewed javelin, and continue the hunt. The same could be done to human enemies. This skill gave the desert Indians a primitive technological advantage for thousands of years. Through time, the bow and arrow eventually replaced the *atl-atl* as a superior and more accurate weapon.

Young One learned about all sorts of desert survival skills and primitive homesteading techniques. He learned to run for miles with a mouthful of water that he could not spit out or swallow. This task taught him correct breathing for high altitude running and self-discipline. Primitive people without a canteen or water gourd could carry a mouthful of life-giving water to a dying loved one, or even to a valiant, dying enemy. To them, a worthy enemy was more valued than a cowardly friend. He also learned about medicinal herbs and poisonous plants. He learned about the movements of the sun and moon and stars and how to travel by them.

Young One perfected their all-but-lost tongue. All of the instruction given to the students was in their native tongue—for there were few places where it was still exclusively spoken. English, the language of the dominant culture, was the verbal medium of communication in their pueblo. It was taught in the schools and was the official language of commerce in their community, although some also spoke Spanish.

Young One always had a slight accent in English, but it was hard to say where he was from, because his language was spoken by so few. Few of his people could speak their own language fluently; many knew only phrases or common expressions in their old native tongue. Speaking good English was their way off the reservation to a life of fast food and air conditioning. But it was also the way to lose their culture.

More than anything, his time in the Last Secret Place taught him to be self-reliant and to live a sustainable life. He learned to live with and love the things of the past. But knowing the old ways did not completely quench the fire of yearning for new things in his heart.

He once asked Grandfather why they must learn to speak in their old, difficult language. He patiently explained, "Our people had no way to make books, and the things of old could be taught only by words. The language of another people does not have the words to express our thoughts, son of my son."

Then he spoke sternly and with great emphasis. "To be a true member of your people, you must think in your own language. If you think like an Outsider, you are not really what they call an Indian. You are one of them in red skin. They can never understand what it is like to truly be one of us. They are like the bat—part mouse, part bird, yet neither one really. Yet they speak for us to the Outsiders. Slowly our people are becoming Outsiders. Our way will be lost then for all time. More and more Outsider blood is entering our people. Soon we will be no more."

>×——×——×<

In the thousands of years of the existence of the Last Secret Place, how many young men were trained there is unknown. For generation upon generation, this starting school kept their way of life alive. If it were not for the Last Secret Place and the network of trails around it, their culture and traditions would have disappeared years ago. While there, they grew food and herbs in waffle gardens or gathered, hunted or raised everything they needed to live. They took and used only as much as they needed. Not more, not less.

Young One remembered something the old teacher once said to him: "When it rains, the people do not get wet, and when the cold wind blows, they do not shiver. The people take these gifts for granted and want more. It is the thirst for more and more that drives the Outsiders to their crazy ways. True happiness comes from within the contented heart, not from the hungry pocket."

But in the world of this and that, there were those whose intentions were not the best, and the school and its good ways attracted the forces of malevolence. Each year a new student was selected, and the witches tried to have one of their own insinuated into the place. But the selection process was very private, and only the very best of the pueblo youth were considered. They must first pass through tests of strength, courage, and spirit. It was a sacred honor to be trained there. To be even considered for selection for training there was an honor. None of the boys knew that they were being trained for a very special way of life that few on Earth experience. To the people who knew, this was more elite than the best Ivy League prep school. And, it was many centuries older. But it was also the path to arduous, lonely, and dangerous tests. It was the way to personal triumph and humiliation, to achievement and failure, each the opposite side of the other. These all-important lessons had to be learned in life in order to remain centered in one's universe.

The examinations of this secret school were as real as the hard life around Young One. He swore an oath of silence, whereby if he divulged any of the secrets, he would be punished severely. In the old days, they would cut out the tongue of anyone who spoke of the place and the ears of anyone who listened. Things were different by the time Young One started. By then they promised to cut off his hands as well so he could not write of it in English either. Young One took the oaths knowing and hoping that he would never face those punishments. He never did speak of the place, and his wisdom grew with his strength. But he thought often of the lessons he learned as a boy there.

He learned to be a hunter in that place. Once, along with other students, he helped run down an antelope in the old way. They chased it around and around in relays, until it was exhausted and winded. They finished it off quickly, and Young One caught its spirit in a stone fetish. Every part of the animal was used, even that which could not be seen.

⋊⋌ ⋊⋌ ⋊⋌

While still thinking, Young One remembered an unpleasant incident from the time before he knew of the Last Secret Place. He recalled it like a dream within a dream. When he was a little boy, perhaps five or six, he saw a horned lizard and threw a stone and killed it. Grandfather witnessed the act and spoke to his grandson.

"Why did you kill the creature?" he asked of him, with an unapproving voice.

"Because it was ugly," Young One replied.

"You took life for no reason. It is not something good to eat, and it could not harm you. Look, it is not dead yet."

Grandfather looked about the ground beneath his feet and found a sandstone pebble. He placed it into the mouth of the dying reptile. They sat there talking while the thing died. This, he explained, "was to capture the spirit of the creature." That way, it did not die without meaning. As the horned toad writhed its last wiggle, Grandfather said, "Now he is in the stone. You must carve the stone to look like it. Then, you will always remember, and you can reclaim its spirit for your use. This way, we make use of everything of the earth. We eat the meat, wear and use the wool, leather and fur. We burn the bones to get the ashes to put in our waffle gardens. We also gather the lost spirits of the animals to use when we need them."

Grandfather was speaking from his heart to the son of his dead son. "When we kill an animal, we capture its spirit in the stone from the earth. It is carried on its last exhaled breath and enters the stone we put into its mouth. This is how we capture the spirit of the animal. We pray and sing thanks to the animal for giving us food, clothing, and its spirit for the future. That way, it did not die without reason."

The rest of the day, and most of the next few days, Young One rubbed different, harder stones over the sandstone, shaping it to look like a horned lizard. At last it was finished. His carving actually looked more like a squat lizard that had been run over by a pickup truck than a horned lizard. If someone didn't know what it was, they would never have guessed, but Young One was both proud and embarrassed by his first religious creation. He thought it was ugly and wanted to throw it away, but Grandfather wouldn't hear of it.

"You look at things with the eyes of an Outsider. You must look inside of a thing to see its real beauty," he told his grandson. "This will be the first charm for your medicine bag when you get one."

Young One placed it into a special red clay pottery vase when he was not carrying it around with him. This was their custom. It had a little hole for it to breathe, for although it didn't need air, it did need to be in contact with the outside, or to be next to the heart of the possessor, to remain viable.

"All the animals the Creator put on the Earth have different sizes, shapes, and spirits. That is good and is the way of things. The spirit of the horned toad gives endurance and patience. It can crawl where no other creature can. When you kill one, you will have its spirit with you. It is caught in the stone. A human can bring it back through breathing it in. Whenever you need patience and strength to endure, you will have it. But use your medicine wisely. It can be used only for good, not evil, or it will backfire on you. The spirit will turn on you, and good medicine will be turned to bad. Just as when throwing a stone into a pool of water after a storm, the ripples from it will come back to your shore. All things in life are connected. Always remember these words."

In the Last Secret Place, they lived off the land, drank its water, and ate its roots, herbs, and meat. It was subsistence survival, but a good life. When an animal was killed, the hunter prayed for the spirit of the beast and gave thanks for the gift they had received from it. The Outsiders hunt by pushing a metal wagon and loading it with many kinds of dead life without knowing or caring where it came from. No one captures the spirits of their animals when they die. No one sings songs to ease its passing to the other side of life. Grandfather once went into an Outsiders' supermarket. He was amazed to see how many things there were in one place to trade for. Grandfather was just like a kid in a store for the first time. When he saw meat in foam packages and plastic wrap, he saw how lost from the true path of life that the Outsiders were. To him, they were pieces of animals in glass paper. No one sang songs for those lost animals. No one captured their spirits. Among his people, selling meat was a sin.

"The Creator gave us the sun, the wind, the grass, the water, and the animals to live on. They are gifts from the Maker of life. We have been given everything we need to live. If a hunter is fortunate enough to kill an animal, it should not be bartered for profit. Chunks of it can be traded to others for foods of lesser value, but the excess must always be given to hunterless families. That way, everyone can eat what the Creator has given."

Young One knew that, in the days of no refrigeration, this made perfect sense. Eat or give away the meat before it spoils. Some would be smoked or sun dried into jerky to be eaten later. The greedy hunter chewing on rancid meat could pay a horrible price in the form of food-borne illness in a world without hospitals.

━✕━✕━✕━

As time went on, Young One became talented in the use of traps and snares, which his people were famous for. He also became proficient in the use of the throwing stick, used to obtain small game. It was similar to a boomerang that did not return to the thrower. It was useful in obtaining a quick meal. He also learned about edible and medicinal plants. He likewise learned which plants were poisonous and to stay away from them.

One of the mystical arts he was taught was how to become invisible. There are three ways to achieve this state of not being seen. The first is not to be seen at all. Move when no one is looking. Or move in the total dark. Or hide behind objects. The second way is to appear to be something else even if someone sees you. This is the art of the deceiver. Camouflage works on this principle. In times of old, Indians would dress in animal skins to sneak up on game. The animals saw them, but did not recognize them as what they were. In modern times, the store clerk does not recognize the shoplifter because she sees a customer. A criminal does not recognize the police officer disguised as a fellow crook, until he arrests him.

The third and most difficult way to become invisible is to move through the shadows. This is known by the Navajos as becoming a skin walker, one who can assume the appearance of another creature. Again, whether they are seen or not, they are not recognized for what they are. They walk through the place between daylight and dark. This is the stuff of witches, and can only be used at night. It is not the way of their tribe, but their lonely desert is full of unwelcome visitors. They believed that the sunlight holds the power of a witch in check. Many youth in the village had taken up wearing Outsider heavy metal tee shirts with devil symbols on them. How much other interest they had in satanic matters was unknown to Young One.

Young One spent almost all of his time in the herd camps or in the Last Secret Place when he was not attending the Bureau of Indian Affairs school that was required by law. He was as Indian as anyone in his pueblo had ever been. He was not only a pure blood, meaning full Indian genetic material, he was well trained in their language and arts. In a way, Young One was one of many seedlings carefully prepared for the future. He slowly grew into a handsome, good-natured, quiet youth. From physical labor and training, his arms and legs became sinewy. His lungs were efficient at breathing at high altitudes. He also underwent spiritual training to strengthen his mystical skills. A true Red Earth Indian is a mystical as well as physical warrior. Young One was rather scary to others, even as a child, because he would suddenly appear next to them, as if by magic. But this was no magic. Their minds were preoccupied with other matters, and he would quietly come up to someone without their noticing. This happened so many times that he was suspected by some of being a witch.

But that was not true. He had merely learned to walk without making noise, while they clomped around in cowboy boots. Several times his wrestling skills were called upon in the schoolyard, and he bested boys much older and larger than himself. Soon, bullies looked elsewhere for their wicked entertainment after he showed a couple of them how embarrassing it could be to be physically bested by someone smaller.

Although he was not large in stature, he was very disciplined and had a strong inner spirit. Young One was quiet, but not timid. There was about him an intensity of life force that was perceptible to others, especially animals. Good animals took to him immediately. Bad animals feared him greatly. The two-legged ones were no exception. An animal will fawn to the strong, and attack the weak. That is their nature. Even older boys left him alone. They felt his presence as a superior creature. His good nature did not lead itself to aggression, and he avoided a lot of it. He kept mostly to himself and avoided trouble altogether.

The Oldest Elder seemed to always know what was in the heart of everyone around him. Once Young One asked his old teacher how many of the things that he could feel were possible. The old teacher sat for a long while, and then he spoke. "All things are connected through their spirits. All living and even the non-living things are a temporary union of body and spirit.

"You may see two people standing in front of each other. What you see are their bodies. Their faces, their arms, their mid-section, their legs, and so forth. They look like two separate things, but they are connected through the ground under their feet. If the earth trembles, they both feel it. We are all connected by the invisible ground of our spirits. The sacred spirit enters our bodies at birth and exits at death. We are as if our bodies were a robe around our spirits. At death our spirits drop their robes and are gone. Our spirits can extend out over great distances like the earth beneath our feet. They are connected through a place where there is no time or distance. You can feel because you believe you can feel. Everyone has this power, some more, some less than others."

Then he said no more about the topic. He got up and walked away, leaving Young One deep in thought, pondering the profound statements he had just heard.

Another time, one of the other boys asked a question about good and bad. The great Oldest Elder took out a large knife and handed it to the startled student.

"Is this good or bad?" The other boy did not know what to say.

"It is both. You can use it to cut your food or to harm someone. But it is you who makes it good or bad, not the knife. For life to be in balance, it must be both. All things are made of opposites. Man-woman, day-night, happy-sad, joy-anger. Each cannot exist without the other. That is the Creator's way. The blade of this knife has two sides. One cannot exist without the other."

The three initiates sat there in front of the flickering flames of the campfire and thought about what they had just heard. They were trying to understand the meaning of the words spoken by the Oldest Elder. They had a lot of time to think, something that is in short supply today.

And then Young One's mind was back to his present time in the Arabian Desert. The sergeant of the guard was checking the posts. Once again, he stood guard duty watching the vast expanse of empty sand in front of him, still waiting for something to happen...

Chapter 9

THE CRAP LINE

For the first month, they soldiered alone. It was lonely and frightening being on the front line. Practically everything they needed was trucked up to them. There was a portable barbershop, a mobile dental office, a bookmobile, and a religious-services trailer the guys called the "Jesus mobile." There were no services for any other religions but Christianity. The Jewish soldiers had to meet in secret for fear of discovery by the morals police. Jones had to worship alone, if what neo-pagans do can be called that. Strangely enough, the morals police had confiscated none of his new-age paraphernalia when his belongings were searched. They must have thought his stuff was for some sort of board game or something. That flipped Sergeant Franklin out. He was overheard stating, "This is some regular army-happy horseshit. The troops can't have Bibles, but that tie-dyed tofu burner can have a damned 'wee-jee' board and tarot cards.

"Jones, if you do not put that stuff away and start soldiering, I can tell you what your future is, and I don't need a crystal ball to do it. You will be meditating in a cell in Leavenworth." It sounded good to Jones, who hoped that the cell was air-conditioned.

Every week, it seemed like more reserve units were trickling in. Their skeleton companies were becoming fleshed out. With each new group, there was fresh news from home and new rumors to exchange. But the truth was, the new guys did not know any more than the soldiers who were already there.

Everyone knew that in the beginning they could never stop the Iraqis if they pushed toward Riyadh. The more soldiers that arrived, the better everyone liked it. At least they would have a fighting chance. A lot of guys thought there was not going to be a shooting war. The roads were literally getting to be like the California Freeway. Lines of traffic went both to and from the front lines back to the airport at Dhahran or the ports of Ad Damman or Al Jubayl. It was one of the busiest highways in the world for a few months.

The reservists pulled guard duty, performed reconnaissance patrols, dug entrenchments, went to training classes; the scariest of all and one of the most dangerous tasks was going on convoy duty. They had a lot of guys riding guard on convoy duty as tons of equipment and supplies were arriving every day. The buildup was really on. There were so many cargo ships in the ports that they worked twenty-four hours a day just unloading them. Ships were berthed all the way out in the gulf waiting their turn to unload their cargoes.

The roads in and out of the port facilities were full of military and civilian vehicles all carting their goods and wares to the front line. So much war material was arriving that the port facilities were also blocked with trucks being loaded. Vehicles of every sort and description were lined up in anticipation of receiving cargoes. Everywhere out in the desert, trucks of all sorts were driven around getting ready, positioning, repositioning, carrying troops, fuel, water, ammunition, supplies, and an unbelievable amount of military equipment. Everything the soldiers needed to live had to be brought into Saudi by boat or plane. The whole country was alive with transportation activity.

Truckers from all over the Middle East made their way to Saudi Arabia for the extremely favorable freight rates. Military transports from all over the world were also arriving daily. The Army had contracted out the job of moving most of the war equipment to foreign national trucking firms. They were paid by the load, and these were boom times for local truckers. The more trips they took, the more money they made. Hence, everyone was in a hurry.

One of the jobs of Young One's battalion was to guard convoys of equipment and supplies. The guys jumped about like dogs begging to go for a ride. It really broke up the boredom. Convoy duty, for all its hazards, was choice duty for the troops. The best thing about convoy duty was that the truck cabs were always air-conditioned. Drivers from all over the earth were hired to transport everything from tanks to toilet paper up to the front lines. Each of the trucks had an armed American guard aboard it to prevent theft, sabotage, and terrorist attack. Once the load was onboard the truck, there was a breakaway seal placed over the door handle. It had better arrive unbroken to its destination.

That was the guard's duty. The driver's was to get it there. It was pretty good duty—no driving, often just snoozing as the driver did all the work. It was a great break from regular guard duty. Riding in the convoys gave the troops the sense that they were going somewhere, rather than merely feeding sandflies.

A contract Saudi trucking company was bringing up their gear. How many of them could be trusted was at first questioned. As it turned out for the reservists' cargoes and their lives—all of them could be. A truck driver's honor is loaded into the back of his rig along with the cargo. He is trusted with tons of expensive things belonging to others, every day. The drivers' loyalty to their honor as men turned out to be more valuable than their political or religious beliefs. Besides, the coalition paid better than Saddam, and no one was shooting at them.

When the motorized caravans pulled into camp, it was almost like the circus coming to town. The soldiers were anxious to see what was brought in. It always meant work details would be formed to unload the trucks. They received ammo, food, needed supplies, mail from home, and fresh rumors to spread around.

Whenever a truck of supplies arrived, it had to be unloaded rapidly so the driver could go back for another load. Franklin would say, "Hey, you. Go over and help unload the vehicles." Soldiers tried to disappear to prevent getting put on Franklin's "Hey You" roster. After the stuff was unloaded, it had to be stored away. Their storage locker was a broken-down trailer that had snapped an axle on the way in. They transferred the cargo and hauled the trailer in for safekeeping. The driver abandoned it. They painted it desert camo and kept it. Although it could not run, it still held gear and supplies. It was the only secure lock-up point and the envy of all the other companies in their battalion.

The worst road was a double strand of asphalt called the Tapline because it ran alongside the main oil pipe from Saudi Arabia to Jordan. GIs called it the "crap line." Because of a lack of regular rest stops, every place where you could pull over was full of piles of decomposing human waste and toilet paper. Its real name was the Trans-Jordanian Pipeline Road. In the beginning, there were no state troopers, no speed traps, and no semblance of highway control. Periodically, there were military police stations staffed with multinational officers ready to assist motorists in almost any language. But no one wanted to talk to them. The world over, a cop is a cop, and, if you're smart, you don't have much to say to them. You certainly don't want them saying anything to you. The drivers would merely slow down while passing, and when "out of town," they would push the "pedal to the metal," as truckers say, and continue juggernauting forward. Young One thought that the roads were almost as bad as those back on the rez. But at least the drivers in Saudi Arabia were not drunk.

Persons of every possible ethnicity from all four corners of the round earth sped past each other, close to death at unbelievable speeds. Seventy miles per hour seemed slow on the straight, two-lane highways. There were people in the military driving large trucks who had never driven an automobile before. One thing was certain. Very few of these folks had ever taken driver's education classes. And from the way the others drove, they must have flunked. There were people who had driven back home, but on different sides of the road. A lot of people got killed on the roads over there.

⟫—✕—⟫

On the long convoy drives, while riding shotgun with the driver, Young One had a lot of time to think and daydream. He remembered his first motorized vehicle. He wanted to buy a pickup truck and went for a job at a trading post run by Outsiders. The black highway brought a daily stream of Outsider tourists through the red hills. The Outsiders were hungry and eager for things of the past of others. They bought stone carvings (not real fetishes), turquoise and silver jewelry, painted pottery, and other art objects. For whatever reason, to satisfy something missing from their lost pasts, or with the hope that the things would increase in value to satisfy something in their futures, they eagerly purchased what was in sight.

He remembered the day he told the father of his father that he was going to take a job in the pueblo at a trading post selling native jewelry and artwork. Grandfather thought silently for a while and then spoke his words.

"Our people have never allowed the Outsiders to draw on paper the pictures of our sacred dancers and *kachinas*. Our people now do this for money. A few generations ago, our people would die under torture rather than give our secrets away. Now, they trade them for dirty, green paper. Never sell the things of our religion. Please promise me that you will never sell pictures of our religious ceremonies to the Outsiders."

"Yes, father of my father. I will never do that."

"Our people have always been traders and barterers. Our people have always been famous for our honest dealings with others. This has been part of our culture since there was anything to trade. Always be honest in your trading, son of my son. Cheat yourself before you cheat others."

Young One saved enough money for a pickup truck, an old Chevy. It was a tan-and-rust colored heap of junk. The pickup truck was irreverently referred to by the Outsiders as a "reservation convertible," because of the usual odd assortment of people and animals transported in the back. Grandfather did not like mechanical things since one had carried away his son "to the other side." He had no use for them, and Young One once heard him say, "The rolling pony is too thirsty a beast to live in the desert because the Outsiders control the underground pool where it drinks." Young One thought Grandfather would buy a truck and join the motorized world if he could just get one that ran on firewood.

"The people no longer walk or run because they found the wheel. Our people used to die because they were too skinny in the snow season; now they die from being too fat in all the seasons."

Occasionally, Grandfather would ride in a pickup truck carrying manure from the sheep camps to his waffle garden in the village. He always rode in the back, not in the cab, on those occasions. The rolling pony frightened him. He never really let go of his dread of motorized vehicles.

Then Young One's thoughts were back in the present, and he was looking through the bug-splattered windshield of a contract tractor-trailer truck. All over the road were crashed vehicles of every description. Luxury cars, early sport utility vehicles and military trucks of all kinds despoiled the beauty of the desert with their wrecked presence. Many well-to-do Kuwaiti refugees had handsomely bribed the Iraqis to allow them through a hole in the lines. Some of them, in their haste to escape, did not make it to safety. One of the Arab truck drivers told them there were people buried alongside the road in unmarked graves. They crashed far away from anything, and this was before the Americans were there. They just buried the people where they died to keep the jackals from getting to them.

The way they heard about the story was when the convoy was on a rest stop and a couple of soldiers went over to the sand to "take a leak." No sooner had they started peeing than one of the Arab truck drivers in their convoy began to scream and indicated with his body language that he wanted them to stop. Some of the other Arab truck drivers were getting very upset about the Americans urinating on human graves. Arabs always bury their dead before sundown. Some of them were never dug back up for proper reburial.

One of the truck drivers who spoke English ran over to see what was going on. He quickly translated to the Americans that people were buried there in unmarked graves.

"Their automobile used to be there, but is not there now. Someone must have picked it up to sell for scrap and used parts. Nothing is ever wasted here."

The worst thing about convoy duty was that if you had an accident on one of those roads, you were a long way from medical attention. There was no golden minute in which to save a victim. You would be lucky to have a golden day. More GIs were killed or maimed on the highway than from enemy fire during the Persian Gulf War. Driving conditions were absolutely frightful there.

Their infantry company had eight Humvees, four of which traveled with the convoys for security as well as for the command and control. The remaining four rode up and down the road between the two-man foxholes that were widely separated. They also had four rented civilian pickup trucks.

Once in a while, they even went to King Khalid Military City, south of Riyadh. The guys called it "the Emerald City." There were even green, irrigated lawns right in the middle of the desert. It was the only green place in the entire kingdom, and it really stuck out in the middle of nowhere. Its location was supposed to be a secret, but everybody knew where it was. It was a two-day trip from their place on the front line.

Sometimes it took a long time waiting for the trucks to be loaded, especially at the seaports. There were long queues of trucks ahead of them. Other times there was next to no one waiting. Sometimes they got the wrong stuff and had to go back to return it. If everything was moving, they could get in and out with a load of war supplies rather quickly. Sometimes, a helicopter would fly in to their area with some cargo hanging below it on a sling. It would drop the stuff and then be off in a blinding cloud of dust.

While the troops were in town, they were warned not to speak to or even look at the Saudi women, whom the GIs called "sand nuns" or "ninja women" because of their long, black traditional dress and the black veils over their faces. Sometimes the soldiers would see them on the street when going into town to bring back supplies. They would get a severe ass -chewing for even staring at them. A catcall or rude noise could get you an ass whooping from a sergeant, or arrested and beat up by the morals police. No one wanted to upset the locals. The police had a reputation for brutality that was deserved.

The reservists got a cheap thrill driving up in their dirty Humvees to where new troops were just arriving. Their "camies" were already starting to fade from constant wear and exposure to sunlight. The new guys stared with awe at the desert-hardened reservists. Their lips were cracked, and they were sunburned and hard-looking from life in the field. They had the look of veterans to the newcomers, who were still wiping petroleum-based Cosmoline packing grease from their equipment.

><-- ><-- ><--

Every time they went anywhere that there was water, one could find Walters. One time they went to pick up supplies in the port of Ad Dammam, and there was a long line of trucks ahead of them awaiting loads. The town of Ad Dammam was a combination of old, Arab-style buildings and modern, western, industrial structures. It had become a major port of entry for everything that the Saudis could not make from dates, sand, or oil. Just about everything they needed came through there. The convoys also sometimes went back to the airport where they originally landed to pick up supplies.

Walters drove the pickup out of line and around the warehouse complex until he found what he was looking for: an unattended hose attached to a faucet. He lined the bed of the rented pickup truck with plastic sheeting to hold water in, and then he placed the hose in the plastic-lined truck bed and turned on the tap. At first, there was a little bit of rust, then it ran clear. He looked around nervously to make sure no one would catch him. He was stealing something more valuable that gasoline. The Kingdom of Saudi Arabia was not a good place to commit the sin of theft, as he was soon to discover.

After filling the truck bed two-thirds up with water, he drove to a shady side of another warehouse, where he could still keep an eye on the convoy he was supposed to be with. He skinned down to his boxer shorts and luxuriated in the water as if it were his private swimming pool. He was relaxing with a can of cold pop he had purchased from a street vendor. The wily Walters had unfortunately enjoyed his private pool time a bit too long. He was nodding off in self-contented satisfaction. He forgot to keep an eye on the rest of his guys. The convoy was loaded up, and everyone was looking for him so they could get going.

Both Franklin and Lieutenant Ramirez had been looking for Walters. They were pissed. Porter and McHugh were sent to find him. When they found him, they did not bother to awaken him; they silently went right back and reported his whereabouts to Sergeant Franklin. He and Lieutenant Ramirez then quick-stepped up to where Walters was asleep in his shallow pool. The whole squad was following them in anticipation of what would happen. There was Private Walters, slumbering like an otter. He did not hear the others creep up on him. He did, however, hear the workings of the tailgate latch as Franklin pulled it open.

All of the water gushed forward in a fall to the asphalt, taking Walters with it like a fish. He opened his eyes just in time to see Franklin's glare, and then he hit the pavement. His head smacked the tailgate and his butt kissed the ground in front of everyone. There he was, rubbing his head and his ass simultaneously while Franklin screamed at him. All the other men were howling in laughter. The great "get over" had been caught. Walters got a great "knowledge knot" on the back of his head. Everyone was laughing so hard that tears rolled down their dry faces and soaked in. His pain and slight injuries only added to their glee. Franklin kept screaming at him all the while his cargo was being loaded. Walters would never live that one down...

>*——*×*——*×*

One frightening funny incident occurred when they were driving some trucks up from the military port. They would pick up supplies and equipment and bring it back to their area. Sometimes it was food or fuel, sometimes water, tents, ammo, or other supplies. An Arab driver named Hassan was assigned to their company. He was a Bedouin who had traded in his camels for some serious diesel horsepower. He spoke English pretty well from his association with so many Brits and Yanks in the oil fields. Possessing a working knowledge of the English language gave him a decided advantage when working with the petroleum expatriates. He translated instructions to the other Arab drivers and was, therefore, an impromptu leader of the Saudi truckers when in convoy. To his credit, Hassan always got the cargo delivered.

Hassan was quite the velocity addict and one afternoon was driving a tractor-trailer truck full of mortar rounds. His truck had a civilian radio and he loved listening to Armed Forces Radio, which had recently begun broadcasting. It provided a mix of rock and roll, country and western, and some rap songs. There were different programs on at different times. Someone during the oldies hour had requested a cruising song that was popular in the mid-1970s. The announcer broke in and dedicated Bachman

Turner Overdrive's "Roll On Down the Highway." It had a driving, pounding beat and was a great tune to drive to. Sammy was his security escort for that run.

"This song is dedicated to Specialist Fifth Class Randy Gardner, from Melissa in Company C of the 192nd Transport Battalion. Randy, I think she likes you," the disc jockey teased playfully.

Following this, the DJ "slammed home" the wild tune. Hassan was the lead driver, as always. This was because he could translate for the other drivers, and also because of his aggressive driving habits. But Hassan spoke English better than Sammy.

He asked Sammy, "Truck driver song?"

"Yeah, truck driver song."

With that, he pulled out his stick he used to hold down the pedal. It was wedged into the front of the seat. He went wild. He cranked the volume knob on the radio up as far as it would go. The speakers were really "bumping out" the tune. He loved the song so much that he was laughing and dancing in the speeding truck. He was actually doing "the bugaloo" in the cab. Sammy was laughing, too. The wild guitar licks and the pounding drumbeats were thrilling. If they had hit anything, they would have been blown to two separate kingdoms come. The rest of the convoy drivers were pushing pedals to the floorboards with their passengers unconsciously pressing boots on the floor trying to slow them down. After the song was over, Hassan pulled his dancing stick out and decelerated back down to a normal eighty miles per hour, still laughing like a madman. He had tears of sheer joy running down his dusty cheeks, hearing an American driving song. Rock and roll music had been forbidden in the Kingdom of Saudi Arabia. Hassan enjoyed the sound of the forbidden fruit. Sammy had such a broad smile, you could shove a whole pineapple into it. He always seemed to have a good time, all the time. He was a simple, happy man. This was all part of riding shotgun on the crap line...

>+—>+—>+<

Once the big divisions began arriving, they had priority to get unloaded and moved into position. The reservists had to "suck hind tit" to the large armor, artillery, and infantry units now arriving. Every day, more troops, more tanks, more artillery pieces, and more trucks were coming in. Everyone knew that all this stuff was not arriving for nothing. Rather than make the reservists comfortable not to be alone, this was scarier. Now it looked like there would be a war after all. This was no mere peace-keeping mission.

Initially, they could do a convoy run in a day. Unless there was an accident or sandstorm on the highway, the big wait was how long it took to load and unload. A lot of stuff went on quick if it was palletized. You had to be careful what they gave you, for mix-ups were common. But now, the big lift was on. More and more troops and equipment were arriving daily. The loading capacity was overwhelmed by the influx of war materials and equipment. Trucks waited in long lines to be loaded. Now, with so many trucks waiting for loads, it took up to three days to make a run from Ad Dammam or Dhahran. There were frequent stops and MPs patrolling the roads along with Saudi police. The roads were crumbling apart from so much traffic. Potholes began to appear in the billiard-table-smooth roads. On convoy duty, they usually got a real meal in a mess hall, and they could purchase back-home goods from civilian shops.

During the down time, they got to stay in a transit barracks. They were usually air-conditioned, had showers you could stand in all day if you wanted, and had television in their large day rooms. The long showers were unreal after their once-a- week dowsing and daily helmet baths in the deep desert. There were even washing machines where they could launder their uniforms. If there was an overnight stay waiting for a load, there were bunks with clean sheets on them. It was like a vacation from the front line.

The men never knew when they would stay over or just turn around and head back to camp immediately. It all depended on how fast they could get them loaded and on their way. The ride was always good; a guy could sleep while the driver did all the work. It was a great break from the tedium of front-line duty. It was an unintended morale booster.

Their squad had a long layover in Ad Damman, which was where they went mostly to pick up supplies. Their trucks were not scheduled to be loaded until the middle of the next day. The infantrymen were sent to a transit barracks. They got to watch television in the day room for the first time in months. The next morning, after a breakfast of real eggs and real milk and sliced bananas on civilian cereal in the mess hall, they decided to go sightseeing. It was a Friday morning. Young One, McHugh, and Jones went out walking in the town.

As they walked along, they could hear the calls to prayer echoing through the dusty streets and whitewashed buildings. They walked around for about another hour just looking at things. After months of sensory deprivation in the desert, everything was eye candy for them. They were very cautious about not getting into trouble. They were going through an older part of town where they had been told was a *souk*, or outdoor bazaar. As the three buddies approached the marketplace, they were astounded to see it empty. There was not a living soul to be seen. There were cooking fires smoking unattended. There were all sorts of goods and wares ready to be bought in the shopkeeper-less stalls. Fruit and vegetables were neatly stacked on rugs for sale.

McHugh spoke first. "There's nobody here. I wonder where they went? Somebody could steal everything."

"You don't want to steal in Saudi Arabia—they cut off your hands, said Jones. "Just one, I think," he continued. "The right one, to keep you from eating in public. At least that is what I heard."

They continued on without touching anything. Several blocks later, they came upon a crowd. The Americans thought it was a parade or a show of some sort. It turned out that it was. It was Friday morning, and this was "chop-chop" square, where criminals are punished in public. There was a Saudi policeman watching them intently. He approached the three Americans and spoke in broken English.

"You want to see? Come, I show you." With that he escorted the three up to the very front of the crowd. In front of them was a woman tied to a post. She was dressed in a gray prison frock. She was not Saudi; she did not look like an Arab. She looked more like a Filipino or Indonesian woman. Her sentence was read to the crowd in Arabic. The policeman quietly translated for the Americans. "She has been convicted of prostitution. She was caught giving herself for money to dock workers. Now the law demands punishment."

The woman was crying and pleading for mercy. The beating started. Her sentence was six hundred lashes, given sixty at a time every two weeks. This was her third trip to the whipping post. The administrator of justice struck her with a long, wooden stick tipped in lead. He did not "spare the rod," as they say. With each whack, a cry of pain came forth from the wretched woman. He hit her as hard as he would have hit any man. Blood streaked through her prison clothes, although the stick did not rip the cloth, only the flesh underneath. The crowd gasped in wicked delight. A sinner was being punished. There was time between each whack to provide maximum pain to the victim and pleasure to the crowd. He struck her on the back, the buttocks, and the back of the legs above her knees.

There has never been a public outcry against corporal punishment in Saudi Arabia, for two reasons. First of all, to open one's mouth in opposition to the law would bring certain punishment. Secondly, it was religious retribution used as wicked entertainment by some. After about thirty whacks, the woman passed out hanging from her chains. The lashing continued to the prescribed sixty. The unconscious victim was dragged back to her prison cell to heal for the next beating. She would receive no medical attention. If she died, it was the will of Allah; if she lived, it was the same.

The next act of punishment involved two convicted thieves. They were dressed in knee-length *thaub* shirts, also prison-gray in color. Their faces showed signs of recent beatings. Crude interrogation techniques prevailed in the kingdom. They were Palestinians and had been convicted of highway robbery, a very severe crime in Saudi Arabia. Their sentence was right-hand and right-foot amputation. They were given no anesthesia to ease their pain.

A wooden block was rolled out, and three guards chained the first prisoner to it. His arm was extended over the block and tied down with leather straps. Tourniquets were tied at his right wrist and right ankle. With the swift stroke of a scimitar, his hand was lopped off and fell on the ground in front of the Americans. The poor wretch shrieked in agony, much to the crowd's delight. The fingers kept wiggling for a few seconds and then stopped moving all together. Next, the foot was chopped off with another single stroke. The second prisoner was likewise dismembered. They were taken to the hospital for surgical treatment, and their severed appendages went another way for disposal. None of the three Americans could believe what their eyes had just witnessed. But the best act was yet to come in this tragic street play.

This was to be a special day for the cheering crowd of faithful Saudi citizens. For the final act of the day, there was to be an execution. That is what brought the crowd. There was a Saudi schoolteacher who had been convicted of sodomizing one of his male students. This crime against morality carried the death penalty. Other crimes that carried death-penalty sentences in Saudi Arabia included apostasy, murder, rape, infidel proselytization, drug or alcohol dealing, and treason. Men were ritualistically beheaded. Women were shot in the back of the head with a pistol to avoid exposing the hair or nape of neck to the sword and to the eye of the unclean.

The man who was soon to have his life functions terminated was also dressed in a gray prison thaub shirt, but had a hood over his face. Unlike western medieval executions where it was the executioners who masked their faces, here the prisoner was hooded. His hands were tied behind his back with silk cord. He was brought forward, and a cleric spoke some words to him. The executioner stood with a gleaming gold scimitar. The attendants tried to get the frightened fat man on his knees. He refused. They tried a second time to get him to kneel down and bend over and expose his neck to the executioner's sword. Again he refused to comply. On the third try, one of the attendants took a gold dagger from his belt and stuck it in his guts. The man let out a groan from deep inside him and slumped forward on his knees. No sooner had his head gone down than the executioner took it off with a single, expert swing of the golden sword.

The crowd was pleased that iniquity had been punished. They had also been forewarned that they, too, could be some Friday's entertainment should they transgress the holy law. The Gulf War was a place where the GIs behaved themselves as in no other time in our military history. They had been warned of the consequences. The crowd began to disperse. The policeman could see that the Americans had been visibly shaken by what they had just seen.

"Do you think it is terrible to kill a man for having sex with a boy?" said the policeman in his broken English to them. "He was not killed because he had sex with a child. That was merely a sign of his real crime—that of betraying the trust that was placed in him by the boy's father. His father wanted him to grow up to be a good man. Children must always do what they are told to do by their elders. Adults must tell children to do only good things. So in a way, the man betrayed the trust that the child had placed in him—that he would help him to grow into a good man. For that, he had to die in front of everyone. He committed his sins in private but was punished in public. This is the will of Allah and has been our way for over a thousand years."

This presented a strange incongruity for, in a part of the world where the hands of poor thieves had been cut off for centuries, the sheiks, emirs, princes, potentates, and presidents had long filled their arms with mountains of ill-gotten treasure without suffering consequences.

Young One went away with a heavy heart, as he had never before seen anything like that. McHugh told the story time and again to anyone who would listen. Each time he retold what he had seen, the story got better. Jones could not eat his vegetables that day, he was so shaken up. They went back and told the other guys what they had just witnessed. Everyone thought it was bullshit, except Simms. He said, "I wish I was there to see the bitch get beat. More of them hoes need it."

The guys from the convoy were coming in. Walters was on the M-60 in the lead vehicle and he was grinning like a possum. After the dust of their arrival settled, Walters gave everybody the good news. "You will never guess the good fortune that is about to befall us, my brothers."

McHugh and Feiny were nodding their heads in the affirmative as he spoke.

"Is everybody listening? There are women coming to our area."

"Bullshit," was the reply from the others.

"No, really. There is a medical company coming right down there," he said while pointing behind them. "I'm not kidding, there is a medical unit moving in, and they are going to set up a field hospital here. We'll be able to go to some hot honeys for sick call."

"You'll probably be down there all the time, you sick bastard."

"I'd take a transfer there if I could. There are going to be nurses, X-ray and lab techs, and female medics. There is a God," said Walters. He forgot, however, that there is also a Satan who would, in the not-too-distant future, change his life through the sins of his flesh...

Chapter 10

DINING IN THE DESERT

Young One was quite fascinated with everything that army technology had produced—the helicopters, the tanks, the weapons, and even the people. He found the food different from what he had been used to. He had experienced many opportunities to taste new foods as far back as in his high school cafeteria and more recently, in the army mess hall. How different an army meal was from those he had shared with Grandfather out in the herd camps. Everything that they ate, they bartered for, they caught, they found, or they grew themselves. It was a life of sparse survival, living from hand to mouth. He remembered one time when Grandfather spoke to him about desert survival.

"There is everything a human being needs right here in the desert. The Creator hid it in many places right in front of us. He has given us everything to feed and clothe ourselves the way we always have. We must learn how to find food and fiber in our land." While he spoke, Grandfather was chopping on a tough, old juniper branch with his metal trading-post knife. He was fashioning a digging stick. It was about three-and-a-half feet long, and the broad end was flattened to make a wooden pry bar. Grandfather then whittled down the other end to fashion a handle. He would use it to dig out the agave roots.

They had already dug a fire pit and lined it with large, flat stones. As he bent down, Grandfather dug around and chopped at the base of the large, succulent plant with a sharp, flat rock to loosen it. Then he pried it from the earth with the digging stick and chopped off the tough leaves from the stem. This activity revealed a crown about a foot in diameter at the base, which was white in color.

He supervised Young One in excavating four more roots. Then they gathered firewood sticks to build a fire. They spent as much energy gathering their food as they got back from it. Any little food stored away as fat was well hidden in them. For his age, Grandfather was in incredible shape because of the life he led. A hot fire of cedar wood was built in the stone pit. They replenished the fire with more sticks that burned down into a pile of hot coals. Grandfather and Young One took turns stoking the glowing embers until the wind began to blow them into ash.

After several hours, when it died down and the coals turned to hot ashes, Grandfather took a cedar bough and brushed them aside. He saved some of the clean, gray ashes for seasoning on their food because of their salty taste. It was also a good source of minerals for their diet. He next laid a mat of wet bear grass stems on the hot stones. Then he placed four of the tuber-like *agave* crowns in the pit and covered them with wet grass and a layer of red earth. They were left to slow-bake until the next day. Young One and Grandfather then went out into the desert to set their snares for the next day's meat.

"We must always take care of tomorrow's needs today. Each day must be planned for. We will come back here tomorrow to eat. Nothing is certain in life, and there are no promises, son of my son." It was a constant theme with Grandfather.

Grandfather showed the son of his son how to pick the *cholla* buds from a plant that looked more like a thorny bush than the cactus that it was. They were about the size of Young One's thumb, and the two men boiled them and ate them like fat green beans. They also ate prickly pear cactus, both the fruit as well as the green pads sliced into strips. First, they had to burn off the thousands of tiny spines. They took two sticks and fashioned primitive tongs. They were used to hold the fruit and the pads over a singeing flame to burn off the spines. The reddish-purple fruit was delicious, but was filled with many seeds that had to be spit out. Also, the juice stained the teeth and tongue for days after. Grandfather also taught his grandson how to make soap and shampoo out of the yucca plant roots. When it was the right season, they roasted the fruit to get a "desert banana." They gathered mesquite beans and ground them between stones to make gruel. Grandfather taught him how to made sweet-tasting punch from the flowers of the ocotillo cactus, and how to gather pinyon nuts and desert sunflowers. Grandfather taught him which grass seeds were good to eat and which were poisonous. It took quite a time to fill just a cup with them. It took all day to get a meal from the tiny grains when they were cooked into a coarse porridge. He also learned where to find ground cherries, hackberries, wild rose hips, and desert thornberries.

Young One learned about wild onions and garlic with which to season the food. He learned to roast buffalo gourd seeds and to crush and boil them to get oil to rub on rough skin. Young One came to realize that the desert was a well-stocked supermarket if one knew where to shop. He also learned how to weave a basket from native materials in which to carry home the groceries.

The next day, they were sitting under their cedar bough sun shelter, which was much like an open-sided picnic pavilion. Young One was skinning a couple of cottontail rabbits he had snared the evening before. They were to be roasted on a stick over hot cedar coals. Young One kept turning them until they were thoroughly cooked. Then he helped Grandfather dig out the baked plants. They were quite hot, and they were soft and starchy and tasted to Young One like potatoes and cabbage mixed together. The roots had a little flavor of each, but not exactly. They were good to eat with the roasted rabbit.

Young One and Grandfather ate two of the roots and reburied the other two for the next day. They had plenty to eat, and some for tomorrow. Grandfather said they would be safe from digging scavengers because they were afraid of the smell of fire. They drank cups of tea made from herbs that Grandfather had gathered. It was a plant the Outsiders call "Mormon tea." Grandfather especially liked coffee obtained from the trading post. He always started off his day with several cups of camp coffee but he also drank herbal tea made from plants he collected during the rest of the day.

⋊—⋊—⋊

Back on the other side of the Earth, if there were ever two opposites in the world who were attracted, they were Private First Class Bernard Feinstein and Private First Class John Samuella. They were known to the other squad members as "Feiny" and "Sammy." Feiny was from the Big Apple on the Atlantic—New York—and Sammy was from the Big Pineapple in the Pacific—American Samoa. Feiny was a small, wiry guy with a quick wit and fast with humorous quips. His dream was to go to Vegas and be a comedian. He joined the Reserve for the extra weekend cash. The closest unit for him to drill with was an infantry brigade; hence, he became a grunt. Samuella was a large, barrel-chested man who did not speak English well. Sammy's great-grandfather had promised that ten generations of his male descendants would serve in the U.S. military in return for the Americans saving his people from the Japanese during World War II. Sammy was there keeping his dead ancestor's vow.

Feiny fancied himself somewhat of a gourmet and was always making deals or scrounging for something to help make the combat rations—Meals Ready to Eat, MREs, or "Rees"—taste better. He was of the Jewish faith and could not eat MRE Number 1 (pork and rice with barbeque sauce), Number 4 (omelet with ham), and especially Number 8 (the dreaded ham slices). Of a total of twelve meals, he could eat only nine, so his desert dining suffered. He did all right trading with other guys, as bartering came naturally to him.

Feinstein was constantly mixing up different accessory packets and parts of different meals. He made a fabricated picnic table from some Ree boxes and ammo crates full of drift sand. He would take his mess kit plate and lay all his food out, presentation style. Eating was a real production for him. He said it "separated us from animals." A couple of times, he talked the guys into pooling their meals, and he concocted something good from them with a combination of very limited civilian food, mostly stuff sent from home or procured from the deals on wheels truck that made its circuit around the encampments. They would then have a family-style meal at his improvised picnic table.

One time Franklin, after seeing Feiny enjoying his combat rations, commented upon his overly fastidious habits. He remarked, "Feinstein, you must have to dip your socks in kerosene."

"Why, Sarge?"

"To keep the ants off your candy ass, son."

Sammy, on the other hand, mixed all kinds of things together into one blob and ate it. He would take the entire contents of a meal and mix it all up. No kidding. All this space-age food was strange to him, so he mixed everything together into a nasty-looking gruel. He would take a main meal and squeeze it into his canteen cup. Next, he would add grape jelly, crackers, cookies, powered beverage drink, the entire salt pack, and just about anything that would fit into the cup and stir it up with the little plastic spoon. His hand was the same color and size as a first baseman's mitt. It made the little eating utensil appear even smaller. He would then gulp the mixture down between large smiles. Everyone around him was either gagging or was actively amused by his eating habits. Somebody asked him why he mixed it all up together. He pointed to his smiling mouth and said, "Here today." Then he pointed to his ass and said, "There tomorrow."

He was a nice enough guy, but one did not want to make him angry. He came from up in the hills where the Samoan native tongue was still predominantly spoken. A lot of modern things were new and fascinating to him. Most of the food was new to everyone, but it was especially different to him. If it was not yanked from the sea or knocked off a tree, it was not like food from back home to Sammy.

How Private First Class Jones, a confirmed vegan, stayed alive just eating cookies and peanut butter, no one knew. He traded food with Feinstein, who usually got the better of the bargain. He would trade his meat entrees for the vegetarian components of the Rees. He got skinnier and skinnier as his body slowly cannibalized itself to remain alive. He was slowly starving himself to death with his self-imposed dietary restrictions.

One time Franklin was talking to him about his vegetarianism. Jones told him it was not healthy or natural for humans to eat red meat. Franklin pointed to his right eyetooth and said, "Son, these canine teeth tell me

I was made to eat meat. And I do not eat red meat. I have my wife cook it until it turns brown. Then I eat it."

Everyone laughed, save Jones. After the first month, he finally gave up and joined the ranks of the omnivores, as one could not permanently sustain oneself on the non-animal portions of the MREs. He was a weird, new-age sort of fellow. He had a tie-dyed scarf of the same color as Desert Storm camo. It was really cool. A woman back home sent it to him. He would wrap it around his head like a damn Genie. It used to drive Sergeant Franklin nuts. Jones believed in the healing power of crystals. He was some type of a born-again Hindu or something. They must have all been born again if they believed in reincarnation.

He had a swami or guru or some other such thing back in Vermont. He was so weird that the brass had him special drug-tested twice. But old Jones was a natural, nothing artificial in him. He definitely was out there on life. He was also an artist, and was always drawing stuff on cardboard from the MRE cartons, using them as his "canvas." He used several colored marking pens and actually made some cool pictures of the Gulf War.

Jones' favorite band was Yanni. Everybody called it "yuppie elevator music." He was constantly reading about magic and new-age religion. Porter called it "old-age paganism."

Sergeant Franklin did his best to accommodate the religious beliefs of his men. He overlooked Young One's medicine bag; he did not say anything about Feiny having his Jewish beanie under his helmet. He didn't even say anything about Walters (who was a Seven Day Hedonist), having some woman's soiled panties in his helmet. He shuddered to think what he did with them when no one else was looking. But this whole notion of neo-paganism did not set well with him.

"What are you going to do Jones, sacrifice a goat at midnight?" Franklin inquired incredulously.

"If there was a goat around here, you know what Walters would try to do with it. He'd give new meaning to getting your goat," said McHugh.

"No, Sarge. We don't do that anymore," replied Jones.

"I should have kept an eye on you during Halloween. Then I'd know what you were up to." Jones just laughed at the thought of Franklin figuring him out.

⸕⸕⸕

It was mid-September, a week after the big sandstorm. It was still hot, and the sandflies were a continual annoyance. The battalion had been there a month. Everyone was uncomfortable and tired, and the sun had the demon testosterone boiling in the men's veins. They hadn't showered in a week. The troops were hot and funky, including their moods. Everyone tried to get along, but sometimes an asshole would get hot under the collar, and trouble would start.

As they were having their evening meal, the sun was setting over the horizon and peeking under the camo netting. The squad was sitting around and eating their field food. Four cases of MREs had been laid out on the hood of the Humvee to get warm in the sun.

First squad finished their duties and got their pick of cuisine from the MRE pouches. In theory, a soldier was to reach into a box with blind karma or faith and take the luck of the draw. Usually, somebody would look through them. Feinstein and Walters had already memorized the packing order of the MREs in their carton and could tell by the position in the box what meal was there. They were almost like kids who can tell where every piece of candy is in a sampler by memorizing its position in the box. The ham slices usually disappeared first, as they were the closest to real food. Most guys had a few extra meals stashed away to fit the mealtime. For instance, you didn't want to get pork and rice with barbecue sauce for breakfast. But, if you were the last guy at the box, that's what you got. For the first month in Saudi, all they ate were MREs.

Each MRE main meal was packaged in a six-inch long, sand-colored pouch that looked remarkably like a heavy-duty, oversized catsup package from a fast-food joint. All of their meals were thermo-treated portions in tubes. To eat one, a soldier merely squeezed out the irradiated-for-freshness space-age food. In addition to these, there were accessory packs that contained all the other things. They held gum, a little packet of toilet paper as soft as sandpaper, matches and the indispensable condiment for the MRE—a miniature bottle of real Tabasco sauce. The meals also contained round, dry, saltine crackers, about which some soldiers said, "The boxes the meals come in taste better."

They also had cocoa powder. It did not dissolve well in cold water; they were not allowed to have fires for security reasons, and there was not any wood to burn anyway. Occasionally, when no one was watching (which was rare), Feiny would make a tiny fire in a scooped-out depression in the sand and burn pieces of cardboard to heat his cocoa. To this he would add coffee and make a cup of mocha.

Of all the guys, Feiny tried to maintain some semblance of civility in the field. It was as funny sometimes just watching him as it was listening to him. He really had a comical nature. He was quick and clever, but sometimes his mouth got him into trouble.

Second squad was next, and the third squad each took what was left of the next best in the cases. By the time the last squad came in, all that was left were meals number 6 and 10, chicken- a la king and tuna and noodles, respectively. The tuna and noodle meal wasn't all that bad in taste, but it sure appeared as though it had been eaten once already. Squeezing the stuff from their containers didn't help matters.

One of the other guys, a redneck from Florida, said, "Hey, who the fuck took all the ham slices?" No one spoke up, so the cracker prick started looking around to see what everyone else was eating. He was one of those guys who, in civilian clothes, wore a cowboy belt with his name on it. Franklin said it was "so he could find out who he was when he pulled his head out of his ass."

Feinstein was sitting with Sammy at his makeshift table, doing his best to make a gourmet meal, and he answered, because no one else said anything, "Don't look at me." Everyone paying attention laughed.

"What did you say?" the grit asked defiantly.

"I said it wasn't me," at the same time pointing for emphasis to his camo-colored yarmulke strategically placed atop the crown of his head.

"Yankee boy, you're real damn smart, aren't you?" Then, with his hand, he swept Feiny's meal from his improvised dining table into the dirt. He grabbed him by his BDU jacket and pushed him back onto the sand. The redneck was about to smash him with his free fist, when Sammy stepped in. He had two white Chiclets from the MRE accessory pack held in his large left hand.

"You hit him, these your teeth," he said in his broken English. When he finished speaking, he dropped them onto the sand. It was a great visual aid, and the troublemaker, not wanting the large Samoan for a dentist, released Feiny.

"I'll see you again," he said threateningly to Feiny over his shoulder.

"You see him every day," replied Sammy. That was almost the end of it.

Sergeant Franklin had been observing from over on the side. He noticed some bullshit brewing and wanted to put a stop to it. Not that he really gave two shits in a dead rat's ass about any of them, but if there was a fight, there would be guys going to the emergency dispensary, and there would be incident reports and disciplinary charges to be filed. To avoid the burden of reports, most sergeants put a lid on the grab-assing real quick. He walked up to the group and said to the redneck as well as to the brown neck, "Are you two trying to make me look stupid?"

"No, sergeant," they both said in unison.

"Now just imagine how foolish I'd look driving you both down to the dispensary in stocking feet, just to get my left and right boots taken out of each of your sorry asses? Your enemy is out there," he said pointing northward toward Smuggler's Berm. "I don't want any more of this shit. Do I make myself clear?"

"Yes, sergeant," said Sammy.

A reluctant, "All right, Sarge," was extracted from the grit dude.

"The rest of you people finish your chow; you're going to need it tomorrow."

The other guys shared their stuff with Feiny, and everyone went on. The redneck never said he was sorry, but he never bothered Feiny again. He was having a bad day, but Sammy had almost made it a little "badder" for him.

"Sarge thinks he's Superman," Tucker said of Franklin as he walked off.

"Despite the 'man' on the end of his name, he doesn't look Jewish to me," said Feiny under his breath. He had regained his composure and was back to his old, humorous self again.

>+—×—+<

As summer turned to fall, one could hardly notice the difference, except the days got slightly shorter. It was still hot, and the nights got cooler. They continued in this way for a long time with boring regularity, as one day became another. More and more soldiers from all around the world were arriving. There were a lot of new neighbors. Still, no one knew for sure if there would really be a war, or if it was just another peacekeeping mission. It might all be just one large show of force. They could be hiding in holes for years. As more and more troops arrived, more and more amenities also arrived. The Army Air Force Exchange System mobile PX went from camp to camp, like the bookmobile, selling items of necessity.

Shoe polish, razor blades, candy, chewing gum, cigarettes, and junk food became available. One of the trucks even had the unbelievable commodity—ice cream bars and frozen ices. No kidding—they even had a camouflaged ice cream truck running up and down the line. It had a little musical, door-bell-sounding thing that played different tunes. They were called deals on wheels trucks. They even had a mobile dental unit that went up and down the front line with a team of tooth fairies drilling and filling.

The roach coach was a roving cafeteria truck similar to those that visit work sites back in the states. It carried cold and hot drinks, junk food, and packaged sandwiches. Some retired general was making a fortune selling the troops stuff they definitely should not have been eating. But it was a real morale booster. They call it the exchange system because that was what it did. It allowed the soldiers to exchange their cash for their wares.

One of the popular items purveyed was the beef frankfurter that all the coalition soldiers supposedly could eat. Sammy had never seen a hot dog before, and this large food vacuum cleaner was suddenly very quiet and not hungry.

Feiny asked his buddy, "Do you want a hot dog, Sammy?"

"No hot dog," was his reply, as he sincerely shook his head to the negative simultaneously. Feiny knew that Sammy sent most of his monthly paycheck home for his mother and sisters; it was getting toward the end of the month, and he may have been short on cash until payday on the first.

So Feiny said, "Sammy, I'll buy you a hot dog. I have some extra money."

"No, no hot dog," he said with emphasis as if he were getting pushed into eating something awful. Several of the guys were standing around the roach coach sipping real coffee and eating their snacks, while listening to them.

"Sammy, why don't you want a hot dog?" Feiny inquired of his buddy with a puzzled look on his face.

Sammy took his index finger and pointed to his crotch. "Same, same. No can do. No can do."

Everyone hanging around burst into fits of laughter. Guys were spitting out their coffee and chunks of half-chewed stuff in hilarity. Sammy thought a hot dog was an animal's penis. People laughed until their guts ached. Even the civilian working the truck broke up when he was told what Sammy had just said. He told the story like an old-fashioned peddler up and down the coalition line. Everybody who heard it laughed like hell. It was hard for them to imagine anyone who did not know what a hot dog was. Sammy laughed too, but was unsure why. He was usually a good-natured guy and did his best to get along with everybody.

>*——>*——>*—

In addition to the regular French Army, there were also French Legionnaires who, strangely enough, seemed to speak every language but French. They arrived right after the reservists and were among the first with "boots on the ground" in Saudi Arabia. They were specialists in desert warfare. All along the coalition line, there was a lot of thievery going on, in a land not known for supporting that profession. But the world over, everywhere soldiers go, stuff disappears. That is why their uniforms have such big pockets in them. Therefore, no one wanted to accuse the Legionnaires of stealing stuff, but it seemed that every time something was missing, there were French boot prints in the area. The Saudis really wanted to cut off more hands than they did, but they needed them too badly to shift gears and pull triggers in the war effort.

One of the Legionnaires, Nichols, was even an American, a guy who said he was originally from Nevada. After Vietnam was over and the old war-horse was out of work, he joined the Legion. Soldiering and fighting had been his true lot in life. He used to come over once in a while with a couple of his buddies, and they would trade stuff. The French had the best chow. They had real food and bottles of Perrier instead of wine with every meal. They made what was called "Saudi champagne" from the mineral water and apple juice. They also compared weapons and traded rumors as usual. They all seemed to be all right guys, but they were all older men, and one could tell they were all tough as hell. They seemed more like convicts with guns than soldiers. Any one of them could clean your clock faster than a Swiss jeweler.

Nichols was about thirty-eight or forty years old. One time he and a couple of his buddies were visiting, and they were sitting around swapping chow and drinking Saudi champagne. McHugh asked him what it was like to be a mercenary. He said it was "all right," as long as you remembered the three rules of being a mercenary. They were simple and must be followed.

"The first rule is that nothing in life is free. Everything costs something in this world. You must pay with your money, with your hearts, with your tears, with your blood, with a chunk of your ass, and with the lost heartbeats wasted listening to the bullshit. There is nothing in life that is free. Never believe anyone who wants to give you something for nothing.

"The second rule of a mercenary is to never completely trust anyone with everything, every time. A person who knows your secret may undergo torture and not reveal you. A week later the same guy is drunk in a bar telling everyone about your bullshit. Many spouses say things in divorce courts that they would never say otherwise if some sweet thing had not gotten between them and their perceived happiness.

"The third rule of a mercenary is to never do anything dangerous or illegal unless you are being well paid for it. There are no weekend sports for us. An injury costs money through lost work. Never do anything for bravado. The good feeling wears off all too soon, while the pain of injury can go on forever."

"So that is why you do it. For the money?"

"No, man; money is just dirty paper. It's what money can buy that's important. It can get for you anything you want, if you have enough of it. It can buy both happiness and sorrow. Usually, they come together. But no, to answer your question, I do not do it for the money. I do it for the love of war. There is no greater feeling and no worse feeling than the tension of battle. It's cowboys and Indians for real. There is no doubt who gets hit. No one jumps up and hollers 'HA, HA, you missed me.' That's because they usually don't miss the second time. It really is the best game in the world. It's hunting for real. That is why I do it." He stopped speaking for a short while and then continued. "You look at me as if I'm full of shit. You think to yourselves, 'If this guy is such a great mercenary, then why is he here with us and a mere enlisted man in the French Foreign Legion?' I will tell you why. Nine governments currently want me for practicing my chosen profession. That is why I am serving in the Legion. I'm hidden."

The young American GIs liked his stories. He told them well, and they were probably true.

"Do you like killing people?" asked Jones.

"Only sometimes, especially when it is someone who really deserves it. The first couple of times were in Vietnam. I found the experience exhilarating. We had them. Tap, tap, tap. They were clearly bad actors. We caught three of them setting up an ambush for our guys. They wore black pajamas, straw lampshade hats, you know, the whole works. One was digging holes in the trail, and another one was sticking *punji* spikes into them. The third one was just squatting there on the side of the trail. I was part of a recon team that just happened upon them. We were lucky we spotted them before they saw us. There were four of us. We raised our weapons and on the count of three, we wasted them. After conducting our ambush, we waited a while, and then we went down to see."

"Why did you wait?" McHugh wanted to know.

"To see if any of their buddies would show themselves and also to give them time to die in peace. I have seen guys full of bullets but not quite dead yet jump up and start blasting. It is always better to wait. Best of all just run away, and set up shop elsewhere. It is always best to split, but we needed the intelligence we could get from reading their dead bodies. When we went down, we saw that we caught them good. They were with their ancestors. The weirdest thing about the whole episode is that the third guy squatting down was a woman, and she was dipping the sharpened *punji* sticks in her shit. That makes a nasty septic wound when you step on it. Gangrene sets in quickly. They certainly deserved it when they got it. That booby trap was clearly intended for an American soldier. Other times, the line between good and bad was not so clear."

"What did you mean, to read their bodies?" Feinstein inquired.

"We had a guy there who could tell how long you were in the bush by the condition of your body. He was an intelligence specialist. A soldier in the bush gets beat to hell by the environment. Scratches, blisters, calluses on the feet, insect bites. They all tell their story to the trained eye. These folks had clean bodies, meaning that they lived in a village nearby and came out every so often to do their dirty work. Hardcore VC running in the bush were always dirty, scared and abused looking. These were locals engaged in guerilla activity."

"What happened to the village?" inquired Jones.

"I heard that there was another incident in the area and the whole thing was napalmed into a smoking hole. There was no more trouble in that sector for a long time after that."

Then Feiny, always the curious comedian, asked Nichols, "What is the funniest thing you have ever seen in all your years of soldiering?"

The expatriate American thought for a moment, and then a great smile cracked his normally somber face. He had thought of a very funny incident that occurred when he was on one of his tours in Vietnam.

"Once, in 1970, we were assigned to protect a hamlet named Duk Luk, or something like that. We were advisors to a company of South Vietnamese soldiers. They were not worth a shit. I remember that one of them wanted to trade his brand new M-16 to me for my camera. I recall he said that he 'did not need it because the Americans were there.' You would send them on patrol, and they would just go out into the bush a couple of klicks, hang around for a while, and then come back in, claiming to have 'reconned' the entire area. They would report 'No VC.' If Americans went with them, they were as likely to be shot by them as by the Viet Cong. They would then say that enemy contact was responsible.

"You could never trust the little bastards. Some of them were even peaceniks like some of the youth in America. They wanted to smoke their dope and were not going to fight. A bunch of them bought these little Japanese motorcycles and spent all day driving around inside camp, because there was nowhere to drive to outside camp without getting killed. So they just drove around and around, annoying the shit out of everyone. They would buzz here and there, making major pains in the ass of themselves, stirring up dust and running into the villagers' animals. I can still hear the damn noise from the things. Their commander would not do a thing about it. He was black-marketing the gas to them.

"Well, they used to chain up the bikes to this huge banyan tree in the middle of camp. One night we came under a 105-mm artillery attack. Rounds landed all over camp, but one of them hit smack in the middle of the bikes chained to the tree. It blasted them to shit, and also took out a good part of the tree. When the South Vietnamese soldiers saw this in the morning, some of them stood there crying great big old crocodile tears. I remember laughing so hard that my sides ached for days. There were those bikes all over the camp, some parts way up in the trees.

"I don't think I've ever laughed so hard as I did that day. For weeks I would look at the spot and burst out laughing again. The best part of the story was that then the lazy ARVN got mad and started soldiering. They started going out for the VC with sincerity after that. It was the funniest thing I ever saw in my entire life." So went their dinner conversation. They were starved for more than food...

Chapter 11

HANGING AROUND IN BABYLON (WHERE IS THE GARDEN?)

Porter was another driver in their squad. He was a charismatic Christian from the back hills of North Carolina. He was a devout something or other and an endless source of biblical information. Once, while sitting around, he was reading from a book of Bible facts someone sent him in the mail. Guys who knew a little scripture themselves used to test him on his knowledge of the good word. He seemed to know the gospel pretty well.

Porter and a couple of the guys were off duty and were lounging around the bivouac area, talking. Sergeant Eliot was teaching Young One how to play checkers at Feiny's sandbox table. The sarge had made a board from a cardboard carton. He used a magic marker to darken in some squares for the black. He let the cardboard's tan show through for the other color. He played with water bottle caps. The caps facing up represented the red checkers, while the ones facing down represented the black checkers. Young One was catching on fast; he really liked the game.

They had just gotten back from convoy duty and weren't ready to turn in. It was almost twilight, and they could be outside in the dimming sun. The Arabian sun cast an orange-red color over the sky, creating a beautiful backdrop for Porter's impromptu pulpit.

Porter was still clutching his book of Bible facts and was reading sections of it. He stopped his reading and unexpectedly said, while pointing northward toward Iraq, "Babylon the Great, Mother of Harlots and the Abomination of the Earth." He nodded his head several times in a sign of silent realization and agreement. The other guys with him stopped what they were doing and looked at him. They thought he was going mad in the heat. He continued speaking, not to himself anymore, but to anyone who was listening. This was not his usual way. He was often very quiet, and, although he was very religious, he kept it to himself. Something must have been upsetting him. Young One and Sergeant Eliot ceased their game to listen.

"Ancient Babylon from the Bible is right over the border in Iraq. This was once part of the lost Kingdom of Babylonia. They had the fanciest gates in the entire world, all carved with animal figures and the like. It's where the Hanging Gardens of Babylon were. They were one of the Seven Wonders of the World because of the rare plants and such that were there. That is also where the Tower of Babel was. The Israelites called it 'Baby-lu.' It was on the west bank of the Euphrates River. It says so right here," he said, while holding up his book of Bible facts for anyone who cared to look at it for verification. He continued without missing a beat.

"The Lord struck them down and sent them all their different ways, speaking different languages for trying to build a tower to Heaven. Only God can allow us into the Kingdom of Heaven. We cannot just decide to go there on our own. The sins of Babylon are why we speak so many languages today. That is why the Lord gave us the English language, to bring all His people under one roof to read the Good Book. It's the language for which the Bible was written. The whole world would be better off if everyone were Americans."

"Wasn't it written in Latin or Greek or something like that?" inquired McHugh.

"I did not say 'written in.' I said 'written for.' The original language was Mesopotamian Sumerian because that was the only written language in the world at the time. Aramaic, mother tongue of modern Hebrew and Arabic, was used for the later books of the Bible. The Israelites preserved the Old Testament in Hebrew. The New Testament was first written on parchment or papyrus scrolls in Greek by the early Christians. Then it was translated into Roman Vulgate, a kind of poor man's Latin. It was first printed on a press in German and put into English by none other than King James himself.

"America is great because we speak the main language of commerce and transportation in the modern world. Do you know that every international airline pilot in the world speaks English? They have to. That is why so few Americans speak foreign languages. It is because God does not want us to speak in foreign languages. America is giving the world a second chance to speak in one tongue, like before the Tower of Babel in the Bible in ancient Babylon. We not only trust in God like our money says to do, but He trusts us in return with His sacred word. My pastor says that every time you translate the Book into another language, it gains or loses something. That is because we don't all think the same."

Franklin was listening to them, and he added, "You're right, Porter. If they want our money, they have to learn how to say 'thanks' in English." He had heard that somewhere, and it sounded like a good time to reiterate it. As a fellow Christian, he was impressed with Porter's knowledge of the scripture. It was not like Porter to be so talkative. Usually he said little. Now he was really on a roll about Saddam and Armageddon.

"Where did you learn all of this, Porter?"

"From different places – some from my parents and pastor back home, and some from reading books about the Bible, but mostly from the Good Book itself. To be truthful, I am not all that smart, but I have been reading the Book and a lot of books about it, so I sound smart."

Porter continued on about the Bible in his thick North Carolina hickory-hill accent. He sounded as if he could have come from Mayberry itself on the TV show. Porter, for all his country ways, was actually very intelligent. He just did not sound smart because of his backcountry accent. But he really knew his Bible. It was strange to hear such eloquent words spoken in such a dialect.

He would just go on and on about the Book of Revelation and the start of Armageddon and all sorts of scriptural stories. For him, this was the real deal. He was going to go to Heaven. He wrote letters home to people telling them he would see them in the Rapture. He told them he would be standing on the right side of the Pearly Gates. He had his doubts about the others but did not express them, for it was not his place to speak about others. As religious as he was, he never pushed it onto others. They had to talk to him about it first.

Porter, wishing to bring the conversation back to his perspective of life on earth, said, "You don't believe me, do you all? We are standing on the same ground that was once part of the Kingdom of Babylonia. Modern-day Iraq had also been the home of the Sumerians, Assyrians, and the Chaldeans from the Old Testament. The lost city of Ur is right over there in Iraq. It was the birthplace of Abraham, the patriarch of Judaism, Christianity, and Islam."

"What is a pa-tree-ark?" inquired Young One respectfully.

"I am not sure, but it says it here. It could be a founding father or something like that. Have you ever heard of Sodom and Gomorrah?" Porter then asked.

"Yeah, where they used to throw wild parties and have orgies. Babylon was the center of world materialism and irreligious idolatry and was the Las Vegas of the past. Those were the days," said Jones the born-again "wannabe"pagan with a hint of false nostalgia.

"Sodom and Gomorrah are just an hour's drive outside of modern Baghdad," added Porter.

"That is where God punished the evildoers for their iniquities. The city was consumed by fire, and it burned the whole town from the inside out. Today, it is believed that natural gas seeping up from a huge oil field below ignited and burned the place down. That was where Lot's wife was turned into a pillar of salt, just across the desert here, a couple of hundred miles to the north," Porter added.

"Yeah, then where is she now?" inquired one of the disbelievers. "It doesn't rain much here, so it wasn't washed away."

Sergeant Eliot, who in civilian life lived on a farm, said, "The animals licked it away." Everybody started laughing except Simms. He said, "You white boys are disgusting." Simms always thought the worst.

"It's not what you're thinking," said Sergeant Eliot. "On the farm, you have to give the horses and cattle and such salt blocks to lick for the minerals. The animals go wild for it. Camels and goats are probably not much different. When the first caravan passed by, old Mrs. Lot was gone, with a smile on her face."

"I wonder where they started first?" somebody asked, and everybody laughed again except Simms. For all the awful things that came from his mouth, he found the topic of cunnilingus very upsetting. Porter continued as if nothing significant had been said.

"Babylon is where Daniel the Prophet from the Old Testament became one of the most powerful people in the then-known world. None other than King Nebuchadnezzar himself had captured him in Jerusalem, along with thousands of other Jews. They were taken captive to Babylon as slaves. King Solomon's temple was burned to the ground. At that time, Babylon was the center of evil power. It was the most evil place in the world. They had astrologers and sorcerers and magicians. Because Daniel would not renounce his God and pray to pagan idols, he was thrown into the lions' den by the king. They thought the lions would eat him or play with him to death as a cat does to a mouse. But old Daniel fooled them all. Have you ever heard that story?"

McHugh said that he had heard it before. He remembered hearing a nun tell him in Catholic school that Daniel noticed that the biggest, meanest lion was limping and acting mean. Daniel went over to him, pulled a large thorn from his paw, and squeezed out the pus from it. Well, that old lion figured he owed Daniel a favor and guarded him from the other lions. After a while, the other lions liked him, too, and they lay down around him. When the Babylonians saw this, they knew it was God's work.

"There was no thorn in the paw. That is a Bible 'add-on.' There was no thorn." Then Porter continued.

"But that night, the king was troubled with nightmares in his sleep. When the guards told him that the Jew from Jerusalem was still alive and was petting the lions, he called him to the throne room to interpret his dreams. Old Daniel did so well that the king pardoned him and cast out the Chaldean magicians. Daniel became the third most powerful man in

Babylon. He saved the lives of the other Jews, and they were eventually returned home to Israel."

Simms had had enough of that shit. "How long are you going to babble on about Babylon? Babylon, that's what the reggae brothers used to sing about. It never brought them any peace and justice. Those brothers are in jail, braiding their dreadlocks and keeping the other niggers off their asses. That is some old shit. The only thing that brings justice is this," he said while patting his rifle. "It's the same as back in the hood. It's better to get caught with it than without it."

Then he laughed at his own supposed cleverness. No one else did. Simms had all the charm of George Jefferson on the 1970s television show. Then he walked off with his characteristic street strut. He never seemed to lose it, even when he was marching—he just sort of "bee-bopped" along as if he were back on the block.

Porter looked hurt. Simms was certainly a sinner like all of them, only a much better one. Private Porter sat there silent for a few moments, and then he laid back on the sand and told the others to do the same. They were looking up into the twilit sky.

"All this sand was once under water. The great flood covered the whole earth. I sometimes lay back and look at the sky." The clouds overhead were orange, iridescent puffballs reflecting the setting sun. "Sometimes I wonder what it would look like to see the bottom of Noah's boat right overhead, as if I were a fish looking up at it."

"Dude, you have been in the sun too much," replied McHugh.

"Do you really think that Armageddon is coming?" asked Feiny.

"Absolutely, but it is not here yet," reminded Porter.

"What do you mean? Do you think that this is the battle of Armageddon, or the Mother of All Battles, as 'So Damn Insane' over there says?"

"There is no battle of Armageddon spoken of in the Book. It will be a series of battles, maybe even many wars. It will end with the Rapture for the true believers in the end time."

"Isn't that what's coming here?"

"Armageddon refers to a fortified place on the plain of Jezreel in Israel called Megiddo, and it is the area around it. Today it is located in the Carmel Mountains in Northern Israel near the Mediterranean Sea. It was at the crossroads where the caravans from both north and east met to run south into Palestine or Egypt. The Philistines defeated King Saul, the first King of the Israelites. They massacred everybody, and the battle was called Armageddon. That is where the last war on earth will take place. This is not Armageddon, but it may be the Mother of All Battles that Saddam predicts.

"We do not know what is coming. God keeps the future a mystery to all but His most trusted prophets. John the Apostle was given a vision almost two thousand years ago about the end times. He wrote about it in the Book of Revelation. It is sometimes called the Apocalypse."

"You mean like the four horsemen of the Apocalypse? I've heard of them."

"That's right."

"Let's see. The black horse is war, isn't it?" asked Jones.

"No, the black horse is famine, like the black hole in an empty stomach. War rides a red horse, all covered with blood. Disease rides a white horse, like the color of nurses' uniforms, and death rides a pale horse, like the bled-out color of a dead body."

"Maybe Saddam is right about this being the Mother of All Battles," one of them said.

"The harlot of Babylon will produce many bastard children," answered Porter.

"War is never really over, is it? I saw a TV show about the great wars, and some guy said 'World War I and World War II were really just one big war. They just stopped for a while to rearm and replenish their vanquished troops, just to get back at it in the next generation.' Could it be the same for World War III?" asked Jones.

"All the signs are not here yet."

"What signs?"

"The first sign has already happened. God's chosen people, the Israelites, will again have their own land. That has already happened, after thousands of years of waiting. The survivors of the Nazi Holocaust founded it after World War II. The second sign has not happened yet. It is reformation of the Roman Empire. All of the countries of Europe have to get together and have a common coin and their own army."

"They would never do that. They have been fighting among themselves too long for that."

"Isn't that what NATO is?" McHugh asked incredulously.

"NATO and the UN are the start of it."

"This new thing the Bible speaks of will be NATO without the United States."

"The countdown to Armageddon will start when missiles are fired from Babylon to Israel."

"You are crazy. No one would do that. Israel has the bomb. They would blast them to Hell."

"The bomb is no protection from God's word. It will cause more trouble than it will stop." Then Porter changed the subject slightly. Feinstein, being one of God's chosen-but-orthodoxly-wayward people, listened intently.

"Do you know the Garden of Eden was in Iraq? It says so right here. Look here." His companion verified the words in his book of Bible facts, but McHugh still wasn't sure if he should believe it or not. The sun had already set, and it was really getting too dark to read, but Porter did not seem to notice.

"Of course, it wasn't Iraq then, it wasn't even Mesopotamia or even Babylon yet. The Garden of Eden was the most beautiful place on earth. Every plant on earth grew there."

His agnostic companion asked incredulously, "Isn't the Garden of Eden back in the Holy Land?" By this, he meant Jerusalem or Bethlehem or somewhere in that area.

Porter replied, "This is all the Holy Land. Or rather, this is the backside of the Holy Land."

"The backside of the Holy Land. Now you're making sense," the other guy said. "This place is where you could give the Middle East an enema," quipped Feinstein, finally having something to say.

He laughed at his own joke, said nothing else for a few seconds, and then looked around and added, "If this place is the Holy Land, then I never want to see the Unholy Land." He laughed again to himself.

Porter said, "You should not blaspheme." He said it just like a preacher.

McHugh said, "I'm not sure there even was a Garden of Eden. And if there was, why would God put it in such an awful place?"

Porter explained that it had not always been an awful spot. "The original sin of eating the apple caused evil to spread out from its original location. During the time of Noah's Ark, this sand was all under water from the great flood. The desert is really the bottom of a lost sea. That is why there is so much sand here. That is why there is nothing but the desert here. Another apple tree will never grow here. God destroyed the world by water last time. This time it will be by fire."

Everyone quit their "smoking and joking" to listen, as if almost spellbound by Porter's stories. McHugh, who was from Pennsylvania, where apples grow aplenty, said he could not argue that an apple would ever grow there.

"You like detective stories, McHugh. I have seen you reading paperback books you got from the bookmobile on the very subject."

"Well, yeah, I do."

"The first murder on earth occurred not far from here."

"Go on."

"It was just outside of the Garden of Eden where Cain killed his brother Abel. He beat him to death with an old bone, they say. His was the first soul cast to Hell."

"Is he a devil?" one of the guys asked.

"No, he is a tormented human sinner, but he has been there so long that he is probably an officer by now," Feinstein added in comic interruption. All of the enlisted men laughed aloud at the thought. Entertainment was at such a premium that almost anything was funny.

Porter also told them of the enslavement of the early Jews and about the hanging gardens of Babylon—forever the name of evil to every good Christian. To Porter, if this was not Armageddon, then it was the start of it. He called Desert Shield the "dress rehearsal for the Apocalypse." The end time was coming. All of Porter's Bible talk and prophecy of doom and destruction got old pretty quick. After a while, people would say, "Yeah, yeah, sure." But no one was really sure what to believe.

><>

Private First Class Simms was a black former gang-banger from Kansas City who temporarily turned in his street colors for camo and joined the Reserve. He came from the back alley of some dead-end street in the middle of the urban core. In his youth, he had been caught up in the unending gang warfare of the hood. These young inner-city warriors declared intertribal warfare on each other for the right to spray-paint unintelligible markings on a wall they didn't own, or ever possibly would.

Next to Franklin, PFC "Dog-Down" Simms had more combat experience in the neighborhood before enlisting in the army than any of the other guys. He shot his first guy when he was twelve. His victim was a grown man, who was somewhere doing something he should not have been doing. Simms was no patriot. He went into the Reserve to find out where the armory was kept. He was going to rob the weapons, machine guns, hand grenades, and all. He and his homies would have some real fun with those deadly toys. Then fate fortunately intervened for the good people of Kansas City. Private First Class Jamal Simms got orders to the Big Sandbox—Saudi Arabia.

Once in the system, he got away with a lot of stuff because he was actually a very good soldier when he wanted to be, and because he was black. It seems that all of his drive-by shooting experience as a civilian was paying off. Simms lived in a world where bad behavior was good, and cold behavior was hot. He had a juvenile record, but it did not count. He never got caught for anything serious. The fact that his transgressions against society occurred before his eighteenth birthday gave him a clean slate for the army. It actually was more like an erased chalkboard. If one looked hard enough, the writing of yesterday's teachings in the hood could still be faintly seen upon the blackboard of his soul. He really never left the hood—he brought it with him. He always hung out with guys from other squads because they were black.

Simms' real problem was that he was born on the wrong side of the tracks. They were on his mother's arm. He was born with nothing, and he, in all probability, would die with nothing. A black sergeant from another platoon was once heard telling him, "Son, if you don't change your attitude toward life, as long as your asshole is pointing towards the ground, you are going to be poor."

>———>⋇——>⋇

Simms was a smart-ass, but he had the wherewithal to back it up with any one. He could be mean and arrogant. He did not fear anything on two legs. At least not anything white. But one thing he had never been around (the human ones aside) were snakes. He feared and hated them.

The squad was unloading some boxes of MREs in the back of a contract tractor-trailer. The soldiers had formed a "bucket brigade," passing boxes of food from one to the other. Simms was kneeling in the trailer and was handing out boxes to Porter, who in turn was handing them to Young One. As usual, Simms was talking shit about how he missed the "hoes and bitches" back home. He really liked upsetting Porter because he knew he did not care for such speech and because he was a cracker. As he continued with his verbal diarrhea, he was cut short in mid-sentence.

He was kneeling and reaching down to pick up another box when he shrieked like a school child and instinctively recoiled back in utter terror. But there was nowhere to go, as he was wedged between full cardboard boxes of supplies. He was so frightened that his normally dark complexion turned ashen. He froze in the hot truck and stared straight ahead at the coiled, sand-colored snake, almost camouflaged atop a cardboard box of MREs. He was literally face to face with death.

The mouth on the large, triangular head opened to reveal two ivory-colored, venom-dripping hypodermics. It swayed back and forth a foot from his face, hissing in warning. It was poised to strike in a split second. Simms could not move. For the first time in his life, all he could do was tremble. He was afraid to speak, to move, or even to blink. The pair of elliptical yellow eyes staring straight back at him did not blink, either.

Porter was working next to him and, seeing what was going on, did a most peculiar thing. Instead of running or calling out for help, he began to pray to the Lord. His prayers and supplications of faith were spoken slowly and softly at first and then gradually became faster and louder until he began to speak in tongues. Simms could hear him but could not see what he was doing. His gaze was locked upon the swaying serpent at his face. Porter raised his arms over his head and continued speaking faster and faster, louder and louder. Porter's body was twitching and jerking as though he had gotten "slimed" with nerve agent. His body trembled with religious devotion as he spoke the foreign words.

Simms was transfixed in mortal terror and horrible fascination as Porter reached down right in front of him, grasped the poisonous reptile in both hands, lifted it up, and then held it over his head. The snake behaved like it was frozen or anaesthetized. PFC Porter's eyes wiggled back and forth in a most unnatural manner, as if he were convulsing. Still speaking in tongues, only softly now, he carried the snake out of the truck trailer, still holding it over his head, and took it to the perimeter, where he let it loose on the sand. The snake began crawling away.

Then, he suddenly came back to the moment and said, with a voice that sounded like somebody else's, "Be gone, child of Satan. Crawl back to Hell where you came from."

The snake instinctively began to crawl away toward the Iraqi border when Simms rushed up with his M-16 rifle and slammed two 5.56-mm good-byes into its head. The body of the now-headless snake writhed upon the sand as if it were break dancing, as blood squirted from what was left of its neck.

"That's just to make sure you get there," he said in defiance. He was back to his usual shit-talking self. The two gunshots brought everyone to the area. All the rest of the members of the platoon came rushing up with their weapons in hand to see what the shooting was about. Normally, discharging a weapon without direct authorization would bring a world of shit down on a soldier. But since he killed a poisonous snake, they let him slide. Sergeant Eliot told him, "Next time, call me. I'll shoot it." That was the end of it.

"Man, did you see that shit? The cracker hypnotized a snake. They were both in a trance. I ain't fucking with Porter no more. The dude's crazy. I can't believe the shit I just seen."

Everyone was both amazed and amused by the incident. It sure broke up the boredom of bivouac. Word spread quickly about what had happened. People listened more intently to Porter's biblical facts after that...

Chapter 12

LIFE ON THE LINE

Youssef was a desert dweller, a *Badawi*—or as the French Legionnaires called them, the Bedouin. These desert folk were a hardy lot: fiercely loyal to friends and deadly to their enemies. They were the Ishmaelites of the Old Testament. They were the other children of Abraham, banished to the wilds of the desert, where they flourished. Today, the Bedouin range in different bands all the way from the Persian Gulf to Morocco. Youssef's people had traveled for thousands of years through those parts of the desert now called Arabia, southern Syria, Iraq, and Jordan, without credentials, passports, political allegiances, and without paying taxes. They moved as if there were no borders. They lived deep in the desert, following their herds of goats and sheep that, in turn, follow the infrequent rains to find the sweet grasses and bitter herbs that spring forth from the sand as if by necromancy. One day their encampment would appear and the next day, it was gone. The desert swept clean all remembrance of their passing on the wind. The Bedouin seemed to come from dust and to disappear into it.

Sixteen-year-old Youssef was a member of the *Rualla* tribe, who today are herdsmen. In years past, his people were nomadic caravan guards or caravan raiders, depending upon the circumstances. Alas, the days of the great caravans, with hundreds of camels loaded with the treasures of the earth, along with hundreds of guards to protect them, had gone. The camel was the ideal mode of transportation in the desert for thousands of years. They were reliable, sturdy, and could fuel themselves along the way as they tread without water on dry sea beds.

They could go for long periods without the life-giving fluid. Some of the Bedouin still earned their living the old way, surviving in small bands, following their herds and flocks. They eked out a meager existence by herding goats, sheep and camels. That was all that remained in the fall of 1990 of a once-proud way of life.

The jeep and the truck had largely replaced the camel as the major means of transportation in the desert. This change had reduced both the prestige and economic status of these proud people. Trucks were expensive to purchase, fuel, and maintain. Besides, they got stuck in the sand, and towing or repair services in the places where the Bedouin went were are non-existent. But most of all, trucks also had to pass through customs stations where cargoes were inspected and embargoed, questions asked, bribes demanded and taxes paid. The Bedouins thought it best to avoid these places if possible. The camel made it possible.

The only thing camels were still good for was smuggling or transporting goods from border to border, without government sanction or taxes being involved. Cigarettes, batteries, chewing gum, radios, television sets, video recorders, Western clothing, and other contraband were carried on the backs of camels to supply the needs of the duty-free purchasing public in the village *souks*.

Anything that was hard to obtain was possible to get if one knew the right Bedouin and was willing to pay the necessary price. Barter had always been the stock and trade of these desert folk, who, of necessity, had to obtain things not known to the desert by trading in the villages. It was impossible for any government to completely close off thousands of miles of desert border, as these desert travelers knew all the back paths in and out of anywhere.

In a twist of ecological fate, following the mathematical laws of proportionality, their old way of life was diminishing. The deserts were growing geographically through deforestation, but the way of life of the desert folk was shrinking correspondingly. The people were not becoming extinct, but their culture was slowly threatened by progress. Their traditions and the attained knowledge of survival in that part of the world was being abandoned by young and old alike, in search of an easier lifestyle in the towns or cities.

As the Gulf War approached, the way of life of the Bedouin was curtailed even further. The borders were more closely watched. Airplanes flew overhead and reported their activity to the authorities. Patrols would be sent out to investigate them. Minefields planted in the trackless sands in past military conflicts were another hazard faced by the Bedouin. The nooses of progress were slowly closing on the necks of these desert people. Soon, they would be on reservations like the indigenous people in America. But Youssef and his people were as free as they still could be. His ancestors were traveling the desert before the great pyramids were built.

At night, they sat around fragrant fires of frankincense and myrrh sticks to bake bread and roast meat. They scraped salt from the rocks where it had waited millions of years to be used. They slaked their thirst from puddles clearly visible after the rains and from hidden groundwater wells deep in the earth. Many had been forced to abandon the old way of life for economic serfdom in one of the overcrowded Middle Eastern cities. That year, however, the warming climate and associated weather changes drove the *Rualla* Bedouins northward into the war zone.

Youssef went along with his father, uncles, and his little brother that morning to the desert village just across the Iraqi side of the border. Their purpose was to trade beautiful woolen rugs his mother and aunts had woven from their goat and sheep wool. They would trade these for flour, eggs, coffee, fresh fruit and other wants and necessities of life they couldn't find or produce themselves in the desert. They also had several young male goats they would trade if the price was good in the *souk*. It was still dark. A breakfast of goat cheese chunks, mixed with grain and water by the fire, got the body started for another day. The sun was just struggling upward as they set off in the direction of the desert town.

There were many houses made of whitewashed plaster, and desert palm trees lined the streets. They were in southwestern Iraq, near the Jordanian border. For those who lived with few material possessions, this offered them plenty to see and to wonder about. There were so many sights, sounds, and smells in an inhabited place. There were piles of fruit, cooking stalls, and heaps of spices, garlic, hot peppers, and melons. There were merchants selling rugs, clothing, and cooking implements.

There were Arab peddlers selling all the necessities of a simple life, while other merchants offered western and Asian electronic equipment. Everything was spread on blankets and rugs or hung on the walls of the shops. Although this desert bazaar was no shopping center, it was the closest thing to a mall that Youssef had ever seen. The incessant din of haggling conversation, so much a part of Arab trading, filled their young ears.

After the goats were sold, Youssef and his little brother wandered away from their father and uncles and began looking around at all the new sights and smelling the scents from the cooking fires. They were soon, however, lost amid the maze of streets and back alleys of the Iraqi village. But, they knew that the town was not that large, and they could find their way back to the animal pens.

An old woman was squatting on the ground, dressed in dusty, black clothing and selling fruit. She was wiping off the dust from her plums by putting them in her mouth to moisten them with saliva, and then polishing them with a dirty rag. She looked up and smiled with rotten, crooked teeth then offered to sell them a plum. The little brother wanted to taste one, but the wiser Youssef quickly pulled his arm back and led him away from the stall. They kept walking down the stone-paved alleyways while looking around at all the new sights and hearing new sounds and sniffing out new smells. They soon reached the other side of the village.

They started back toward the marketplace to rejoin their family members when, suddenly, they saw several older boys running down the street with frightened looks on their faces. As they sped past Youssef and his brother, one of them shouted with winded breath, "Run, the conscriptors are coming," in Arabic. Fear is a very contagious emotion. Neither Youssef nor his little brother knew what that meant, but they ran as well. They only got halfway down the narrow, dusty street when a military vehicle pulled in front of them from a side alleyway and jerked to a screeching halt before the fleeing boys. A soldier jumped from the passenger seat and pulled a semi-automatic pistol from its holster, cocked and fired a single shot into the air. The sharp crack of the pistol report froze them in their tracks.

A tan-colored military truck pulled up from behind them with its tailgate down. The sergeant spoke while armed guards kept automatic weapons trained on the soon-to-be-kidnapped youth. Several other soldiers, who had been chasing the fleeing boys down the street, soon caught up to them as well. Youssef's little brother slipped around the vehicle and, while looking over his shoulder, kept running down the street. The sergeant who fired the pistol towards the sky said, "None of you try that." They knew he meant it. Youssef's little brother was regarded as a small fish released from its net. The sergeant knew he would be back for him later when he was of larger size. Youssef was glad his little brother had slipped away, as he would be able to tell his family what had happened. His father and uncles would rescue him, he thought.

"Get in the truck," was the laconic order harshly given to them. It was punctuated with a swoosh, followed by a whack across the legs with a long, thin stick about the size of a broom handle. In size and function, it was a cross between a club and a whip. The boy who had been hit winced in pain and obediently followed his directions. Although each of the other boys obeyed, they were all given a quick taste of the stick across the backs of their thighs while climbing into the truck. Once aboard, the sergeant sat in the back along with two guards and ordered them to keep their mouths shut. Soon, they were driving on a bumpy road toward destiny. They had been picked up from the streets with no more concern than had they been stray dogs. Youssef and his unfortunate companions were prisoners of war, before it even began.

In the back of the truck, one of the other boys began to become hysterical with fright, saying that this was all wrong, he was guilty of no crime, and that his family would worry about him. His protestation of innocence was interrupted, however, by a sharp slap across the face by a mean-faced corporal. The other soldier, sitting as guard in the back of the truck, locked and loaded his AK-47, indicating he was ready for trouble. The sound of an automatic weapon's lethal mechanisms slamming a round home is a universal attention getter. There was no more trouble in the truck for the rest of the drive.

They were taken out of town to a military camp, where the truck braked to a halt on a bumpy dirt road. There the driver spoke to someone in Arabic, probably a gate guard, and soon the vehicle started moving again, this time more slowly than before. The truck stopped again, and, almost immediately, the canvas cover was torn open, and a blast of bright sunlight shot in, temporarily gluing their eyelids shut with solar radiation. As the tailgate was lowered, the sergeant shouted in harsh colloquial Arabic, "Out of the vehicle. Now!"

After literally blindly obeying the sergeant's orders, they were directed to form a line in front of a sun-faded canvas tent, where they waited. Youssef thought his bladder would burst, as they were not allowed to relieve themselves. He was led into the canvas tent by a sergeant who handled him roughly and stood behind at parade rest as an Iraqi Army officer sitting behind a small wooden desk spoke to him. One by one, the recruiting commander interrogated them.

"You have been detained upon suspicion of being a Zionist spy," said the officer. This was the same lie he told each of them during their private interview. Youssef responded that he was merely a poor desert boy who went to the market with his family to barter.

"Silence," he screamed and slapped his automatic pistol down with a hard thump on the wooden table in front of him.

"You were with the others, and one of them is suspected of being a subversive," he continued. Of course it was not true, but merely a ruse to encourage Youssef's enlistment in the army. It had worked countless times before, and it would work this time as well. Youssef didn't know what a subversive was, and he protested his innocence. Individually, they were all told that they had but two choices. But in reality, they had only one. Each was told he would be tried as a subversive element, and this would, of course, involve their families. The other choice was to show their true allegiance to the regime in Baghdad and set the matter to rest by proudly enlisting in the Iraqi People's Army.

Recruiters the world over tell hot lies to gain warm bodies to hold cold weapons, but this was a particularly egregious way of doing it. Whether to save themselves, their families, or their bursting bladders, they all signed voluntary enlistment papers and were allowed to experience the relief of painful urination after several hours of being forced to hold it. In this manner, the whole Iraqi Army had "voluntarily" enlisted. There was no need for a draft, because for these unfortunate young men, there was no Canada to go to. Also, none of them had rich relatives to purchase a deferment for them.

Baghdad has always been famous for its thieves, but now, the secret police and "enlisters" had stolen the greatest wealth any nation possesses, the treasure of its youth. In a land where there is no social security system, the young must take care of the old. Each generation nurtures the young and in turn are taken care of in the twilight of their years by their offspring. Without children, especially sons in that part of the world, the old ones wouldn't get much older. By taking the youth and throwing away their lives in the sand, the Butchers of Baghdad were destroying not only their country's future but its past as well.

After a cursory enlistment ceremony, each was given a cup of tea, then they were taken by truck to a larger military post and billeted in old canvas tents that smelled of waterproofing chemicals. The place was more like a concentration camp than a military barracks. It was two weeks before they were issued uniforms and boots. Youssef had never worn boots before, and to date his only footwear had been leather sandals. He didn't like boots because he felt they confined and gave blisters to his feet, but they were required. After a while, he almost got used to them.

After a month of military training that consisted of marching and saluting, he became a soldier. Part of their training was listening to propaganda speeches, both of a political and a religious nature. They were to help the troops get their minds right. The uniform that he had been issued was old and baggy, but it had been laundered. It may have belonged to a deceased soldier, but there were no bullet holes in it as reminders of its previous occupant. They received rudimentary rifle and war-skills training.

There were really two armies in Iraq: the Republican Guard, which was the elite of the Iraqi Army, and the People's Army. The former was well led, trained, armed, and supplied. The ranks of the Republican Guard were filled with the sons, nephews, and friends of the powerful government officials, rich businessmen, and those who showed extraordinary zeal in pursuit of their military duties.

The People's Army was a collection of religious fanatics, hate mongers, weary old men, and frightened young boys purchased or purloined from throughout the country. They came from the streets of the capital city, the dusty villages, and swampy marshes.

There were students taken from their classrooms, their open books abandoned on empty school desks. Fathers went to work and never returned. Teenage boys were snatched from their play or chores. They were enlisted through trickery, appeals to patriotism, religious fanaticism, threats, and violence. Young and old, good and bad alike soon found their way into the ranks of the unfortunate. On the line, most were farther away from their homes than they had ever been before. All would go no farther, and most would not return. Those who were fortunate enough to return home would never be the same.

There were men or boys all along the line in the sand who spoke several dialects of Arabic, all thrust together. There were swamp Arabs, city dwellers, mountain herdsmen, Kurds, Turks, and desert nomads. These were the poor, bastard children of the "Mother of All Battles."

What really troubled Youssef were the hours the army kept. A Bedouin day begins at sunset, after sleeping through the hot day. The nomad day is divided into segments. They would cook and travel in the night air. The desert can change a hundred degrees Fahrenheit from day to night, although less varying ranges are the norm. They would work until after midnight, and then go back to bed to stay warm until just before sunrise; then they would work until around ten or eleven in the morning, and then go back to bed to escape the heat. In this way, they worked with the desert climate, without suffering from it.

But the Iraqi Army followed Western ways of life. Up early in the morning, work and train until dark, then go to bed. This was the hardest adjustment for Youssef's biological clock. The Saudi Arabians, following their Bedouin roots, even have clocks and watches with Arab time and Western time on them. Depending upon who they were talking to, Arab or Westerner, it was a different time of day. Being there gave one the sense that it was not just the hours that were off; the centuries were off as well in that ancient land.

After a month of rudimentary training that consisted more of indoctrination than fighting skills, Youssef was shipped by truck to the front line, where he soon found himself in an infantry company. The People's Army was ill-trained, improperly equipped, and led by madmen. Their main function was to man the line in the sand Saddam drew across the border between Saudi Arabia and occupied Kuwait.

The life of a private soldier in the Iraqi Army was truly wretched. Youssef and his comrades labored under the most miserable of conditions. Minor transgressions invariably resulted in beatings, while more serious offenses brought bodily mutilation or execution. Corpse displays were common and served as putrefying reminders of both the importance of discipline and the punishment for disobedience.

Youssef had no moustache, meaning he was not a full-grown man in their society. It was like being a hornless calf penned in with steers and bulls. Every dirty job, he got it. Every dangerous assignment, he got it, because he was unmarried and had no children to support, and because he was a *Badawi*, an ethnic inferior.

Three things kept the Iraqi Army in line: fear, pain, and fear of pain. In front of them were the elite forces of the most militarily advanced nations on the Earth, and they were frightened of the coalition army, but they were more afraid of the soldiers who stood behind them. Each company had a special officer assigned to it. Each had a Republican Guard in addition to their regular sergeants and field officers. They could be spotted by the bright red triangular shoulder patch and by the evil expression on their faces. Every one was a cold-blooded killer who had earned his rank in the Iran-Iraq War. They had proven themselves to be brutal men in the past and would surely be so in the future. These special soldiers were well armed and trained as special guards, prepared for violence.

Their duty was not to shoot at the advancing enemy, but to keep their own frightened, deluded, and starving Iraqi soldiers on the line. They were there to keep them from deserting or cutting and running under fire. But that was how Saddam kept the bricks in his first line of defense in place. These evil men were his cement. And there was no more evil man among them than Captain Kasim, the Republican Guard assigned to Youssef's company...

Chapter 13

DRY HOLIDAYS

September became October, and October came and went. They had been on the front line for two and a half months. For recreation, the American reservists played checkers, chess, and other games fabricated from anything they had at hand. Walters had a Monopoly game set sent to him, but Simms stole the dice to play craps with. So, they had to draw numbers on slips of paper enumerated from one to twelve to play the game.

Simms took the dice and drilled tiny holes through the black dots on each die and filled it with melted lead that he had scraped from the battery terminals from one of the vehicles. He then repainted the dots with shoe polish. By this device, he planned to cheat other players at craps by surreptitiously switching dice. After getting caught by a larger brother in another company, he got "lumped-up" pretty good. He wore sunglasses and walked around with both eyes swollen shut. Word got around fast but no one seemed sorry for him; in fact, most everybody felt glad that Simms got some "wisdom welts." He was not well-liked, to say the least.

They also read a lot, wrote letters home, and read and reread the ones they received. It was their greatest morale builder. A vehicle would pull up and the Christmas-like mailbag would bring the guys around. The company clerk would hold up a letter and call out a last name.

"Harris," would be shouted by the clerk reading the name of the intended recipient.

"John A.," was the correct response from the would-be letter recipient.

"Wilson."

"Harold B." In this manner, they would receive their correspondence from the outside world. Sometimes it was a newspaper or bill from home. Bill collectors seemed to find them in the middle of nowhere, halfway around the world. Sometimes, the correspondence was a perfumed love letter from back home. The clerk would occasionally smell an envelope and comment favorably upon the lovemaking ability of the fortunate soldier before delivering his mail.

A lot of the other guys got letters from sweethearts back home. Young One did not have a girlfriend, but there was a bronzed beauty back home that he had had his eye on. While he went into the army, she went into her first year of college in Albuquerque. He did not stay in touch with her, but sometimes thought of her. Part of him regretted not consummating a relationship with her before going off to war. Another part of him was glad that he had not.

He wrote home often, and his words on paper were translated to Grandfather in their language. The father of his father would nod his head and smile when he heard of his brave grandson in a large war party halfway around the world. Grandfather would speak his message to Young One, and one of his nieces would translate in her mind and write it down in English to be mailed. Their language had never been written down, so it had to be done that way. Their language was passed down word of mouth to ear for as long as it had been spoken. Grandfather was impressed how the clever Outsiders had managed to put words upon paper, thereby turning sound into sight.

As time progressed, more and more soldiers arrived. They were coming from all over the world. The reserve units had bought the time the rest of the coalition needed to build up sufficient forces to initiate the ground assault. Major U. S. Army divisions were starting to arrive, but they were kept in the rear. This was to keep the Iraqis from gaining intelligence about their strength and composition. Also, the mechanized and armored cavalry were more mobile and could be used to plug holes in the line or to move rapidly into position to head off a major Iraqi assault. The soldiers assigned to convoy duty noticed whole tent cities had appeared, where just a few weeks before, there was nothing but barren desert.

October became November, and the days of the calendar were falling off one at a time like the leaves from the trees in McHugh's Pennsylvanian woods. As the weather cooled ever so slightly, more new troops kept arriving, and with them came more amenities. It was still hot during the day, but not the asphalt-bubbling temperature of August. They even got one hot meal a day. No one knew if it would be breakfast, lunch, or dinner. At first it was just a tray pack meal. They had whole dinners in one big foil serving pack. The contents of each looked like a tube of leftovers. They heated them up with an immersion heater in a garbage can. Each was enough for a whole squad of hungry soldiers. A guy never knew what meal he would get, but whatever it was it beat the hell out of warm Rees squeezed out of a pouch, which was all they had eaten for a long time.

><--><--><

It was a little more than a week before Thanksgiving. Their company commander called the men together. He gave them the bad news. Their original ninety-day call-up had come to an end. They were informed that they were not even going to be rotated to the rear, never mind back to the States. They would be stuck there for at least twice as long as they had expected, and it did not appear that they would see any action. This was another damn peacekeeping mission after all. Continuous guard duty was what that meant.

President Bush had signed into effect Executive Order 12733 extending the reservists' call-up for another ninety days. He also signed into effect a stop-loss authority automatically extending the enlistments of critical personnel beyond their normal estimated termination service date. The reservists' butts were staying in the great ashtray for a while. That automatically extended their date of estimated return from overseas. For guys who had been in college or trade school, it meant missing another whole semester. They were there for the duration of hostilities and certainly would not be home for Christmas.

There was no end in sight. At least the weather was getting better. The days were only in the eighties, but it felt like a cold spell. At night it started to feel downright chilly. November was sliding away. Thoughts of the holidays began to come into the guys' minds. Everyone hoped that they would be back home in the States with their families. With all these soldiers pouring in, Saddam would surely pull out of Kuwait, and they could go home. There was still a hope that diplomacy would prevail.

Thanksgiving Day rolled around, trucks delivered Thanksgiving dinner for the entire battalion, bringing striped caterers' tents and folding tables like it was a graduation or wedding party. The troops got to eat from paper plates, and it was a genuine sit-down dinner. There was real turkey and dressing. The mashed potatoes were instant, but damn near everything else right down to the holiday pies had been cooked in the rear and trucked up to the front in large thermal containers. There was even whole milk, ice cream, and real brewed coffee. Everyone ate until they almost burst, and they got to take the leftovers back to their positions for later consumption. The event was formally over with the company police call. Sergeant Franklin lined them up and gave them their orders to police up the area.

"If it don't grow, pick it up. If it moves, don't touch it. If it's too big, we'll paint it. Move out troops."

Every scrap of litter was removed, and the routines of soldiering resumed.

The sand was even raked with a garden rake, and soon even the footprints were erased by the wind. It had been a good day. Young One was not sure what to think about Thanksgiving. The Indians gave their food and knowledge to the Outsiders with belt buckles on their hats and got screwed for it. But those were not really his people. It was good to eat so many fine things. It was like a feast. He was thankful, however, to be alive that day as he was every day.

December came and things got worse. There were so many new units arriving that they overwhelmed the water resources. Saudi Arabia had twenty-six desalinization plants working overtime, turning seawater into potable water. Their showers were cut back to once a week again because there were so many troops to wash and keep clean. Everyone knew something had to happen soon, but nobody knew when.

><—><—><

There were parades of military officers from all over the world driving up and down, looking over the front line, as well as passels of politicians coming around to get their pictures taken. They were disappointed that there were no babies to kiss, but the women had not been there long enough yet.

As Yuletide approached, everyone's hopes revived that they would be rotated back to the States because so many new troops had arrived. Instead, they got word that they had been extended beyond the 180-day mark. Merry Christmas from the president.

Trucks of packages from home were sent to the front. They even had some soldier dressed up like a skinny Santa Claus who arrived in a helicopter, passing out presents. Many were from strangers. Guys wept as they read cards from third-graders in Wisconsin wishing them well and hoping they didn't get killed over there. Many packages were merely addressed to "Soldier, Persian Gulf War." One package contained a battery-powered artificial Christmas tree from a veterans' wives group in Ohio. It even had little twinkling lights. It was a strange sight looking at it on Christmas.

Although displays of the Christian holy day were forbidden, there probably would have been a riot if the morals police had tried to interfere with Christmas. The troops had tried hard to observe the Muslim religious customs, each and every one of them. But they were not going to let the rag heads ruin Christmas for them without a fight. One guy from another squad had a guitar, and they sang Christmas songs. For most, it was the first time they had sung carols since their boyhood. The spirit of the season in that seasonless place hit them hard. It was the loneliest any of them had ever been in their lives.

The commander allowed the tree to be erected only on Christmas Eve and only under the condition that it be taken down when the batteries ran out. No one was to put new ones in. It went two days straight, blinking day and night under its camo-net enclosure to conceal it from the Saudi morals police, who drove all over looking for religious infractions.

Also, there were more and more female troops arriving, and they really kept the morals cops busy. The driver of one of the roach coaches said, "I heard some marine dyke punched out two of the morals police in Riyadh who smacked her with a stick for having her sleeves rolled up. They were so surprised they just stood there while the bitch was beating on them with both fists. She knocked out one of them and pounded the shit out of the other, before anyone broke it up. They say the brass had her ass on a plane and out of the country before the sun set."

No one bothered about the troops in the front line anymore. The morals police did not have time to keep up with all the newcomers. Besides, being so far out in the desert, they were away from public view. Arrangements were made to have their mail and Christmas presents smuggled directly into the country. The soldiers did not know it, but Christmas mail had to be specially delivered to keep the morals police from confiscating it. Any cards depicting the Nativity, or angels, or Christ were taken and burned. Cards with pine trees were allowed, as were snowmen, jingle bells, and snow-covered natural scenes. Any Christmas music on Armed Forces Radio had to be instrumental only.

Some guys got bottles of booze disguised as mouthwash sent in the mail. Franklin's brother-in-law sent him three bottles along with toothbrushes, dental floss and toothpaste. Each of the bottles was full to the brim with Jack Daniels. McHugh got a rum cake from his aunt in Pennsylvania. It came in a metal cylinder and was vacuum-sealed inside. The booze was dripping from the cake as they removed it. One slice would hammer you. Everyone in the squad had a slice except Young One. "What are they going to do if they catch us, send us to war?" asked Sergeant Eliot as he wolfed down his piece.

As a morale booster, arrangements were made for the troops on the front line to call home for the holidays. A tractor-trailer full of pay phones was brought to their area. It had a satellite dish and its own electric generator. Young One spoke briefly to Grandfather halfway round the world. Arrangements were made to have Young One call the trading post at a certain hour where half the pueblo was waiting to hear from their warrior native son. Young One established contact, but had time only to tell his Grandfather that he loved him and that everything was going well. Then an operator broke in and informed them in English that the phone call had to terminate for security reasons, and the line went dead. A computer had picked up a foreign language that it did not recognize, and the decision to terminate the call was made by an anonymous intelligence officer.

The men traded presents with each other from what Simms had left. He was the driver on the mail run from the battalion headquarters. He pulled over to the side of the road and went through the Christmas mail. Anything that looked like it was valuable, he put aside for himself. He filled his duffel bag with presents marked "any soldier." He was smart enough not to have taken any packages sent to the soldiers with their names on it. For the next few weeks, he sold the stuff to anyone who would buy it. He was a real dick. Just when you think that human nature has found its lowest level, Simms could find a crack and crawl down just a little deeper.

Still, there was a lot of stuff left in the "any soldier" piles. Most of the men got packages from loved ones back home. Some got nothing. The troops were also treated to a Christmas Day dinner, much the same as Thanksgiving. It was great getting hot chow in the field. The more they tried to make it like back home, the more homesick they were. After

Christmas came and went, New Years dawned and their hopes of going home grew dimmer than ever...

Chapter 14

THE BOOZE CRUISE

Someone who had a portable radio was listening to Radio Baghdad—the Mother of All Battles Radio, as it was called. It operated out of a captured civilian radio station in Kuwait City. Technically, it was forbidden to listen to it, but this being the original land of forbidden fruit, it was irresistible. At first, the coalition commanders wanted to jam the signal, believing it would be demoralizing to the troops. But the bullshit was so thick that at times it brought comic relief.

Two of the popular propagandists were nicknamed "Desert Dotty" and "Baghdad Bill" by the troops. Dotty hosted the ladies' hour for the female troops, which made up about eleven percent of the total coalition war force. She would excoriate them about working for male chauvinists. To her credit, she never finished the insult with the "pig" suffix. No Arab would dare call even an enemy a pig. She told them how cruel it was for them to have to face the dangers of driving large trucks in a country where their own women were forbidden to "get behind the wheel."

"You are here driving trucks and helping a country that does not even allow their women to drive. You are part of the continued imprisonment of women." She told them the morals police would punish them for their wickedness. She said how the army would turn them into lesbians by cutting their hair and by making them wear pants like a man. They showed their hair and faces and ankles like whores. She reminded them how they could not even purchase anything without going through a man.

"You are making money for men, and you cannot even buy things yourself without their permission. You cannot shop here," she laughed derisively.

Somehow this rhetoric did not turn the tide of feminism. Women of combat age already had their sexual preference marked in their genes, as this was pre "don't ask, don't tell" days. The enlisted and officer women did their jobs. They would not allow propaganda to spoil their contribution to the war effort. They felt Desert Dotty should have been speaking in Arabic, because that was where the real problem was—among the Arab men and especially among the women for putting up with it. She should be telling them, not the Americans. But solving social problems was not Dotty's aim. Demoralization of the troops was.

One of the funniest episodes on the Mother of All Battles Radio occurred when Baghdad Bill was trying to plant the seeds of homesickness and suspicion in the minds of the troops. "While you are over here waiting to die alone in the bloody sands, your wives, girlfriends, and sisters are making love to Hollywood movie stars like Tom Selleck and Bart Simpson," he told them. It was meant to demoralize the troops, but it had the opposite effect. There were howls of laughter and guffaws of glee all along the line. It showed everyone how far off the Iraqis were in their assessment of the American fighting folks.

One of the sergeants walking away said, "When I get home and I find one of those rubber Bart Simpson dolls, my Class A Dependent is in for some serious shit." Everyone thought it was pretty funny.

Predating Tom Selleck and Bart Simpson by at least two generations was "Jody," the army's archetypal stateside seducer of your wife, girl, sister, or mother while you were away. Jody was every no-good, two-timing son-of-a-bitch rolled into one. Whenever they marched anywhere, they sang in cadence about him.

"You left your girl and your Cadillac.
Now Jody's humping her in the back.
Sound off (ONE, TWO), sound off (THREE FOUR).
Bring it on down now, ONE, TWO, THREE, FOUR.
ONE, TWO —THREE, FOUR."

Another heart-breaker was:

"Ain't no sense in looking down.
Jody's got your girl and gone.
Ain't no sense in being blue.
Cause Jody's got your sister too.
Sound off (ONE, TWO), sound off (THREE, FOUR).
Bring it on down now, ONE, TWO, THREE, FOUR.
ONE, TWO—THREE, FOUR."

No one knows how many guys named Jody got their asses kicked because of these songs when the soldiers came home. But it was certain that nothing old Baghdad Bill could say hadn't already been said and sung by GIs for the past three wars.

Nat Turner was a brother from Houston. He was generally quiet, did not bother anybody, and he wanted nothing more than to get back home into the arms of his girl. He carried a picture of her and showed it to everyone. She was a beautiful young woman of mixed Euro-African ancestry. Some of the guys said she looked like Vanessa Williams, but she was heavier, built in the right areas. Some wondered how Turner managed to land her. He was a nice guy but was not in her league in the looks department.

When they first went over, Turner would receive a couple of letters a week. Then the letters arrived less frequently and were less steamy than before. Then, after she had not written for a couple of weeks, a letter came telling him she didn't want to continue a long-distance relationship. He had become geographically undesirable. Jody had her in his Cadillac, and she wasn't coming back. He thought about killing himself.

He finally wrote to her mother, who in turn wrote back. She explained that she tried in vain to get her daughter to respond, but from shame or some other reason, she refused to explain herself further. Turner just took the letter and folded it up and put it into his pocket, unrealistically hoping that if he read it later, it would say something different. He was a shattered man, ready to give up his hold on life.

Turner could not eat or sleep for days. It was as if he were a car running on two cylinders. He was ready to crack his block at any moment. Young One thought he was going to shoot himself out of desperation. Turner kept writing letters to his girl, but did not send them. He kept them with his gear. He was just sitting there all alone with his rifle across his legs at the perimeter. The splinters of cupid's arrow were festering in his heart. The man's mind was poisoned by emotional pain. He was a broken person. Young One approached and spoke to him.

"Turner, are you all right?" The big guy from Houston slowly nodded his head in an unconvincing gesture.

"You were thinking of shooting yourself, weren't you?" He hung his head in painful shame and said nothing. Turner was seriously thinking of checking himself out.

Young One continued, "We cannot leave life just because we want to. It is for the Creator to give and take life. It is very bad medicine and a betrayal of those who came before and of those who will follow you."

The Bureau of Indian Affairs school where Young One attended high school had a basketball court with an old, electric scoreboard. He had noticed that Turner enjoyed watching basketball games whenever they had a rare opportunity to watch television on a layover trip for supplies. Young One explained to his buddy that, "Life is like a basketball game counting backwards. With each heartbeat and every breath, a point comes off the scoreboard. Just as the game eventually runs out of time, so do our hearts stop beating and our lungs run out of breath.

"One day, for all of us, the game of life will be over, and the Creator will call us to the other side. We all have our own scoreboard set by the one who gives life. Sometimes a player gets fouled, but he cannot give up. We must play the game to the very end the way it is intended. You cannot walk away and stop playing. The great buzzer will sound for you when your time is up. You will know it is finally the time to go to the other side. None of us can say when we are born, and none of us can predict the moment of our own death."

In all his twenty years, Turner had never heard life summed up so succinctly. Although he had not been a deeply religious person, it made sense to him. Back home, he had been hymned to, hallelujahed at, and "say it, reverend-ed" into disbelief. And here, this young Indian, in a few sentences, had explained the mystery of life better than any Bible-thumping preacher he had ever heard. Turner rejoined the other guys and forgot about self-homicide, at least for a while. For weeks, he would just stand around during mail call and hope that a miracle would happen. It never did.

><><><

It was the beginning of the second week of January, a week before the January 15 deadline for the Iraqis to withdraw from Kuwait. The guys heard cheering from Alpha Company next door. About ten minutes later, a Humvee pulled up, and their battalion commander, Colonel Coltrane, told the company commander to have the men gather around.

"All right, every swinging dick, fall in around the head shed," shouted Franklin. The whole company not on guard duty fell in to find out what was up. As the guys were straggling up, the colonel, who was standing atop the sandbagged head shed, made his welcome announcement.

"Men, I have some very good news. I thought the higher brass was joking when I first heard it, but after checking it out, it seems it's true. It seems that some rich Hollywood types have chartered a cruise boat, and we're going to have three days of R&R out in the gulf.

"The boat will take us into international waters, where drinking and gambling are legal. We'll be able to eat 'civie' chow three meals a day and get to sleep in beds with real sheets. All the first units in country will have had their turn. We are next in line. Our turn is tomorrow. There are enough other soldiers to hold our place in the line for a couple of days. There will be buses here for you at 0530 hours. Be ready." He finished with "Gentlemen—pack your bags." Everyone howled in delight and threw their boonie caps in the air.

"We're going on the Love Boat?" one soldier asked incredulously.

"Yeah man, a booze cruise," said the other in disbelief.

"I wonder if there will be dudettes on the boat?" asked Walters.

"Just you, Walters," remarked Simms.

The next day, after they had packed up everything they owned, which was less than they came with, thanks to the sandstorms, they were bussed to the military port on the gulf. The entire battalion was going on a three-day vacation. Their weapons were locked inside a trailer guarded by soldiers from their sister battalion. A convoy of buses took them to the sea. They ate MREs on the way down. They were taken by motor launches out to the cruise ship. It was the most fascinating thing Young One had ever seen: a real ocean-going boat. He had taken numerous convoy trips to the port of Ad Damman and seen the waters of the Persian Gulf. One time, when there was a layover at the port, he even tasted the Persian Gulf water. It was salty, like the rainwater back home in an earth-salt pond.

The soldiers were berthed two guys to a room. McHugh was his roommate, but Young One did not see much of him, as he was either out drinking or sleeping one off. Young One sat on the side of the boat in one of the deck chairs. He was absolutely amazed with the ocean. Its vastness and the salty scent in the moist air were almost intoxicating. He had never seen the big waters before. He had never been on a boat before, not even a canoe. The largest body of water he had seen in his entire life was a small lake.

The boat was like a floating motel, he thought. The clever Outsiders had found a way for even iron to float. He was fascinated with modern technology, even though he knew little about it. As far ahead as he could see, there was water. Porter also seemed fascinated, probably looking for the spot where Jonah was swallowed by the whale.

In addition to tankers, supply ships, and freighters, once in a while, a navy ship would steam by with its propellers in its wake. Sometimes an old Arabian boat would sail by. It was a strange blend of the old and new that deeply impressed Young One. It was a very fine experience for Young One and his buddies. It sure beat guard duty or convoy duty.

While they were loading up the boat, the wakes of passing ships rocked the moored cruise ship on its keel. The movement gave Young One a slight seasick feeling. After a couple of hours, the anchor was pulled in, and, with a loud blast of the horn, they were off into the gulf. Once the boat started moving, the uneasy feeling in his stomach disappeared. He was going to ride a ship upon the great waters. He felt the cool, salty air fill his lungs, and it intoxicated him with its newness. Grandfather would be so proud of him. He was so amazed that there were sea birds flying so far out in the gulf. They soared like hawks or vultures, without flapping their wings to stay aloft.

An all-you-can-eat buffet had been set up for the soldiers. This was real living after months of field rations. Even Franklin seemed to have a good time. Most of the guys had never eaten expensive chow like this. To most of them, the fanciest thing they had ever eaten was their recently catered prom dinner. After months of dining on MREs and tray pack dinners, this was as close to Heaven as they were likely to get. Sammy was especially happy to be near the sea again, to smell the salty air and feel the moist breeze on his skin. He had been bred from people borne by the sea. It felt like home to him.

They had a theater on board that showed almost-up-to-date films. There was one theater that showed sports events exclusively. For most, it was a dream come true. Literally, it was the thrill of their lives, limited up to this point by lack of funds and experience. Beer was a buck for a sixteen-ouncer, and it was the real deal—not the 3.2% stuff—because technically they were out of Saudi Arabia and not on an army base. Some guys just slept in their cabins, glad for the privacy and the chance to sleep without fear of getting bitten by something or having their throats slit. There were teams of roving MPs making sure that propriety was maintained. For some, however, it was pure hell on earth. They drank too much the first day and spent the next two fighting off seasickness and hangovers. Their livers were out of shape, and some of the guys were no drinkers at all.

Some guys did not drink and got seasick, nevertheless. Simms spent the three days on his bed, seasick with the dry heaves. Three days later, they returned to port and were on their way back to the front lines. It was going to be some other battalion's turn next. They soon found themselves back in their holes in the ground, waiting endlessly for an enemy attack that would never come.

It was January 11, 1991. Four days later, they were officially at war. But their morale was high. They were "fat and sassy," while the Iraqis grew "lean and mean." More and more, everyone could feel a tremor of war starting to itch all along the coalition lines. Still, there was no negotiated settlement. Saddam had two days to pull out of Kuwait, or Desert Storm would begin.

>—×—×—<

Three days after returning from the booze cruise, their company commander called them together. Everyone could tell from the look on his face that he was not there to announce that they had won another all-expenses-paid sea cruise. He had just returned from a battalion briefing about the latest developments on the war. Captain Nelson climbed atop the sandbagged head shed and when the troops quit milling in, he announced:

"In case you do not know the date, it is January 14. Tomorrow morning when you wake up, we will be in a state of armed conflict. United Nations

Resolution Number 678 will go into effect while you sleep, though not the sentries on guard duty I hope." The reservists laughed nervously at his attempt at humor.

"In case you are not aware," he continued, "UN 678 authorizes all necessary means to compel Saddam's withdrawal from Kuwait. January 15 was set as the last date for him to comply with previous United Nations resolutions to leave the Kingdom of Kuwait and withdraw back across the border. That is tomorrow. At midnight tonight, the United States and its coalition partners will be in a state of armed conflict with the nation of Iraq. It does not appear that Saddam is going to retreat. No one is really sure what he will do, but hostilities are anticipated."

Then Captain Nelson continued, "I expect each of you to do his duty as you have throughout Desert Shield. Effective at zero hundred hours, the rules of engagement of Desert Shield are suspended. The regular rules of combat engagement will go into effect. I don't want anyone getting trigger-happy. I don't want anyone shooting anything, unless you are shot at, without noncommissioned officer concurrence. We don't need a friendly fire incident ruining our fine record here. We have been on the front line longer than damn near everyone. It looks as if we are going to be here for a while longer.

"Effective immediately, all personnel will wear their helmets and flak jackets except when sleeping. At least we had three days of boozing and cruising. As far as I know, there will be no rotation south." Audible groans arose from the troops.

"Keep your eyes open and your heads out of your asses. If I hear any more, you will be informed. Platoon leaders, take charge of your people." Lieutenant Ramirez told Franklin to dismiss the troops, as the CO was through with them.

"On your feet."

Then the men stood up at attention, and cried in unison, "CROSS THE LINE, YOUR ASS IS MINE." It was something somebody saw on a tee shirt, and they adopted it as their company slogan. They had been saying it for some time, but now they had enough firepower to back it up. The company commander smiled when he heard it. It was good for *esprit de corps*. He jumped down from the roof and went inside to conduct officers' business.

Everyone went on full alert with the news. Their peacekeeping mission had come to a halt. Maybe they would finally get to see some action. Everyone expected all hell to break loose that night. The sentries on guard duty at midnight checked their watches at the stroke of low twelve as Desert Shield became Desert Storm, but not much else changed. In fact for two days more, nothing at all happened. Then the war began...

Chapter 15

WAR IS HELL AND HELL IS HERE

At first, the bombing was in the distance from Youssef's unit, but soon the rolling thunder of war was over their heads. Bombing was done around the clock. Attack helicopters shot anti-personnel rockets and strafed with canon and machine-gun fire during the day. At night, the jets would shoot the Iraqi tanks from the sand. With tremendous explosions that rocked the earth itself, their defenses were disappearing into deadly debris. The bombs and missiles exploded with nerve-numbing blasts that shook their very souls.

Sometimes, burning tanks loaded with fuel and ammo would continue exploding as the flames hit live rounds. The worst job for the young privates was shoveling sand and liquid on top of the burning tanks to extinguish the flames and stop them from exploding. There was no fire department, and water was too scarce to waste. They would save barrels of urine and drop the stinking stuff over the burning tanks. If it spilled on someone, as it invariably did while they were slinging it, the stench remained for a long time and was continuously renewed.

With each helmet full of sand Youssef shoveled or each bucket of urine with which he doused the fire, he prayed that the ammo would not explode when he was close to it. The hearing in his left ear was damaged when a burning tank's artillery shell exploded behind a sand pile very near him. He just sat there in a shell-shocked fetal position, trembling and sand covered, until another, larger private came up to him and kicked him like a dog to bring him back to his senses. He was immediately forced to continue the task, although he couldn't hear anything in one ear for days. He absolutely hated the life of an Iraqi soldier. Besides, he was not an Iraqi citizen; he was a stolen boy.

Among the Iraqi troops, there was a rumor that the devil had given the Americans "an evil eye in the sky" to allow them to see in the dark. It could feel your body heat and hear your heartbeat from the air. No fires were allowed along the line because they could give away their positions, but there wasn't any firewood anyway. They were forced to cover themselves in multiple layers of clothing taken from the dead in order to stay warm. The bullet holes and gore they could see in the stained uniforms didn't bother them as much as the lice and the scabies mites they couldn't see. As they huddled in the cold winter night air, the Iraqi soldiers shivered, regardless of how many layers of borrowed clothing covered them.

From lack of sleep and shell shock, from disease and demoralization, they moved through each passing day as zombies in an evil dream. Most were merely limping or crawling through life. With one foot planted in the past and the other falling into the future, they tried to make their stay in the present as brief as possible. There is no group of human beings in greater psychological denial than an army of men experiencing mass disintegration. They thought of their families and of the good times they had in the past. They also thought of the future and hoped they would see their loved ones again in this life.

Along with bombs, the coalition planes dropped leaflets explaining how to surrender. Being caught with one of these by the Republican Guards was a very punishable offense. Some Iraqi soldiers hid them in seams of their uniforms and in their body as if they were a sort of "get-out-of-jail-free card." Whenever they were dropped, the soldiers were ordered to gather them up and burn them so they could not infect the minds of the troops. The worst airmail they got from the coalition were warning notices to abandon their positions. Psychological-operations leaflets would be dropped explaining that their area was to be carpet bombed at a certain hour and that this was their last warning. At exactly the appointed hour, precision bombing obliterated their positions. It was particularly demoralizing to have that happen. The Iraqis could set their watches on the timing. Their morale was shattered along with their sandcastle field fortifications.

Some of the Iraqi soldiers deserted and tried to go back home. Usually they would be returned a day or so later for punishment. Some of them never returned. Either they got away or were lying dead in some hidden place in the lonely sands. The flies, vultures, and jackals would be their only undertakers.

There were squads of Republican Guards scouring the desert looking for deserters, and they invariably found them. The first time that deserters got caught, their feet were smashed beneath the butts of rifle stocks to discourage them from running a second time. Second desertions were punishable by locking the victim in a metal box to bake in the sun. There was no last, heroic cigarette and blindfold before the firing squad. A screaming and cooking victim is not likely to inspire heroism in others. The suffocating pleadings for mercy from those locked inside still echo in Youssef's nightmares.

There were reports of officer assassinations and whole platoons deserting. With everything being in short supply on the front, there were not enough metal boxes to go around. Consequently, whole groups of deserters were severely beaten, forced to dig their own graves and promptly machine-gunned as ceremoniously as the circumstances would allow, in front of battalion headquarters. Along with desertion, suicide was another problem that added to the attrition of their ranks. Although killing oneself was against Koranic law, to be killed in battle defending the faith was an act rewarded with Heaven. Martyrdom and eternal bliss were assured in Paradise. Some soldiers merely stood there in the open with their arms outstretched to receive the machine gun bullets from the shooting helicopters or airplanes. It was a common belief that it was better to die a quick martyr's death and go to Heaven, than to continue suffering in Hell on Earth.

There was no more bold shouting, no more mad passions and evil vows; there were only a few hopeful thoughts. As they huddled together in the dark, fireless encampments, under constant bombardment, artillery shelling and machine-gun strafing, it was hard to tell a tremble of fear from a shiver in the cold desert nights. The boastful and the timid, the foolhardy and the cowardly, victims and villains alike trembled together in the bomb shelters. At times the very desert itself trembled along with them.

"Oh, why has the Almighty visited us with such sufferings?" they would ask one another each night. But, every morning there were fewer of them to answer.

While the coalition forces had satellite broadcasts of their favorite radio and television shows, long distance calls home, and morale-building mail call, the People's Army soldiers didn't have any word from home. Any letters they wrote were either lost or blown up by coalition airstrikes.

The only news Youssef had from home was from the Mother of All Battles Radio, which switched from bloated lies about victories to claims of untold human suffering from the bomb attacks upon the civilians. They were intended to enrage the troops and make them want to fight harder, but they had the opposite effect on the Iraqi soldiers. What bothered them most was not being home to protect their families.

Youssef was particularly demoralized. He could not read or write very well, his father even less. He had learned to read and write ancient Arabic, from the time of the prophets, from the religious Imams. He and his fellow students had memorized verses of the Holy Koran using gray board tablets with ink made of ground charcoal, water, and gum arabic. When freshly written and still wet, it first appeared quite black. When the tablets were baked in the sun, the ink turned light gray and finally disappeared altogether, leaving a mere shadow of the holy message. But that Arabic was like Roman Catholic Latin to a Westerner—the religious tongue of the past. It could not be used for modern communication. Writing holy verse and reciting it back did not make a letter writer. Where could Youssef send a letter to a Bedouin? Who would he write it to, and who would read it?

Some of the soldiers had pictures of their loved ones, their wives and girlfriends. Youssef never had a picture of his dear mother, the only woman he ever loved. He prayed more for her safety than for his own. He thought of his mother and his aunts baking unleavened bread draped over a round skillet upon a small fire of *arfaj* or frankincense sticks. His stomach growled in demanding protest for a taste of what his brain was enjoying, but there was nothing to share. He hoped his little brother was safe and had gotten away to tell his grieving parents what had happened to him. He used to cry himself to sleep and had to scrape away the crusty remains of dried tears from his eyes, upon being woken up for guard duty...

><del>— ><del> — ><del>

Whenever possible, Iraqi enlisted men were forcibly encouraged to listen to the Arabic version of Mother of All Battles Radio to obtain religious as well as political information. All the propaganda they heard on the radio was a mixture of religious songs, holy readings, and bloated, boastful speeches that promised the enemies of Iraq would be broken and defeated. There would be lines of American bodies with a beginning, but no end. At first, the soldiers in the People's Army were bold, having been pumped up psychologically by the propaganda, but soon their fervor flagged. They even broadcast news of great Iraqi victories that never occurred. It made the men feel good to know that, somewhere, they were doing well, because where they were, the war was terrible.

Youssef saw a boy not much older than himself have his ear cut off for secretly listening to the lies on Armed Forces Radio. He could not even understand English; he liked to hear the music. Captain Kasim would not listen to his explanation that it was the only channel he could tune in because of coalition radio jamming. "Discipline must be maintained!" screamed Kasim, but the poor wretch was only half-listening.

Depression slowly and surely took the place of bravado among the Iraqi troops. The sophisticated weaponry and target-acquisition devices of the coalition warcraft soon sealed their fate. With each bombing and strafing sortie, there was less and less of the line remaining. The People's Army was being blasted to oblivion. Every night there were fewer and fewer bunkers and military fortifications filled and more mass graves to dig.

All along the line in the sand were miles of nightly destruction, and the air was full of the scent of death from unburied bodies, putrefying under sun and moon. The army of the righteous ones was slowly becoming a horde of the unclean. Their vast army was slowly and surely being reduced to scrap. Around them was the greatest junkyard in the world, and not a scrap dealer in sight.

Water was in such short supply that it had to be rationed only for drinking purposes. There were no showers or baths. Human body odor became so bad that it no longer was noticeable, as their noses became inured to the stench. When a forced smile came over their weary faces, teeth that hadn't seen a toothbrush for weeks made others blush. Food ran short and water was low, even for washing before customary prayer. Some worshippers had to ritualistically wash their feet in sand for prayer because of water scarcity. Without water, the Iraqi soldiers were forced to scrub their uniforms with sand to remove salt, oil grime, and gore from them. Without this necessary treatment, their uniforms would turn stiff as boards from dirt and salty sweat.

On the coalition side of the line, the Americans were training and practicing, eating steak and potatoes, fresh salad and a luxury unknown in the desert: ice cream. The poor, illegitimate children of the Mother of All Battles on the wrong side of the tank tracks dug trenches with hand tools, prayed to the Almighty, and buried the remains of the latest wave of martyrs. Youssef had blisters so bad that the loan of a pair of gloves from a dead man seemed a blessing. He secretly prayed that he would never have to return them.

They dined—when they infrequently ate—on dried fruit and chick-peas, with an occasional bit of grizzled, greasy, boiled meat that invariably had hair on it. No one asked if it was from the goat or the cook. They ate it anyway, as quickly as possible to avoid losing it. A warm meal without a beating or an air attack was a gift from above. But this was not a diet upon which to go to war. If it is true that an army "marches on its stomach," these troops were next to bootless.

Soon, the cough of influenza drifted in the air, and dysentery ran up and down the line in the sand. Scorpions, spiders, and snakes plagued their encampments, flies tormented them incessantly in the day, and body vermin kept them awake at night. Desertion became commonplace. But where could they go? They were surrounded by the greatest deterrent to escape on earth, the limitless sands of the Arabian Desert, and by unknown mine fields planted all over the place. The Iraqis were reported to have planted nine million land mines, many around the oil wells to deter production if captured by the coalition. The mines were also buried to keep their own soldiers in, as well as for keeping the coalition soldiers out. They had many varieties from several different nations. A single misstep would mean a lonely, lingering death in a pool of their own blood.

The Arabian sands did not cooperate with Saddam's plans. In some places, protected from the winds, the mines remained hidden and very dangerous. In other places, after sandstorms, minefields were completely exposed. Other minefields would be completely covered with windblown dunes, and a human could safely walk over them without setting them off. It was a continually changing danger and depended entirely on the whim of the wind. Some minefields were marked, and some were not. Some had their warning signs blown away by the coalition bombs. It was a place where a soldier literally had to watch his every step...

Chapter 16

A PARTING OF FRIENDS

The squad was sitting around on field-fabricated benches made of MRE boxes full of sand. Everyone was on full alert. They were under a large camo net that gave partial shade from the skin-searing sun. A weird patchwork of shadows was produced by the wind blowing on the netting and shifting the sunlight. If there was a breeze and one was out of direct sunlight, the heat was bearable. They also had a makeshift table of boxes and had their rifles out and field stripped for cleaning. Busy fingers with wire brushes, toothbrushes, and solvent were cleaning every bit of burned carbon from the mechanisms of the guns. They had their rifle target practice that day.

The air was full of the scent of gun solvent and wiping oil. The guys had condoms and used them to cap the barrels to keep fine sand from getting down into the weapon. There was nothing else to do with them there. As usual, some soldier in the group was jacking his jaw. He told them that he heard that the Iraqis had crossed over the Saudi border and had taken the town of Khafji. The marines were fighting them back. There had been no action in Young One's sector, but they knew anything was possible. If trouble came from across the border, they were ready for it.

Young One had his rifle stripped down, and he was busy cleaning all the internal parts. Walters was sitting around, sipping a canteen cup full of iced pop and reading a comic book.

"Walters, aren't you going to clean your rifle?" asked Young One.

"No dude, I didn't shoot it since last time."

"Didn't you re-qualify today with everyone else?" asked Young One.

"Yeah, dude, but I used McHugh's rifle. He wasn't paying attention, and I switched weapons with him after he already qualified. They were stacked, and I was the temporary guard. I switched rifles in the stack and kept mine nice and clean. It was not zeroed for my eye, and I didn't shoot my best, but it saved a lot of cleaning.

"Besides, we must just pass, not shoot marksman. It won't affect my rifleman's badge. I'll just give it an oil wipe for inspection." That was Walters, always the weasel trying to find a way to "get over" on the system and his buddies.

>——>——>——

It was the second day of Desert Storm, and the coalition forces were on high alert. No one was sure what would happen. That night in camp, they were awakened by shouting and small-arms fire coming from the Syrian and Moroccan camps nearby. At first, the Americans thought that they were under Iraqi attack. Alarm was called, and thousands of sleepy GIs wiped eye snot from their vision and peered into the darkness for invisible foes. It was the full battle rattle. Even the support troops took to the trenches, fearing attack. The infantrymen went balls to the walls for an hour.

They were sent back to their tents. A little later they learned that the coalition Arabs were cheering and shooting their guns at the news of the first Iraqi Scud missile attack on Tel Aviv. It seemed that their long-standing war with Israel was not over yet, merely put on hold till they could get back to it. There was a real possibility of the coalition falling apart if they sat there much longer.

The officers sent the men back to their bunks, with the exception of those on guard duty. Franklin told Private Feinstein, "Those are your cousins out there," referring to the common Semitic origins of both peoples. "We're doubling the guard so they don't sneak in here and circumcise you all the way with one of those big knives they carry, son." Everyone in the squad laughed, including Feinstein. But Feiny didn't really think it was funny. He secretly hoped they would triple the guard. He slept a nervous sleep the rest of that night, lying on his stomach.

As the convoy duty was about over and the reservists' sector of the line to guard had been greatly diminished by the new troops moving in, a new dirty job was assigned to them. They were to conduct motorized reconnaissance patrols of No Man's Land between the warring armies.

Their patrols became more penetrating and frequent in what was called "limited source operations." Each had a more aggressive nature than the one before it. There were more Iraqi recon patrols being discovered. Visual reconnaissance was the only intelligence left to the Iraqis about the location of coalition forces. The bombing had intensified, and the Iraqi Army was blind. With no technical intelligence capability, they had to resort to probing patrols to reconnoiter the coalition lines. It was dangerous because the soldiers never knew what to expect when they met Iraqis. Sometimes they surrendered en masse, and, other times, they ambushed the coalition soldiers.

Although there was a thirty-mile buffer strip between the warring armies, the roving patrols were getting closer and closer to the Iraqi lines.

Sergeant Eliot was leading a motorized patrol. He was in the shotgun seat and was talking on the radio when it happened. McHugh was driving, Feinstein was the machine gunner, and Sammy was the assistant gunner. Feinstein often wondered to himself what he would do if he had to shoot another human being. He asked himself, "Could I do it?" He was about to find out just over the next hill.

Up to this point everything had been quiet, but, seconds later, all that changed. The Americans had driven up upon a dismounted Iraqi reconnaissance patrol. There were eight of them, hiding in the sand. They had heard the Americans coming and deployed a hasty ambush behind some low sand dunes. They waited as the Americans drove into the killing zone, then opened up with a fusillade that burst through the windshield along with a hailstorm of shattered glass, killing Sergeant Eliot outright.

Instinctively, Feiny pulled the charging handle on the M-60 and began to return three-round bursts that dropped two of the bad guys. McHugh slammed the Humvee into reverse but got it stuck in the deep sand. Sammy jumped out behind the vehicle and was trying to lift the wheel from the rut, but it was useless. The wheels of the Humvee screamed and threw clouds of sand into the air as bullets whizzed all around them. One round smashed through the windshield, and whizzed so close to McHugh's ear that he heard the bullet sing by. A split second later, another round tore into his right shoulder, and a third pierced his right arm. He reached for the radio with his left hand and gave a distress call with the GPS coordinates while protected by the engine block. He took another round in the left leg that tore a large piece of flesh from it. Bullets were hitting the vehicle and ricocheting all over the place.

With enemy bullets buzzing by like angry hornets, Sammy ran up to check on Sergeant Eliot from the protected side of the vehicle. It was no use; he was clearly dead. Feiny was still returning fire with the machine gun when they got him. He took a hit directly in the chest and his limp body slumped down into the vehicle. Another round hit him in the muscles of his upper shoulder near his neck. A split second later, two A-K rounds slammed into his Kevlar helmet, and dropped him down into the vehicle. Miraculously, they both hit high on the helmet and did not penetrate his "brain box."

Made nearly berserk by the sight of his friend being gunned down, Sammy hastily stuffed the dead sergeant's flak jacket into the chest of his own for double protection, and then jumped atop the vehicle. Using his large fingers like vise grips, he tore the mooring pin from the gun mount and ripped the M-60 machine gun from its moorings. Holding the heavy gun in his right arm and the link belt of the weapon in his left, "he went to work". His helmet was shot off his head along with a piece of his ear. Rounds slammed into his chest, arms, and legs, but he kept advancing, hosing the enemy with a 7.62-mm stream of lead until the last Iraqi stopped moving.

The gun ran dry, but he kept pulling the trigger as if it were still working. He slumped into the sand bleeding and hurting from fourteen wounds. Most had hit his chest, where the vest protected him, but the ones in the arms and legs did real damage. One of the Iraqis was not quite dead and was lifting his rifle when from seemingly nowhere a single shot rang out. It was the wounded Feinstein coming to the aid of his fallen friend by putting the Iraqi's "dick in the dirt." Feiny was to learn that he had a cracked sternum and two smashed ribs from the force of the bullets hitting his flak jacket, but he would live. Sammy was all shot up.

Overhead, two Apache attack helicopters had moved in and were circling in protection. A medical chopper was called in to remove the wounded and to retrieve the American dead. An intelligence team was coming for the Iraqi dead. While they waited, Feiny hobbled up to his wounded buddy who had just saved his life and kept him alive with reassuring talk. But Sammy was out of it. Feiny kept hollering, "Sammy, don't die, please don't die." He got down on his knees and prayed as tears streamed down his dusty face. His arms and legs were a mess of bloodied flesh and punctures.

"You've got to see my show in Las Vegas. You can't die," he kept repeating to his buddy. Feiny didn't know if Sammy heard him or not. But right before being loaded into the medevac chopper, Sammy's large hand reached out and grasped the smaller one. They were transported in two different choppers and flown to two different hospitals. Flight surgeons immediately stabilized their wounds on the way to the best-equipped surgical hospital available.

The rest of the squad members were sad to hear about Sergeant Eliot. He had been a good dude, and they would miss him, but they were glad that all three of the others lived and were going home. Young One was especially sad to hear about Sergeant Eliot. McHugh, Feinstein, and Samuella were going home via medevac plane. Feinstein was even cracking nervous jokes to the medics working on him. He was a real trouper, with entertainer in his veins, while the medics were trying to stem his blood flow to prevent this from being his last act. Soon, for them, the theater of war was washed away in morphine and rotor noise. The war was frighteningly over for them...

Chapter 17

HIGHWAY TO HELL

The Humvee was the army's replacement for the jeep. Humvee is short for High Mobility Multipurpose Wheeled Vehicle. The one they were going on patrol in was an infantry-configured model that had been brought in from Germany for the real conflict, after a career in the military participating in war games. Its forest-green camo paint had only recently been sprayed desert tan. It had no camo splotches as the regular army troops' vehicles had. This "Hummer" was a banged-up older model, with so many bugs in it that it needed an entomologist, not a mechanic.

It was one of a huge fleet of hastily refurbished military vehicles garnered from around the world and sent to the Persian Gulf. After they were done with it, it would probably be given to the Kuwaiti or Saudi armies. It would be too expensive to transport it back, unless they sold it to a salvager, who would sell it to a rich Arab for some real bucks. Needless to say, the Hummer was expendable, and so was its human crew.

The silhouette of a pot-bellied sergeant stood next to the vehicle with his hands on his hips as the strange soldier approached him in the early morning darkness. It was Franklin. With Sergeant Eliot gone, the platoon sergeant was filling in until a replacement could be found. He asked with a strong southern drawl, "What's your major malfunction? Who the hell are you, troop? Where's Walters?"

"He's on profile, Sarge. Spec-four Mizzi. Top sent me as a replacement," said the affected voice from behind the concealing brown muffler and sand goggles.

"Just get on board, specialist; we're already late because of you," he spat out as he rejected the thrust-out handshake. Sergeant Franklin wasn't simply being mean to spec-four Mizzi; he was mean to everyone around him.

Mizzi's gear was tossed aboard the Humvee, and no sooner had the last crew member boarded than the vehicle started off with a lurch. It was soon heading out of their temporary encampment toward enemy lines. This was the best sport utility vehicle ever made, but they weren't going on this ride for sport.

Young One had been standing up and leaning on the M-60 machine gun in the back. He popped down the hatch and introduced himself to Mizzi.

"I'm the machine gunner; you're the assistant gunner," Young One informed Walters' replacement. Usually he and Walters traded off. Today was Young One's turn to man the machine gun. "It's very simple," he said. "It's our job to drive around and wait for the enemy to shoot at us so we can mark their position for air or artillery strikes. If we get enemy contact, the sarge radios in the coordinates. If we're close enough, you mark their position with a yellow smoke grenade. The ammo is in the canvas bag," he said, pointing to a drab olive green satchel on the floor. Inside were several green canvas bandoleers of assorted grenade-launcher ammo. There were high-explosive, fragmentation rounds and smoke grenades. Walters had filled the cartridge loops with his favorite loads. He used to wear them like a south-of-the-border bandito, with two strapped cross-wise on his chest.

"Your weapon is hanging from its strap on your side of the vehicle. It is signed out to Walters, so take care of it."

Mizzi merely nodded as Young One spoke. It was an M-16 fully automatic rifle with an M-203 grenade launcher affixed to its underside. Young One had never met Mizzi, and he thought he sure was a quiet guy, almost unfriendly. The sarge should have found out who the new guy was, but there were so many new replacements trickling in all the time that someone new or unknown was commonplace. Young One was still very upset about Sergeant Eliot, McHugh, Feiny, and Sammy. It was a loss to everyone. But this was no time or place for a sentimental journey. Thoughts of the missing Walters consumed most of Franklin's mind. Everyone knew Walters was a "skater." Franklin wanted to square his ass away for sure. First, Walters performed unauthorized modifications on a company vehicle, and then he scammed out of duty. He was supposed to be on this patrol. Maybe he could book him for AWOL. It was an appealing idea, Franklin thought.

"No one told me he was on profile or on authorized leave." He made a mental note to get Walters as soon as they got back. If Walters needed a little personal time, he simply should have asked. Franklin would have told the specialist, "No."

Mizzi's face was still wrapped in a brown GI-issue scarf, and sand goggles hid a pair of eyes the color of ripe olives. A Kevlar helmet hid the tar-black hair under it. It was a cold February night in the open desert. It wasn't at all suspicious for Mizzi to be covered up, as the cold night winter wind in the Humvee could cut right through your clothes and suck the heat right out of your body.

A cursory glance at Mizzi would reveal nothing different from any other infantryman in the army. The goggles really helped keep sand and bugs from smashing the eyes at fifty miles per hour, but they also hid the dark, telling eyes. The helmet could help in an accident, as well as assist this unknown soldier's anonymity. Therefore, nothing was questioned. With the camo flak jacket, Mizzi was visually indistinguishable from any other soldier in the war.

Young One saw Mizzi looking at the floor of the vehicle. He explained that sarge was real mad at Walters for going over to the British Tank Battalion next door and trading several cases of MRE rations and three camouflaged poncho liners for a tank-hardened steel plate. This, they cut to fit and welded to the floor of the Hummer. Atop this, Walters had added a layer of OD green sandbags. He was extremely paranoid about landmines since one of the other Hummers in their battalion had hit one, injuring all the occupants.

Those guys were lucky; they only hit an anti-personnel mine. An anti-vehicular mine could turn them into "assholes and elbows." Mizzi just returned a disbelieving shake of the head and presented upturned palms of gloved hands in a gesture of innocence. Gesticulations served in place of verbal conversation and sufficed for communication. Nothing was questioned.

In the front, the mouthy sergeant continued to speak. This took the focus off Mizzi, who desired to remain anonymous above all else. Franklin was talking to Simms, but he may as well have been talking to himself.

"I'll take his young ass behind the motor pool for a counseling session for this bullshit." The sarge, for all his redneck bravado, meant well, but sometimes he was like a mother hen clucking with its head up your ass. He wanted to throw away the sandbags, but they were already late when the driver told the sarge about it. He told the soldiers in the back to throw out the sandbags, but Simms interrupted.

"That's littering," he said. Not that he gave two shits in a dead rat's ass about the local ecology; he merely did what he could to thwart Sergeant Franklin every chance he could. The sarge had more rank and experience, but Simms had a secret weapon. He could throw down the race card and trump any charges Franklin cared to fill his white hand with. Simms liked sliding right along the edge of life, always one slip short of going too far.

Its close-set headlights and short, narrow bumper gave the military transport vehicle an animated appearance. If it were a living creature, its mechanical-beast face would have been described as looking forlorn at that moment. As they passed through the checkpoint, Private First Class J. Simms gave a clenched, left-fist wave out the open window to his black brother on guard duty, as a greeting sign of racial solidarity.

Their mission that day was to drive northward toward Kuwait on a paved road for a few miles and then northeastward up an old oil service road for about a half-hour, hang around and report any enemy activity, and then return the same way. With the obligatory chat with the new guy over, Young One poked the upper half of his torso up through the gun port, while standing on the floor. As he stood in the back of the Humvee, he felt the crisp night air biting into the front of his uniform. He pulled his goggles up from over his eyes. There was something wrong with the sky that morning.

Young One was constantly looking at the stars whenever he was outdoors. As they drove northward, he noticed something strange. It was becoming more and more difficult to see the stars to their north. The stars that were in the southern sky behind them could still be seen.

Ahead, only the brightest stars were still visible. Something was hiding the heavens. It was as if a black blanket had been thrown over the sky.

He had never seen anything like it in his life, and he did not understand it. The few stars left in the sky began to dim as they drove farther and, finally, their twinkling disappeared altogether. No stars at all were visible overhead. This made the shivering soldier shudder in the predawn night air flowing over the moving vehicle. Something was very wrong. It was not light yet, and the stars should be visible.

As the Humvee sped forward with increasing acceleration, Young One had a strange feeling. For weeks, he had been watching the clouds form on the horizon and blow away. He knew the rainy weather would soon come. Everyone said the rains were late this year because of all the bomb concussions. In past wars, the claim was that cannon blasts simulated thunderclaps and could make it rain. If that were true, the coalition warplanes had already dumped enough explosive tonnage to create a monsoon in the desert.

He was no military practitioner, but he knew the weather in the desert, even this one. The armies just couldn't sit there and sink in the late winter and early spring muds. The one thing that separated the coalition forces from the Iraqis was their ability to move quickly. Mobility would be impossible in the mud. The meteorologists had the last word, as many of the high-tech battle systems were extremely weather sensitive. The cloud cover up north had already caused canceled air attack sorties because of lack of visibility.

These reservists had been driving around taking enemy fire and reporting its location for weeks. They had lost men to hostile action. They had already seen more action than the bulk of the regular forces, which were still staged in the rear, poised for the big assault, which hadn't yet started.

The active-duty lifers call this activity "dragging bait," and they said it was the perfect job for those "damned reservists." They had been peppered with small-arms fire from a distance two nights before. No one was hit, but the old Hummer had two AK-47 pockmarks in her rear, placed there by Iraqi infantrymen too far away to get a good shot with their automatic rifles, as the Americans hightailed it to a safe place to call in air support.

Soon, after calling in the coordinates of the enemy position, coalition aircraft swooped in for the kill. The reservists did not know if the planes hit anything, because they were not about to go back there to see. Their job was to get the Iraqis to shoot at them from hidden places in the sand and then mark the spot for air force jets or army helicopters to move in and finish them off.

They were supposed to be driving with their lights on, but it was common practice to use night-vision goggles to avoid being shot at by a sniper. Franklin told Simms to drive without headlights and to use the goggles. Unlike the traffic-jammed Crapline, the straight-line north road was not well traveled, and they could meet danger with every turn of the wheel.

Wearing the goggles was like looking at a black-and-white television, only it was green and white, and Simms barely saw the green image of a vehicle careening toward him through his night-vision goggles. Just in the nick of time, Simms swerved hard to the left as a Mercedes careened by at eighty or ninety miles per hour past their right side. The startled and blinded occupants of the civilian vehicle just kept coming. They passed so closely on the wrong side of the road that a mere second coat of paint was all that separated them from a collision. The driver of the Mercedes immediately flipped on his headlights and kept speeding south towards Riyadh. The driver had probably learned to drive in Great Britain, as

Kuwait was a former British protectorate, and many Kuwaiti youth had attended British universities.

Sergeant Franklin shouted, "Turn your damn lights on."

"You told me to turn them off," Simms protested.

"Well, now I said to turn them on! Things change, son."

"Yeah, but you're always putting me through the changes," retorted the defiant PFC.

The more the driver and the sarge got to know each other, the more they disliked each other.

Young One stood up through the roof gun port to the outside. The flak jacket covering his chest wasn't exactly a down-filled vest, but it helped keep in some body heat. The 7.62-mm machine gun didn't have a blast shield and couldn't offer much protection from the bone-chilling wind, either. Since not much was going on, he slipped down into the vehicle and whispered to the silent Mizzi, "Why don't you sleep, and I'll wake you if something happens." With Mizzi settled down in the back, and with the sarge and Simms at it again, he had the opportunity to quietly sing his religious songs to energize his medicine charms. He must have become too loud, for the driver and the sergeant temporarily stopped their shit-talking to listen.

"What is that?" demanded Franklin.

"Just the chief back there singing his medicine prayers. He says it brings him good luck," Simms said.

Sergeant Franklin didn't tell Young One to stop because of the army's policy of religious diversity.

Simms was a sinner, and he knew the Indian songs and prayers bothered the sarge, so he liked the machine gunner's ancient chants immensely. Besides, Chief Alphabet was a brother of sorts. Simms didn't like the feel of this mission, but then again, he had done a lot of things in his life he hadn't felt good about, before or after the event.

Young One just kept singing the prayers of his people in the open air, bidding the night sky good-bye. Meanwhile, Simms was pushing Sergeant Franklin just an inch short of Article 15 charges. He knew just when to stop, and then when to start on a new hassle.

Simms looked at Franklin and thought, *This dude looks like friendly fire to me.* Things between them went downhill from there.

"In the desert, you need to move fast and keep moving," Franklin said to Simms, still in a pissed-off mood at Walters for loading down the ass end of his Humvee. The extra weight really did diminish the vehicle's acceleration. He was now blaming Walters for reducing their maneuverability, and he believed that is what caused the near-accident.

"I wonder where those guys were coming from?" Simms inquired to change the subject.

"From Kuwait. They must have driven on dirt roads through the desert, maybe on a smuggler's trail or something. Chief, keep your eyes open for a dirt road with fresh tire tracks."

A couple of miles up the road, they saw it.

"Turn here," said Franklin.

As they turned off the paved road, Franklin was complaining about the GPS handset not working properly. It was something about triangulation. He would have to read the map and compass the old-fashioned way. Simms couldn't find his way around anyplace, unless graffiti was spray painted everywhere and there were familiar drug dealers or pimps selling one sort of crack or another, strategically placed on street corners for landmarks. He was the pilot, not the navigator, anyway.

"Sarge, I don't think we should go up there."

"I told you about that thinking, didn't I, private? You don't have enough rank to think, son."

He took his finger and counted the two stripes of his PFC insignia. "One, two," he counted sarcastically. Then in a mocking manner, he counted from one to seven the stripes on his own sergeant first class rank insignia. "Yep, I outrank you. Take off, skipper," he said, pointing toward where the Mercedes had come from.

They began following the tracks of the mysterious vehicle through the desert. They could be spies, or terrorists. They could be refugees who bribed the Iraqis or found their way through the desert on their own. Their tracks were unmistakable and were easy to follow in the sand. The tracks led them northeast, deeper into the desert, directly toward the Kuwaiti border.

In actuality, they had crossed over the Saudi-Kuwaiti border without realizing it. There were no signs, no border guards, merely a vast, empty track of rolling sand dunes. The ground was firm, and they followed the tracks of the luxury automobile through the empty desert. Around and around huge sand dunes they drove, this way and that way, following the tire marks in the sand. Young One thought it was a perfect place to get ambushed, and began to slap the roof of the vehicle to get their attention. They stopped to get a look. Young One ducked down and said, "There is something out there. It looks like open graves or something. "There it is," he said, pointing toward something in the sand ahead of them. They got out to look at the area.

"Keep us covered up there, Chief."

Cautiously, with live weapons drawn, they approached the spot to which he had gestured. As they stalked closer, they could see what it was. They were not graves, but places where the privately owned vehicle had gotten stuck in the sand. Wheel ruts were filled with expensive clothing and crushed luggage. The contents of their suitcases had been used to give the tires a grip in the loose sand. The vehicle's occupants were in such a hurry that they did not even pick up the stuff.

Franklin and Simms looked through the items, while Young One stood ready on the machine gun should trouble erupt. Simms and Franklin pawed through what turned out to be Arab garments of remarkable quality. They were crushed and stained with tire marks. Whoever the occupants of the car were, they had some money. Franklin found a passport in a soiled western suit coat. It bore the name and photograph of what appeared to be a wealthy Kuwaiti businessman.

There were business suits, and, in one of the pockets, a money clip full of Kuwaiti, Saudi, and U.S. currency. While Franklin was busy looking through the stuff in the other wheel rut, Simms shoved his find into his pocket without telling the others. He would count it later, when no one was looking.

They got back into the Humvee and continued following the mysterious track back to its source. As they drove up the crest of a sandy hill, they noticed the whole northern horizon seemed on fire. "Will you look at that?" said Franklin, as he motioned for them to stop. Simms decelerated the Hummer to a halt.

From their slightly elevated position, they could see a long distance away. Franklin took out olive-drab green, rubberized binoculars, and his eyes bulged out almost as far as the binoculars' lenses when he realized what was happening. He established radio contact with his headquarters.

"Mother Hen, this is Chickadee Three. Over," he said with an anxious drawl.

"Chickadee Three, this is Mother Hen. Over."

"Mother Hen. How do you copy? Over."

"Chickadee Three, we copy you, Lima Charlie. Over," answered the battalion headquarters radio operator.

"Mother Hen, situation report follows. Large fire on northeastern horizon. Could be an ammo dump burning or something shot up by the air force. Over."

"Chickadee Three. Be advised that enemy forces have set fire to the oil fields. Over."

"What? Why the shit did they do that?" Franklin said not bothering to add "over."

"Chickadee Three, be advised to maintain radio protocol. The reason is unknown at this time. Over." This was to caution Franklin that they were on an open channel, indicating many other people could be listening.

"Roger that, Mother Hen. Wilco. Over."

"Chickadee Three. Stand by for official transmission."

"Roger." Franklin's mouth dropped as the radio operator tersely informed them that the Iraqis had begun setting the Kuwaiti oil fields on fire as a military diversion.

"Chickadee Three. Maintain surveillance of situation and report. Over."

"Roger that, Mother Hen. This is Chickadee Three. Over and out." Franklin put down his radio handset and watched the burning skyline with disbelief. This was Armageddon, the Mother of All Battles, as the media said. The desert was on fire. Hell was coming up from the earth itself.

Grandfather's dream was unfolding right before Young One's unbelieving eyes. The earth and sky were on fire. That was why he could not see the stars—smoke was blocking them from view. A shiver ran through his soul as he saw his life and very possibly his death unfolding before him. At that moment, he was more frightened than at any other time in his life. Darkness was just giving way to light.

Back in the Hummer, Franklin informed his people. "Listen up, troops. Headquarters indicates that the hostiles have set the oil wells on fire for purposes unknown. It is our duty to investigate this situation."

A chill ran up and down the spine of the already-shivering Young One as Sergeant Franklin spoke. PFC Simms didn't feel anything, because he was already so "bad and cold." Mizzi was sitting up, listening. When it was over, the mysterious soldier once again assumed the prone position and pretended to sleep. But Mizzi heard every word.

"Let's go see this bullshit," said Franklin.

>————×————×————<

The Arabian sun was shining low on the eastern horizon through a lead-gray sky. Everything to the north of them was aflame. It certainly was a strange-looking morning. All night long, the Iraqis had been blowing up the oil fields. The oil smoke blowing overhead continued to squelch Franklin's handheld GPS receiving unit, or "slammer." He couldn't get his bearings from at least three overhead satellites, as was required. He had two, but the third was on the side of the Earth with the oil smoke. He stopped and tried to determine where he was with map and compass. The problem was that in a world devoid of terrain features, all the maps looked alike. Franklin was rooting through a stack of tan-colored papers. There were thirty maps in the case. He had them spread out all over the hood of the vehicle, flapping in the morning breeze.

"They may as well issue this shit on large sheets of sandpaper with grid lines on them," he muttered.

"Everything looks the same here. Shit, this can't be right. This compass is screwed up. We took two rights and a left, we can't be heading in this direction."

Holding the field-issue compass in his right hand, he beat it several times on his other hand, not believing what it was telling him. He ordered Simms to drive up the trail heading toward the oil fires, still following the mystery tracks.

"Sarge, I don't think we should be going there. We're lost."

"We're not lost son, just temporarily mis-oriented." It was something he heard as a kid that Daniel Boone or Davy Crockett said. That was good enough for Franklin because he still held onto a black-and-white view of life. It had to be good enough for Simms.

⟩⟨⟨⟩⟨⟨⟩

"Pay attention up there, Chief. Keep a sharp eye for enemy activity." Then he shouted over his shoulder at the FNG. "Wake up, sleeping beauty, it's time to go to work."

Mizzi began to stir in the back.

Simms asked, "Sarge, who do you think those guys were who almost ran into us? Terrorists who blew up the oil wells?"

"Don't know. Could be. Keep your eyes open and your mouth shut, private. The Iraqis must have pulled back," Franklin said as he scanned the horizon from a distance with the binoculars. "Drive over to that little hill to the right." The Humvee moved slowly through the soft sand. Simms was worried about getting stuck. There was no towing service there.

236

They drove right up to Smuggler's Berm. "I don't like this, Sarge." They were driving right up to the Iraqi front door. They stopped, and Franklin took another look on the horizon. It looked as if nobody was at home.

He said, "Get the grenade launcher." Franklin took it and rammed a high explosive round into it and shot it far in front of them. It exploded with a blast of sand. There was no sound of return fire from the enemy.

"Chief, hose down the area with some M-60 rounds."

Young One charged the machine gun and fired a long, continuous burst. Its spray created a line of dust in the distance. There still was no sound of return fire from the Iraqis.

Franklin ordered Simms to drive forward. Reluctantly, the soldier obeyed. Evidently, the Iraqi troops had pulled back to a second line. The Humvee was moving through an area of abandoned trenches.

They began to enter a startling panorama of military devastation. Blasted emplacements were littered with destroyed military vehicles. Some were in groups, while others were scattered here and there in hideous disarray. All were in a state of ruin. As they drove closer to the source of the fire, everyone was both fascinated with and disgusted by what their eyes took in.

This wasn't the first time the Iraqis had torched the petroleum-producing equipment. Their soldiers had set the refineries near the coast on fire weeks before. In their withdrawal from southern Kuwait, they had a scorched-earth policy that destroyed what the desert couldn't. Refineries, pipelines and pumping stations were blasted and abandoned. Simms stopped the Hummer, got out, and began to rummage through some war debris.

Franklin warned him, "Be careful for booby traps." Simms stopped and got back in the vehicle. Franklin almost felt sorry. A booby trap taking Simms out would have made his life easier. Franklin would even help write the letter home. They continued following the mysterious tracks. They were driving deeper into Iraqi territory...

Chapter 18

FALL FROM GRACE

Meanwhile, across the desert, a short distance away in space and time, other scenes in this tragic play were being enacted. In the tactical operations center—referred to by helicopter pilots as the "TOC"—near the forward line of the U.S. troops, Colonel John "Madjack" Washington was already sipping his third cup of hot, steamy coffee as the morning sun was just struggling skyward. He laughingly called himself a "Java Junkie," and said that he liked his coffee like his women—strong and black. That's because that is what he was.

He was once even heard to say, although not too loudly, "Thank goodness Nancy Reagan wasn't a Mormon, or we wouldn't even have coffee here." It got a laugh, but he wasn't really trying to be funny.

He came from a black, broken home in Philly and pulled himself up by the bootstraps. He'd had three tours of duty in Vietnam, flown sensitive combat missions in Grenada and Panama, and had extensive experience in counter-drug operations in Central and South America.

Colonel Washington was the commander of the attack helicopter battalion assigned to the tank division of the First Corps that was to spearhead the attack upon the Iraqi Republican Guard.

"Colonel, we just received a Mayday call from a medical evacuation helicopter up north. And they've activated their emergency locator transponder. They were returning from picking up the wounded from a special operations firefight."

"Can you locate their position?" the senior pilot asked.

"They disappeared from radar a few minutes ago, over the Minagish oil field."

"That's inside hostile territory. Isn't it?"

"Yessir," was the executive officer's only response.

"Get the air force on the horn. Patch us into AWACs," the colonel ordered.

After several minutes, which seemed much longer, the air force confirmed that a medevac helicopter returning with wounded had been lost from their down-looking radar as well. The aircraft had fallen from the sky and was believed to have been shot down into the smoke from the burning oil wells inside Kuwait. They had already dispatched two "fast movers" (meaning jet aircraft) overhead, but they were unable to penetrate the dense smoke. Their windshields fouled up with oil, and the wipers smeared it further, creating next-to-zero visibility.

Two electronics aircraft capable of pinpointing the location of the radio beacon were too far away to be of immediate use, as they were searching for the remains of an F-111 shot down deep in Iraq. All of the colonel's Apache attack helicopters were out on missions north of Kuwait City. Someone had to get in close under the oil smoke to get a good look and possibly perform a rescue.

It was at that moment that the colonel made the most fateful decision in his career; indeed, in his entire life. His attack-helicopter battalion was the closest flight unit to the location of the crash. Washington could imagine the unwashed hands of the Iraqis manhandling the dead and wounded in this crashed air ambulance. There might even be females aboard. Technically they didn't have combat status, but they could be lost in the battle nonetheless. He could also imagine the Iraqi gunners aiming at the red cross on the side of the medevac chopper, as if it were a bull's-eye. His anger clouded his judgment.

Normally, this would have been a routine order. But this was not a routine day. He had been sitting around polishing a chair with his ass and flying a desk too long already. Colonel John Washington knew no one senior to him would authorize this flight, but he was the closest qualified pilot available. He knew this was his last war. All the young guys were getting all the action. He remembered when he was a young pilot in Vietnam that he got more action than he wanted.

Washington knew he was fast approaching the age of forced retirement. His career in the military would soon be finished. It had been his whole life. He really couldn't see himself as a crop duster or a news-chopper jockey in civilian life. This was his last war, and he knew it. Normally, he would have, should have and perhaps could have sent someone else. He could have said to himself, "This isn't my problem."

He had to go up or out, as they say in the modern military. And to Washington, headquarters was a place where there was so much ass-kissing that they had to issue scented toilet tissue. No, that wasn't for him, but neither was military insubordination. He was torn between duty and honor, between bad and worse. He was too valuable a human resource to waste on a search-and-rescue flight into hostile territory. Also, the Apache should not have been operating alone. Attack helicopters operate best when in the accompaniment of others.

I've got to help those people, he thought.

He picked up the landline phone. "Get Johnson, and fire up number three," he said to one of the mechanics on the flight pad.

"But, sir!"

"That's an order, specialist."

"Yes, sir."

Then the executive officer broke into the conversation. "Colonel Washington, I do not authorize this mission. You do not have flight approval."

"So noted, major."

Then he walked away, out the door, to where the last Apache was waiting. The XO should have immediately called higher headquarters to inform them of the incident. Washington was senior to him in rank, and he could not legally stop him. He finally did call his superiors, and was informed that his general was out doing his morning physical training. By the time they got hold of him, Washington was already long gone. He had boarded when the weapons officer pulled away from his breakfast, ran onto the steel-plated parking surface and began climbing aboard.

"What's up, colonel?" he inquired.

"The Iraqis shot down a medevac flight. Saddle up," he said, authoritatively.

"Yessir," the young warrant officer replied enthusiastically, as he put on his flight helmet.

With one crew member reading the checklist, and the other doing the checking, they completed the call-and-response preflight check, right by the book. It sounded like a cross between a riddle and a rhyme.

"Anti-collision/position lights—as required?" the checklist reader asked.

"Anti-collision lights, both night; position lights steady bright." This was the response straight from the technical manual. Both pilot and copilot hurriedly recorded all the appropriate entries on the required forms. Other questions were more straightforward.

"Systems check?" was the next cursory inquiry.

"All within normal operating range."

The entire ground crew was on its toes because the old man was the pilot that morning. There was no good-humored joking around the preflight procedures. It was also early, and no one had expected this flight. The ground crew had been up all night preparing the helicopters for their nocturnal hunting mission. The sun was just coming up, and the men's eyes felt gritty from the sand and the dawn light. They knew something serious was up to get the commander from his desk. The urgency in his voice was commanding in and of itself. Everyone sensed something was wrong. The Apache was taking off. The twin engines strained under the whak-whak-whak of the hardened steel rotors. The ground crew wore safety goggles and averted their gazes as an additional precaution against the sand and gravel washed up by the rotors, surrounding them in a temporary dust dervish. A pebble could take your eye out in "half a heartbeat."

Having selected a reference point to maintain ground track, the pilot had both cyclic and pedals in the neutral position, and increased power. Green, Nomex flight-glove-covered hands adjusted the cyclic to obtain the desired rate of climb, while foot pedals were used to adjust the trim. The colonel's eyes scanned the orange plastic windsock that indicated surface-wind direction and velocity.

The seven-ton, tan and brown camouflaged helicopter leapt from the sandbagged landing zone with its peculiar nose-down flight configuration. It had remarkable mechanical agility. As the metal wasp emerged from the windblown sand, it presented an ominous sight. The prominent engine casings on each side of the upper fuselage completed the image of a flying insect. Equipped with an M-230 chain gun, it also carried Hellfire anti-armor missiles and 2.75 inch antipersonnel rockets. It was a flying tank-killing machine.

Both crew seats were surrounded on the bottom, front, rear, and sides by Kevlar plates. All the operating systems were duplicated, with piping, wiring and cables widely separated from each other to make them less vulnerable to battle damage. The chain gun was controlled by the pilot's helmet. Whichever direction he looked, the gun moved in the same direction. The pilot flew the bird and fired the chain gun, but the co-pilot gunner shot all the heavy stuff. With the CPG sitting in front and the pilot sitting higher in the back seat for visibility, the chopper rose skyward into action. The war wasp was soon in the air, and its loud operating noise was diminished as it got farther and farther away. In the pilot's cockpit, nimble hands and pedal-pumping feet, like an old-time pipe organ player, soon changed heading and altitude and maintained airspeed changes necessary to navigate to the location of the downed medibird. Occasionally, the pilot's eyes shot down to the aeronautical map on his kneeboard. But it wasn't that important, as, once airborne, he could see the burning oil fields dead ahead. The oily cloud was beginning to film his windshield. They had to keep out of the smoke by flying around the thickest of it. It was a short flight as the crow goes, as the lone Apache flew into the smoke and began circling the burning oil wells like a giant dragonfly searching for prey.

Although his personnel file was marked with courage and valor, those who knew Washington spoke quietly of his foolhardiness in the face of danger. He had made a distinguished career in the army: Nam, Grenada, Panama and now the Persian Gulf. Wherever the shit was hitting the fan, anywhere in the world, Madjack Washington was usually there, shoveling it in. He had been relatively recently promoted to battalion commander.

He knew that a warrant officer would have sufficed for this mission, and probably would have performed better. The army, in his twenty-four years of service, had probably spent over a million dollars training him. Secondly, he had been privy to top-secret briefings where technology was unveiled by the superspooks and cloak-and-dagger folks. These included satellite intelligence and the new plan to use infrared technology to find and destroy Iraqi tanks by their heat signature. Finally, and most decidedly, he knew about the plan for rapid penetration of armored columns creating a pincers movement to trap and destroy the Republican Guard.

If he were to be captured, these very intricate war plans could be jeopardized. The lives of many could be lost through his bravado. But he went anyway, to save the lives of fellow soldiers. He thought of the few, oblivious to the risk he presented to the many.

He and the gunner could not tell day from night under the oil cloud; only the oil flares and burning debris lit their way through the deadly place. Periodically, the smoke would shift, and a ray of sunshine would poke through the burning oil clouds, illuminating the darkness below with an eerie light. It certainly was a surrealistic scene. The heat, rising from the petroleum-smoke plumes, created meteorological conditions conducive to their own continued combustion. Air was continuously rushing in to fill the vacuum and fanned the flames

The winds periodically shifted the billowing smoke from the burning wells, causing them to dance upward like giant dervishes swirling in time to the tune of the screaming winds. Some smoke was white, some was gray, but most was jet black. Sometimes it shot straight up from its hole in the earth, and sometimes the wind blew it in a sideways direction, spreading it over the ground in a thick, black, sickening fog. Some of the wells merely gushed forth unburned oil. Others resembled smoky candles, while some of those with high natural gas content had no visible emissions at all.

Washington noticed that a pipeline had been shot up with machine gun fire. Everywhere a bullet had pierced it, a flaming spot formed as hot gas and burning oil rushed for release. In the distance, a storage tank was completely engulfed with burning oil spraying from its rooftop and down its sides that gave it the look of a grotesque birthday cake.

The desert-camouflaged mechanical wasp, with its multi-functional stingers, buzzed angrily among the burning oil wells. Keen eyes searched the sandy floor for signs of the downed medevac. The pilot had to keep the helicopter out of the thickest of the smoke both to maintain visibility and to keep it from stalling. Meanwhile, no signal was being received from the downed dustoff chopper. The burning oil was erasing the electronic signature of its distress beacon.

Seeing the needless destruction of such a valuable commodity, the pilot said to the gunner on their inboard intercom, "Wait till the folks back home see the price hike at the gas pump for this one."

"Unbelievable, sir," were the last words the warrant officer uttered.

The Apache was equipped with electronic sensing systems. These could pick up on even the most modern lock-on from a radar-controlled antiaircraft battery or an incoming missile. But below the protective canopy of the burning oil smoke, an old-fashioned danger awaited them. Their electronic detection systems were useless against it. This hazard was an old quad machine gun; it had no radar.

It was an optically sighted, Soviet-built weapon, supposedly not suitable for modern warfare, but if the gunner could see his target for at least ten seconds, he could engage it. Knowing the potential direction of incoming aircraft, he could spray it with Warsaw Pact bullets larger than a 50-caliber machine gun. The weapon's four barrels could simply be aimed in front of a moving aerial target, so it would fly through a storm of lead.

The Iraqi crew had been left behind to shoot up any helicopters investigating the fires, or to deny access to ground personnel intent on extinguishing the oil wells. They could hear the helicopter coming before they saw it. From the air meanwhile, there was so much war debris on the ground that neither Washington nor the weapons man in the front saw the Iraqis on their forward-looking infrared radar before it was too late.

Orders were barked in Arabic, and the gun jerked as it furiously spit its heavy bullets skyward while red-hot brass casings spewed on the ground. Green Soviet tracer rounds looked like a laser show flashing through the blackened sky. Inside the Apache, Washington could hear the bullets hitting the bird. It was a sound he had heard many times before, but not as intensely as these close-range hits. It sounded like four jackhammers pounding on the outside of the helicopter. Most frightening was the hollow, sucking, whistling noise of the rounds exiting the rotary wing aircraft. It was like driving through a hailstorm, but much worse; this hail could kill. In seconds, the chopper was chewed up. Wires were hit, cables snapped, and the second engine was perforated.

The correct response would have been an immediate ninety-degree turn in direction followed by another ninety-degree turn and altitude change. This would put the aircraft in position to be able to apply suppressive counter fire. But the Apache didn't respond. It spun more than 180 degrees and kept on spinning, taking further damage. The front of the chopper was seriously chewed up by the heavy weapons fire.

The pilot screamed through the onboard communication system, "Triple A!"

There was no concealment available other than heading into the oil smoke. Washington was desperately attempting to maintain revolutions-per-minute rotation to keep the wingless bird in the air. Thick black smoke emanated from the port engine.

The pilot called out to his weapons man over the onboard intercom, "Forced landing autorotation," but the words fell literally on dead ears. The gunner had been killed instantly. He took a round through the side of the head. His gore was splattered on the shattered side window.

The helicopter, spinning like an out-of-control carousel, began to spiral downward, its remaining engine able only to slow its decent. The pilot's eyes watched the instrument panel intently. It was the only thing not spinning. He had no time to get off a mayday distress call. The AH-64A was armored, but was no flying tank. Although it had redundant systems, with everything shot to hell, it would no longer fly. Thick smoke swirled from the wounded bird as it spun out of control.

A helicopter pilot couldn't bail out like a jet pilot, abandoning his wounded bird for the chance to look up the skirts of a parachute. The twisting and turning rotors would catch the silk and pull the chutist up into the blades. A helicopter pilot must stay with his failing ship. Madjack knew his only chance was to try to set the coughing helicopter down in some safe place. But no such place presented itself in the limited time Washington had in which to set down.

Spatial disorientation, the choking smoke, and the simultaneously triggered multiple alarms inside the chopper combined to overwhelm the pilot's skill with confusion and terror. The helicopter was crashing. Like a child's whirligig toy out of control, the helicopter fell through the thick smoke. It swirled as it hit the sand nose first. The chopper augured into the ground very hard.

The pilot had no time to get the landing gear down. As he nose-dived in, the chain gun collapsed under the belly of the dying bird to keep it from digging in and flipping over upon itself. The last thing Washington remembered before losing consciousness was a splash of sand over the bursting windshield.

Although the smoking aircraft plowed into a sand dune with terrific force, fully loaded with ordnance and fuel, there was no explosion, no fire. It just hit the ancient sand like the worst car crash imaginable. The rotors kept whirling around slowly, as if the grounded war wasp was not dead, merely mortally wounded, and was trying to leap back into the sky again. The one operating engine was still straining in desperate gasps to regain flight. The chopper was listing to its right side, with the whirling rotor still spinning overhead. It gave an ominous appearance to the crash, as if anything could happen at any moment...

Chapter 19

PATH OF DESTINY

The Humvee kept driving on the dirt trail, toward the burning oil wells. The sand was covered with spent carbon clusters of soot that fell like black snow. The sand got dirtier the closer they came to the oil wells. The wheels made tracks that looked like two chalk marks on a blackboard in the coal-colored surface. It was already full daylight, but it was still dark under the burning blanket of oil that covered the desert like a funeral drape.

Franklin and Simms were in the front, still arguing. Simms turned on the windshield wipers, but they only smeared the glass into an opaque mess that was impossible to see through. They stopped again while Simms cleaned the windshield with a rag and some diesel from the extra Jerry can of fuel. He was talking to himself in anger as he went about the task of removing the oily film from the windshield. For all his macho-sounding speech, he could bitch in a high-pitched voice worse than one of his "hoes." After finishing cleaning off the windshield, Simms looked at the burning horizon in front of him, and when he realized what he was seeing he said, to himself, "Homeboy, this is some real eerie-looking shit."

Franklin was standing outside, again trying vainly to get a GPS reading. The burning oil smoke had thwarted technology. While Franklin was looking at the maps on the other side of the Hummer, Simms stooped down by the driver's tire, pretending to check something. Franklin would not be able to see what he was doing from there. Instead of inspecting his vehicle, he looked at his newfound wealth.

He removed the clip and thumbed the currency. They were all large-denomination bills, a total of $2,000 in U.S. greenbacks. Simms did not know what the foreign currency with it was worth, but he would find out when he got back. The money clip was marked 24 karat and was of a rich Middle Eastern design. It would make a great souvenir for back on the block. He stashed the huge wad of money more securely in his buttoned BDU-shirt pocket. That would keep it safe. Then he got back into the vehicle and waited for Franklin.

Anxious to divert Franklin's thoughts away from what he was doing by the tire, he asked, "Sarge, do you believe this is the Holy Land?"

"Sure I do. Porter told me so," he replied.

Simms did not think it was that funny. He then asked Sergeant Franklin if he had ever been saved. Franklin said yes, he had been saved three times. "Once by the Lord when I was sixteen years old. The other two times were in Vietnam, by tactical air support. And that's only because I was praying."

Simms was anxious. He still wanted to keep Franklin's attention away from his recent find.

"What did Porter do, read it in one of those holy books of his? You don't believe that shit, do you, Sarge?" Simms asked, having already forgotten about the snake a few months before. Young One remembered the incident with Porter and the snake, and recalled it in his mind.

"You had better keep your eyes on the trail and drive, private. That's what I believe. You were not talking all this shit about him the day he saved you from the snake. I thought that made a believer out of you." With that said, Franklin began laughing at Simms for the fool he had been that day. He rolled his lips back over his teeth, held his head back and laughed like a horse. Simms hated the sarge's guts.

Back in the Humvee, Franklin really did think this might be the start of Armageddon. Everything around them at that moment certainly had an evil, hellish appearance. Young One kept looking at the burning oil wells and the black carbon deposits on the sand. He had never seen anything like this. This was worse than Grandfather's dream. The future was unfolding for him. It was dark, as if a cover of gloom was drifting on the wind.

The tan-colored Humvee, contrasted with the black soot, stood out like butterscotch-colored shoes on a nun. They had gone farther into enemy-held territory than any other army unit with the exception of the Special Forces, who were conducting covert missions deep in country.

Young One was the first to see the Apache helicopter flying overhead, off to the right. It was flying low, but not moving fast. It looked as if it were searching for something, because it was flying around. He secretly wished that he were a helicopter pilot, instead of just an infantryman. He could then swoop like a hawk flying over the battlefield. He slapped on the top of the roof of the Humvee to get his sergeant's attention. Franklin had already seen the helicopter and was pointing in its direction. It was flying low, heading deeper into the smoke, and had almost disappeared from view, when all of a sudden they heard the sound of machine-gun fire. It echoed across the empty sand. They could not see the gun but could approximate its position and distance from the direction of the shots.

Simms said, "Somebody's rock and rolling up there."

"Yeah, I heard it too," said Franklin.

They watched as the Apache circled in and out of the thick oil cloud and then disappeared from the sky. It landed with a crashing sound about a kilometer away.

They set off in the direction of the crash, straight into the smoke, but made it only a couple of hundred meters. The last thing Young One remembered was a little click, followed by a loud BOOM, as the Humvee ran over a hastily deployed anti-vehicular landmine. The left front tire hit the pressure plate, and a deafening and deadly detonation ensued. The blast blew a billowing cloud of sand into the air. Young One thought he could see the front of the Humvee blasting apart from the rear as if it had been cut in half. The front half was explosively thrust about in pieces, and a smoking hole marked the end of its tracks. The back end of the Hummer flipped three times through the air and landed about ten meters away from where the front of the vehicle had been.

If it weren't for the tank plates Walters had welded on, they all would have been dead. They offered protection from both the concussion and the shrapnel. The machine gun was ripped from its supports and smashed into Young One's helmet and face. Young One took half a somersault before being dropped hard on the ground out of the roof gun port. He hit the ground flat on his back, like a dead cat.

The concussion, the blast, the flight through the air, and then the hard thump in the sand almost did him in. For what seemed a long time, he lay there watching the oil smoke float overhead. He wasn't knocked out cold, simply neurologically stunned, like receiving a whole body slap from an invisible, giant hand. His head throbbed, and blood from his head wound ran into his eyes. He began to move as soon as he was able. He first started to move his feet, his legs, his arms, and then his head and neck.

Nothing is broken, at least not my backbone, he thought. His whole body had a numb sensation, like a leg that had gone to sleep from lack of circulation. At first, he thought he was blind because the lenses of his sand goggles were shattered by the blast. Little by little, his nervous system began to come back to life. He could see he had landed about twenty-five feet from the smoking hulk of the Humvee. He didn't know what had happened. There was a split in his helmet where it had been smashed by the machine gun. Without the helmet, the blow would have crushed his skull. Blood ran down his face. It tasted salty as he licked his lips. He could smell the explosive residue that reminded him of blasted fireworks. He began to crawl forward in a semi-conscious state, not realizing the dreadfully dangerous position he was in. There probably were other landmines around, but he didn't set any off. On hands and knees, he made his way back to the remains of the vehicle, collapsing face first in the sand, and falling into unconsciousness next to the smoking hole where the front of the Humvee should have been...

>←→←→←→←

Back at the Tactical Operations Center, the alarm was sounded. The flight controller, a specialist fifth class with close-cropped hair and an incredulous look upon his face, cried out to the on-duty non-commissioned officer, "Sarge, we've lost Colonel Washington's signal. He may be down."

"Tell me that again, soldier," his sergeant demanded while looking over the shoulder of his subordinate at the radar screen. "Verify this with AWACs immediately."

After confirming the news, the sergeant picked up the landline phone and contacted his superior officer. Within minutes, the entire chain of command along the phone line was electrified as they learned of the missing link.

In his concrete command bunker, Washington's commanding officer, a one-star general, was visibly upset.

"Who authorized that pilot's flight?" his commanding voice demanded into the duty phone.

After a short pause, others in the room heard, "He what?"

"Find him!" was the general's final order before slamming down the handset so hard the bell of the telephone sounded a single ring. He rubbed his balding white head with his right hand and wondered, *How am I going to explain this to General Command?* He would soon be catching a royal ass-chewing and seeing stars for this incident, but none of them would be going on his shoulders. However, the call had to be made. After taking several minutes to compose himself and his thoughts, he contacted his headquarters.

"Walt, this is George," he said to his fellow general with the first-name familiarity not known anywhere else in the U. S. Army's chain of command.

"We've got a situation here."

"What's that?"

"Colonel John Washington of First Corps' Attack Helicopter Battalion has been lost in flight. His aircraft signature disappeared a few minutes ago from the AWACs radar screen, and his emergency locator transponder is non-operational at this time."

"What the holy hell was he doing up there? He knows all of our invasion plans. If he falls into enemy hands, we'll lose more than one chopper jock. You find him and do it ASAP!"

"Yessir." He hung up and punched the number to the Tactical Operations Center hoping to find out it was merely a malfunction and he had not really lost his attack helicopter commander and his chance for further promotion at the same time.

He thought, *The colonel is going to be wearing his ass for a flight helmet for this one.*

"Any news of Colonel Washington?" he asked hopefully of the executive officer on the other end of the line.

"No, sir. His signal disappeared about ten minutes ago, somewhere in the black shit from the burning wells. Air force electronics can't penetrate the oil smoke, and we can't risk any more helicopter overflights of the area." That was the rest of the bad news.

>——×——>×—<

A regular army spec-six was at the computer console, simultaneously monitoring six screens of telemetry data. Each showed a different parameter of measurement from the others.

"We have a lot of activity in that sector. It's the remnants of the Takawalna Mechanized Division of the Republican Guard. They were shot up pretty badly two days ago. The two helicopters are down there amid the debris of battle in the vast Minagish oil fields in southwest Kuwait." After a moment of silence, he continued.

"Both choppers disappeared from AWACs in the same vicinity, approximately twenty-three minutes apart. We have had no radio contact with either bird. We must assume the worst. Colonel Washington must have augured in pretty hard.

"We know the general area where Colonel Washington went down from his last reported AWACs position, but not exactly where. His radar signature started going fuzzy as he flew deeper into the smoke and just disappeared. We also have the functioning distress beacon from the medi-bird. We're hoping that it is still sending out enough signal to pick it up."

While he was speaking, he was replaying the information from the last radar contact with both helicopters. It showed the medibird's position and where the attack helicopter disappeared.

"They've got to be among the burning oil wells southwest of Kuwait City," the computer operator interjected. "They just fell into the oil smoke. They simply disappeared from radar view and never reappeared."

"Do we have anyone else in the area who could assist?" the senior officer asked. "The infantry had a recon patrol out there at that time, but they lost radio contact with their people also. We fear the ragheads got them as well, sir." His officer gave him a dirty look. "Sorry, sir. The Iraqis may have gotten them as well."

They could bomb them, strafe them, shoot them, blow them up, or bayonet their guts, but they could not refer to the enemy with a disparaging term in that war. They might have offended someone in that insane mess.

✶✶✶✶

Mizzi had been hiding in the back when the explosion took place, and lay in a stunned condition for a long while. Centrifugal force held the soldier in the remaining shell of the Hummer. Mizzi's eardrums were injured by the concussion that echoed around for microseconds inside the acoustic shell provided by the back of the Humvee. The impostor remained conscious throughout the explosion, but barely so. After several minutes, Mizzi's hearing improved somewhat but did not clear completely. The trembling soldier got up and began crawling and then stumbling around the scene, also oblivious to the possible presence of other landmines.

Off to the right Mizzi saw Sergeant Franklin and went over to him. His legs were completely blown off, but he was still alive. His uniform and face had been burned in the blast. His face was bleeding, as if he had gotten the shit kicked out of him by a street fighter. He just sat up in a pool of his own blood, supporting himself with his arms, life fluid slowly draining away into the sand. The realization came to Mizzi's mind that the explosion hadn't happened too long ago, or Franklin would have bled to death already. They must have just been stunned, not knocked cold. Franklin was shaking uncontrollably. Mizzi screamed, "Sarge, what happened?"

"We hit a landmine, asshole. What do you think happened?" he said. While still holding himself up on his arms, he motioned to his left pocket, where he kept his smokes. Mizzi knew what he wanted and took one from the packet, pulled up the concealing eye goggles, and removed the muffler to light the cigarette. The lit cigarette was then placed in his shivering lips. Franklin was unable to smoke it, but there seemed to be a look of appreciation in his eyes. He looked into Mizzi's face to give thanks, and his eyes widened in disbelief.

"Why you're, you're...," Sergeant Franklin said as the cigarette stopped moving in his lips. The sarge was dead. His flak jacket hadn't saved him, merely given him a longer death. He just sat there dead, with a lit cigarette in his lips. It finally extinguished itself at the filter.

Mizzi just left the burning cigarette in his mouth and looked around quickly to see if anyone else had been looking.

Not finding Simms and seeing Young One unconscious on the ground nearby, Mizzi quickly replaced the muffler and goggles and crawled back to the rear end of the Hummer. It was no use to try to call for help, for the radio was gone, the dash was gone, everything in the front was gone.

Simms was nowhere to be found, or, more correctly, he was everywhere to be found. It was over the front wheel on his side that the blast occurred. The government paid for his birth, everything in between, and now it was going to pay for his death. The only things left of Simms were part of his head in the Kevlar helmet and the torso protected by the flak jacket. Laying unnoticed on the sand was the Arab's burned and bloodied wad of money. Stolen bills were fluttering in the wind, their burned edges still held securely by the golden clasp.

Mizzi came back to Young One. He looked dead because he was not moving, just lying face down. However, it was evident that Young One was breathing slowly. After several attempts to arouse him with words, nudges, slaps, and screams, he finally began to move his eyes. He had trouble focusing at first, and his hearing was damaged. Young One's eyes were full of blood from his head injury. Mizzi took out a canteen and flushed them out with water. Young One's ears were ringing. Then he remembered. They had seen a shot-up helicopter crash in the sand and were heading for it when they ran into an enemy landmine.

"Where's the chopper?"

Mizzi motioned with one hand to the right ear indicating that the hearing in that ear was gone. No answer could be forthcoming. Both of their ears were ringing from the blast.

Young One got to his feet, motioned toward the direction they had been heading when the explosion occurred and gestured for Mizzi to follow him. If they were in the middle of a whole minefield, the possibility didn't come to their minds. They were in shell shock from the blast. Their bodies were starting to stiffen up from their injuries. They moved with the dexterity of mummies, as they pressed forward to the downed helicopter. Their weapons were left in the back of the vehicle remains.

><-- >< ->><

They could see the chopper had crashed into a sand dune from the cloud of sand it was throwing into the air. The helicopter kept jumping as if it could at any moment leap back into the air and fly off. The rotor blades were still spinning slowly, and it gave an eerie effect to the site, as if it could explode at any instant.

Young One's goggles were gone, and the spinning rotors blew sand into his eyes. He could not see. Someone had to crawl between the fuselage and the swirling blades. They had to see if anyone had survived the crash. Mizzi, who still had sand goggles and a helmet, went first. The giant blades made a "swooshing" sound as they whizzed overhead, throwing bits of sand like stinging sleet. After carefully crawling up to see inside, and taking great care to avoid the turning blades, Mizzi looked at the front compartment, and saw what remained of the copilot. Fighting waves of nausea and the urge to vomit, Mizzi checked the higher back compartment, ever mindful of the main blade swinging a few feet away. One misstep or a fall could mean immediate amputation or death. The whole front of the chopper was smashed and riddled with large bullet holes.

Mizzi could see that the other man in the back seat of the helicopter was unconscious; at least there was no blood on him if he was dead. They had to make sure before they left him. He was covered with sand that had blown in through the open canopy. While brushing sand from his shoulders, Mizzi saw his rank insignia. He had full bird eagles on his flight suit. Several slaps on the face brought movement. He was alive. The specialist tried to pull him from the chopper but could not do it alone. Mizzi next tried the chopper radio but couldn't make it work. Mizzi crawled back and motioned from the swirling sand for Young One to come and help.

The task of removing the pilot was blinding. Young One had to keep his eyes closed because of the rotor-generated sandstorm.

Young One climbed up to the pilot's compartment and pulled the pilot up, taking great care to avoid getting sucked up into the rotors. Together, they finally got his dead weight out of the helicopter and plopped him onto the sand. He moaned unconsciously as he hit the ground hard.

Regaining their breath, they dragged him from the blinding and choking cloud of rotor dust. Young One examined the pilot for broken bones as best as he could. If there were any, he could not feel them sticking through his flight suit. There was a rip in his flight suit and a large burn mark across the exposed midsection, but no blood was evident. Mizzi removed the pilot's cracked fight helmet that had saved his life. He had taken quite a bash on the head at the moment of impact. They were anxious to get away from the helicopter both in case of explosion, and also because the Iraqis who shot them down could be coming. They knew this was a high-ranking officer, and should not be captured.

The blades were still spinning wildly in the swirling cloud of sandy dust behind them. They made their way back to the remains of the Hummer, carrying the unconscious officer with his arms over their shoulders. He was taller than both of them, and they dragged him along, with his flight boots plowing dual furrows in the sand. They rested back at the remains of the Humvee for a while. Immediate rescue did not seem likely, as help would already have been there.

They each retrieved their chemical-protective gear hanging in bags from the side of the demolished vehicle, and Young One grabbed Franklin's for the pilot. They had been trained by military inculcation never to go anywhere without chemical protective clothing. Mizzi grabbed the rifle with the grenade launcher and its ammo.

Young One took his M-16 and checked it out. He worked the actions of the weapons to see if they had survived the explosion. Both rifles seemed all right, but firing them could have attracted enemy attention. Young One felt the blood-crusted bump on his forehead and looked at what caused it. The machine gun was too heavy to carry, and had been damaged in the accident.

Young One slung the bandoleer of grenade-launcher ammo around Mizzi's neck. The silent spec-four nodded approvingly. They each carried water on their pistol belts, but one of Young One's plastic canteens had burst when he fell upon it as a result of the explosion. He had a sore spot on his right buttock from the trauma. He grabbed a gallon-bladder canteen of water and carried it as well.

The burden they now bore included three sets of chemical protective gear, an extra gallon of water, their rifles, ammo, and field gear, in addition to the unconscious pilot. Thus encumbered, they weren't going to set any speed records wherever they were going.

The pilot was a large man and heavy to lift. It proved a difficult task. Instead of putting him down, they would carry him twenty paces and catch their breath while standing upright. Stepping off the road to avoid more landmines, they began heading southward back to coalition lines, or to a safe place where rescue could be expected. It was laborious work lugging about all their gear, water, and the pilot.

They had to keep moving, because the crash was sure to bring the enemy. No one wanted to be guests of the Iraqis. Young One and Mizzi communicated with shouts and gestures, as their ears were still "over-amped" by the explosion.

※——※——※

A few hours later, one of the many subordinate officers was briefing the commander. "Sir, we must assume Colonel Washington is down. He disappeared from AWACs in the oil smoke. We've been unable to raise him on the radio, there has been no mayday call, and his emergency locator transponder is not sending out code."

"Any other word of Colonel Washington?" asked the senior officer of the others in the briefing room.

"No, sir. As far as we know, he's still missing."

"Get the air force on the horn and brief them of the position and request surveillance overflight of the area where he was last known to be."

"Although we do not want his information to fall into enemy hands, I'm also worried about the man. Madjack Washington has had a hell of a career in the army. His loss would not only be to the service, but to all of us."

"Why do they call him 'Madjack?'"

"I only heard this secondhand. It seems that he returned from a mission in the Nam with a chopper so shot up that it looked like a kitchen colander with blades on it. He landed in a hot LZ that was under heavy fire by North Vietnamese regulars. The guys on the ground were surrounded, and three helicopters were downed trying to get them out under a heavy hosing. His copilot was severely wounded."

"So that's why they call him 'Madjack.'"

The other officer took a sip of his coffee from the heavy mug in his hand and continued:

"No, that's just the start of the story. There was no one else to fly back. His ship was so shot up that it was a miracle that it flew. There was one chopper left in the repair hangar. It had not been cleared for flight because of engine trouble. Alone, with no copilot or crew, he fired the old Huey up. The mechanic who helped him get it ready kept warning him that he might not make it. He had no machine guns. It was low on fuel. The mechanic told him that it would be suicide, especially alone.

"The mechanic wished he had kept his mouth shut because Washington invited him aboard and gave him his CAR-15 rifle that he never flew without. He told the mechanic to jump in and ride shotgun for him. The mechanic had seen no combat. They were both black and the mechanic supposedly said, 'You must be mad, Jack.' He then climbed in, and together they took off.

"Some of the men who were rescued said they thought they were done for when Washington and his new sidekick came. It was a hot load, under fire. Rescued soldiers already inside the chopper were returning fire, shooting with one hand while pulling wounded buddies inside with the other. They say Washington shot an NVA soldier with his 38-caliber service revolver who was running up with a grenade in his hand. The mechanic sat shooting from the side window as if he were on a stagecoach in the cowboy movies. They wound up bringing three loads of soldiers. They each got a Silver Star even though Washington did not have an authorized flight plan."

"That's quite a story. He's almost a legend in his own time."

"Let's hope this is not his last chapter," the general replied...

Chapter 20

FLOOD OF BAD NEWS IN A DRY LAND

The senior officers in crisp, starched, desert-camouflage BDUs were walking with a purpose in their steps. Their morning was half over, and they were headed to a nine o'clock briefing about the situation. Their normal PT had been cancelled because of the smoke, so after breakfast, they headed directly toward a nondescript concrete building that looked very much like an ammo bunker. At its doors, two guards snapped to attention and presented arms with their weapons at the officers' approach.

The officers entered the elevators and pressed the down button, as there was no other way to go. Soon, they were descending in the elevator, deep into the entrails of the earth. It was the Saudis' bombproof military headquarters, shared with the coalition commanders. It had been refitted with the latest of communications and intelligence equipment. The place was full of charts, computer screens, and air force brass. They called it the "Black Hole." It was eighty feet underground, buried beneath tons of reinforced concrete. It had all the charm of a D-Day bunker. It was here that all of the high-level air command decisions were made. The situation was very tense that morning.

The elevator doors opened up into the war room. It was ultra-modern and full of computers, television screens, radar readout devices, and all sorts of high-tech command and communications equipment. The shakers and movers of all the U.S. military services were involved in this important meeting. In the briefing room adjacent to the war room, a technical briefing for the commander was being prepared. All the top brass were there. Washington had managed to "shake the top of the flagpole," as soldiers say. None of the coalition partners had been invited. For the moment, the news of Colonel Washington was to "stay in the family." If the situation did not resolve itself soon, the command and intelligence elements of the coalition partners would eventually have to be told, but then only in secrecy. But for right now, the commander wanted a lid put on it. They especially did not want the media to be made aware of such a grave situation.

A survival, escape, resistance, and evasion operation involving a high-ranking officer would make a great human-interest story, but one that could jeopardize the ground assault and possibly the outcome of the conflict. It could also seriously endanger Colonel Washington. For now, everyone was ordered to secrecy. During periods of armed conflict, it was a most serious order. All present were briefed on the situation in a cursory manner, and were being told only what they needed to accomplish their missions. No more and no less. But the CEOs of war could fill in the dots and knew there was something big going on to have commanded the attention of the entire general staff.

After informing his subordinates of the situation, the general entertained comments or suggestions from the participating services or agencies present.

"Don't we have anything already up there that can help us right away?" the commander inquired of his subordinate officers from the air force. After a short pause, an air force general spoke up. "We can redirect returning reconnaissance aircraft to conduct overflights of the area after completing their regular missions."

The commanding general contemplated this for a moment and then said, "Thank you, General Meister. Please inform your people to go ahead, but no aircraft is to penetrate the oil smoke unless I authorize it. We've got enough trouble there without adding to it. For all we know, they may be just looking for dead bodies." The air force general nodded his head, excused himself and moved briefly to the back of the room. Via landline, he ordered that returning intelligence aircraft look for two downed army helicopters amid the burning Minagish oil fields. They were authorized to shoot up any remaining gun camera film on the way in, over the area where the helicopters were believed to be lost. The general knew that it would take time for the planes to land, to retrieve the film, to process it, and to interpret the images.

General Baer, the highest officer present, inquired if satellite technology could be used to locate the two downed helicopters. He knew there were many satellites positioned over the Kingdom of Kuwait at the time of the war, and new ones with all sorts of intelligence-gathering capability had been repositioned in non-synchronous orbit in anticipation of hostilities in the Gulf. There were weather, communications, intelligence, and earth-mapping satellites constantly peering down upon that part of the world. The interwoven network of military intelligence satellites carried the most sophisticated optical and electromagnetic sensing capability in the world.

The general staff knew every military planner watched the weather satellites. It was a basic part of planning and operations. Each service had its own weather satellite, and their folks watched the progress of the weather fronts as anxiously as they read intelligence reports. Without clear weather, they could not bomb or do battle-damage assessment of targets already hit. Without air support, the coalition could not be assured of total victory in the ground assault that was to take place as soon as the weather broke. The general also knew they had mapping satellites up there looking for potential trails in the trackless sands.

"Can the weather satellites be reconfigured to look for the downed aircraft?"

"General, sir," one of the subordinate air force technical resource officers spoke up. "NOAA has an atmospheric Landsat over the area right now. I'm afraid it is not going to be of much help to us."

"I'm listening."

"Weather satellites' missions are to look at clouds and track large storms, not to search the ground. NOAA's assets can give us an idea of what the area looks like, but it won't be much use for anything else. Meteorological satellites simply aren't designed for this type of information gathering. They are configured for weather-radar readout back on earth.

"The problem is, their best optical capability has a surface resolution of only 50 meters. The Apache attack helicopter has a length of 14.8 meters, and its width at the midsection is too thin to bring it up to the needed 50 square meters. It presents too small a target for successful acquisition and resolution with that technical asset. It is the same problem with mapping satellites."

"Are you telling me they have so many satellites up there that they are practically running into each other in space, but none are of use to us?"

"General, sir, defense-mapping satellites can see closer and in more detail, but they can't look through the oil smoke. The only chance we have is to use our more sophisticated intelligence-gathering platforms." By this, he meant utilizing spy satellites to attempt to locate the downed aviators.

"Photographic-intelligence satellites have much greater ground resolution. They can resolve a ten-centimeter object from the edge of space. On a clear day, their photo-optical lenses are powerful enough to see a tennis-ball-sized object on the ground."

But the problem was that there wasn't a clear day to be had.

"Why can't we direct Desert Star assets to locate his helicopter?" the general asked. There was a noticeable silence in the room. Desert Star was the code name for the vast intelligence-gathering satellite network roving over the Persian Gulf at that time. In a twist of historical irony, the land that had invented astronomy was now being spied upon from the stars.

"General Baer, such an adjustment of our technical-intelligence resources will compromise our acquisition of primary targets." By this he meant that military intelligence would not be able to locate the Scud missiles, which were the Iraqis' offensive weapon of most concern. The other target was the Republican Guard Divisions, who were Saddam's shock troops. Baghdad had already shot Scuds at Israel, and there had been "whooping and hollering" reported in the coalition camps when some of the Arab troops heard that Tel Aviv had been hit.

"General, what about the security of our troops from Scud attacks?" one of the staff officers inquired of his superior.

There was complete silence in the war room. Only the almost imperceptible high-pitched hum of the computers could be heard.

"As commander, can I authorize the use of all our satellite assets?" he asked the air force general after taking a breath.

"No, sir. All of the intelligence satellites in the theatre of operations are under the control of the air force. We control and, in essence, own the U.S. satellites in orbit.

"To complicate things further, their intelligence product is the property of the National Photographic Interpretation Center in Washington, D.C. Any movement or reorientation of the satellites has to be OK'd by both agencies."

This was not going to be a quick task. General Baer knew each sister service had its own intelligence needs, and there was already fierce rivalry between branches of the armed forces for the imagery data, considered so essential for the conduct of modern warfare. Another person in the room, in a civilian suit, added, "Any or all of the changes must be done with the approval of the Joint Chiefs of Staff, the Secretary of Defense, and possibly a congressional subcommittee. The best we can do is to hope that they will debate and argue in true partisan fashion, and finally gave a 'wink and a nod' to make the changes in the satellites' trajectories."

"General, it's going to be difficult to juggle all of our intelligence needs. There are currently four synchronous orbiting military intelligence satellites operating over the Gulf. Each of the major services—army, navy, and air force—has a Kennan KH-11, and the superspooks in Langley have a newer and more sophisticated Lacrosse satellite. All of these technical-intelligence resources already have pretty full dance cards. But we will do what we can."

"Get working on it, Al. I don't care if you have to light fires under their chairs. Get them up and moving."

"I'll do my best, general."

✄ ✄ ✄

It was several hours before the civilian returned to General Baer with the details. He looked haggard, as if he had just worked like hell since the briefing.

"General. I have news, but it's not all good. None of the sister services are willing to relinquish their satellite capability. They are using their technical-intelligence resources for target acquisition and battle-damage assessment. Ongoing operations could be seriously compromised, should we shift our strategic assets. We've twisted arms, called names, and even tried to call in old markers. Everyone feels it is not a prudent expenditure of such valuable intelligence resources on just one man."

Then General Baer got frustrated and angry. "That one man knows too much about our attack plans. He was present at several high-level staff meetings. He even knows about Hail Mary."

This was the code name for the invasion of Iraq and the liberation of Kuwait. It could save thousands of coalition soldiers' lives if it worked. It entailed a feint by a marine armored assault along the coast followed by a grand armor charge through the western Iraqi desert, then cutting back east into Kuwait. The diversionary force of marines poised to invade from the sea was to keep the Iraqis uncertain about where the invasion would actually originate.

U.S. Army tanks and armored personnel carriers had been secretly moving behind the lines into western Iraq for days. Their purpose was to penetrate Iraqi territory and then swing to the right, behind their retreating enemy forces, to bottle up and destroy the main divisions of the Republican Guard. Then the remaining Iraqi forces would be cut off from their communication and resupply lines, and forced to surrender without bloodshed. It was a complex and grand maneuver having the entire playing field in action. If the deception worked, it would be a hard blow to the Iraqi war effort, and Madjack Washington knew enough of the plan to endanger its success.

Everyone was silent as the civilian added solemnly, "If the enemy gets hold of Colonel Washington and interviews him with sufficient persuasion to encourage his cooperation, we'll be filling up a lot of those 40,000 human-remains pouches in the warehouse by the airport."

"You do, however, as commander, have the authority to order the army's technical intelligence resources to be repositioned over the area for a special operation. You'll have to get Washington's okay to redirect strategic assets. It's going to be a hard sell, sir."

"Then you'd best get your plaid pants on, son, and start making some calls," the general noted emphatically.

"Yes, sir," was his reluctant reply.

Unknown to any of them, Colonel Washington and his new companions were being stalked by hostile Iraqi patrols amid the burning oil fields...

Chapter 21

HOWLING HELL

The two American enlisted soldiers stumbled forward, carrying the unconscious pilot. They had to stop and rest continually, as it was physically taxing work. They were out in the open, with no cover or concealment from enemy fire. They were forced to head directly into the burning oil fields to gain the protection from enemy observation offered by the smoke. It would only be a matter of time before an Iraqi patrol found the chopper crash or the remains of the Hummer and begin tracking them.

They set off on a course they thought was parallel to the road, to avoid detection, as well as to keep from stepping on another landmine. They had no compass, no map, no global positioning system to guide their steps. They could not even see the position of the sun. Young One relied on dead reckoning to set their path. They set their sights upon the only landmark available: the fires that lit the blackened sky like evil tiki torches.

Not knowing that the pilot had a survival compass in one of the pockets of his flight suit, the best they could do was to keep going in the direction away from where they thought the Iraqis were. For all they knew, they could have been moving straight toward Baghdad. Unable to carry the pilot any farther, they stopped and rested standing up, each with a shoulder under an armpit. At first, they tried laying him down, but it was too hard lifting the large, unconscious man up again.

"You are the spec-four, and I am only a private first class, but I think we should head in this direction," Young One panted, while pointing to the burning oil fields. The specialist responded with a nod of approval and accompanied him without protest. Overhead, the thick black smoke roiled in the air. It was like nothing either of them had ever seen. From time to time, the wind shifted direction, and the drifting smoke clouds allowed a stray ray of sunlight to pierce the smoky canopy and light the artificial twilight beneath it. They were the only points of light in the hellish darkness.

If they remained on this course, Young One hoped it would take them to the backside of the Iraqi front lines. They did not know if that section of the line was still occupied by enemy soldiers or not. But it was the only chance they had to stay alive. They had drunk most of their water, as hauling the large man was very strenuous and caused them to perspire profusely. They would have to find water soon. They were losing too much fluid through sweat and their exhaled breath.

As they got closer to the oil field, a backdrop presented itself that all the special effects experts in Hollywood could hardly have duplicated. More than 1,000 oil wells, petroleum tanks, pipelines, and pumping stations were damaged, destroyed, or explosively obliterated. They were literally in the hottest part of the war.

The burning oil wells crackled, and the heat from the hot oil pools rushed skyward, as the surrounding air rushed in to fill the vacuum created by the hot, rising columns of air. The flames shot upward and iridescent red-orange fingers of fire grasped at and ignited the black smoke.

The rushing wind greatly assisted the oil in its combustion. If there are two things that are plentiful in the desert, they are sand and air. And now both were polluted with petroleum. The air was filled with poisonous vapors and combustion gases.

Rivulets of boiling crude petroleum hemorrhaged from the sabotaged oil wells, escaping after eons of confinement in the earth. The thick, black, viscous fluid bubbled and fumed forth with a malodor somewhere between roofing tar and hot asphalt. The atrocious aroma filled their nostrils and created a choking sensation. The oil-well gases were overwhelming.

Most of the burning oil turned into particulate matter—sooty carbon clusters. The rest became converted to carbon monoxide and carbon dioxide gas in the flames. The particulates, being dark in color and buoyant because of the warm air rising gradually, rose into the sky, where they cooled and became coated with the moisture in the winter air. This created black soot and ash that fell from the sky.

They felt like they were in a dark warehouse or some other vast building whose walls were so far distant as to be invisible, rather than feeling as if they were outside. With so many volatile hydrocarbons in the crude oil, any ignition source could spark the air around them at any moment. Also, much of the atmospheric oxygen was being consumed and replaced by toxic chemicals. They felt trapped in the open. Terrified, they pressed on. Young One remembered that Grandfather had seen all of this in his dream.

With burning eyes and choking breath, he said to Mizzi, "We had better put on our chemical protective gear." Again Mizzi agreed without words. They had three suits of chemical protective gear. Young One and Mizzi had their own, and they put Franklin's gear on the pilot. The protective clothing and masks made them look like space creatures. It did help them breathe cleaner air, however.

Young One had taken the bandage from his forehead because the gas mask couldn't get a good, tight fit. The rubber pressed hard against his throbbing head and reopened the wound. He wiped blood from his face with the sleeve of his BDU jacket.

The burning fires also consumed the limited supply of available oxygen from the atmosphere. Their respirators could not make oxygen; they could only filter out pollutants. Classic symptoms of slow toxic atmospheric poisoning began to manifest themselves: parched throats, pounding headaches, labored breathing, coughing, and shortness of breath. Their masks filtered out much of the oil smoke, but they did not make oxygen. They were becoming simple-headed from anoxia. Animal-like fear to stay alive drove them onward.

In addition to those belching smoke, some wells burned very cleanly, like screaming blowtorches from the sand. The sound of the rapid release of petroleum gas escaping from its million-year residence in the earth was horrifying. Other wells merely issued a high-pitched scream of unignited gas and potentially deadly, flammable vapors.

Even from a distance, they could still hear the harsh sound in their injured ears. How much further damage the noise from the screeching oil wells did to their already injured ears they could only guess.

Some wells were burning so hot and brightly that their radiant heat could be felt a great distance away. Other wells weren't burning at all, and the oil gushing from them created flowing rivers of oil that filled depressions in the earth, forming oil lakes up to thirteen kilometers long and six meters deep. Some of these oil rivers and pools were on fire and covered everything in their path; others were mere sticky tar traps waiting to burst into flame. The creeping oil floods swallowed up all the fragile desert sand, its botanic and animal life, military emplacements and minefields alike.

The part of the desert they were in had been badly overgrazed by herd animals for too many years, and the only plants left uneaten were either noxious enough to cause a camel to puke or spiny enough to gag a goat. Everything was overused in this land of temporary luxury and continuous want. But now the sparse desert vegetation was covered with oil and set aflame. If Porter had been there, he would undoubtedly have had something to say about burning bushes in the Bible. Saddam promised to "reduce the Arabian Peninsula to ashes." Perhaps this was his way.

Finally, the wind shifted, and carried the noxious vapors away and brought fresh air. They followed the black, sticky stream of oil, trying to get in front of it so it would obliterate their tracks and make it harder for an Iraqi patrol to catch up. They continued to struggle until neither of them could go farther. They collapsed on the sand right out in the open. There was nowhere to hide. They were leaving a trail like a cornrow in the soot-covered sand from dragging the pilot, but at least they were in an area where the smoke was blowing the other way, and could temporarily breathe clean air again. Young One removed his gas mask and smelled the air. It was fresh for the moment. After seeing this, Mizzi also doffed the hooded, protective mask, quickly wrapped the muffler and replaced the helmet, and then removed the colonel's mask.

Young One pulled a handful of crumbled MRE cookies from his pockets. He carried a whole meal in his pockets. Some of the pouches had burst in the explosion. He gave Mizzi the remains of the cookies and, with his fingers, ate much of the ruptured food coating his pockets. It was salty from his dirty fingers and gritty from sand. But it was food, and Young One knew the best place to carry it was in his stomach before it spoiled. They ate and drank sitting back to back for security. After their meager repast, both fell fast asleep on the sand...

>*— >*— >*—

"Lieutenant Ramirez, we have a serious situation here." Ramirez heard the words of his company executive officer. There was no first-name bullshit this time, he noted.

No, something is wrong here, Ramirez thought. He was being addressed by his proper military designation, and the XO delivered it with a tone of warning in his voice. It was that intonation of army voice that says, "You have just tap danced on your dick with golf shoes, son." The captain was already getting his ass chewed by his superiors over this situation. The young Mexican-American second lieutenant had no idea what was going on.

He was quickly briefed of the situation in battalion headquarters. More soldiers from his platoon were missing. They had missed their radio check and were not in their designated patrol zone. It had been only several days prior that another one of his patrols had been shot up by an ambush. A squad leader was dead, and three soldiers were badly wounded and out of action. He had just finished pushing through the Purple Heart paperwork for his wounded and writing the letter to Sergeant Eliot's loved ones.

He read the duty roster for the day. It read Sergeant First Class Virgil C. Franklin, Private First Class Young One Asabathithez, Private First Class Jamal R. Simms, and Specialist Fourth Class John Walters. Lieutenant Ramirez felt genuinely sorry for all the guys, even Walters. He hoped they just had radio trouble. He did not want to write any more letters home. He silently prayed this time all he would have to do was give a good ass-chewing to the wayward troops. He did not want anybody to get hurt. He always said, "Everybody is going home." He hoped he had not lied again.

He was the platoon leader, and the worst thing that could happen had just occurred. He had been blindsided by his men, and it was evident to his commanding officer. People were missing, and he didn't know why or how many. He did not know where or why they were not where they were supposed to be. He had been given the task of figuring it out. And figure it out he would. If you do not know where your people are, you are a poor leader.

With a heavy heart, he quick-stepped it back from the Battalion Headquarters to his company area. Captain Nelson had stayed behind. That was a bad sign. If he had been escorted in and walked out with his company commander, he would have known they were on his side. Now his superiors were talking about him. This had been a hard week, but it was getting harder.

>*—*×—*×*—<

Young One was the first to wake up. He remembered looking at the pilot's watch when he got up. They had been escaping and evading for almost six hours. Leaving Mizzi with the pilot, he walked around to reconnoiter the area. He cautiously approached the burning oil field ahead of him. There did not seem to be anyone around. No tracks, no sound or sight of Iraqis.

The cloaking smoke gave the place an unnerving gothic appearance. A sudden shift in the wind cleared the smoke and revealed a military graveyard. Every type of military equipment, gear, petroleum-purchased paraphernalia, and vehicles, all painted the telltale tan of the Iraqi Army, lay in ruins around them. Battle tanks, fuel tanks, and water tanks alike were smashed and lay broken on the battlefield. Everything in view was destroyed. Wrecked vehicles lay about in various states of mechanical humiliation. Blasted military equipment of every description despoiled the landscape further.

Perhaps the Iraqi commanders erroneously believed that the coalition would not bomb them near the oil wells, as if the well fields were a sacred place to the unholy western world. But, for whatever reason, the Iraqis desperately needed office and storage space, and the ancillary buildings scattered here and there along the pipelines were chosen for the headquarters. They had electricity and phone lines. To the coalition war planners, they were enemy command-and-control centers. Thus, the well houses and pumping station buildings were to prove to be no protection. Their value to world petroleum production was not considered, and their corrugated sheet-metal walls were no deterrent to a bullet or a bomb. It was apparent to Young One that many Iraqi units in the vicinity of the oil fields had been hit hard. He went carefully from destroyed vehicle to vehicle, looking for food or water or something to aid in their survival.

He remembered a class he had taken, where he was warned not to go too near where depleted uranium or D.U. rounds had hit, and now he wondered how many of the destroyed military hardware around him had been hit with it. Those rounds were harder and heavier than lead, and could penetrate any known armor. They were the waste of nuclear fuel rod processing. When they hit, they vaporized into radioactive powder called "DU-dust" by the troops.

He saw no sign of live Iraqis, but the remains of the dead were everywhere. He explored around the blasted vehicles; one was an ambulance. Everything of value had been removed to treat the wounded, except a pair of wooden crutches that had been discarded. One of them was broken. Young One took the other for the pilot, thinking he might find it useful to help support his weight, now that he was starting to come to.

Young One then went back and woke up Mizzi. The colonel was semi-conscious but did not seem to know what was going on. They got him on his feet and began to move. They struggled deeper into the hellish junkyard, half-carrying and half dragging the badly injured pilot. All around them were the hulks of destroyed tanks, armored personnel carriers, infantry fighting vehicles, trucks, and Iraqi jeeps, and everywhere lay the dead.

The bodies of those covered with oil, or who had been burned beyond recognition, resembled the remains of Pompeii, or asphalt statues reaching toward heaven. Other bodies looked as if they were trying to grasp and catch, in their last thoughts, the airplane that had just killed them. Some enemy dead had been vaporized into a chocolate-pudding-colored mass of stuff and rags that had been their uniform. They coated the insides of their tanks and infantry fighting vehicles. Going into one of these to hide was unthinkable. The smell of death hung under the smoke.

Burning tires on one of the water tanks boiled the water in it like a ghastly steam kettle. Mizzi took the plastic water jug and filled it with the steamy stuff. It was full of paint taste from the boiling tanker, but it was water. It was also dissolving the plastic material into their drinking water, giving it a horrible taste, but they would need it desperately.

Because of the noise and the gushing oil, they stayed away from the well heads. That was good because the vicinity around the wells had been heavily landmined by the Iraqis before starting the fires. Now the landmines were under hot, burning oil. Periodically, they would explode in the sizzling stuff.

Ammunition of all sorts, both large and small, exploded as flames wrapped themselves around their casings. Rifle cartridges, machine-gun bullets, mortar shells and tank and artillery rounds exploded in a fantastic fireworks display as the hot petroleum set them off. The most frightening thing of all was a stream of hot oil that was "cooking off" a whole field of antitank mines. Smaller explosions accented their detonations, while the staccato of toe popper mines filled in between. They hunkered down and watched this horrible spectacle from a safe distance, like the grand finale of a fireworks display.

After crawling through the destroyed vehicles, they took shelter behind a blown-up hulk of a T-62 Soviet battle tank. The colonel was moaning and starting to revive, rocking back and forth as if he was dreaming, and occasionally coughing and gagging from the smoke.

Unexploded cluster bombs created another hazard. They were like bunches of large, deadly grapes, each about the size of a softball. They had been set with delayed fuses to deny the enemy access to the area. Periodically, one would explode, scattering the others further. Like giant hand grenades, they would go off here and there in the distance, and sometimes very close. They knew why there were no Iraqis around. No living thing should have been there. It simply was too dangerous.

They continued on, changing direction to escape the flowing oil and smoke clouds. Everywhere the three Americans went, their footprints were marked in the oily, soot-covered sand. The sticky stuff attached itself to their boots much as metal filings do to a magnet. Each step left an unmistakable trail of clean sand behind it. It was like walking through black snow. They would be very easy to follow if an Iraqi patrol came upon their tracks.

With the sand burned black and the sky glowing orange, it evoked powerful images of Halloween. After carrying the pilot as far as they could, Young One finally collapsed under the weight. As the colonel hit the ground, he began to moan, and slowly opened his eyes for the first time since his crash...

Chapter 22

TWO-WAY FIRING RANGE

Lieutenant Ramirez was still trying to find out what had happened to his missing men. There was still no radio contact, and other patrols sent out could not find a trace of them. They must have driven right past where Simms turned off into the sand. The ground was full of Humvee tracks that all looked alike. Another patrol had driven across their tracks without realizing their significance. They thought it was also someone looking for them. Their track was hidden in plain view.

Two enlisted men were walking by. They gave snappy salutes to their lieutenant, which Ramirez returned with the mechanical motion of one lost in thought. Then, he stopped in his tracks as if he had been stungunned when he saw Specialist Fourth Class Walters walk past, going in another direction. It was like seeing a ghost.

"Walters," he exclaimed in joy. "You're all right!" His men were not dead after all. Now he would find out what had happened and give the commander the good news. He had hoped that there was an easy answer for the loss of contact with Franklin and his people, such as a broken radio or communications interference from the oil smoke. Mechanical failure or something must have forced them to return to camp early. But then he saw in Walters' eyes that something was very wrong. He had a guiltier look than usual. He also looked puzzled.

The hung-over soldier didn't know what the lieutenant was talking about. The dehydrating desert air didn't help the malaise he was experiencing. He thought he was in trouble for missing transit that morning.

When asked, "Is everyone else okay? What happened out there?" Walters had no response. He had no clue what had happened to the patrol he was supposed to have been on.

"I don't know, sir."

"What do you mean you don't know? Didn't you go out with them this morning?"

"No, sir."

"Why not, specialist? Your name is on the duty roster for patrol today."

"I know, sir, but I overslept."

"Where is your shoulder patch?" Ramirez shouted angrily

Walters looked at the bare spot on his shoulder where his unit insignia was supposed to be. The patch had been cut off. It had been removed expertly. A few hanging threads were all that remained. Its outline could be clearly seen, as the cloth around it was profoundly sun bleached, while it still bore the color of the original camouflaged cloth.

"I want to hear all about it, troop, and I want to know it now!"

The Mexican-American officer's bronze complexion blanched as he heard Walters' explanation of why he wasn't where he was supposed to be. He closed his eyes and slowly shook his weary head.

"You left the company area and spent the night with a woman? That's AWOL, mister."

Then Ramirez asked the million-dollar question: "If you didn't go on that patrol, then who did?"

"Don't know, sir."

"Your shit is weak, soldier. You are restricted to the company area immediately." He had missed his mission that morning. He'd already heard rumors that the others were missing in action. Walters knew that his ass and the wallet riding on it in the pocket of his britches were both on the line.

"Lieutenant, what did happen to Sergeant Franklin and the others?"

"We don't know, specialist. I am sure the captain will want to speak to you when he gets back from the battalion commander's ass-chewing. Stay in your tent. That's an order."

"Yes, sir."

Finally the officer said, "Don't make me go looking for you, Walters. Your shit's already flaky, troop. If I can't find you, it's going to be flying in the breeze along with the rest of your sorry ass. Do you understand me?"

"Yes, lieutenant," said a frightened voice. Walters had never heard the LT speak with such hostility before. Something big must have been up. With that, Ramirez set out to inform his superiors.

He thought that maybe this was good news, at least partially, because he would have to write only three letters home to loved ones. *But who the hell is missing?* he asked himself. *And what was the significance of the missing shoulder patch?*

><-><->-<

Youssef's company was one of the last left on the Iraqi line. It was they who planted some of the explosives in the oil field. They set off in a convoy of three military trucks, led by a Soviet-made armored vehicle. One of the Iraqi patrols had spotted the Americans' sooty tracks in the sand and informed their leader. Captain Kasim, the revolutionary guard assigned to their platoon, thought the tracks were from infiltrators or spies. Neither Kasim nor his men knew of the helicopter crash or the Humvee accident. They just recognized the boot prints and knew they were of an American make.

They drove their convoy as far as they could when deep sand made it impossible for the wheeled vehicles to proceed. Next, Kasim dispatched a ten-man squad of infantry from the lead vehicle to follow the Americans' tracks. Had the patrol followed the tracks in the other direction, Kasim could have scored big points in Baghdad by capturing a downed American Apache helicopter with all its radios, radars, and special weapons still intact. But they followed the footprints to where they led, oblivious to where they came from, thus missing the prize.

>—✕—✕—

The three Americans had to stay under the smoke for protection from potential Iraqi sharpshooters. An Iraqi rifleman could pop up from anywhere at any minute and blast them. They were behind enemy lines, which had to be crossed before heading southwest, the direction back to coalition lines.

The Americans had to continue through the burning oil fields if they were to escape alive. They found it wasn't always possible to maintain their direction because of detours and directional changes necessary to negotiate their way around the oil pools. Their M-17 gas masks afforded partial protection from the smoke, but could not provide needed oxygen, so they had to avoid the thickest of the smoke to continue breathing.

Behind them, a full squad of dismounted Iraqi infantry was slowly making its way through the wrecked vehicles, following the Americans' telltale footprints and drag marks in the soot-covered sand.

The Americans were resting behind a blasted-out infantry fighting vehicle and catching their breath. Mizzi was trying to give the pilot a drink of water. He coughed at the first swig, spat out the second, and swallowed the third. He had regained full consciousness. Young One explained what had happened to him, while talking as well as he could through his respirator.

Young One "felt" them before he saw them coming through the smoke. An Iraqi patrol must have discovered their tracks. He tapped Mizzi on the shoulder and pointed to the shadowy figures following them. Through the steamy lenses of the gas mask, Mizzi also saw the Iraqi riflemen approaching. The enemy patrol found the pilot's helmet, which had been thoughtlessly left behind when Mizzi placed the gas mask on him. The Iraqi riflemen knew they were stalking a downed aviator, an American colonel.

The Americans were not spotted by their pursuers until they stood to move off, and the Iraqis caught a glimpse of their silhouettes against the burning horizon. Through a break in the smoke, the point man opened up on them with sporadic AK fire.

Although the young Iraqis had fired their guns before, it was only at paper targets, because until that moment, they'd had nothing to shoot at. The coalition planes flew too fast, too high, and shot too much back at them. Now, after a month of bombing and strafing by the air force, they could not contain their enthusiasm at finally having an opportunity to do some killing, and their premature fusillade temporarily saved the Americans. Amid the misdirected and undisciplined gunfire, the Iraqi sergeant tried to contact his superiors, but the coalition jamming interfered with his radio.

Each bullet threw up a tiny puff of black and tan dust as it disappeared into the soot-covered earth around the Americans. Instinctively, Young One and Mizzi fell to the ground and assumed the prone position as they had been taught in basic training. The colonel moaned from being dropped on the sand between them.

Young One worked his way on his belly around the side of a nearby demolished tank and began to fire single shots toward the Iraqis, who ducked for cover. It was difficult to get a bead on the enemy through the steamed eyepiece of his gas mask. Young One's return fire spoiled the Iraqis' plan of a quick kill. Instead of rushing the trio, they were deploying among the wrecked military vehicles and slowly making their way forward in two groups. One group was coming straight on, while the other attempted to flank them on the left.

While lying prostrate on the sand behind the corner of a blasted tank, Young One gave the advancing Iraqis a full twenty-round burst of M-16 automatic fire. Although he had been taught in boot camp to shoot only single shots or three-round bursts to save ammunition, he wasn't in an economical mood just then. They were on one end of the two-way firing range that infantry both crave and dread.

Young One wasn't sure if he hit anything, but he wasn't really trying to. He just wanted to make the Iraqis stop shooting at them. His rounds landed in the sand around the enemy soldiers. They, too, hit the ground. They kept the firefight active with sporadic bursts of automatic and semi-automatic AK fire. Stray rounds ricocheted off the armored hulks and whistled past like angry hornets. Mizzi was so frightened that it was difficult to get a magazine of ammo into the rifle. The soldier's trembling fingers finally managed to do it.

The Americans kept low and crawled away, pulling the pilot behind them, and trying to put a piece of destroyed war machinery between them and their pursuing enemy.

Mizzi thought, *If Walters were here, he'd be shooting at them right now.* Through the fogged chemical protective mask, a dark eye took aim at the Iraqi patrol. They were still a hundred or so meters away but were closing fast. Their silhouettes could be faintly perceived through the gray veil of oil smoke.

Mizzi rose up on one knee and fired several M-16 rounds in semi-automatic mode. This forced the Iraqi riflemen again onto their bellies, and they began firing back, temporarily stalling their advance. Bullets were ricocheting and singing all around the Americans off the thick-skinned tanks and propelled howitzers. Young One responded with another full automatic burst, but he could see that the Iraqis had assumed their continuous assault, this time crawling forward on their bellies as they fired.

Young One screamed, "Use the M-203 grenade launcher." Then he returned fire in three-round bursts as he had been taught in boot camp. His shot discipline was returning. These shots kept the Iraqis' heads down, but they could have easily rushed and overwhelmed the Americans. *Why don't they?* Young One wondered.

Mizzi, who had only rudimentary knowledge of the weapon and its various munitions, wondered the same thing. The bandoleer of ammo had both smoke grenades and high-explosive rounds. The frightened soldier forced a high-explosive round into the chamber of the shotgun-like mechanism. It wasn't a very complicated weapon, about as complex as a single-shot shotgun. Aiming it with the side sights was tricky, however, especially through the eyepieces of the gas mask.

Mizzi took the best aim possible and fired the first grenade at the advancing Iraqis. It exploded with a loud bang, and the grenade launcher gave a quite startling recoil. Its high-explosive projectile overshot its mark and landed behind the enemy soldiers, who were surprised to have a grenade detonate so very near them.

A second group of Iraqis were following the track alongside the burning river of oil. They appeared and disappeared among the destroyed vehicles like shadows in the smoke. Also hidden in the smoke was an abandoned gas truck, still full of its highly combustible liquid. How it had survived without exploding was a mystery. Shrapnel had pierced the upper side of the tank. The gas had leaked slowly to the point of the openings, but it was still two-thirds full. The Iraqis were fanning out in front of it. They were taking up firing positions.

The other group of Iraqi soldiers was stalking around the Americans' flank and were closing in for the kill. Then Young One realized the Iraqis he had been shooting at were just a diversion to keep them busy so the rest of the foot patrol could sneak up on their side.

The grenade landed near the Iraqis, but missed taking out any of the enemy soldiers. Shrapnel from the grenade splattered against the wrecked gasoline truck's thin sheet-metal side. Gasoline poured from the gaping breaches, and rivulets of the flammable liquid ran onto the soot-covered sand. Another grenade was snatched from the bandoleer and jammed into the breech of the weapon.

This was hastily fired at the group of Iraqi infantry attempting to come around them on the left, in an effort to outflank them. It landed right among the advancing Iraqis, but in haste a smoke shell had been grabbed mistakenly. Had it been a high-explosive round, it would have killed or wounded a number of them. It hit near them, but instead of an explosion, a hissing sound and yellow smoke began to spew from it. Young One hollered through his respirator that was difficult to talk through, "You shot a smoke shell—grab a high-explosive round."

Sometimes, good fortune is born from a mistake. When the Iraqis saw the smoke, they thought it was an American chemical warfare grenade and conducted a hasty retreat. They knew they had chemical warfare weapons and figured that the coalition did as well. This pushed them back, giving the Americans a chance to hobble away under its temporary protection. Unsure what to do next, the Iraqis sent a runner back to report to Captain Kasim. This gave the Americans time to crawl farther away.

When the other group of Iraqis saw the thick, yellow smoke they also thought the Americans had discharged chemical warfare agents and likewise pulled back near the gasoline truck, and took up defensive positions. It was then that one of their number noticed they were in a river of gasoline from Mizzi's first shot that hit the fuel tanker, and they performed another hasty retreat. They had just gotten clear when Mizzi's third grenade was fired. It hit the vehicle mid-center with a tremendous bang, followed by a terrific whooshing noise produced by an enormous fireball of expanding vapors that ripped the truck apart in an instant.

The wall of heat and the severe concussion from the explosion frightened the Iraqis, who withdrew to a safe distance. The sergeant in charge decided now it was his duty to report back to his superiors. Given that the radio no longer worked, he felt reasonably sure that this would provide a face-saving justification for retreating from the fiery scene. This decision allowed the Americans, temporarily at least, the opportunity to make their escape.

✂— ✂— ✂

The Iraqi patrol returned to Captain Kasim to say that the Americans had disappeared into the burning oil. They showed him the aviator's helmet. This was a big prize in Kasim's eyes. He read the name "Washington" on the helmet and, with his rudimentary knowledge of English, thought it meant the American capital city, rather than the aviator's last name. *This must be a very important pilot*, Kasim thought, *a crack aviator.*

The soldiers from the foot patrol also informed their captain that the Americans had used chemical weapons. They seemed to be heading in the general direction of the rear of the Iraqi front lines. The Iraqis could not drive through or follow on foot, but they could anticipate their quarry's direction and set up an ambush in the abandoned trench complexes.

Kasim ordered his men to don their chemical protective gear. He had seen firsthand during their eight-year war with Iran how deadly the air itself could become during a chemical attack. No more men were to go near the blasted tanks. It was too dangerous. They would go around the area of wreckage and catch them near the trenches. He would make a trap for the three Americans and wait. Soon, the Iraqi infantry company was back in their vehicles and heading to intercept the enemy infiltrators.

✂— ✂— ✂

In place of the Iraqi riflemen, the Americans were now being pursued by burning petroleum. Like hot lava, it followed their trail, slowly smothering everything in its way. All around them, ammunition was cooking off in the burning hulks. The hot, burning oil was igniting everything in its path. As they rested in a hulk of a smashed self-propelled howitzer, Young One saw something disturbing. It was a chemical-munition round. It looked just like the pictures he had seen in training. How many others may be the same type of shells? That is why the Iraqis did not advance any closer after them. They must have known about the chemical munitions. They knew it was too dangerous to go into the area. Among such dangers, the Americans had unwittingly found the safest place in the battlefield.

Off to their right, the ammunition from a self-propelled artillery piece exploded. A sickly yellow-green smudge issued forth from it and drifted upward to mingle with the oil smoke.

Fortunately for them the wind was blowing a different direction. Colonel Washington was in full command of his wits once again, and knew they had to get out of there immediately. He also felt concern for those unfortunates downwind who would be breathing the stuff. It would be commingled with the masking oil smoke so as to render it undetectable until its lethal effects took hold.

The Iraqi nuclear, biological, and chemical warfare capability consisted of biological agents as well as chemical agents. Each Iraqi battalion had its own decontamination stations. They had many different types of chemical shells. Neither Young One nor Mizzi knew what kind of chemical munition it was. But the shells scattered about, waiting for the burning oil to set them off, clearly had the physical configuration of chemical shells. They had to get out of there immediately. They proceeded in the direction away from the prevailing wind to avoid the deadly chemical cloud. They did not want to breathe the poisonous stuff. It was indeed fortunate that it was winter in the desert, and, through a weird twist of fate or shrewd military planning, this was the only time of year a soldier could wear protective clothing and not die of heat stress.

><del>-><del>-><del>

An air force intel briefing officer was speaking to his superiors via landline.

"We can attempt horizontal photo reconnaissance, sir, with an aircraft positioned low enough on the horizon to look under the oil, but high enough on the horizon to overcome the natural curvature of the earth."

"So you can look sideways under the oil cloud."

"Yes, sir, we think so, but we can't be sure of success."

Just give it your best shot. The mission is authorized."

"Yes, sir, General Meister."

Meister had been given orders to resolve this situation with everything at his disposal. He felt truly apologetic about not employing the air force's more advanced satellite technology, but the decision was not his. It came from higher up than this one-star air force general. He also was quite sure that the aerial surveillance capability at his command would actually help find the helicopters better than the satellites could. It certainly would be quicker.

He would do all he could to bring back the flying soldier. Everything he could do, short of jeopardizing national security, would be done. He called the operations center and ordered overflights of the area with sophisticated aircraft loaded with the most advanced equipment in the world, authorizing the flights in the name of national security. It was the best he could do at the time on short notice. Let the pilots earn their pay.

><del>-><del>-><del>

Upon his command, down-looking, battle-damage surveillance aircraft capable of operating from 5,000 to 60,000 feet in altitude were called in.

They photographed and re-photographed the terrain looking for changes that might indicate movement by the downed pilot.

Trained interpreters peered at the photos, but due to the obscuring smoke, none taken by normal recon aircraft with straight-down or oblique-angle optical equipment were of use. They would have to try something more sophisticated. The general ordered his people to deploy the most advanced ground-search platform they had.

The recipient of the general's directive immediately passed the word. "The commander has given orders to look for a downed helicopter pilot. Activate J-STARS. Mission information will follow once you are airborne."

The Joint Surveillance Target Attack Radar System was a modified 707 jetliner loaded with top-secret aerial-surveillance equipment capable of visualizing objects from as far away as 150 miles, looking from the side, with a variety of remote sensing capabilities. The J-STARS surveillance aircraft could be likened to a ground-searching AWACs, and it was now being deployed to look for the two missing helicopters. Two hours after ordering it to the sky, it was flying over the horizon a hundred miles away from the burning oil field, attempting to peek under the smoke veil that covered the desert's face.

It had on board the perfect tools to find the lost choppers. Along with other intelligence-gathering assets, it had been especially configured to look for Iraqi tanks hidden in the sand. This was the evil eye in the sky that the Iraqis feared. It was essentially a flying metal detector. But although it could see right through the smoke with its metal-detection capability, in the area it was searching, there was too much metal on the ground. Amid the pipes, oil derricks, and war debris, the two missing helicopters and the remains of the Humvee were impossible to distinguish. It was like trying to use a metal detector to find a missing class ring in a factory full of washers.

Other classified aircraft capable of using side-looking airborne radar (SLAR) in the X-band range were also of no avail. Forward-looking infrared radar (FLIR) was likewise useless. There were simply too many hot objects. "Failure to resolve ground target," was the official reason given.

The advanced surveillance aircraft did manage, however, to pick up the emergency transponder locator or homing device from the medical helicopter, but it was a weak signal still faintly transmitting its grounded location in anticipation of rescue. (The Apache's emergency beacon was as dead as the proverbial doornail.) The problem was that anyone with the correct transceiver could also track the signal. The rescue teams had to beat the enemy to the crash site.

The Coalition leaders didn't know if the Iraqis had the electronic capability to detect the signal, but they could not take any chances. Nor did they know where the Apache was down, only that it had been heading for the medibird, and so must be nearby or somewhere along the azimuth vector from his base to the other chopper. They now made the decision to send in attack helicopters, the only aircraft capable of flying low and slow enough. It was starting to look like their last, best hope...

Chapter 23

TEQUILA RUNNERS

The pilot was awake and requested more water. He washed out his mouth with the first gulp and spat out a spoonful of sand. Then he drank deeply from Young One's canteen. He remembered being shot at by the Iraqis, but nothing else. He talked with Young One for a while as they rested. Young One explained how they got acquainted and gave him the crutch; he stood up and tried it out. His right hip was severely injured. Every movement was a painful experience. His head pounded with each heartbeat, and he wanted to lay down and go back to sleep, but they had to get moving or face capture.

The three struggled closer to the fortified Iraqi emplacements. There was still military debris around them, but it was sparser than the mechanical graveyard behind them. The three lost Americans had no idea what might lie ahead. They could see the area had been heavily bombed and appeared deserted. Young One knew that just because the enemy trenches were empty when they first came through, there was no assurance they would still be empty on the way back. But they had to take their chances.

Some sections were full of dead and wounded, and some were empty but stank as bad as the ones filled with death. All were dark, filthy, fetid places reminiscent of World War I newsreel footage. Some Iraqi units had been totally destroyed, others had run off, while still other portions of the Iraqi trenches were either fully manned or held by skeleton crews.

Off to the Americans' left, the burning river of oil kept streaming forward. Slowly, surely, the black ooze was inexorably moving ahead, swallowing and setting flame to everything in its path. They were in danger of being cut off from their only means of escape. They had to keep moving to stay ahead of both the faster-moving Iraqis and the slow-moving oil spill. The dark, rolling smoke added to the dreadful surrealism of the place.

How did Sergeant Franklin get us into this awful situation? Young One asked himself angrily. Then he realized it was not good medicine to curse the dead. They couldn't go back the way they came because it was the first place the Iraqis would probably look. They weren't sure if where they were going was safe either, as it was farther off to the left from the place they had first crossed the line. The limping colonel slowed them down considerably.

Leaving Mizzi and the colonel to rest, Young One cautiously crept forward, using his best desert hunting skills. There did not seem to be any movement or sound other than his own. After about fifteen minutes of reconnoitering, he returned to report that there were no Iraqi soldiers in their immediate vicinity.

> ✳──✳──✳

The Iraqi line in the sand was really a large pile of sand pushed up with bulldozers. At first, it had been eighteen feet high, but the desert wind was slowly leveling it down after months of no ground assault. It was believed that the coalition tanks were soft in their bellies, like the

Americans themselves, and it would be easy to shoot them there as they drove up the sand berm, exposing their vulnerable undersides.

In front of these were minefields and concertina barbed-wire barriers. Also, behind the wall of sand were various field fortifications, such as trenches, concrete-pipe firing positions, and sandbagged, crew-served weapons positions. Further behind these were tank and artillery positions. There were also underground command centers that were dug into the stone, beneath the sand. They were used for ammo dumps, field hospitals, and storage areas. The Iraqi sand castle had been wall-to-wall carpet-bombed and seemed thoroughly deserted.

Young One and Mizzi lowered themselves into a World War I-style slit trench that ran along behind the berm, and then helped pull the colonel in. It was quite painful for him. The trench ran from one triangular sand fort to another. In some places, the Iraqi trench was open to the air, and other portions of it had corrugated metal roofing for concealment and protection from the elements. There were living hovels dug into the sand, which were shored up with corrugated metal of a similar construction as the roofing. Along its length were crew-served weapons revetments. It had been blasted apart from air attack.

The area around it was full of bomb craters, and there were live cluster bomblets scattered about the ground. It was a very eerie feeling being in enemy fortifications and not knowing if there were enemy soldiers around. But they had to take a chance if they were to make it home. The pilot limped along as well as he could supported by his one crutch and Mizzi's sturdy shoulder.

Some sections of the trench were completely empty, and the only reminders of their former occupants were the dried, stained remains of their sweat, tears, blood, and urine. The only living things there that were happy were the flies. The walls and ceilings were covered with them. After months of Iraqi occupation, with its abbreviated sanitation procedures, and weeks of bombings and strafing, huge populations of the devil's pets prospered on human waste, garbage, death, and putrefaction. They had found shelter from the winter winds in the emplacements and decaying flesh, and their life span was extended. It never got cold enough to kill them off, just cool enough to slow them down a bit. War has always been good to the flies. This one was proving to be bountiful.

The Americans were not aware that they were caught in the trench between a classic infantry pincers movement. Soon, the patrol that was tracking them would find their way through the oil flow and get them from behind. The Iraqis were pouring into the long slit trench and continued moving toward them from opposite directions. Any moment, the Americans would be spotted, and gunfire would punctuate their hostile intentions. There was a machine-gun port they could crawl out of, but they would be down range of the enemy in a killing zone. As they ducked into the recessed weapons position, they realized they were trapped. They would soon be wounded, captured, or killed.

There was a large machine gun in the trench that had been hit by a nearby bomb that rendered it useless. Its barrel hung in wounded disgrace from its tripod legs. Young One tried its charging handle, but it was jammed shut. It was scrap metal for sure. It would be no help in their defense. The Iraqis were converging upon their hiding place and were closing in for the kill. In all, sixty Iraqi infantrymen were descending upon their position. The Iraqis weren't sure exactly where the Americans were, so they were sweeping the entire length of the trench complex, while Kasim kept his reserve force watching the rear so the Americans could not double back and elude capture. They would be on them soon.

Young One's heart pounded faster and faster in his chest and resounded in his ears like ancient drumbeats. It was as if he had astral-projected out of the place for a short while. In the eyes and ears of his mind, through memory, Grandfather was retelling him a story he had heard years before as a boy. It was one of many stories he had heard of his ancestors, for remembrance of those who have gone before is very important to any people without a written language.

His great, great uncle was a tequila runner from Mexico during the Great Depression. They would go south across the border into Mexico, buy cheap, pure tequila, and transport it back across the border for sale up north for much higher prices. They would walk for weeks, carrying barrels on burro-back. They would hide in arroyos and dry washes and under scrub brush to avoid being caught by either the Mexicans or the Americans. Young One could hear the old man's story spoken in their ancient language through the ears of his memory as if he were back home with him once again...

>―― ✕ ―― ✕ ――<

"Your mother's, father's, father's brother was leading a train of *burros* out of Mexico toward the border going to Albuquerque. He and his sister's daughter's husband had a Mexican guide helping them to find a safe place to cross the river. Even though this was the time of the rolling pony, there were still many places where they could find no trail in the desert for their round feet. So the Mexican cavalry used horses and were hunting the smugglers the old way. The mounted soldiers found their track and were on their trail, overtaking them on swift horses.

"Not known to them, the American cavalry soldiers were off their horses and were hiding in the rocks across the river, waiting in ambush for the smugglers to try to cross. They were stepping into a trap, but did not know it. This was the most dangerous part of the journey, the river crossing. The tequila smugglers had managed to evade capture until the sun started to sleep. Then, just before dark, they started to move out of the *arroyo* that concealed them and headed to the river crossing. The only noises to be heard were the clicking steps of the twelve burros on the stones and the sloshing of the liquor in the barrels.

"Then something strange happened. The smugglers were anxious for the cloak of darkness to conceal their crossing. The Mexican cavalry wanted to capture or kill the tequila smugglers before they could cross the water that separated one place from another and before the night came. But twilight fell upon them, and darkness slowly followed. The smugglers did not know it at the time, but they were trapped between two enemies. They were also caught in the twilight—that strange time period of transition between light and dark when shadows lengthen. Their shadows could be faintly seen in the red-orange western sky. Its last light disappeared into the star-speckled blackness, as the sun gave its place in the sky to the rising moon. The Mexican cavalry soldiers were using kerosene lanterns to stay on the tracks of the wily smugglers.

"The Mexican soldiers had at last found their track with the lanterns and were on the verge of hunting them down. The *burros* of the smugglers were hot and tired. They needed to get to water soon, or they would die of thirst. It was the start of evening, and the cavalry had to find the smugglers soon, before they crossed to the United States, where they could not follow.

"Their Mexican guide, not wishing to spend long periods of the rest of his life in a south-of-the-border prison, pulled out two pistols and fired at several Mexican cavalrymen who were walking on foot, leading their horses. He shot one but missed the others. The return shots from other

Mexican soldiers killed the guide, and both of our people ducked down into a depression in the earth, while the bullets sailed overhead, as the soldiers kept shooting wildly at where they thought the smugglers were. Other dismounted Mexican cavalrymen heard the shots and were soon shooting in the direction of the smugglers and the pack animals, but they were shooting over their heads, into America.

"They moved down to the river, and the *burros* began to drink. They would not continue moving on. The stubborn animals would not budge even with bullets sailing over their backs. They were so thirsty, and the smugglers knew they could not make noise or they would be caught. Fortunately, the sound of the animals' drinking was drowned by gunfire. Normally, they would have run from the sounds of gunfire, but the pack animals knew instinctively that it was drink or die. What none of them knew was that the American cavalry was waiting for the smugglers on the other side of the river. When they saw the lantern light and gunflashes from across the river, and as the stray bullets going in their direction whizzed past and ricocheted around the rocks they were hiding behind, the Americans thought the tequila runners were shooting at them.

"The American soldiers shot their guns at the Mexican cavalry, who they thought were the smugglers, already across the river. A serious gunfight ensued. Bullets whizzed and whistled over their heads from both directions. While the Mexican and American authorities were shooting it out, each thinking the others were the bad men, the barrels of tequila sloshed across the water at another location a little way up the river. The smugglers snuck away half chuckling and half not daring to make a sound while bullets sailed over their stooped backs. They both promised never to do that again, and they never did. That is the way it was,"

Grandfather used to say at the end of one of his stories.

><——><——><

Just as quickly as the memory came into his mind, it was gone. Young One was once again back in the middle of the Persian Gulf War and was being stalked by hostile enemy patrols. Reality brought him back to the present as a hail of Iraqi bullets buzzed angrily past him. The dust from several close hits peppered the emplacement next to him. Sand poured out of the bullet holes in the sandbags near Young One's head like grains from a draining hourglass. It was a ghastly reminder of how time was running out for them and what a dangerous life situation they were presently in. They could hear other Iraqi soldiers shouting behind them. As they ducked into the recessed weapons position, they realized they were desperately trapped. Coming down the trenches on either side of them were armed Iraqi infantrymen on a deadly mission. The enemy was upon them.

Young One pressed his back against the side of the gun emplacement in order to gain protection from the bullets. He looked out to see if any Iraqi soldiers were coming down the other way. They were. The enemy was closing in fast upon them from both directions. As both Iraqi patrols advanced on their position, Young One had a new idea from the past. He took his rifle, and from the relative safety of the gun emplacement, he held it with extended arms, out into the trench. He first delivered a couple of shots at the group charging from the left, and turned the rifle and fired again at the enemy coming from their right. Shooting the M-16 rifle to the right side got his face burned from the hot brass casings spewing forth rapidly from the ejector port on that side of the weapon. He did not think that he hit anything, but he really stirred up the Iraqi infantrymen.

An old trick worked once again. Each group of Iraqis approaching from different sides thought that the other group was the hostile Americans, and they returned fire. They began to shoot at one another. They literally mowed each other down. Youssef was toward the back of the line on the right side and fell down as several of his former buddies with bullet holes in their bodies fell back on top of him. He was knocked to the ground by the dead that fell upon him. Bullets whizzed over him as he lay buried under the bodies, and then the shooting finally stopped. He thought, *Now I am buried alive with the dead.* Of all the evil things that had happened to poor Youssef, this was the worst.

>+—×—+<

The Americans hunkered down in the sandbagged emplacement along the trench as the Iraqis kept returning fire at each other. Amid the furious firefight, they crawled through the shooting port of the machine gun emplacement in the Iraqi trench. They were soon crawling away from the battle to temporary safety. For a short while, it sounded as if the coalition invasion had already begun. Automatic-weapons fire filled the air, and grenades punctuated the moment, as fellow Iraqi soldiers committed fratricide upon one another, each thinking they were shooting the Americans in this brief but deadly trick.

All the while, the three Americans clawed their way forward, ever mindful of the bullets whizzing around behind them. The pilot assisted by pushing with his crutch and with his good leg. The sounds of automatic and semiautomatic small-arms fire and the shouts and screams of the wounded and dying Iraqis provided sufficient noise suppression to allow them to move unheard, even though they were held back by the pilot.

Instead of moving straight forward, they traveled in a diagonal direction along the back of the sand berm.

Orders were shouted in Arabic to cease fire, but the shooting continued and became sporadic, then stopped altogether. A dozen and a half Iraqis lay dead, and seven had been wounded by each other. Unfortunately, Kasim was not counted in their number.

Meanwhile, the three escapers and evaders continued to crawl away from the Iraqi trenches until the last Iraqi finally ran out of ammo or realized what had happened. The Americans could hear words shouted and screamed in Arabic once the fighting had stopped.

The Iraqis finally realized what had happened. They were aghast when they understood that they had been tricked into shooting each other. They were not likely to fall for that one again. The mood of the surviving Iraqis ranged from shocked embarrassment to bitter outrage. Many of their friends were wounded or dead because of them. These Americans were devils from the entrails of the earth.

"See how they have clouded our minds with evil spells to force us to kill our brothers," they said. Kasim shined a flashlight on the sand and could see the Americans' tracks. They had been there just a minute before.

"These infidels have caused us to shoot our brothers," one of the other surviving Iraqis shouted.

"We must have them," screamed another furious survivor. The moaning wounded were quickly sent to the rear; the dead were left where they fell. The walking wounded were ordered to stay with their squads. The seriously wounded were loaded onto one of the trucks. A medic was all they had. There was no medical evacuation, no doctor or emergency room.

Captain Kasim cared not for the dead or the wounded; his zeal was both religious and political. He believed that each day was a page pre-written in the book of life, and each of us merely reads it. What was written on the pages by the hand of the Almighty was what was read and what was going to happen. He believed in destiny, but not in free will. His concept of life involved reading each line, moment by moment. His problem was that the head librarian was Saddam, and it was he who scripted the tragic comedy.

After exiting through the machine-gun firing port, the three Americans limped to and assumed the prone position behind a sandbagged heavy-weapons emplacement, about twenty-five meters out and fifty meters to the right of where they went through the machine-gun port. The Iraqis were still in shock from the trick that Young One had played on them. The confusion put a handful more of sand back in the hourglass for the Americans. It gave them time to escape. The Iraqis knew the Americans were out there not far away, and Captain Kasim wanted them.

He wanted his revenge, but also, it could mean a trip out of the war zone if he captured American prisoners. He had to have something to show for such a loss of his men. He could report to his superiors that he captured the Americans in a terrific firefight. He just stood there, seething in his anger. The remaining Iraqis cautiously approached the gun port, anxious to get the Americans, but they were gone. Through the dark haze of the oil smoke, they could see the tracks where one of the Americans had been dragged through the sooty sand. They thought, erroneously, that their patrol had wounded or killed one of them.

But when the mind's eye of Kasim saw how Satan had whispered such trickery into the ears of the Americans to perpetrate upon his soldiers, his anger knew no bounds. He was already an evil man; now he was an angry, evil man. He wanted revenge; he wanted to taste the blood of the ones who had made a fool of him. He wanted to stab their hearts and lick the blood off the knife. Evil fantasies of what he would do to them danced in his head, and thoughts did not come clear for him. He was blinded with vengeance and deaf from his own self-righteous thoughts.

Youssef was trembling and frightened half out of his wits. His near-death experience was shared with the remaining soldiers. But no one cared particularly about Youssef. After the firing was over and he was dug out from the bodies on top of him, he was called a coward for not being dead also. He was immediately pressed into the service of moving the wounded to the rear. His mind was at the point of cracking. The dead were left where they fell. Death had fallen all around them for weeks, but it was now on top of him.

He was totally demoralized and depressed by almost having been painted out of the picture by a brush with death. His fellow soldiers had foolishly shot each other. They nearly killed or wounded him as well. Youssef knew for them, the war was lost—for him it was over. And for everyone, it would be over soon, one way or another. These Americans were not his enemy. Kasim was his enemy. It was not the Americans who took him from his family. It was not they who beat him to get more work from him and starved him to skin and bones. He made up his mind to escape if he could before he, too, was killed.

Kasim wanted these Americans, and it was personal. So many of his men were killed and wounded by these demons. He stood in the gun emplacement that a few minutes before had been filled with his enemies. The shifting smoke had temporarily concealed his quarry. The remainder of Kasim's shot-up troops were taking up positions along the trench, waiting for the wind to shift so they could get in some shots at them. By the time the Iraqis got their composure and the smoke cleared enough for them to visually acquire their targets, the Americans were a hundred meters away off to their right. The oil smoke further reduced their firing distance by obscuring their field of vision. The rest of Kasim's riflemen had finally dispersed along the trench, trying to locate the escaping Americans as he had ordered. Their angry eyes searched through the smoky haze for their targets, as their fingers wrapped around anxious triggers.

Youssef and a couple of other privates were sent to the far end of the Iraqi flank. They had to step over dead bodies to get down the trench. Youssef looked at the Americans, silhouetted against a wall of flame from a burning tank trench. He was the only one who saw them. One of the privates with him had lost his eyeglasses in an air raid, and the other had a bandage over one eye from a previous wound. Youssef's sharp eyes saw all. One of the Americans was limping. Kasim wanted him to shoot a wounded man in the back.

Is there no end to this man's evil? Youssef asked himself in his thoughts. They were little more than dark silhouettes on the horizon. One of the other soldiers, who was very angry because one of the victims was his cousin, must have spotted the Americans and fired his AK-47 in their direction on full automatic. Its bullets sprayed wildly around the human targets without hitting any of them. The AK has a notorious sidepull as it kicks back. Unless this is understood and the weapon forcibly held on target, the assault rifle sprays wildly, and only a lucky shot would hit. Kasim ran up behind him and hit the over-zealous rifleman in his helmet with the butt of his pistol. It smarted and rang startlingly loud in the ears, but it didn't break the skin or leave a lump. It was intended more as an attention getter. It worked like a charm.

"Shoot single shot," he ordered to all with authority in his voice and a sneer upon his face.

"You shoot them," he ordered to Youssef and the other privates, who switched to semiautomatic and began to pull triggers. Youssef thought he could have hit the Americans if he had been better trained on the use of his weapon or perhaps if he were lesser trained as a boy in religious belief. He just couldn't shoot a retreating enemy in the back. He shot near them instead. One of his shots into the ground struck something. There was an explosion as a buried landmine was hit with his stray bullet, and it exploded with eardrum-breaking concussion. No one was hit with pieces of it, but the windborne sand was thrown on the fleeing Americans as they struggled ever forward, trying desperately to make it home...

Chapter 24

DESERT STAR

The Lacrosse was the most sophisticated intelligence-gathering satellite that had been made operational during the first Gulf War. Its extraordinary vision was capable of looking through natural fog and clouds, but smoke or sandstorms presented acquisition difficulties. It was hoped, however, that visualization would still be possible through even more advanced, but classified, technological enhancements. In addition to its normal optical capability, it also could beam microwave energy that assisted in resolving objects on the ground when photo-optical means were precluded. But its use had been saved for the ground assault for security reasons, and the general lost precious time cutting through several tough layers of bureaucracy before obtaining authorization for its premature deployment.

Then still more hours were lost before the order was given to actually make corrections in the orbiting satellite, and the nimble fingers of computer programmers began racing over keyboards to move the satellite's orbit, and instructions were beamed to the Lacrosse via a secret communications satellite on the other side of the earth.

Finally, the sophisticated spacecraft was prepared for tactical realignment to conduct a concentrated search, which meant moving the satellite from the low-altitude orbit it had been put into by the space shuttle two years before. (The maneuvering thrusters had enough fuel to adjust the satellite's orbit several times in case its orbit began to decay or in case of attack by enemy killer satellites.)

Far out in space, the satellite's systems lit up, as it was remotely ordered into flight position. The 150-foot wingspan of the solar panels folded back upon themselves as deftly as metal bat wings. Maneuvering rockets ignited, and thrusters began repositioning the satellite into firing position. The kicker rockets then ignited, and the satellite shot into space, to be positioned in geosynchronous orbit 23,000 miles above Earth. There, spinning at the Earth's same speed, it could hover over its target for an indefinite period of time, with only the hand of the Almighty capable of swatting it back to Earth.

Once in high orbit, the maneuvering rockets gently nudged the satellite into the exact position over the Persian Gulf. The solar panel wings unfolded and began storing the energy of the sun itself, while a smaller but more advanced version of the Hubble telescope (designed to account for the distortion of light in the Earth's atmosphere), reached down to survey the surface below.

Finally, as a microbiologist views a drop of pond water, the unblinking eye in the sky focused its God-like gaze on the Kuwaiti war in search of the lost colonel and his enlisted companions.

One of the many secure cellular phones rang, and a subordinate informed his commanding officer that a demonstration was ready. The official entourage was ushered into the photo-interpretation center where

they would get their first look at the future of warfare. The large projection screen looked remarkably like a big-screen TV in a sports bar. Even the techno-officers were impressed. They had heard about the capability for instant viewing, but now they could see it. Warfare had turned a new corner, and it would be hard for any enemy to follow.

The new satellite technology made the intelligence product instantaneous, something that had never happened in military history. But the security concern was that while Iraq lacked its own satellite capability, it might have ground equipment capable of intercepting and decoding the encrypted data. That capability, if it existed, could have doomed the rescue effort. The telescope was adjusted, and its focus was brought closer to earth, visualizing everything from the Persian Gulf to the other side of Kuwait. The whole Kuwaiti side of the Persian Gulf was stained with a waterborne, black ooze running all the way down the coast of Saudi Arabia. Meanwhile, a thick pall of smoke had crept so far inland that Kuwait City could not be seen at all, though the orange specks of the oil fires themselves glimmered like evil stars piercing the inky veil. Yet through the dirty cloud cover it could still be seen how the face of the desert had been scarred by trenches and tank tracks and pock-marked with bomb craters and artillery shell holes.

It was shocking to see the extent of environmental damage the Iraqis had inflicted on Kuwait. The greatest oil spill in world history was plainly visible from the heavens. It was clear that it was Saddam's intent to poison the water intakes of the desalinization plant that provided the drinking water for Saudi Arabia. Then the coalition would dry up and blow away.

Already, the spill was twenty-five times as large as the *Exxon Valdez* disaster and was growing. Hidden in the dark, chocolate-mousse-like stuff were thousands of live, floating sea mines and dead, floating sea life. Under the golden sands of the beaches were thousands of landmines, each awaiting the tread of an unfortunate marine's boot.

In addition to spilling oil into the gulf, the Iraqis had also set the very earth afire. Was it to hide concentrations of troops waiting under it in surprise? Was it a diversionary trick to catch the attention of the coalition while they carried away the booty of war from Kuwait City? Was it to provide an effective smoke screen to prevent satellite and aerial reconnaissance of Saddam's Republican Guard units? Was it to show the world that if he couldn't have the oil they so desperately wanted, that he would save them the trouble of burning it in their automobiles and furnaces? Was it the final revenge upon those thieving Kuwaitis to make them spend exorbitant sums of money to rebuild all the expensive pumping and refinery equipment? Or was it simply the act of a madman?

"Can you get us a closer look?" the general asked the operator.

"Absolutely, sir," replied the female technician.

The eye in the sky blinked and refocused to get a closer look, and individual oil well fires and large pools of burning oil became visible where the smoke was thinner. But even this secret technological marvel could not see the helicopters, nor could it find a glimpse of the lost aviator and his companions. The operator continued to adjust the focus and tried several different technologies in an attempt to pierce the veil of smoke over the face of the desert.

"I'm sorry, general, the smoke is masking our photographic-acquisition ability. Even the satellite's starlight-optical capability is unable to penetrate it, and the microwave transmissions are too scattered."

"Can you try to enlarge the image?"

The operator zoomed in until the visible ground objects were five hundred times their original size, but it was no use. In exasperation, General Baer turned to a nearby orderly.

"Sergeant, please find the senior intel officer on duty and ask him to join me."

"Yes, sir"

A minute later the orderly returned and addressed Baer's back as the general continued to peer at the display.

"Excuse me, sir, Lieutenant Colonel Whitehead is here."

Baer turned. "Colonel, tell me why the most advanced satellite surveillance equipment on the planet can't cut through the smoke and help me find these people we're looking for. We know they've got to be down there."

"Sir, we even tried using the far infrared thermal imagery, which should locate a warm human body, but there are so many hot and smoking objects down there that we are seeing too much to make an accurate determination."

The general gestured toward the burning oil wells and flashes of ignition in the clouds.

"What is that?"

"Autoignition flashes, sir."

"That is the strangest thing I have ever seen. What causes it?"

"Differences in dielectric potential from the various chemicals in the crude oil. It's very similar to lightning. In fact, you might consider it chemical lightning."

"So it's interfering with your acquisition of the targets?"

"Partially, sir, but not completely."

"Explain."

The colonel paused for a second to gather his thoughts. "All objects above absolute zero emit a thermal heat that can be detected from space by the use of far infrared-detection capability. This allows the sensors to differentiate between warm and cold objects on the Earth's surface. In normal situations, we can see people on the ground from their body-heat emissions. However, a human body is next to impossible to locate with so much combustion heat masking their thermal signature, as is presented to us here. Our infrared imaging systems were overloaded looking at pools of burning oil and the blanket of hot smoke giving off a brighter heat signature than a mere warm body."

He pointed to a telemetry image of an infrared scan. It was a blur of bright colors indicating heat sources.

One of the senior officers interrupted. "So it's like trying to see a polar bear in a snowstorm, or a piece of licorice in a coal bin?"

"Yes, in a manner of speaking from a visual perspective. But here, we are trying to visualize the infrared heat portion of the electromagnetic spectrum, not the visible color component." He paused again, then continued.

"Another way to conceive of it is that it's like trying to listen to someone at a rock concert with a hidden microphone. There is simply too much background interference to successfully differentiate the desired signal."

Looks of disappointed understanding slowly appeared on the faces of the senior officers present in the room. This was the best intelligence-gathering capability on Earth, and it was useless in locating the helicopter or its missing pilot.

"To make matters worse, our weather folks predict that conditions are ideal for sandstorm formation. This will further obscure our field of view and curtail aerial reconnaissance of the area of operations."

As he spoke, the intel officer marked the places he was talking about with a laser pointer. The tiny red dot jittered over the board as he continued in a nervous, but technically confident voice.

"In addition to the smoke obscuration, the soot-covered sand and chemically similar smoke overhead make it impossible to discriminate objects on the ground using optical photographic means. There simply is no contrast for the lens to capture. We have several photographs that were taken when the smoke was thin enough for our telemetry to penetrate. But they are negative. The ground is covered with lampblack, and everything simply blends together."

An eerie silence had fallen over the room full of ambitious men, who normally were eager to hear themselves talk, as long as someone superior was listening or someone inferior was obeying.

Finally, the general responded. "How about weather satellites? Can we use them for this purpose?"

"NOAA has systems capable of differentiating thermal energies, but we don't think that they will be of use to us in locating the downed chopper. They were designed to study erupting volcanoes or large forest-fire spread, and they simply can't resolve small targets."

"Are you telling me that all of the technical-intelligence assets we possess cannot pick up a trace of these lost soldiers?"

"I'm afraid not, general, but we still have some other tricks we can try. The satellite can transmit its own invisible microwave energy to illuminate the ground invisibly. The signal hits the ground and is reflected and scattered back. We know the technology can't see through the sandstorms here, but it may be able to see through the smoke," Colonel Whitehead explained as the operator attempted to enhance the images using digital multi-spectral scanner equipment.

"The oil is composed of thousands of different chemicals. Each molecular species in the oil smoke had its own transmission wavelength, and the imagery data we're collecting from the multiple bands of the electromagnetic spectrum just might give us a cleaner picture."

But moments later the operator shook her head.

"I'm sorry, sir, still no luck."

"Sir. Perhaps he's dead," said the colonel hopefully to his general.

"If he's not, he'll wish the hell he was when we find him. When I get hold of that colonel, I'm going to chop the wings off his shoulders myself, whether he's dead or alive."

The other officers in the room exchanged covertly amused glances, knowing what trouble the pilot was in, suspecting that he indeed might better remain missing for his own good.

Another technical-intelligence officer present in the room ventured, "Sir, we've also tried collection assets such as passive electronic surveillance sensors and high-resolution radars that can transmit in real time. We've looked at more than 100,000 pieces of strategic-reconnaissance intelligence in an effort to locate the individual in question. It's as if the desert has swallowed him up."

"Then you had best give it a large enema and make it shit him out!" With that, the general turned and strode out of the room, leaving behind an uneasy silence.

>*-->*-->*<

The three Americans heard the thunderous roar of jet engines overhead, and Colonel Washington speculated that the planes were detouring from other missions to search for them. Some actually flew directly over the survivors, but the thick smoke kept them from being seen. Other aircraft were farther off and could barely be heard as they flew off presumably to resume their attack or reconnaissance sorties against the Iraqis.

Once in a while, the smoke would temporarily thin out to allow the ghostly bottoms of the warplanes to be seen as they roared overhead. The Americans could not know that most of these aircraft were sortieing specifically in search of them, either to help effect their rescue, or to kill them if they had already been captured. But whenever the planes got low enough to make a visual sighting possible, the oily film fouled their windshields forcing them to return to altitude, where they were as blind as was the top-secret satellite technology being deployed in the futile search.

Through the smoke, Washington saw the shadowy forms of helicopters flying off to their left. He asked Young One to help him pull out the emergency radio from his survival vest. The pilot's PRC-112 radio had taken a direct hit when he was shot down when an Iraqi bullet tore through its electronic guts, mere centimeters from Washington's own. He clawed open his shirt near his belly, and saw the long burn mark stretched across the width of his abdomen. The tracer had passed so close that its heat had seared his skin. He had been in shock and was unconscious and didn't feel it as it happened. He could feel it now.

If I had a potbelly, I'd be pushing my guts back in right now, he thought.

Although the survival radio was damaged and unusable, the pilot still had several pin flares that could be used to alert the overhead aircraft. The trouble was, the Iraqis were so close that if he "popped off a flare," they'd surely find them. Their real advantage was to remain unseen and hope that trouble passed by, or the helicopters came back for them.

><-><-><

Down in the war room, another military-intelligence briefing was underway. The photo-intel folks had finally been able to piece together a composite picture of the same place over time. It was the visual product of much human and electronic genius. All of the images that had been taken by over-flying planes were integrated into one computer-enhanced assembly.

"The photo collage had found Colonel Washington's helicopter," proudly announced the general's aide. He showed his superior a grainy, computer-enhanced radar image of the helicopter half-buried in the sand.

Before responding, the general made an effort to conceal his excitement under an outward show of calm command leadership.

"Do you have those coordinates?"

"Yessir. We know where the bird is down."

"Then send in rescue parties to retrieve them dead or alive."

Chapter 25

TO THE RESCUE

A special antenna mast protruded above the top rotors of the recon Black Hawk as it sped low over the desert floor. Onboard was ultra-sensitive equipment to detect the medibird's emergency beacon and side-looking radar to locate enemy tanks and other armored vehicles. Close behind flew four Apache war wasps spread a hundred meters apart to present more difficult targets. Astern of these airships came five more Black Hawks. This comprised the aerial task force dispatched to retrieve the downed crews.

Having switched to night vision in an effort to improve visibility, the pilot of the lead helicopter was picking up the homing beacon from the medibird, despite being half-blinded by the oil film collecting on his windshield and running like black raindrops down the armored glass. Finding that the windshield wipers only smeared the viscous coating, he turned them off and pressed on through the roiling clouds of smoke.

The Apache attack helicopters were likewise blinded, and kept their radars locked on the observation bird that cleared a corridor for them to fly through safely. Back on the lead ship, the windshield had become so dirty that the pilot stuck his head out of the chopper's side window to see ahead. Soon his helmet's face shield too, was oil-streaked, and his efforts to wipe it clean only managed to smear it further.

He borrowed the copilot's helmet, resigned to placing blind faith in his radar image to lead them to the crash site. Suddenly, directly below them, the downed medibird materialized out of the black fog just as the pilot heard the stutter of bullets striking the hull. He jerked his head back in, slammed shut the armored glass window, and immediately ascended. The copilot radioed to the Apaches that they had just come under fire. The lead attack helicopter pilot picked up the heat signature of the machine-gun barrels through the smoke and fired a pair of antipersonnel rockets that instantly silenced the enemy gun.

The lead Apache then circled directly over the medibird and shot off a yellow smoke grenade near the crash site. This guided in the other helicopters. But it could also attract the enemy. The lead Apache remained hovering under the smoke as the other three ascended into the sky to avoid getting more blinding oil soot all over them. They, too, had been blinded by the beeline straight through the hot oil.

The three Black Hawks circled one by one in a descending spiral into the thick oil smoke. They could see where the marker grenade's yellow smoke blended and finally disappeared into the black oil smoke. As soon as the helicopters touched down amid a cloud of sand spew, squads of heavily armed infantry departed from two of them and disappeared into the sand clouds from the rotor wash. The security element quickly and expertly established 360-degree security around the dustoff chopper, while another rescue chopper landed with the forensic team, who went about the task of recovering the dead and searching for wounded.

One of the victims was a female medic. The Iraqis had gotten to them before the rescue team. Judging from the number of boot prints, there were several squads of dismounted infantry that had ransacked the contents. The Americans took pictures of the scene for intelligence purposes with the skill of a crime investigation team.

They also accurately mapped the location so a large recovery helicopter could be brought in to retrieve the remains of the medibird. With expert precision, the recovery portion of the team went about their work. The scene was photographed with both still photography and video tape for later analysis. After they were done, the bodies were bagged and loaded onto another helicopter for the first leg of their journey back home.

A half-hour after finding the medibird, the site was cleaned up. There had been no Iraqi contact, and the area seemed deserted. It did not appear that the Iraqis had done anything more than look for personal souvenirs and remove medical supplies. They came in trucks and went back north, the same way they drove in.

The recovery team then discharged star cluster flares to illuminate the smoke, then radioed the map coordinates. These were marked by the command chopper and radioed back to headquarters, from which a heavy-duty Chinook helicopter would be dispatched to retrieve the medibird's remains.

The scout helicopter then lifted off and flew around the former Iraqi gun site in an ever widening circle until they located the wreckage of Washington's Apache. They were surprised to find only the dead copilot aboard the aircraft. One member of the recovery team took out a specially filtered video camera and took pictures of the footprints around the chopper for intelligence analysis.

There were no Iraqi boot prints around the Apache; only American boots had stepped there. But there was something wrong with one of the sets of boot prints. There were two sets of tracks and what appeared to be the drag marks of the pilot's flying boots. One of the boot prints was from American-issue desert infantry boots; the other was wearing old-style jungle boots, the kind they used in Vietnam. This was all very confusing, but it was not their job to interpret the intel, just to gather it.

One of the security squads from the rescue team following the footprints spotted the wrecked Humvee, as well as Franklin and Simms. A helicopter landed, and the recoverable remains of Franklin and Simms were flown back to their company for burial procedures and notification of next of kin. Another chopper took the copilot back to his unit for the same procedures. Not much of value was left with the Hummer; they retrieved the machine gun and the ammo and what few personal effects were left in the wreckage. The rest of the Hummer's mechanical carcass would be picked up later for scrap.

✄ ✄ ✄

Two hours after the rescue team had completed its duties, the operations chief burst into General Baer's office and announced in a proud but nervous tone, "The rescue party found Colonel Washington's helicopter. It was pretty badly shot up and had crash-landed. The Iraqis had a quad heavy machine gun hidden in the smoke. It chewed the shit out of the Apache. They must have also shot down the DUSTOFF chopper. All aboard the medevac were dead, both the previously wounded passengers and the crew."

The officer directed his superior's attention to the aerial reconnaissance photographic montage.

"General, sir, this is the crash site of the Apache."

Using a laser pointer, he indicated first the downed chopper, then the crash site of the destroyed Humvee, the laser darting like a red firefly to the part of the screen he indicated. Next he moved the pointer to a cluster of vehicle tracks and boot prints outlined against the soot-blackened sand. What looked like a thin tan line on a dirty chalkboard could be seen meandering off in a direction away from the wreckage.

"As you can clearly see, the tracks commence here at the crash site and have their termini here." He pointed to the Iraqi trenches. "Some unknown person, or, actually persons, as one can see by the number of footprints, carried Colonel Washington straight into the Iraqi front-line bunkers. We must assume the worst. An Iraqi patrol has captured him." His red laser pointer shot along the line of entrenched emplacements. There was a hushed silence in the room. The worst had happened. The enemy had Madjack Washington. All the invasion plans needed changing immediately.

The general stood there, not sure what to do. If this important officer had been captured, there would be severe problems for the coalition forces. The only alternative, really, would be to carpet-bomb the area to ensure everything in its path of destruction was removed as a threat.

"How many enemy communications have come in and out of that part of the line?" he inquired after a thoughtful pause. He was answered by one of the other intelligence officers present in the room.

"Counter-intelligence assets have intercepted nothing from that part of the theater, except that strange blip coming into their field radios from Baghdad. It is believed to have been the signal to set the oil wells afire. It came from a converted AM radio transmitter. The fly folks took it out a couple of hours after it went active. There has been only low-power tactical traffic and some cell phone communications. It's mostly battlefield stuff: requests for supplies, for reinforcements, and for medical attention. To the best of our knowledge, and in these matters it is considerable, no messages have been sent into or received from that sector of the front concerning Colonel Washington. Not a sound of this matter has been heard, and we have had our ear to the ground. But we'll keep listening."

And listen they would, with a big ear-trumpet satellite capable of picking up radio, telefax, and both landline as well as cellular telecommunications. It could handle up to 70,000 conversations simultaneously and continuously send its information to another satellite computer that converted the data in it to energy and relayed it to a secure receiving station in Maryland. There other computers combed the messages for key words of military or political importance. Another superspook in the room who was a civilian added, "There has been no word from any of our operatives in Baghdad of an important officer's capture. If they have him, their capital city doesn't know about it."

This was encouraging, as it meant that even if they had managed to torture the pilot and extract his information, they could not send the extracted intelligence to their higher headquarters for action. But it also meant tying up a lot of technical resources that could at that time have been used elsewhere. Nonetheless, at that moment, Madjack Washington was the most important person in the war zone.

"Widen your search area. We really need to find out what happened out there."

The general then turned to the air force commander of the sector. "General Meister."

"Yessir."

"I want a cork put on that area. Nothing in, nothing out."

"Will do, general, sir."

This would mean that any movement of vehicles bringing in interrogation specialists, or any attempt to move the captured pilot to a place of interrogation would be eliminated. If Colonel Washington were in an enemy truck, he would be destroyed with it. His secrets would be kept, one way or another. A new battalion commander to support the ground assault could be found more easily than repairing all the damage Washington could potentially create.

Another officer in the war room interrupted. "General, we're receiving taped video footage of the crash site from the rescue team."

"Patch it through." Moments later, the footage was being viewed in a private premiere performance. The officer continued.

"Sir, this is Colonel Washington's helicopter, as it was found by the downed aviator rescue team. An Iraqi antiaircraft machine gun was sitting on it, waiting for someone to effect rescue. Some serious shooting went on before our team could go in for a look-see. The Apache was all chewed up by heavy machine gun fire, and Colonel Washington was gone. The weapons man was found dead."

"What do you mean, gone?"

"He'd been removed by persons in GI-issue boots, possibly survivors from the Humvee."

"What Humvee?"

"This one, sir," he said, as he handed the general a photo of the remains of the Hummer.

"Well, there's some hope."

"There were two other soldiers on that patrol, but they are unaccounted for," interjected a second major. "There were American boot marks around the aircraft. They may have rescued the pilot."

The general agreed. "He may have had help from the survivors of the patrol."

"The reservists were conducting a limited source operation in the area and had come up missing this morning. They ran over an Iraqi landmine. It appears that two individuals survived the explosion, removed the pilot, and are believed to be operating in the survival, escape, resistance, and evasion mode.

"There were two sets of boot prints in the sand. Also, the remains of two other soldiers, an E-7 named Virgil Franklin and an E-3 named Simms. Another man was a private first class from a New Mexico Reserve unit. The question is: Who was the man who left those strange footprints? One was wearing Nam-style jungle boots, and the other current desert-issue infantry boots."

"Reserve support troops are the only ones in the war zone wearing the old-style footgear," noted one of the officers present, "so one of 'em must have been that PFC from New Mexico."

"Don't know, sir, but if they got Colonel Washington away from the crash, we don't think the Iraqis have caught them yet."

"Why is that?"

"After this many hours, Baghdad would surely be broadcasting that they'd captured a high-ranking American officer. Also, the Iraqi infantry would have stripped the copilot clean of any valuables."

"All his belongings were still with him when his body was found, and there had been no attempt to remove sensitive electronics."

"But if there was no evidence of Iraqi presence after the shoot down, why would our people leave the crash scene? Isn't it SOP to remain as long as possible with the crash to facilitate rescue?"

"Yes, general, sir. That is the standard operating procedure."

"If they were in the vehicle when it ran over the mine, they all probably received considerable concussion force from the blast, causing temporary neurological distress. They probably were not thinking clearly."

"There's also this, sir," he said, showing the general a plastic bag filled with blood-spattered currency. "A large amount of Kuwaiti and U.S. cash was found among the remains of the dead from the patrol."

"Where did it come from? What does this mean?" groaned the general.

"We don't know, general, sir, and I'm afraid there is even more mystery here. The Humvee had been specially armored with British tank plating."

"What?"

"And the final mystery is, why did they leave their assigned patrol area, acting individually? They drove into Kuwait, right through enemy lines."

"What were they up to? I want to know everything about this incident, and I want to know it right away."

"YESSIR!" rang out everyone in the room as the commander exited with his security detail. The investigators would be busy for a while.

><----><----><

Walters knew he had seriously messed up. He just sat there on the edge of his bunk with his face in his hands. He'd "screwed the pooch" for sure with this one. If he only knew that the others were all right, he could feel better. He should have been with them. But if he was with them, he would be in a lot worse position than he was right now. He would get an Article 15 for sure. Maybe even a court-martial.

As he lay back in his bunk feeling sorry for himself, the company clerk came and told him, "Bugaloo to the headshed. The old man and top want to see your ass ASAP."

Walters felt his young life had just about come to an end. But if he could have seen Franklin and Simms in the desert, he'd know what coming to an end really meant. The company clerk escorted him to the commander's bunker. He stayed outside while Walters went inside.

Two military police officers and a military intelligence officer, along with his company and battalion commanders, interrogated him for hours. This was some serious stuff. He was advised of his rights under the Uniform Code of Military Justice, which weren't much, and the third degree began. Walters thought this was a lot of fuss about oversleeping. Something else must be wrong.

What he didn't know was that his platoon sergeant and squad buddy Simms were dead. Neither did he know that Chief Alphabet and some unknown person were escaping and evading at that very moment around the desert in the middle of the greatest oil spill in history with a high ranking officer with classified information. And he had conveniently missed all this. "Why?" was all they wanted to know.

At first they sat incredulous at learning of his nightly escapade. The female medic, the contraband booze, the blackout. They asked the same questions over and over, hoping to catch him in a lie.

"Who was that other person? How much have you been paid? Oh, he didn't pay you. Why not? How much did you pay him to pull your guard duty while you slammed your salami with that medic?"

The investigators found Simms' and an unknown person's fingerprints on the gold clasp. It was possibly an Arab's. Everyone's question was, "Where did it come from?"

"Walters, where did you guys get all that money? Did you have a black-market scheme going on with Simms?"

"No, sir."

"Come on, Walters," Captain Nelson said, "you are constantly up to something."

"What were you up to? Where did your buddy get ahold of large-denomination Kuwaiti dinars?"

"He is not my buddy, and I wasn't up to anything with him."

Walters did not even know what a dinar was. He had never seen one. "I don't know anything about any money. I just wanted to get a piece of ass."

"Were you prostituting any of those females?"

"No, I wouldn't do anything like that."

"In view of your past activities, it is a suspicion," the investigating officer added coldly, "one that we are not inclined to dismiss immediately." Then he quickly snapped. "What's your connection to Simms?"

"There is none; he's a real dick and no one, not even the other blacks, can stand him."

The other officer switched channels on him to inquire, "How much did you pay him not to go on the mission and why? Who is it that took your place?" Walters really didn't know who took the ride in the Hummer. "The guard at the checkpoint reported four soldiers on that patrol. Someone else went on that mission instead of you. Who, and why? We want to know who it was, Walters."

"I don't know who the other guy is."

Finally, they were done questioning. The bewildered spec-four was dismissed. After his departure, the military policeman spoke first. "I don't think he knows who went on the patrol in his place."

The military-intelligence officer responded, "I concur, major." They, too, had been hoping for a simple answer. They hoped that Walters had simply scammed out and paid someone to take his place on the patrol or that someone owed him a favor and went in repayment. But that did not seem to be the case here. They were going to have to get their shovels out and dig deeper.

"We've got Arab nationals on both sides of us. Is it possible that one of their people slipped onto the mission?"

"It's possible, but how would they know Walters wasn't going to be there?" the other asked. "And how could they possibly have known about the helicopter crash? No, there are far too many coincidences at work here."

They both shook their heads slowly in a gesture of mutual misunderstanding.

"We really need to find out who went on that patrol. We need to find out now! This is going to the top."

"It'll take some doing, but I'll put some Saudi intel officers on it."

Every battalion commander in the American sector had all of his or her morning reports checked and double-checked. No one was missing from duty that day. The word was sent up and down the line. The Marines, the Brits, the Syrians, the Egyptians, the Moroccans, and the French Legionnaires all reported no missing personnel. Everyone was present or accounted for. Whoever was on that patrol was still a mystery.

>—✳—>←

They also questioned Walters' date for the evening. Private First Class Lola Harris was escorted into her company commander's tent and interviewed vigorously. She immediately flooded with tears of fear and regret for all the trouble the previous evening's dalliance had created.

It was embarrassing to have the whole world know with whom she slept. But tell she did.

As the investigators spoke to Harris, several MPs were taken by her sergeant to search her belongings. Her bunk area looked like a Munchkin Bar the military policeman thought when he saw the little empty, airline booze bottles next to her teddy bear collection. She had saved them as souvenirs. The teddy bears were reminders of her long-lost innocence, and the bottles of her recent indiscretion. The MPs confiscated them all.

A little later, when confronted with the evidence, she confessed that she and Walters had finished off all of the little bottles between them, with Walters actually guzzling most of the booze. She also admitted that after the "eventual affirmative" was mutually authorized and the "mission" completed, they both collapsed into a state of exhausted oblivion. Other than that, she couldn't tell the MPs anything, except she remembered Walters looking for his helmet and gear in the morning, but they were missing. It was daylight, and he had to drive back to his area without his headgear. He was very upset about that. She said he acted as if he had somewhere to go in a big hurry.

"I don't think he'll go out with me again. I'm afraid that this is the last time I'll ever see him."

The MPs and officers agreed. She would never see him in Saudi Arabia again...

Chapter 26

SNAKE SONG

Mizzi was looking anxiously behind them for signs of enemy movement from within the trenches. They had to move quickly, as the sounds of Iraqis running down the trench could be heard. Then the Iraqis shouted. They knew they had been seen. There was an Iraqi minefield blocking their way. They would have to cross it in order to escape. They could not yet see the Iraqis, but Young One knew they had to do something soon.

The wind shifted and the smoke helped block the view of their silhouettes from the Iraqi riflemen. It was now well past four in the afternoon, but still gloomy as twilight. The canopy of smoke downwind from the well field completely blocked the sun. They looked like mere shadows from fifty meters off. They had to be mindful, however, of not further silhouetting themselves in front of the burning oil trench.

Still, they had to move before sharpshooters could be brought up or a patrol was sent after them. They would have to traverse the minefields while dodging enemy bullets. They could hear shouts in Arabic, followed by bursts of AK-47 and then more automatic-weapons fire, then silence.

Mizzi started to crawl toward them when another hail of small-arms fire raked the sand around them. Mizzi remained behind at the sandbagged weapons embrasure and, from the protection of the sandbags, returned fire with single-shot M-16 shots. That put the heads of the Iraqis down, but not for long. Young One called to Mizzi, "You hold them off. I'll carry the pilot forward." Mizzi responded with another fusillade of rapidly delivered single-shot fire.

The Americans continued crawling slowly to the right until they passed through a blasted opening in the concertina barbed wire. The pilot and Young One started to low-crawl over to a bomb crater, but somehow the Iraqis discerned their shadowy figures through the smoke.

First, one or two enemy soldiers opened up on Mizzi's position. Then, many of Kasim's riflemen fired simultaneously, discharging more than a thousand AK rounds at Mizzi in a few seconds. The sandbags jerked and were shot apart as Mizzi was buried alive under a shower of cascading sand. The frightened soldier wiggled and burrowed into the sand like a crab, while the sandbagged emplacement gradually disintegrated under the stream of bullets.

While Mizzi was catching all the fire, Young One was struggling away with the pilot, still hobbling on his single crutch, traveling at a diagonal angle to the sand berm and the trenches. Though the pilot's crutch sunk into the soft sand each time he leaned on it, causing him excruciating pain, they were making remarkably good time. Reaching a bomb crater, they pitched themselves headlong into it and lay still for a few moments, gasping for breath.

From the relentless staccato of gunfire being directed at their buddy, they momentarily took Mizzi for a goner. Then, they heard the characteristic pop, pop, pop of an M-16 rifle fired on semi-automatic. Mizzi was still alive and returning fire. For a moment there was silence, followed by a full twenty-round continuous burst from Mizzi's weapon after which the soldier got up running and dove headfirst into the bomb crater, landing on top of Young One and knocking the wind out of him. Saying nothing, but extricating himself from under the body of his breathless companion, Young One peeked over the edge of the crater but could see no Iraqis advancing on them. Suddenly, the enemy opened up again toward the spot where Mizzi had just been.

Young One knew this was a good time to get out of the bomb crater. The Americans made their way to the edge of the minefield. They were still hidden by the smoke. Suddenly, the pilot spoke up, "We've had it, men. We are going to have to surrender; we're trapped."

After a moment of awkward silence, Young One said, "No, we cannot surrender. We must go on. I will get us through the minefield." As he spoke, he unzipped his chemical protective coat and slowly unbuttoned his BDU jacket underneath and pulled out his personal medicine bag. It was a homemade goatskin purse, held around his neck with a leather thong. Inside were the many treasures and mementos of honor in his life.

On a deeper level, the things in his medicine bag were spiritual symbols and powerful objects of religious belief, and the object he selected was his snake fetish. There it was, just as he had earned it as a boy.

Technically, such items were considered contraband by the military, but when he had submitted to the mandatory search before getting on the plane to Saudi Arabia, the sergeant conducting it found his medicine bag. After a tense exchange with the non-com over whether the contents constituted "religious paraphernalia" or "mementos from home," he'd been allowed to board with the bag still in his kit.

Once in country, he could have been severely dealt with by the Saudi morals police had they found his medicine bag on him and recognized what it was. Now, it was time to take advantage of the fortunate circumstance that the mystical tokens were still in his possession. He took the green stone carving of a rattlesnake and held it in both hands, then slowly drew two swift inhalations of breath across it into his lungs. Instantly, he felt the snake spirit enter his body, and he knew it would guide him.

As bullets whizzed past him and his companions, Young One's head began to reel; in less than a blink, his mind transcended thousands of miles and many years into his past...

>‑‑×‑‑×‑‑×‑‑<

He was seven years old and was being initiated into the snake clan in his village. The old men sat in a circle around the fire in the mountain cave. It was part natural alcove with an extended chamber carved into the sandstone toward the back. Close inspection of the wall showed where elk and antelope antlers had been used as primitive tools to hew the dark, smoky room into the belly of the red and white sandstone. This had been a place of religious observation for more generations than all present could remember. The smoke and holy soot of countless sacred fires coated the roof of the cavern and its upper walls.

Young One waited with two other boys outside the mouth of the cave, each with an elder male relative as a spirit guide. The two boys were near his age, with one in the same grade and the other a year junior to him in the tribal school. Each of them had their father, but Young One, whose own father was dead, had his father's father to act as a spiritual second.

The three young initiates shivered in the cold desert air. They were dressed in fawn skin thongs to conceal their immature manhood. On their feet they wore soft skin moccasins not unlike bedroom slippers. This was the ceremonial clothing of their ancestors. The older men inside were singing ancient songs to the slow rhythmic beat of three different-sized drums carved from cedar logs and skinned with antelope hide. These were beat with single, leather-headed drumsticks. Each drum had its own "voice," and together they beat the mood of the moment. They began to beat faster and faster, and the songs became louder. Young One thought they almost matched his own rapid, anxious heartbeat, pounding itself out of his bare chest.

Three elders with appropriate traditional ceremonial garb for the occasion came out with three stone bowls, each filled with some unknown plant material. In the first, green leaves had been smashed into a pea-colored pulp. The first elder came to the oldest of the three boys and ceremoniously wiped the material with his fingertips in designs like war paint on his face. The process was repeated with Young One and the other boy. Then, the next elder approached them and used a dried gourd dipper to sprinkle brownish water on their heads, upper bodies, and arms. The elder spoke in an older version of their ancient tongue, handed down from old devotee to young initiate in a language retained only for religious ceremonies.

The third elder took a bowl of dry powder and, with a hollow bone, blew a shot of it into the face of each boy. To Young One, the green paint at first felt cold to the touch, but once upon his skin, it began to feel warm, then burning hot. The dousing of the liquid was cold at first, but it felt even colder as it evaporated into the night air. The dry powder blown into his face through the hollow bone choked him and almost made him gag in revulsion. After this ceremonial anointment, the three elders disappeared back inside, and the sound of their quiet footsteps was lost in the drumbeats.

Each boy was then grasped on his upper arm by his spirit guide and led to separate locations, close enough to each other for protection, but not close enough to hear each other's low voices. His grandfather took him to a rock ledge and began to slowly chant in an ancient language, which he was told was as old as time itself. For hours, Young One listened, repeated, was corrected, and re-repeated the ancient chant. It was the language their ancestors were taught as they came from the darkness of the earth into light.

Only the elders and religious ones knew the words and their meaning. Young One's head began to swim, and the ceremonial mixture ran into his eyes and burned them terribly. He began to spin and felt a twinge of nausea. He could not see through blurred eyes and had a great urge to vomit. This, his grandfather told him, must not happen, or the spirit would be broken. He fought wave after wave of nausea and thought he would swoon. He was learning his first sacred song—the Snake Song. His grandfather explained to him that soon he would intuitively understand the meaning of the strange words in the ancient tongue.

"The snake is our protector and enemy alike. Brother snake has a powerful spirit inside it that must be understood. Unlike other animal spirits which must bite many times to kill, like the bear, the wolf or the coyote, the snake needs to bite only once. For this reason, it is considered the most powerful among the spirits of desert life. Brother snake kills and eats mice, rats, and young rabbits that not only eat the food of our herd animals, but also carry disease. Brother snake has one bad habit, however. He does not like to be surprised or touched, or he will bite you. His spit can be deadly. That is why you must learn the Snake Song. That way, you will never surprise brother snake, nor will he surprise you."

All night long, each of the boys listened, half in and half out of consciousness, to his spirit guide's song. It was the same group of sentences repeated over and over, but each time with a different accent on each syllable. It was a secret language further encoded by its speaker. As the dawn approached, and after many hours of listening and repeating, his grandfather was satisfied that he was ready to try the snake test. It was the time between darkness and light.

Grandfather took him back to the cave, as did the two other spirit guides, who brought their young charges to the mouth of the smoky alcove. Deeper in the cave, where they could not see before, were large ceremonial jars that looked like fancy terracotta flowerpots. A religious elder they had not seen before, with his head and face concealed in a leather ceremonial mask, walked toward them with the largest rattlesnake any of them had ever seen. The elder laid the writhing snake across a wooden chopping block, holding its head in his left hand and its tail in his right, as another elder swiftly chopped the rattle off its tail. The head elder held the snake over his head with outstretched arms. It was more than three feet long. Blood dripped from its amputated tail.

The sight of the large, venomous serpent struggling in pain and anger was frightful to the youthful initiates. This, his grandfather had explained earlier, was necessary because brother snake sometimes talked with his tail, and sometimes did not, before he bit. The tip of the snake's tail was removed to ensure there would be no audible hint of its location, and to anger the snake with pain, so it would surely bite.

To be successful, the Snake Song singer must listen with his heart and not with his ears. One who has completed the Snake Song ceremony is able to "feel" where brother snake is hiding in the tall brush or under rocks. For those trained to understand it, this sort of recognition becomes intuitive. To most outsiders such a feeling is dismissed or suppressed as mere paranoia because it is not a sense that they have been trained to use from youth.

Grandfather also explained to Young One that he would have a leather hood placed over his face because brother snake lived in darkness and could only be seen with the mind, not with the eyes. He was also told that inside one of the nine jars was a stone carving of a snake. In one of the other nine jars would be the infuriated, rattle-less western diamondback ready to bite the intruding hand.

Young One had seen rattlesnake bites before. His mother's sister had been bitten in the leg while picking berries, and although she received prompt medical attention at the Indian Health Service Hospital, she still walked with a limp decades later and still bore the tiny fang marks of the small, immature rattlesnake that nearly took her life. This large snake would certainly kill or cripple any of the three boys for life.

The three young initiates were told to turn around while a ceremonial eyeless mask was drawn over each of their heads. When the old leather hood was placed over Young One's face, he could smell the stink of sweat, dried spit and tears, which had been inside of it for years.

The nine jars had been set up in line. Inside one was success obtained by finding the tiny stone carving. In another, waited certain pain, possibly permanent injury, and the risk of slow, agonizing death. The other seven jars were empty and each boy had three tries to find the snake fetish, or fail the test.

It was time for the snake ceremony to begin. First, it was the older boy's turn. His father brought him forward into the cave, and he was told to sing the song he had been taught the previous evening. Inside the mask, he could hardly breathe, and the smell choked him. He was told to keep singing the song and to find the stone statue of the snake. He tried as well as he could to sing the song of the snake, but his mind was clouded with fear. Although he could say the remembered words, he did not place the accents correctly. Young One strained to hear through his own leather hood, but the pounding drums muffled the sound and he could not make out the sounds the other boy was singing.

As the drummers slowly beat the cadence of the Snake Song, the first snake singer was led over to the jars, and while still singing, he bent down and reached his hand into the earthen vessel. To his disappointment as well as relief, it was empty. His fingers searched hopefully for the object, but it was not there. Two more times he tried, but each time he grasped only air. He was ceremoniously escorted outside the cave and told to practice his Snake Song with his spirit guide and come back next year.

Next, it was the youngest boy's turn. As his father took him forward, his six-year-old body began to tremble uncontrollably with fear. The elders watched disapprovingly as a trickle of warm urine ran down his cold, bare leg. He was promptly pulled outside and beaten with a yucca stem, originally as thick as a broom handle, which had been pounded with stones into a lacerating mass of fibers resembling a horsetail tied to a stick. Young One could hear the words of rebuke mixed with the child's screams of pain and protest outside the cave. Now it was his turn.

He was frightened, but did not want to embarrass his grandfather or to endure the harsh touch of the yucca whip. He felt his grandfather's firm hand grasp his upper arm as he was led forward, his legs wobbly and about to collapse under him. He kept saying the words of the Snake Song over and over in his mind the same way he had been taught it. So great was his love and respect for the old man that his fear of disappointing him was greater than his fear of the snake. Struggling for breath inside the suffocating leather hood, with the rhythmic singsong echoing furiously in his ears, he told himself, *Sing the song as Grandfather has taught you.*

Suddenly, a terrible and wonderful calm came over his him. This was the first time he had been really in touch with his inner self. He thrust out his arm to reach into one of the jars, and felt some impalpable resistance to the movement of his hand, as if the vessel were sealed with an invisible lid.

Without thinking, he withdrew his arm and thrust his hand deep into another of the earthen vessels, next to the one he almost chose first. He felt a small hard object in his grasp. There was a howl of approval from the older men. Young One had found the carved-stone snake fetish on his first attempt. The hood was torn away and warm sweat dripped from his swooning head and flushed face onto his cold, bare shoulders, back, and chest.

"You have found it," the senior elder said triumphantly. This exclamation was punctuated by a loud, rapid pounding on the drums in triumph. Then, there was silence. Young One's heart was still beating as fast as the drums had been. The clean air smelled particularly sweet and his heart was filled with the thrill of pride. Grandfather presented him with a hand-tooled, goat-leather medicine bag. It was large for his small stature, but Grandfather told him that he would grow into it. The bag, Grandfather explained, was to hold his power fetishes when he traveled. As they turned to walk away, one of the other medicine men addressed Young One.

"Why did you hesitate at that first jar?"

"Because the snake was in it," Young One answered. The eyes of the elders flashed with surprise and delight. They remarked among themselves, "He felt the snake. His spirit is strong. He has the power of a mystic warrior." Grandfather was proud beyond speech and also relieved. A snakebite is not a quick or painless death, but if a boy could not survive in the medicine cave, he would never survive alone in the snake-filled desert. The son of his son was becoming a man. The snake was dumped from the jar and its throat skillfully slit to cause it to die. When the snake's thrashing was almost over, the snake fetish was placed in its mouth to catch its spirit.

Over the years, Young One grew into a fine snake feeler, one who could sense the presence of the legless one. On several occasions, he even warned other children of the presence of snakes. Once, an older, mean boy looked for and killed the rattler. Young One had told him where it was hidden. It made Young One angry with himself because he had betrayed brother snake. He only wanted to warn the others to stay away, so as not to be bitten. He learned from his own kind to keep his special knowledge to himself. But that was long ago.

>←—✕—→←

A split second later, the stark reality of the moment brought him back with the speed of awakening from a dream. He screamed through the gunshots to Mizzi, "We should make a break for it. The Iraqis will send out troops to see if they got any of us. I will walk forward. You keep the Iraqis' heads down and step in my footprints." From the protection of the bomb crater, Mizzi opened up with continuous single shots, as Young One led the pilot to the minefield...

Chapter 27

SATAN'S STAIR STEPPER

While the Iraqis were busy shooting at Mizzi, Young One took hold of the pilot and, placing his shoulder under his midsection, lifted him off the ground. He was carrying him as a fireman carries a victim. The pilot protested, but Young One gave him no choice. Under his breath, he kept singing over and over in his mind the old Snake Song he learned in his youth. He must concentrate. He silently hoped the smoke would continue blowing the same way, so the Iraqis couldn't get off a good shot at them. He must sense where the mines were so as not to step on one of them. He did not know if the Snake Song would work on landmines, but he had to try.

They could hear shouting in Arabic and knew the Iraqis would be coming for them soon. They had to get across the minefield. Young One's heart pounded loudly in his chest like an ancient ceremonial drum. What could they do?

He started quietly singing the ancient Snake Song, using the same mystical skill he had used to feel for the snakes to sense where the land-mines were, or rather where they were not. His primitive instincts were working overtime, using intuition in place of conscious thought.

A statistician could measure the odds and calculate the probability of any action. The entire surface of the minefield was not a pressure plate. There were more spaces in a minefield to set the foot than places not to place the foot. There are recorded cases of people walking right through a minefield without knowing it was there. There are other cases of a person's first step hitting a mine. Whether Young One's carefully placed steps were just a "random walk" through statistical probabilities, or if they were guided by some unseen force of nature or the guiding hand of a divine figure, or if were they the result of his primitive "psychic radar," one may never know.

Without knowing it, by Young One carrying the pilot, his weight was greatly increased, as well as his risk of death. Stepping on an anti-personnel mine can kill, but, more often than not, it blows off the leg and genitals, leaving the unfortunate victim with no hope of a career in ballet. Ordinarily, a human being can tread on one of the larger, anti-vehicular landmines that require greater weight to set them off. (The enemy prefers not to waste them on a mere foot soldier.) Here, the extra weight of the pilot produced sufficient pressure to detonate one of the heavier anti-vehicular mines that could literally blow both men to pieces. And since a mixture of mine types was often deployed in the same area, there was lethally explosive potential in every step Young One took.

Young One kept singing softly the ancient song of his peoples' belief as he struggled against the paralyzing fear that any misstep or fall could prove fatal. While he concentrated on the words, his feet stepped correctly. They were finally across the minefield, but their path to escape was blocked by barbed wire. Young One and the pilot fell on the ground next to the concertina wire. There was an opening about thirty meters to the right that a bomb or artillery shell had previously blasted open. They were out in the open, but he could no longer carry the larger pilot. Beyond the wire was a flaming tank trench and, in front of that, a fifteen-foot-high anti-tank sand berm they would have to climb.

They were through the hole in the Iraqi concertina wire by the time the enemy opened up on them. A small sand drift had collected around the blasted wire, and it provided a temporary refuge as bullets spattered the sand around them. The pilot groaned from the hard thump on the ground, and Young One lay panting from physical as well as spiritual exhaustion.

Moments later Mizzi caught up to them by running through the minefield, carefully stepping in Young One's tracks. They were behind the burning oil trench and its smoke and flames provided concealment; but the Iraqis were still taking pot shots at them in the dark, shooting haphazardly in hopes of striking the injured and exhausted Americans. Young One told Mizzi to take the pilot ahead, while he would try to hold them off. Mizzi relieved the panting private first class of his burden and took the injured pilot forward. They hobbled behind the flaming tank trench and began to ascend the sand berm. They were in Satan's sandbox, but no one was playing.

Young One could not see the enemy but could see their muzzle flashes in the darkened sky. It had been ten hours since the chopper crash. Washington's hip and back were wracked in pain. Washington was moaning under the rough treatment of being carried while being shot at, and he could feel the pain from the chopper crash. Though the pilot's crutch was useless as it sunk halfway down in the loose, shifting sands, he helped climb with the one good leg he was still able to move. Supporting him under a shoulder, Mizzi began to ascend the berm. It was only about fifteen feet high, but was composed of loose sand that had been pushed into a long windrow by heavy equipment. It was the last defensive position they would have to negotiate before being clear of the Iraqi front line.

They were making their way toward the berm when the Iraqis opened up again. Bullets sprayed around them. It was frightening seeing the projectiles thump into the sand, and knowing that the little puffs of dust showed how close death was. Washington moaned as they labored up the shifting wall of sand.

With each labored step, the sand collapsed under their feet, and it took ten steps for one foot of upward progress. They were fighting the sand and losing. The faster they tried to step, the more the dry, loose sand flowed over their legs. Mizzi's legs ached from carrying the injured pilot, who was damned near dead weight. It was a mad three-legged race up the sand berm, and they were losing it.

Nearly exhausted from carrying the large officer, Mizzi finally reached the sandy summit and heaved the rifle with the grenade launcher to the other side of the berm; then, with every bit of exertion possible, Mizzi dragged the colonel the last few feet, and rolled over the top to the temporary safety of the other side.

Meanwhile, Young One had been keeping the Iraqis busy from behind the low dune by shooting off intermittent three-round bursts. Braving another burst of Iraqi small-arms fire, Young One jumped to his feet and began sprinting up the berm, his feet churning in the loose sand. He finally made it to the top and dove over to the other side. Although he hadn't been wounded in the Hummer explosion, he had been pretty badly beaten up by it. The tumble down the other side was painful.

Young One caught up to the two and panted until his breath came back. Temporarily protected by the berm, they got the colonel to sit up. Young One pulled his mask off, and they drank some water. The drink revived the pilot. Mizzi retrieved the grenade launcher and shook loose sand out of the barrel. Young One leaned the colonel up against the coalition side of the berm and began manually reloading his detachable box magazines from his spare box of shells. They were almost out of ammo.

Mizzi had only a few rounds left for the M-16 rifle and was out of rifle grenades except for two smoke rounds. There could be no more firefights. Young One knew they had to get going because the Iraqis were not far behind. They were again forced to head into the oil flows for protection.

The pilot had taken a rough tumble over the berm and the rough handling was aggravating his injuries. Had he not been fully conscious, they would never have been able to move him.

※─※─※

Kasim ordered Youssef and two other privates to look for the Americans. The three Iraqis crawled out of the trench and began cautiously tracking their quarry. Youssef carefully went over to the sandbagged position. He thought they got at least one of the Americans, but there was not even a trace of blood to be seen. There was just a pile of sand and the remains of the bags. Expecting to recover an enemy body but finding nothing there, the three Iraqis went back to their enraged captain.

When he heard that the Americans had managed to elude capture, Kasim's eyes flared, and he shouted with frightening authority as he looked at Youssef and two other privates, "Go get them!"

The other soldiers protested that they would have to run through a minefield to see if they hit the Americans.

"Don't you remember where you put the landmines?" he questioned in evil accusation. Although the three men were not even on the front line when their combat engineers placed the minefield down, explaining that fact would only have aggravated the situation.

"Who do you fear most, the minefield or me?" he asked of one of the privates while pointing the pistol in his face. All three men ran back to the concertina wire and were soon on the edge of the minefield. They could see where the Americans had gone through the wire and then cut back behind the burning anti-tank trench.

The three looked with dread at the ground in front of them, and with worse dread at each other. They had to do something quickly, or Kasim would shoot them to make an example for the others. One of the soldiers told Youssef to go off to the left of the sand dune because they could flush the Americans into him to shoot or capture. In truth, the crafty Iraqi thought that the right side of the dune line, the one he had chosen for himself and his buddy, had fewer mines. Also, he intended to walk through the minefield in the American's steps. Mizzi's running had torn up the sand so that it was difficult for the soldier to determine exactly where the original step had been. The darkness and flickering firelight also aided in distorting his visual perception of the footprints.

Youssef obeyed blindly, for his eyes were of no use in the smoke. He started forward, slowly stalking his way through the minefield. Youssef was already half-crazed from recent events, and he was not really thinking well. He stepped cautiously into the edge of the minefield. He did not have the tracks of the Americans to follow. With every footfall, he mumbled a prayer to the Almighty to guide his steps, hoping to prevent the Devil from reaching right up from the ground and dragging him down to Hell!

It happened quickly. Off to his right, there was a loud explosion as one of the other privates stepped on a concealed anti-personnel landmine. Moments later, missing a leg, the man began crawling back toward the emplacement on his hands and knees. Seeing the bloody remains of the leg flying through a puff of exploding sand, the sergeant decided that they couldn't afford to lose any more men to the minefield, or to desertion, or to braving the wrath of Captain Kasim, so he ordered the soldiers back to their positions in the trench.

The other Iraqi private accompanying the minefield victim turned heels and ran back to the dugout trench and tried to get back in. Kasim was screaming at him in Arabic. The young man was pleading for mercy. Whether the explosion had deafened him or if he was in psychological shock, one will never know. He did not heed the words of Captain Kasim, however.

"Please do not send me back there," he pleaded. He was covered with gore from the landmine victim. Kasim shouted another order. A single pistol shot between the terrified youth's eyes ended the debate. Meanwhile, the man with the missing leg kept crawling toward the dugout. Kasim took an automatic rifle from a nearby soldier and emptied a full magazine into the minefield victim. It seemed to the dazed onlookers to be the most compassionate act they had ever seen him perform.

>+--><--+><

In the distance behind them, the three Americans could hear harsh words shouted in Arabic amid scattered firing. Then the shooting stopped, and there was no more sound until a landmine explosion reminded them of the urgency of their situation. The Iraqis were entering the minefield to capture them. A minute or two later, they heard the sharp report of a single pistol shot, followed by automatic weapons fire.

>+--><--+><

Back among the Iraqis, when Youssef saw Kasim shoot the two Iraqi privates, he assumed he would be next. With his heart racing, he sprinted right through the Iraqi minefield, his meager military gear and possessions spilling all over the place from unclasped pouches and opened pockets as he ran.

Whether it was thanks to the sloppy arming of the landmines by ill-trained Iraqis, or to a heavy windblown covering of sand providentially redistributing his weight, or the magnificent hand of the Almighty guiding his footsteps, Youssef traversed the mine field without triggering more detonations or feeling the impact of a bullet in his back. Whatever happened, it was over so quickly that Kasim would have had a hard time getting a shot at him. In fact, Kasim wasn't going to shoot him. Seeing how blindly the young infantryman had obeyed a potentially fatal order was a good demonstration to the other soldiers of how important an iron fist can be in combat. Kasim thought that he would reward that private if he lived.

Youssef kept running right up to the sand berm, jumped over it, and rolled down the other side. The Americans were off to his right. Once safely on the other side of the berm, he kneeled on one knee to catch his breath. Youssef thought, *If I can capture the Americans, I will be a hero.* Maybe he could even find his family again. But then reality began to sink back into his young brain. Kasim would surely claim the prize for his own. There would be no mention of him. Without a doubt, Kasim would torture the Americans in a worse way than he did his own men.

Not sure what to do next, Youssef sat down on the side of the sand berm hidden from the other Iraqis and waited. His heartbeat, pounding from the dual stresses of physical exertion and psychological fear, gradually began to slow back to normal. His lungs stopped heaving so hard in his chest as he caught his breath. He was so glad to still be alive. He closed his eyes and began to pray both in thanks and in supplication to Allah for help.

"What should I do?" he asked with the voice of his soul, "I do not want to go back there." His answer came quickly. He opened his eyes, and through the thick smoke saw three figures in front of him, moving toward him: two Americans carrying a third wounded one. They were laboring so hard that they did not notice him until they were almost on top of him. They were wearing their chemical protective gear and were not paying attention. Their weapons were hanging from their straps as they helped their wounded companion along.

Youssef was on his feet in an instant. He took the safety off the old rusty rifle and took aim. He could have killed all three right then. The Americans kept struggling forward with their burden, oblivious to the presence of the Iraqi soldier with a fully loaded automatic weapon aimed directly at them. The pilot had further injured his hip rolling down the sand berm. Young One and Mizzi didn't notice Youssef until they practically walked into him. Had they acted differently, they could have been shot. The pilot looked up and saw what was happening. He simply stated in labored breath through his gas mask, "This is it, men."

The Americans stopped and stood there staring at their Iraqi captor as the adolescent Bedouin stared back with fright at the sight of the oil-covered demons. In their protective masks with their bulging, plastic eyepieces, they looked like monsters from a science-fiction movie.

The pilot slowly pulled up his oil-covered gas mask and revealed his face. Youssef took off his own gas mask and looked at the pilot and was even more amazed. He had never seen a black man before. He thought the pilot was badly burned because he was as black as some of the dead, burned soldiers lying about the battlefield. While keeping aim at the Americans by holding the rifle by the stock handle, he walked right up to the pilot and rubbed his left hand over the colonel's face and looked at it. The black color didn't rub off.

He smelled his hand, and it did not have a burned aroma. Then he knew. This was a black one. His people had long told tales around the campfires of the unbelievable exploits of black Arabs from North Africa. They were the legendary warriors and carriers of the sacred word to the people of that part of the world. Youssef thought he would never see such man in his lifetime, yet one stood before him.

He dropped his rifle from the aiming position, placed the selector switch on safety and slung it over his back by its carrying strap. He said in Arabic, "I will help you. In return, you must take me from this place if you are able to do so." Young One and Colonel Washington could not speak Arabic, and only the silent Mizzi understood him. Youssef knew that this was his chance to escape. If he took the Americans back to Kasim, the chance would be unlikely to come again.

The Americans were not sure what to make of their new acquaintance. He could have killed them outright or held them captive. Instead, he was offering to assist their escape. What was he up to? Unknown to them, this was the second time he could have killed them. These were not his enemies, even though his leaders said they were. He was stolen from his family and left to die by people to whom he held no allegiance. He was not an Iraqi citizen and should not have been there. He felt he should be at home, wherever that was at the moment. He just knew it was not there.

They worked their way around the burning oil flows, Youssef helping the pilot keep moving by supporting him under one shoulder. Young One supported his other shoulder, as Mizzi walked ahead and keeping lookout all around them. They were approaching a sand dune-dotted portion of the desert, and the pall of smoke that had done so much to help conceal them from Iraqi sharpshooters was beginning to thin...

Chapter 28

CRAWLING THE
BURNING SANDS

Kasim sent out a foot patrol to track and report the whereabouts of the Americans. Instead of carefully following the foot tracks that Youssef had made in the minefield, they probed for mines, and it slowed them down, allowing the Americans a little more precious time to escape. The Iraqis finally made it across the minefield without mishap and crawled up the top of the sand berm, searching the horizon for a sign of the Americans or their missing scout, Youssef. But they were not to be seen through the veil of smoke. There was no sign of blood in the sand to indicate that any of the Americans had been shot. Kasim would not let his soldiers go farther. He was ever vigilant against desertion, and still held hope that Youssef would return and report the whereabouts of the American dogs.

Instead, Captain Kasim called his sniper team to the top of the berm. The three men took up offensive positions atop the backside of the crest, which afforded them a commanding view had the smoke not shortened their range of fire. The team consisted of a sharpshooter with a powerful Soviet Dragunov sniper rifle, a spotter and a security guard to protect their backs while they were looking forward. The spotter peered through binoculars, but they were hardly better than the unaided eye at piercing the smoke. The targets drifted in and out of view of the powerful lenses. Nonetheless, after scanning the area, he thought he saw some movement.

He waited a minute and then whispered to the sniper, "There are two, no three, possibly four of them out there. It is difficult to tell with the shifting smoke."

The shifting, billowing oil smoke was difficult for the shooter to contend with. Besides, he was not a real sniper; Kasim had given him the rifle when the real sniper was killed in an air attack a week before. His targets would appear and disappear into clouds of smoke or behind dunes. For a moment, he had the chance for a good shot at them and was about to take it, but the blinding smoke again shifted and cloaked his targets from view. The targets were like ghosts or mirages to the Iraqis' eyes.

✖ ✖ ✖

The four new companions were resting behind a low dune that provided cover and concealment from enemy fire. After swallowing several mouthfuls of plastic-tasting water from Young One's canteen, the pilot unzipped one of his pockets and took out his blood chit. This was a small rayon American flag with an inscription in Arabic that identified the bearer as a member of the United States military and promised a reward for assisting that person back to U.S. control. In Arabic, it read, "I am an American. I do not speak your language. Misfortune forces me to seek your assistance in obtaining food, water, shelter, and protection. Please take me to someone who will provide for my safety and see that I am returned to my people. I will do my best to see that no harm comes to you. In return, my government will reward you with 100,000 U.S. dollars."

362

Down in the right hand corner was a distinctive serial number whereby it was registered at the colonel's headquarters. It would be used to verify authenticity. Next to this was a place for the bearer to affix his or her payroll signature with the indelible marker. The pilot took the pen, signed his "John Hancock," and handed it to Youssef. Youssef knew what the American flag was, but could not read the words in colloquial Arabic. He could only read the Koranic Arabic, and that with limited ability. Alas, he had been home schooled without a permanent home. The words may just as well have been Chinese.

Youssef handed the flag back to the pilot because he thought that taking it would make him a coalition soldier. He just wanted to find his grieving family and be with them. He was explaining this to the pilot in Arabic, but Washington did not understand. The only one who knew both Arabic and English was the mysterious Mizzi, who remained silent, but was intently listening. Also what they did not know was that the enemy sniper was waiting for one of them to show himself for just a moment.

Combat fliers also carry a pointee-talkee aid to communicate with indigenous persons. It is a book with common phrases in English and the same thing written in the native language. The pilot next produced this item from his pocket, but Youssef was not able to read it, either.

The colonel decided that Youssef did not understand and that there was no point to continuing. He folded up the blood chit and placed it back into a zipped pocket of his flight suit. Youssef kept the marking pen as a souvenir. With their impromptu conference concluded, they left the comparative safety of their sand dune and continued on their journey.

>*—*>*—*>*—*<

"There they are," whispered the spotter as he pointed out the approximate location of the targets to the shooter.

The sniper scanned the area where he had pointed. "Ah, yes, there is one of them," he replied softly, as the spotter continued searching the area near where he saw the first American. The smoke shifted again, and the targets disappeared into it.

The sniper then saw his chance to get a round off at the magnified military mirages in his scope. While a bloodshot eye peered through the rifle's scope, a greasy finger pulled the trigger. The heavy millimeter Soviet round exploded in the chamber, and a millisecond later the projectile slammed into Mizzi's rifle, shattering it and ripping it from the arms of its holder. It was broken in half and flew onto the ground in a useless condition. The force of the hit knocked Mizzi to the ground. Young One also instinctively hit the ground, taking the injured pilot with him. Youssef looked confused for a moment and then he, too, fell to the ground.

A deafening echo reverberated in the ears of the sniper. He muttered a curse in Arabic.

"I think I missed him," he said to the spotter.

"He went down like he was hit," his colleague replied.

His spotter was again scanning the horizon with large binoculars for the next shot, but his prey were hunkered down. The spotter was talking to the shooter in soft Arabic, half rebuking him for missing, half coaching him in preparation for the next shot. The sniper rubbed his right eye to bring tears to it to clear the fine sand from his vision, and he twisted the scope to focus it for the next shot.

Their quarry were about three hundred meters away, protected by smoke and the low profile they were presenting on the horizon. They began to low-crawl on their stomachs, dragging the injured pilot behind them, at which point the sniper managed to recover them in his sights. Every time they raised their heads or butts, a bullet tried to find them. Forced to crawl back into the thick oil smoke they huddled together on the ground, afraid to move, but knowing they could not stay there—an Iraqi patrol was sure to be sent after them.

It was getting darker, and the burning oil provided the only light. The heat made the air on the horizon shimmer, as a highway appears in the distance on a hot day. The enemy had again vanished from view, and both the sniper and his spotter realized that this was becoming an increasingly difficult kill.

※—※—※

Amid the rivers and pools of burning oil was a high spot in the sand that the escapees needed to cross. The problem was that it was covered with snakes that had been driven from their holes by the hot oil and were in no humor to surrender ownership. These were Arabian saw-scaled vipers and false-horned vipers, two very poisonous reptilian species. While less than two feet long, they had large fangs filled with very potent venom reported to be three times as lethal as a cobra's. Being small and sand-colored made these aggressive snakes still more dangerous, as it would be easy to step or crawl over one in its concealment. Moreover, necessity had forced the writhing reptiles together on the patch of high ground, and they were in an especially nasty mood.

Finding a long, shallow, trench-like depression about eighteen inches deep running alongside the high spot, the Americans began inching forward on their bellies, with the hot, flowing oil slowly following them.

Young One reverently removed his horned toad fetish from his medicine bag. He had carried the spirit of the toad in it for years, and now it would give him the strength to lie flat and crawl forward unseen by his enemies. He held the fetish between his two hands and drew two long breaths into his lungs. The spirit was now in Young One. His head felt dizzy, and his vision blurred. Then he felt better, and softly sang a song of thanks.

The young Indian resumed crawling, pulling the pilot, singing his old songs. Mizzi, following behind, was puzzled. The pilot had relapsed into semi-consciousness but was still alive.

Off to their left, the burning oil spill was inching inexorably toward them. They had to keep moving through the narrow gully, but the sticky oil beneath them was clutching at their prone bodies like liquid flypaper. Mizzi kept struggling forward, pulling the pilot along and keeping low for fear of a sniper bullet. The oil stuck to everything, and sand stuck to the oil. Youssef followed along, keeping a low profile to remain out of sight of the sniper.

Unable to change positions in the cramped defilade, the four escapees had to stop for frequent rests, because dragging the colonel along was so fatiguing to Mizzi. Meanwhile, just above them and on both sides, angry snakes twisted and contorted with serpentine agility and began striking at each other, while directly in their path, spiders and large scorpions also sought refuge from the black flood. Though the petroleum they were moving through was cool enough to be passable, it soaked right through their chemical protective suits and uniforms, fouling their skin. At any moment, it could burst into flames. Their only consolation was the knowledge that they could not be hit as long as they stayed in the depression.

But a large-caliber bullet was already in the sniper's chamber awaiting the next shot at them.

The four were keeping their heads and butts down while crawling along, with Washington holding on to Mizzi's web belt, when it happened. One of the snakes off to the left of the low-crawling soldier saw the bulbous eye of the gas mask and struck at it, quickly and violently. Its fangs hit the plastic eyepiece but did not pierce it. Two streams of straw-colored venom ran down the left lens. If the strike had hit an inch or two away in any direction, Mizzi would have been bitten in the face, and at the very least, the stab from the venom-filled fangs would have brought hours to days of agony, as the poison worked its way to the heart. The chemical protective suit was no armor against the deadly kiss of a venomous serpent.

Mizzi scrambled away, abandoning the others and almost urinated out of fright. The colonel lost his grip and was left alone. A quarter of a mile away, noticing the sudden movement, the Iraqi spotter directed the sniper to fire off a round that slammed into the sand close enough to its target to make the panic-stricken specialist spring up and run away in sheer terror as another sniper bullet was expected.

Young One and Youssef pulled and pushed on the injured colonel to get his body through the oil. He was on his side and assisted by pushing himself forward with his good leg. They just kept crawling ahead, until the snakes were behind them. There were no more sniper shots because they were again concealed by thick smoke.

The colonel was in temporary shock. He did not like snakes, and had been praying that he would not get bitten. Once he got the pilot to a safe place, Young One spotted Mizzi huddled behind a dune a dozen yards away, and dashed over to join the terrified soldier. Having seen the snake strike, he had feared that the fangs had pierced the lens of the gas mask and was relieved to find that although badly shaken, his buddy was unhurt.

Deeply embarrassed, and feeling the need to attend to a body function, Mizzi crawled to a discrete distance from the others and, still concealed from the sniper's view, squatted in the sand. After Mizzi got up and moved away, Young One, who unbeknownst to Mizzi had observed these actions, noticed the soldier had made no move to cover up his body waste. This breach of field sanitation would give trackers positive indication that they had passed this way, and he decided that for the safety of all, he should rebuke the soldier for his carelessness. But first, he needed to make sure. Scrambling over to the area, he stopped in stunned disbelief, staring for a moment at the wet spot in the sand.

"You're a woman!" he exclaimed.

Mizzi knew it was up for her. She took off her chemical protective hood and gas mask to reveal a woman in her mid- to late-twenties. She clearly had Arab blood. She smiled sheepishly, realizing she was in a doubly bad spot. Youssef crawled up with the colonel to the protection of the dune.

When informed of the situation, Colonel Washington was likewise astonished. He had no idea that Mizzi was female. She had pulled her weight like any man he had ever seen. Youssef's olive complexion paled, and his eyes were swollen with disbelief to the size of hard-boiled eggs with the revelation of Mizzi's gender. Some of the propaganda with which he had been brainwashed was a notion that the Americans had special female troops, who because of Muslim men's supposed special reverence to women, would not be shot by the Arabs. The women could walk up to a man, stab him in the guts, and then amputate his manhood. He would keep a special eye on this one.

Recovering from the shock of the disclosure, the colonel remembered that as the senior officer he was technically in charge. He asked Mizzi how she had gotten there and for what reason. She explained that she was from the medical company crewing the emergency field hospital in their sector.

"Walters went out with a medic in my company, and they got drunk on contraband liquor. After they passed out, I knew what I was going to do. I felt women should not be denied the opportunity to serve their country in combat, sir. I was going to change things." Young One explained to the colonel who Walters was.

She revealed that she knew Walters' unit, where to go, and what he was supposed to do. She saw her opportunity and took it. She had promised to wake up her old friend's new friend in time to go on his mission. She further explained how she had carefully cut off Walters' shoulder patch and glued it to the shoulder of her own uniform. She had just wanted to see some action, to see what war was like. Now she did not want to see any more. Young One and the colonel listened with anxious concern to her narrative.

Mizzi had another surprise for everyone, especially Youssef. She abruptly began speaking to him in Arabic. The dialect she spoke sounded different to Youssef, but not impossible for him to understand, and he was shocked to hear it from the mouth of an infidel woman.

Then the benefits of this revelation struck him: She could become their translator. Through her, Youssef could speak to the others. He answered many unanswered questions. She explained the missing pieces to Youssef about the deal they had worked out with the blood chit. Now he understood. He was more frightened than ever. Now he would be tortured and shot as a spy if caught. But it was his only chance to escape and find his way back to his family.

When pressed on how she had come to understand Arabic, Mizzi explained that her grandparents were Lebanese Christians, and Arabic was the language of that lost land. She had spent several years there as a child because her father was an American importer-exporter who had married a Lebanese woman. After the fall of the most culturally advanced country in the Middle East to various warring factions in the early 1980s, they went back to the states, taking the grandparents with them. They fortunately did this before one of the various Palestinian militias could murder them in the name of religious expression.

Her grandparents could not speak English, and young Mizzi could communicate to them only in Lebanese Arabic. Although she couldn't read or write the backward written Arabic script, she could speak and understand colloquial Arabic quite well. This was how she knew what Youssef was saying.

Together, in a safe spot in the sand, they worked out the details. They all retained their uniforms and arms. They would work together for the common good. Whichever army they came upon, they would pretend to be each other's prisoner. If the Iraqis found them, to keep them from being shot outright, Youssef would act as if he had captured the Americans. If they came upon coalition forces, they would hand him over to the proper authorities. Once understood by all with the help of Mizzi's translation, the agreement was concluded with handshakes and smiles.

All of a sudden, their conversation was brought to an abrupt halt. Kasim ordered his two remaining machine guns be brought up to the berm, and ordered his gunners to open up blindly into the concealing smoke. For almost a minute, they strafed the ground with hundreds of rounds blindly in hopes of hitting an uncovered target. Green tracer bullets streaked by in a deadly fire stream. Their sand dune protected them from the stray rounds as they waited out the storm of lead.

After the shooting stopped, the pilot spoke up. "We'd better get going. The Iraqis will probably send out a foot patrol to see if they hit anything. We should head into the smoke. It's our only chance." With that said, they again moved deeper into the oil flows that provided the only refuge...

>⋙—⋙—⋙

Back on the coalition side of the line, it got dark early in the company area. The oil smoke had migrated over their position and brought early night with it. Toward evening, the remains of Franklin and Simms were brought into the company area. Back at Young One's unit, Captain Nelson was apprised of the situation and was told to have a red smoke grenade lit off, so the chopper could land close to the company area to complete the grim task. With the bodies delivered and signed for, the Black Hawk was off in a blinding cloud of dust. Its noise and the sight of it were soon lost over the horizon.

There had been no news of the others. They were presumed missing in action. The company first sergeant took Walters out to see the remains. "Take a good look. Your buddies are dead because of you." After seeing what was left of Simms, Walters turned away and vomited. *But who the hell made the other set of boot prints?* thought Ramirez, who had had his ass well chewed by higher command. Now he must find out what had happened. There was no word of his other missing soldier. Something was very wrong. *What had happened out there? How had this happened? Who was this other person?* A second roll was called all along the line. A female spec-four medic named Nirada Mizzi had disappeared. She was the tent mate of Walters' date the previous night and was nowhere to be found.

If the missing medic had been with a combat unit, it was a breach of U.S. Army policy, which was plain and straight forward: No women in combat, period. Mizzi had been missed in the first count because she worked the night shift. She had not shown up for her duty. What was her angle on this?

><—><—><—

As the four recently introduced colleagues trudged along amid the devastation and destruction, in the distance they heard a buzzing sound under the oil fog. It was a Marine Corps unmanned reconnaissance vehicle. It was really a large remote-controlled airplane with multiple cameras and radars. The UMRV was a strange-looking aircraft, with a wingspan of seventeen feet but only fourteen feet long. It was powered by a twenty-six-horsepower snowmobile engine, could fly for five hours, and had a range of a hundred miles. It was equipped with forward-looking infrared radar, real-time television, and remotely transmitted optical photography. As it flew low under the oil smoke, it continuously sent back real-time pictures of what it saw.

What the Americans did not know was that the UMRV, normally used for target acquisition and damage assessment in areas deemed too hostile for manned flight was part of the support the sister services were providing to look for the pilot. It was flown by a marine corporal seated in a military trailer miles away. A joystick and electronic box sent information to steer and guide it, while a computer tracked its exact location, normally to send information to shipboard artillery, but in case of malfunction, so it could be retrieved. Each cost a million dollars, with its cameras and classified transmitting equipment.

After passing over the Americans' heads, the UMRV flew back toward Captain Kasim and his troops at the sand berm, who saw it buzzing along in a straight line, low, and realized it was vulnerable to small-arms fire. "Shoot it down," Kasim shouted, and in response his men threw up a wall of AK fire in the path of the uncrewed aircraft that quickly became full of holes like a piece of flying Swiss cheese. Whining and sputtering as it fell, the UMRV dropped over the horizon and vanished in a puff of dirty sand, with only a dull thud marking its passing.

The Iraqis were jubilant, thinking they had shot down a cruise missile on its way to Baghdad. Even Captain Kasim seemed pleased. This was the first triumph he and his men had achieved, and he decided it was worth suspending the pursuit of the Americans in order to seek out physical proof of his victory.

At first, Young One and Mizzi hadn't known what the aircraft was, until the colonel panted between painful breaths, "It was a drone. Operated by remote control, like a radio-controlled model airplane. It's filled with cameras and radar transmitters."

"Maybe they're just trying to see what the Iraqis are up to under the smoke screen, or maybe they're looking for us."

This gave them some hope of rescue as well as a chance to crawl farther away toward coalition lines while their enemy, moments before in hot pursuit, was now off in the opposite direction, going after the "cruise missile."

><-><-><

When the screen went blank with electronic static, the marine corporal back at the uncrewed aircraft control trailer adjusted and twisted the control knobs, but the picture was gone. Presumably, the Iraqis had gotten the aircraft, but there was no way to confirm that it had been shot down. It just stopped sending back intel, and the worst had to be assumed. The corporal reported the incident to his gunnery sergeant, and made the mistake of adding a comment on the loss it represented in terms of taxpayer dollars.

"What the fuck are you, a marine or an accountant?" the gunny responded, clearly expecting no answer. The corporal, who until relatively recently had lived in a peacetime world where some supply sergeant counted every sheet of toilet paper, said nothing. The important thing was that live pictures had been received before the drone met its demise. The electronically transmitted, monochromatic pictures taken by the flying camera were being processed and would soon be on their way to headquarters.

Following instructions in the standard operating procedures manual, the two non-coms armed the self-destruct explosive device in the drone, which could be detonated from afar by radio signal, to prevent valuable intelligence equipment from falling into unfriendly hands.

Moments later, as Kasim's troops were almost upon it, the drone exploded into bits in response to the secret coded radio message to destroy itself. It was converted to scrap with a deafening bang and a shower of smoking sand. This was followed instantaneously by a secondary incendiary explosion just to make sure nothing was left. Although the blast was strong enough to have taken out a couple of the approaching Iraqis if they had been a little nearer, it only threw sand in their frightened faces. Now Kasim's thoughts turned to the fleeing Americans. By wasting time chasing after what he thought to be a valuable war souvenir, he had allowed the Americans to widen their lead.

No matter, he thought to himself, *they cannot evade me much longer.* After ordering his troops aboard the trucks, he took command of the armored vehicle. He would move out ahead and angle off to the side, he decided, to get ahead of his fleeing prey. Meanwhile the force coming up from behind would flush the Americans into his waiting grasp. Though the sniper had eventually failed, Kasim had reason to hope that the sustained machine gun fire had wounded or killed at least one of them. If he could spot a blood trail, take a prisoner, or even return to his superiors with a dead body, the entire unit might be rewarded with a transfer to the rear echelon. He was starting to feel good again...

Chapter 29

THE PETROLEUM POOL

The oil flowing over the sand was like an asphalt highway melting into a flowing bubbling stream of tar, blocking the Americans' way. Yet, the oozing oil had also flowed over their tracks and concealed their hiding place, and they knew they had to stay near it to avoid detection and capture. They also needed the light of the burning oil by which to travel. Still, though they did not yet realize it, they had inadvertently trapped themselves.

As they skirted the oil flows and cut between two petroleum pools, the escapees came upon an old dirt road that had not been used in some time, probably left from when oil exploration had occurred there years before. They knew it was dangerous to walk on the road, because the Iraqis could drive up on them and because it might be landmined. However, they had no choice because there was no other place not covered with burning oil.

Staying on the side closest to the burning oil, and being mindful of the wind, which brought with it the choking, acrid oil smoke, they proceeded cautiously along the unpaved surface. As soon as the sun went down, the winter night became very cold, though the flaming oil kept them warm.

Though they were unaware of it, the swelling pools of burning petroleum on either side of the road had begun to close behind them, filling the low spots like floodwater in a storm. But, unlike rain, this runoff didn't sink into the sand. It flowed like hot, bubbling, black lava, igniting everything in its path.

None of them could catch their breath because of the choking fumes, and it was clear that the colonel had had it. He could not go any farther, and collapsed again into semi-consciousness. The other three were also exhausted as well. They needed rest, nourishment, and water. They stopped to rest, safe for the moment, but sure that the Iraqis were still in dogged pursuit. There was no moon and no stars shining overhead. There was no horizon to be seen, only billowing clouds of oil smoke that blackened everything from view.

Their uniforms were drenched in perspiration, and as the cold of the February night deepened, they became wet and chilled, and their only means of staying warm was the restless flames. The colonel's teeth chattered in pain as they wrapped him in their ponchos. Although he had sustained no bullet or shrapnel wounds, every ligament and tendon in his body was hurting. His hip looked as if it were broken or had been dislocated in the crash. Even as he slipped in and out of delirium, he was conscious of the fact that his command was aware of his lost flight, and that he was in serious trouble if he survived and made it back. He was in great pain, both physical as well as emotional. The desert floor was a cold bed and offered little rest. He felt as if he were sleeping in the bottom of a refrigerator.

The legs of all four fugitives ached as the blood drained from them to keep their body cores alive. They had to periodically keep turning over like a two-sided rotisserie to stay warm. One side, exposed to the flames, was overheated, while the other was chilled. The injured pilot gasped audibly when Mizzi turned him over to get his other side warm. All in all, it was the most miserable night that any of them, except Youssef, had ever spent.

The only light was from the orange fire flames rising from the burning petroleum, creating weird flashing figures whose shadows and silhouettes danced a devilish step in the shiny, tar-colored pools, whose surfaces, upon meeting the cooler air, developed a mirror-like evil black sheen. Flame demons cavorted with their reflected doubles upon the shining, anthracite-like surfaces. The orange flames were continuously changing shape, creating reflections on the evil, black mirrors that had a hypnotic, hellish appearance. The fluttering fires and dancing smoke added to the appearance of a mad discotheque to their weary eyes.

Young One's head pounded from being struck by the machine gun when the Hummer had exploded. His crusted blood was stuck to the inside of his gas mask, and his skull throbbed with each labored breath. He was going to have to change the filters, as one was clogged with pollution. He took off his mask and found he could momentarily breathe the air because the smoke was blowing in a different direction. His head wound started to bleed again, and the blood ran into his eyes. He changed the filters and replaced the mask. It was then easier to breathe. He could not have both a gas mask and a bandage on his head because the dressing interfered with a good, tight face seal. Essentially his only choices were to bleed or choke.

The only thing that kept the blowing sand out of their eyes were the goggles of their gasmasks. Although the M-17 respirators were stifling, they filtered out a lot of the pollution. Youssef had his Iraqi gas mask, but although it was not as good as the American type, he had not been wearing his as long as the others had worn theirs that day, so it was still working.

By now they could see that the oil flow behind them was getting larger creeping slowly but inexorably forward, as relentless as their human pursuers. Young One began alternating between short spells of sleep and wakefulness in a pattern called the "ranger rock." The head keeps nodding as the individual tries to stay awake. The voluntary mind, in an attempt to maintain consciousness, jerks it back upright. It occurs when one is fatigued after sleep deprivation. The mind tries hard to stay awake, but the body wants to rest and recuperate. A tug-of-war for his consciousness was being waged between mind and body.

No one set the guard; perhaps everyone expected someone else to stay awake. They all were too weary and battered by the day's ordeal. Over and over, Young One's head dropped on his chest. In time, his conscious mind lost the struggle to stay awake. He fell on his side and was soon fast asleep, as were his other companions, as the burning oil pool crept closer, growing in breadth and depth, encroaching ever deeper onto the sides of the road.

The slightly elevated road bed was the only high ground left, and would soon be completely surrounded by burning oil. The viscous flow filled in the low spot and then began to cover the roadway itself. The three Americans and their Iraqi companion were about to be trapped on a shrinking island, in a sea of oil.

While they were asleep Kasim's patrol came within twenty-five meters of them without seeing or hearing them. Had one of them been awake and moving about or making noise, they might have been discovered. The Iraqi patrol was looking for tracks, but the flowing petroleum had swallowed them up. Never suspecting that their quarry might be found so close to the flaming pools, they continued past the sleeping soldiers and were soon on the other side of the oil flow, lost in the smoke. It was as if the Americans had disappeared.

⟫⟶⟩⟶⟫

One of General Baer's junior staff officers approached the commanding general with enthusiasm in his eyes.

"What have you got for me? Some good news, I hope."

"Yes, sir, general. The good news is we have a photographic image of Colonel Washington."

The younger officer handed the general a photo of the unarmed pilot standing next to an armed Iraqi soldier. It had been taken by the UMRV just before Kasim shot it down.

"The bad news is this," he said, pointing to Youssef in the picture, holding his assault rifle.

"There is an armed Iraqi soldier next to him."

"I want this looked into with every resource at your disposal, Major Johnson."

"Yes, sir."

>―――>―――>―――<

While the others slept the sleep of the almost dead, the injured pilot was in and out of sleep, or more correctly, consciousness and unconsciousness, throughout the night. His troubled mind was a kaleidoscope of worried thoughts. As he lay with his body wracked in pain and his mind filled with woeful memories, he dreamed of his youth on the streets of Philadelphia.

He remembered the roasted aroma from the chestnut vendors on the street corners. He thought of his mother's sweet corn bread, which she laughingly called "Georgia wedding cake." She worked as an operator for the telephone company and was away nearly every day, and it was tough for a young black male in a section of the city that was decidedly deficient in "brotherly love."

It was after nine, one night in the early 1960s, when young John Washington was fifteen years old, that the direction of his life changed forever. His mother could not afford a TV during those times, and he was returning from watching television at a new friend's house. Wanting to get home before his mother started worrying, he took a shortcut down an unfamiliar street and witnessed a violent assault.

It later turned to murder when the victim died in the hospital. A street gangster had been collecting a debt of some sort, obviously involving a considerable amount of money. A fight ensued, a knife was pulled, and moments later young Washington found himself starring numbly at the prone body of the victim, and the upright figure of the knife-wielding assailant: a hoodlum, wearing an iridescent, blue-green, sharkskin suit, and looking like he belonged in it. He glanced up and saw young Washington staring at him in shocked disbelief.

"What the fuck are you looking at?" Washington was so frightened that he couldn't answer.

"I axed you a question, boy. Come over here," the man said with a thick, southern, black accent and motioned with the first two fingers of his right hand. The youthful Washington remained frozen in fright. He had never seen anything like this, even in the movies. The gangster walked toward him with a menacing look on his face and a bloody switchblade knife in his right hand.

"I said come here, boy! Don't make me chase your sorry ass." His survival instinct suddenly activated, Washington turned and fled with the speed of a sprinter. The hoodlum, too, was fast and pursued him with carnivorous agility. But the flashy suit and point-toed, Italian shoes hampered him enough to ensure the escape of the terrified youth.

After a circuitous route through several dimly lit streets, the fleeter-of-foot young Washington thought he had eluded his desperate pursuer and slowed to a walk. He was lost in an urban jungle. It was an industrial part of town, and all the factories and businesses were closed, and though he had never been there before, he recognized it as a part of town his mother warned him to avoid after the sun went down. He banged and screamed at locked doors, hoping to rouse a night watchman or boiler stoker. He was answered only by ominous silence, underscored by the faint whine of a distant siren.

John Washington rested uneasily in an alleyway behind a restaurant, feeling far from safe, but fairly confident that the man in the sharkskin suit had given up the chase. Suddenly, he heard approaching footsteps echoing off the brick walls of the close-packed buildings. Ducking behind some garbage cans, he listened with mounting terror as the sounds refined themselves into the ominous "click-click" of metal cleats on the heels of expensive shoes on the asphalt.

The teenage Washington was too frightened to look, although the killer was clearly silhouetted by the streetlights at the opening of the alleyway. In fact, he was so terrified that he was afraid to breathe in case the hoodlum could hear him. For a moment, the footsteps halted, then resumed drawing closer. Without warning, he heard the cardboard cover over him being ripped away and an exceedingly menacing voice saying, "Well, well, well. What do we's have here? I told you not to run, boy. Now look, you've made me overheat myself, and I'm sweating like a pig on my new suit. I was just going to kill you; that was all I was going to do. Now I'm going to cut you bad before I kill you."

A ring-decorated fist grabbed Washington by the front of his shirt and ripped him from his hiding place. There was congealing blood from the last victim smeared on the ring. Washington was in shock. The man threw him up against the brick wall behind him. The blow was hard enough to knock the breath out of him.

"First, I'm going to cut your nuts off."

Regaining his breath in short gasps, Washington began also to regain his wits. He might let himself be murdered, but he would not be gelded by a street surgeon quite so easily. The hoodlum poised the knife to strike and was just about to bloody his new sharkskin suit further when the sound of the siren abruptly amplified to an ear-splitting scream and a police car pulled up into the alley. It seemed that someone had heard the screaming youth and called the cops after all. The alleyway was now ablaze with light from the squad car's spotlight. An officer jumped out, aimed his revolver, and fired without even giving a warning shot. This was back in the "beat 'em and book 'em" days when, if the arm of the law was not long enough, it could be extended with a bullet, and on this occasion it ended the career of Washington's attacker with a single .38 round to his brain.

Washington still remembered the look on the bad guy's face as he slumped to the filthy pavement next to the garbage cans. His knife clinked on the dirty asphalt beside him. His black straw hat, knocked askew on his shattered head, was crushed in the filth of spilled garbage. Now, his last crime was littering a city street with his hemorrhaging corpse.

Young John could not believe what had happened. It was a moment that he would never forget. It was branded into the soft hide of his soul. Later, a doctor came to his house and administered a sedative so he could sleep.

In time, all that was left of the incident were crime-scene chalk marks on the pavement in the alley. After several hard rains, they, too, were almost gone, but the episode left a mark on the teenager's consciousness that would ultimately lead him from the streets of Philadelphia to the desert in Kuwait.

Washington had to testify in court how the officer had saved his life, and that was the end of it. The criminal who had almost killed him had an extensive police record, the cop got an award for the action, and Washington resolved never to put himself on the wrong end of a policeman's gun. He even wanted to be a cop for a while, but, once he went into the army, he found his true niche in life and never left it.

>―――>―――>―――<

A nearby explosion was the colonel's wake-up call back to the real world. The blast occurred at the same instant as the report from the policeman's revolver went off in his mind. The pilot was jerked from his nightmares. At first, no one knew what had happened. They all thought Iraqi mortars were being fired on them. Youssef was the first to raise his frightened head. A second explosion occurred near the first.

Once again fully alert, Washington told the others, "It sounds like landmines cooking off in the burning oil." Then they realized how much trouble they were in, and how fortunate they were to have stopped and rested where they did, or they may have walked on a landmine hidden in the sand.

Young One stumbled to his feet and walked forward. As he approached the spot where the explosions had gone off, he suddenly found he could make himself advance no farther. His feet literally would not move. It was as if his nervous system wiring had been clipped between the brain and feet. For a moment he thought he had stepped into the flypaper-like oil ooze, but when he looked down, his feet were in dry sand. He tried to raise his foot, but something deep inside him said, "Do not move."

Then he looked around farther on the ground. There was the pressure plate of a hastily deployed Iraqi mine, a mere footstep ahead. He had "felt" the mines with his heart, as the old Indians would say. One more step would have been his last. Looking around more, there was another, and a little farther, there was one more.

Originally built to provide oil field workers access, the old dirt road was considered a potential invasion route for coalition forces, and this stretch of it had been heavily mined. He knelt down and began to gently scrape away the thin covering of sand from the first landmine. He had the top of it completely exposed and was about to lift it out when Youssef screamed in Arabic, and Mizzi screamed the translation a moment later.

"No, no, stop. Do not pick it up!!!"

Young One froze with the pose of a department-store mannequin. Soon Youssef was next to him, pointing under the landmine and explaining through Mizzi's translation it could be booby-trapped. He had seen this done by his former Iraqi captors, who had placed small pressure plate charges under the main explosives. Anyone attempting to lift the mine out would release the undercharge, which had sufficient force to detonate its bigger brother sitting atop it. Military-ordnance specialists would never attempt to defuse these loaded surprises. They would either shoot them or explode them with their own charges from a distance, in a controlled manner. Young One wisely discontinued his excavation of the deadly device.

There were too many to try to walk through, and they were too dangerous to try to disarm. They were trapped within a trap. Young One had an idea. He took off his helmet and filled it with sand. Telling the others to duck down, he threw the helmet of sand straight upwards, sending it about eight feet into the air.

Almost simultaneously, Young One spun around, sprang two strides forward and dove headlong for safety, feeling that time, along with his hurting body, had been momentarily suspended in space. The mine exploded with an ear-deafening and tooth-rattling concussion. His Kevlar kraut cap was blasted to smithereens as the explosion propelled him forward. He landed hard in the sand. As he hit the ground large chunks of the mine could be heard splattering in the sand around him and plopping with a hissing sound into the oil ooze.

The others congratulated him for a good idea, but he was in too much pain to appreciate their praise. Besides, it was a trick that couldn't be repeated: He was pretty badly beaten up by recent life already. He couldn't do that again. Mizzi's helmet was the only one left, and she had placed it over the pilot's head for protection.

No, this will not do. We must think of something quickly because we're trapped, he thought.

They needed something with sufficient weight to detonate the mines, but that could be heaved from afar. Mizzi had an idea. With her instructions and the pilot's survival knife, they cut off the arms and legs of their oil-soaked chemical protective gear and fabricated tubes that they filled with sand. They were tied into crude pouches by thin strips of the same material. With their hands they managed to fill them.

The pilot warned them to avoid putting rocks in the pouches because it could create a shrapnel hazard. Each weighed about twenty pounds and it took all of Young One's strength to heave them with enough loft and distance to make them descend at a steeply arched angle, like rounds from a trench mortar, onto the mines. As frightening as it was when the devices exploded, it was even more nerve-wracking to have to retrieve the bags that narrowly missed the mines. After they had blasted a path through the minefield, they were able to move out. They proceeded forward, as hot oil lapped at their boots. There seemed to be nowhere for them to go, however, and the Iraqis heard the explosions and could approximate their position from the sounds of the blasts. Their choice was to keep moving or die...

><----><----><

Back in the sleepless war room, another act of this deadly drama was being lived. The general had been racked out on his GI-issue bunk in the war room. He hadn't really been sleeping, just "checking his eyelids for holes," as they say in the army. This is the way a dog sleeps all the time, but humans can manage it only in times of crisis. He had been asleep, but not soundly. Now, he was awake, but not completely.

"Sir, I've got further reports of the missing colonel."

"What time is it?"

"It is 0237, sir."

"What is it?" said the tired, grouchy bear of a man, clearly annoyed by having his nocturnal hibernation interrupted. Anyone fatigued and under stress would have acted with less discipline under those circumstances.

"The missing soldier was from the medical company crewing the emergency field hospital in their sector. A female field medic named Nirada Mizzi is the only soldier not accounted for in the entire country. She was scheduled..."

"She?" the commander gasped in incredulity at the use of the female pronoun.

"Walters and another female medic in her medical company, a private named Harris, had played a busy game of 'hide the ham' on her bunk."

"Where is Specialist Walters now?" demanded the general of the intelligence-briefing officer.

"He's in custody, being interrogated by his company commander, with a couple of our folks overseeing. So far, he hasn't had any answers to our many questions."

"I want him charged with violation of a direct order and immediately removed from the theatre of war."

"The paperwork is being typed by his brigade commander as we speak. He will also be charged with dereliction of duty, which in times of war can bring a heavy penalty. At the most, he could realistically get ten years in the Federal Disciplinary Barracks and at the least kicked out of service. PFC Harris will probably get a serious Article Fifteen."

"Retain them in custody until this incident is through—one way or another.

"Yes, sir."

"And major."

"General, sir?"

"Not a word of this is to leak out. Those news correspondents are swarming all over the place looking for a story. If this leaks out and the Saudis get hold of it, there could be serious unraveling of the fiber of the coalition. Do you understand?"

"Every word, sir."

The big bear blanched, and then, his face went florid with rage. Here was a command officer, privy to secret invasion plans, being dragged through the sand by an armed enemy in the accompaniment of a woman, perhaps an enemy agent. He knew the threat had to be neutralized as soon as possible.

"Retrieve that officer one way or another."

Chapter 30

BOILED IN OIL

After passing the landmined section of the roadway, the Americans and Youssef had to keep moving. Additional landmines were cooking off in the hot oil behind them. What the fleeing survivors did not know was that across the burning lake of oil behind them, Captain Kasim had heard the explosions and could approximate their general whereabouts. With each succeeding explosion, their location was narrowed down. If only he still had his mortar section, he would have blasted them right then.

The hot oil would flush his prey into the hunter's sights. His plan was a bold one, but he was a bold man. The oil smoke gave him concealment from the probing eye of sky patrols. Once through the minefield, he would cut back east, get in front of the Americans, and block their advance. He was certain that he would soon have his trophies.

If they got too far out into No Man's Land and out of the smoke, he and his troops would be an easy mark for coalition aircraft, yet they needed to move quickly to get around the escapees and set up in front of them for the kill.

Minutes before, Kasim had dispatched an infantry squad ahead on foot to try to find a way through the oil; and though they were far closer to the Americans than they knew, his men had not yet spotted them through the thick smoke.

The sounds of Iraqi voices close behind them, froze Youssef in his tracks. Knowing he would be shot as a deserter, or tortured as a spy and then shot, he dreaded capture as much as did the Americans. Instantly he dropped into the sand and knelt in the direction that his trained instinct—invariably accurate—told him that the holy city of Mecca lay. He did not want to be shot by his own men like a crying child. But no matter which way he ran, one group or another of approaching Iraqis would shoot him in the back. Praying gave him some strength, and he began softly murmuring pleas to the Almighty as his companions crouched silently near him.

The Americans could hear the shouting of orders in Arabic but could not see their enemy because of the thick smoke. Also, it was difficult to see through the steamy respirator lenses of their gas masks.

Youssef kept looking anxiously over his shoulder, expecting any minute to catch a glimpse of the Iraqi patrol emerging from the blinding smoke. Then, hearing the orders of the patrol leader, he stopped praying and pointed in another direction, indicating that the Iraqis had split up in their attempt to capture them. They must move, but how and to where?

What was certain was that they could not stay where they were, stranded on a small island of high ground that kept getting smaller and smaller as oil continually flowed into the low spots around them. Upstream, one of the burning rivulets of oil managed to spill its flaming contents into the large pool. It burst into fire with alarming speed. The flames raced along the top of the jet-black oil toward the stranded survivors.

Young One used Mizzi's helmet to scoop up sand and tried dumping a helmet of it into the pool. The sand merely disappeared into slow-flowing oil. "A dump truck couldn't fill that in," he heard the pilot say with painful, labored speech.

But they were tired, injured, and out of water. Heat-related illness and dehydration would kill them as surely as a bullet or a landmine. They had to get away from the flames to cool down. At least it seemed that the Iraqis had passed by again without spotting or hearing them.

Seeing a flame front rapidly approaching, Youssef and Young One abandoned the shrinking hillock and sprinted across the hot oil pool. A moment later, as the air around her ignited, Mizzi shouldered the pilot and started wading through the knee-deep flaming oil in the direction taken by her companions. The hot oil burned her legs, and she yelped in agony as it splashed up her legs and ran down into her boots. The calves of her legs were on fire. The pilot must have gotten splashed because he winced in pain as well.

Step after painful step she crossed the thirty-meter-wide pool. The thick, asphalt-like stuff under her feet felt like walking through flypaper and slowed down her every step as the oil seeped through the water drainage holes in her old-style jungle boots.

She didn't know if she would step on a landmine or step into a deep depression and drown in oil. The weight of the pilot bore her down farther. With each laborious step, more of the viscous hot liquid found its way to the bottoms of her feet. Flames lapped with burning tongues at her thighs.

She was on fire, but kept on walking, carrying the pilot until she could not walk or carry him any farther. The smell of the burning oil and her smoldering uniform was suffocating even through the respirator, as she gasped for breath in the oxygen-deficient air.

Finally making it to the other side, but nearly asphyxiated, Mizzi collapsed under her burden like a loyal prospector's mule. She could go no farther and fell face down into the sand with the pilot on top of her. Her respirator was torn from her face as the rubber straps snapped from the force of her collapse.

The pilot struggled to get off of her, but his dislocated hip hampered his efforts. She lay trembling in pain and shock while Youssef and Young One, belatedly recovering from their own panic-stricken dash to safety, ran over and pulled the colonel's body aside, then began frantically scooping and tossing sand onto the flames that enveloped Mizzi's lower torso. Mizzi had sand in her eyes and in her mouth and spat it out between moans.

Young One pulled up her pant legs. Her calves looked bright red and had already begun to blister. She wanted to scream but knew she couldn't for fear of being heard by the Iraqis. Her abdomen heaved in painful reflex as her mind fought her body's urge to shriek in agony. She stifled the urge by sucking air across her parted lips. Young One started to take off her boots.

"Don't," injected the pilot.

"She will never be able to get them back on with the swelling. A barefoot soldier is a dead soldier."

With suppressed winces of pain, they regained their feet and limped onward, working their way forward until they found a gully away from the oil spills. There they rested, clear at last of the oil, out of sight but by no means out of danger from the Iraqis, whose forward scouts had been joined by dismounted troops from the vehicular column that had completed its flanking maneuver.

The Americans had no choice but to keep moving. Mizzi had first- and second-degree burns to her legs and feet. Each step caused excruciating pain as the leather inside her boots abraded away the thermal blisters and raw flesh touched rough army socks.

Young One's feet were burned too, but his leather infantry-issued boots had given him better protection. Youssef also had heavy Iraqi-issued boots, and his feet were all right; but, like Young One, his legs were burned above the boot tops. Mizzi trembled like a wounded dog and panted painfully, suppressing the urge to scream. She was going into shock. Now they would have to carry two people. Young One and Youssef looked at each other. The three of them had hardly managed to carry the pilot; now twice the load would have to be borne by just the two of them, and they would need to work in relays. They began with the pilot, carrying him about fifty paces, then propping him up on his crutch, and returning for Mizzi.

With their feet and legs badly burned and the sand stuck to their oil-soaked boots, they plodded onward, repeating the back and forth shuttle at the speed of deep-sea divers. (And in fact, the surface over which they moved so painfully was an ancient seabed.) When a thick-enough coat of sand had collected on their boots, they scraped it off with the pilot's survival knife, only to have more of the grainy tar attach itself minutes later. Both Mizzi and the pilot should have been in the hospital, but there was no medic, no medicine, and seemingly, no way home.

As the burnt oil hardened on their trouser legs, they assumed the texture of roofing tarpaper. Each movement caused abrasions. Youssef rolled up his sand-covered military pants to expose badly burned calves, but the wind on the burns caused immediate pain, and he rolled them back down. The swelling blisters robbed their bodies of their already-meager stores of water, and they were all going into shock; but to stop would mean death, and for the moment, at least, the pain and exhaustion and dimming hope of survival still offered the better alternative...

>-×-×->×

There was a knock on the suburban Los Angeles door. It was around 10 a.m. Pacific Time. Nirada Mizzi's mother answered the door. There were two men standing outside.

"Good afternoon, ma'am, I'm agent Henry Wilson with the Federal Bureau of Investigation." He showed her his official credentials through the screen door. There was a soldier in an army uniform next to him. "This is Captain Ted Smith of the U.S. Army military police. May we come in, please? It is very important that we talk with you about your daughter." In a shocked mood that only a mother with a child in war can know when the government unexpectedly knocks, she led them into the living room. Then she garnered the courage to ask the fateful question.

"Is she dead?"

"No, ma'am. As far as we know, she is officially missing in action, meaning we do not know her exact status," the army officer answered.

"What do you mean, you don't know?"

"I don't know exactly how to say this, but we are not sure if she has been captured, has been killed and her body has not been discovered, or is escaping and evading capture behind enemy lines."

These were not reassuring words, and the woman broke out into a wailing sob. In the other room, a baby began to cry in response to her guardian's anguish. The grandmother excused herself and a moment later returned with the toddler. Wiping away the baby's tears, she sat down with the child on her lap.

"This is Nirada's daughter. She's twenty months old and misses her mother."

"Mama," the child whined at the mention of the word.

The FBI agent paused and cleared his throat awkwardly. "Ma'am, we must speak to you for another reason."

"What is that?"

"Your daughter is under investigation for a breach of military conduct."

"What do you mean?"

"She disappeared from her duty station."

"You mean, she is—what do they call it—A-W-O-W-L, or something like that?"

"AWOL, ma'am. Stands for 'absent without official leave.' And yes, she is charged with being AWOL by the army. And being that we are in a state of war, she could be charged with desertion, a court-martial offense."

The grandmother said nothing, but the news clearly devastated her. Even if her daughter were found alive, she could be shot or put into prison by her own people.

"When was the last time you heard from Nirada?"

"I got this letter three days ago." She took an envelope from the coffee table and removed a letter from it. Two photographs fell out. They were from Nirada.

The agent said, "May I?"

Her mother nodded.

The first photo was of a field hospital. The other was a group shot in which several other soldiers, both men and women, crowded around Nirada. They were her buddies in the Persian Gulf.

"Did she say anything in her letter that might give a clue as to what happened to her?"

Her mother shook her head in negative reply and then said, "You can read it if you would like to."

The agent read the letter. It held nothing of importance to the case. The writer was bored. They had taken no casualties. They spent their time reading, playing volleyball and waiting for wounded to come in.

Her mother had been glad to hear that. The agent refolded the letter and handed it back to her, saying, "Thank you."

He gave back the photograph of the hospital and asked if he could take the group photo. He said it would be returned when the investigation was completed. The mother said, "If you promise to return it."

"Ma'am, has your daughter shown any interest in Middle Eastern politics? Has she joined any pro-Arab groups or does she have friends who are in any groups?"

"Officer—what did you say your name was? I am afraid I forgot it."

"That's all right. It's Agent Wilson."

"Agent Wilson, we are not Arabs, strictly speaking. Our family came from Lebanon, where Arabic was the official language. But we are Christians, driven from our land by Arab gunmen. We are not Muslims. Nirada would not be welcome at their meetings. They would greet her with the same enthusiasm as they would a Jew."

She stopped to blow her nose in a tissue from a holder next to the coffee table.

"Excuse me," she said, with a note of chagrin in her voice. "I do not know about her political views, except that she voted for George Bush last election, and she was proud to vote as an American."

"What about her friends? Are any of them interested in Middle East politics?"

"She has been going to nursing school while raising a baby. She did not have much time for friends. Her husband is the same way. He is a good man; he works all day and goes to night school." She did not know it, but at that moment her son-in-law and her husband were being questioned by the agent's counterparts. They would get to the neighbors and Nirada's teachers at her school next.

"Have you seen her read any Arab literature?"

"Nirada can speak Arabic because of my mother, who died last year. It was her only language and Nirada was very fond of her grandmother. But she cannot read or write Arabic script very well. I tried to teach her when she was young, but she found writing backwards confusing. Her American teachers at school discouraged it. They thought she had that medical condition where a child sees letters backwards. So I did not encourage her."

"Has she received any unusual amounts of money?"

"Not that I know of. She joined the Reserve to get additional cash to finish nursing school. She went into a medical company to learn more skills, and maybe become a full-time army nurse when she finishes school. It has been hard on everyone financially with her gone, but she has her Reserve check. It is direct-deposited into her bank account."

"Has she made any unusual purchases of expensive items?"

"I told you that money was not plentiful."

The FBI agent thought it better to break off the interview. The mother was getting upset, and understandably so. She seemed sincere. They would double-check everything she said and compare notes with everyone else. The baby held out her arms and asked, "Mama, Mama?" It made the government men very uncomfortable.

The captain said as they were leaving, "I don't know exactly what happened over there, but I promise you I'll check with army sources, and, if I hear anything more about her, I'll call you. What is your phone number?" After jotting down the woman's phone number, he handed her his military business card. "Thank you, ma'am. Although I have no word public or private that binds the United States government, I promise you I will do what I can to find out what happened to your daughter."

"Thank you, gentlemen," said the tearful mother clinging to both the baby and her composure as she closed the door behind the men. That night, she would weep herself to sleep in grief and fearful imaginings of her daughter's fate...

Chapter 31

CAUGHT

Still under the cover of the protective smoke, Captain Kasim set up his ambush. The Iraqi riflemen rapidly dismounted and spread out to form a U- shaped perimeter. Once inside, the Americans would be trapped and taken. The foot patrol left behind would drive them in.

The injured Iraqis remained in their truck along with their medic, who was busy triaging the wounded and treating them with what little medical supplies he had in his kit. He knew that many would die from blood loss and shock. There was no medevac by air available to the Iraqi soldiers. They would have to be driven to Kuwait City for treatment, under constant threat of air attack. Many would not make the ride. For the moment, the smoke provided concealment from coalition air power, but any shift of the wind would make Kasim's force vulnerable. He knew he had to capture the Americans quickly and get going.

>────×────×────×─<

Back on the other side of the coalition lines, a specialist with earphones and a digital display of the area in front of his position suddenly sat upright. One of the electronic devices had picked up the presence of the Iraqi detachment. The surveillance devices were high-powered motion-infrared and sound-detection equipment, much like an automatic light that switches on when someone moves near it. It gave a silent alarm that intruders were in the area.

"Looks like we've got sappers coming in, approaching from the north." The reference was military jargon for any small enemy unit engaged in forward operations ranging from scouting to mine laying.

"Roger that," the other on-watch technician, a spec-five, said in confirmation.

On the consol in front of them, the sound signatures of four vehicles were displayed electronically.

"I read it as an armored personnel carrier and three trucks," said the first technician with certainty. "Definitely heading south. It's probably an infiltration team. I'll notify the lieutenant."

Moments later, the officer of the day was standing next to the two specialists.

"Are you certain it's not just camels and goats walking around like last time?"

The enlisted man smiled surreptitiously and handed over the earphones to the young officer.

"No, sir, we're sure it is a Soviet BTR 70 and three smaller vehicles."

The lieutenant held the headset to his ear for several seconds. "You're right. These are not animal sounds." He handed the phones back to the specialist and called his superior officer on the radio.

"Major, we've received positive indication of a possible enemy infiltration team approaching our positions from the north. They appear to be presently halted. They're probably delivering dismounted infantry. Here are the coordinates."

"I'll call H.Q. to see if any of our allies have authorized patrols in the vicinity," the officer on the other end replied. "Standby." Two minutes later, a choppy radio message confirmed that no friendly troops were known to be in the area.

"Contact the forward observers to find out if they've spotted anything." The major ordered. Within the next few minutes, dugout positions in and around the specified coordinates had been alerted to be on the lookout. They all reported seeing and hearing nothing, but the oil fog obscured their vision beyond fifty meters.

With the protocols completed, the steps required to initiate an artillery barrage began with a call from the command center to the fire control center.

"Green Team, this is Nosy Neighbor. Over."

"Go ahead, Nosy Neighbor, this is Green Team. Over."

"Green Team, be advised of an Iraqi patrol approaching our lines. Standby for a fire mission. Over."

"Roger that, Nosy Neighbor. Over."

After being provided with the approximate position, the fire center calculated the range and elevation and gave the gunners their orders. The artillery crews adjusted their weapons using directions from the fire control center and were soon shouting, "Number one gun up, number two gun up, number three gun up." This indicated that the three 105-mm howitzers were ready to fire.

"Commence firing," the main artilleryman shouted. Miles away from the escapees, lanyards were pulled, and the 105s jerked and scraped the ground in backward recoil. There was a whistling noise as the lethal rounds sped forward in a high arc, then landed in volleys of threes. The ground shook as blast after blast slammed into the desert. The first shells exploded about seventy-five meters in front of their targets, sending concussive waves rippling through the sand.

In classic creeping barrage fashion, the second volley landed fifty meters away, and the third set hit a mere twenty-five meters away from the hunkering soldiers momentarily uniting Americans and Iraqis alike in speechless terror. The moving curtain of fire advanced blindly towards the Americans and Youssef, raining pieces of hot, sizzling shrapnel into the sand all around them.

In front of them was a long crevice in the desert floor. Whether it was from an old earthquake or from being eroded by the region's infrequent but torrential rains, they neither knew nor cared. It was there for their immediate survival. Young One and Youssef jumped up and helped the pilot and Mizzi scramble forward and tumble into the natural trench, just as another salvo blanketed the ground they had occupied moments before, each shell blasting a crater the size of a small house foundation into the trembling earth.

"What is going on?" shouted Mizzi.

Raising his chin from the sand, the pilot pitched his voice above the shattering din. "Friendly fire. Our side must have picked up the Iraqi rolling stock and took us all for bad guys.

"They're shooting at us?" screamed Mizzi in questioning disbelief. "Our own people are trying to kill us?" Her answer this time took the form of another teeth-rattling explosion.

The artillery barrage took the Iraqis completely by surprise. Kasim was sure that the smoke concealed his men from coalition observation, and concluded that the fleeing Americans must have called in the fire mission on a radio he hadn't known they were carrying.

The driver of the truck holding the wounded began frantically turning the ignition key, pulling the choke and stomping on the gas pedal. To no avail. The vehicle would not fire up. An instant after the continued whirling of the starter went silent, a direct hit blasted the truck into smithereens. All of the injured men and their medic went with it. There would be no need for a burial detail for them.

>——>——>←

Young One and Youssef, squatting in the deepest part of the crevice, got partially buried under a huge chunk of earthen wall broken off by an exploding shell. Young One's rifle was lost in the sand as he struggled to free himself from a gritty grave. Youssef had his AK strapped over his back, so it stayed with him, leaving his the only working weapon the fugitives possessed, except for the survival pistol which the pilot, unbeknownst to his companions, still carried.

They quickly dug out Young One, choking and spitting out sand. Youssef gave him the last swig of his canteen water to wash out his mouth. Fearing that the next shell would fall upon them, the pilot rolled over and fired one of his red pen flares from his survival kit. It cracked like a child's cap gun, and soon a tiny, glowing missile was shooting upwards through the smoke. Weighing the risk that the signals would be seen by the enemy against the need to try to alert the distant battery that they were firing on friendly troops, he reached into his survival vest and grabbed his second and last flare.

>——>——>←

"Look at that!" The most observant forward lookout said as he pointed to a pair of far-off threads of pink color suspended in the night sky. The masking smoke had subdued their normally bright red glow, intended to be visible to an air-rescue team, and the lookout wasn't sure what they were. The automatic trip flares that shot upwards to alert forward crews that the enemy was approaching were white, but these had a definite tinge of red. The alert PFC called his superiors, who immediately knew the alarming implications. The Iraqis used green, Soviet-style flares. There was something wrong here.

One of the other forward observation teams saw the flare and reported it as, "Blue on blue, blue on blue. Check your fire. I repeat, check your fire!" This was a NATO term denoting that one friendly component was accidentally shooting at another.

The artillery commander ordered the crews to cease fire as the next volley of shells was be about to be rammed into the guns, rounds that would have would have hit directly on top of the escape-and-evaders, cowering in the crevice. But the pin flares produced a negative effect as well. Had the barrage continued, it might have killed Kasim and the rest of his men. The cease-fire gave the Iraqi infantrymen the opportunity to close in on the Americans. Kasim saw the flare and now knew the Americans' exact whereabouts.

>+—>+—>+<

The command staff had given explicit orders that any hostile actions were to be reported immediately to headquarters. The buzz went all the way up the chain of command.

"General, one of our land sonar devices has picked up infiltrators, and an artillery crew from the 192nd opened up on them. They reported seeing red flares in the sky."

"What's the location?" The general demanded of his operations chief, immediately thinking of the missing helicopter pilot. The answer sent a tinge of hope and excitement racing up his spine.

"Contact the commander of that sector; inform him not to fire again. I say once more. He is not to fire again."

"That has already been done, sir."

"Redeploy the DART. Send them to that location."

>―――×―――×―――<

The Americans were half-oblivious and hard of hearing from the explosions, and it was Youssef who first looked up and saw the Iraqis standing at the rim of the crevice, their AK-47s trained on the four fugitives. Instantly recognizing the scowling visage of Captain Kasim, he reflexively rendered a snappy salute to his former superior. He thought it was up for him, and did the only thing he had been taught to do in the presence of an officer. Had he done anything differently, he would have been dead.

Kasim stood silent for what seemed a long time, then returned the private's salute. It appeared to the surrounding Iraqis that Youssef had captured the Americans, as he was the only one with a weapon. The Iraqi captain studied the situation for a few seconds more, then did something that none of his men had ever seen him do. Delighted that one of his privates, a Bedouin, was presenting him with this coveted prize, he smiled.

He cleared his throat and mustered his most authoritative voice. "This son of the desert itself has tracked and captured the American infiltrators. He is to be praised!"

Youssef looked as surprised as anyone did, and his silence was taken for an affirmative.

A weary cheer went up among the Iraqi soldiers. They were hungry, dirty, filthy, pest-ridden, and shell-shocked, but they were nonetheless temporarily happy to have some reward for all their suffering.

The Americans were searched and relieved of their meager possessions before having their hands tied behind their backs with rough cord. Corporal Baalira found the pilot's revolver and rebuked Youssef for not checking more closely.

"These devils could have killed you when you were not looking," said the non-com.

Youssef had by now recovered his wits, and answered without hesitation. "The American artillery started shooting just as I captured them."

The corporal looked at him intently. Some insignificant thing he had previously noticed was stuck in the back of his mind. Now the pilot's pistol had not been taken by the private. He became very suspicious, but could say nothing for the time being without incurring the wrath of Kasim. He would think about it further and wait for the right moment to speak out. He had long speculated to himself that as a Bedouin, Youssef would have the best chance to escape into the sand should he decide to desert. For that reason, and because of ethnic prejudice, Corporal Baalira had never trusted Youssef, and now he trusted him less.

The sight of the American pistol kept them from looking closely at Mizzi. They all wanted it. It was an old-fashioned 38-caliber revolver, similar to those carried by police officers. Kasim kept it for himself. Not being buxom, and with her face covered in petroleum and her hair pasted to her head in oily strings by a mousse of greasy residue, Mizzi was not recognized as a woman.

The Iraqis were in a hurry. They needed to move out before coalition warplanes could discover them or the Americans resumed their shelling.

The injured captives were roughly prodded to where the vehicles were parked.

Kasim allowed Youssef to continue guarding his prisoners. They were quickly whisked away to Kasim's armored command vehicle while the rest of the Iraqi detail was ordered to their trucks. Now treated as a hero after his run across the minefield and his single-handed capture of the infidels, Youssef was given salve for his burned legs. The Americans received nothing. What little medicine there was would not be wasted on the enemy. Youssef knew he was being watched by a jaundiced eye.

The corporal stared at the Americans. He noted that two of them were enlisted infantrymen and one was a colonel wearing an aviator's uniform. There was a quick discussion about shooting the two enlisted men and keeping the officer.

Kasim said, "No!"

His thirst for revenge had been temporarily satiated with hopes of personal glory and military advancement. All three were thrust into the armored personnel carrier. Corporal Baalira was assigned to guard them as well as the vehicle. The driver was of Turkish extraction, while the mechanic was born a Kurd. They maintained the vehicle and operated it. The corporal watched them as intently as he did the Americans.

He knew that everything was not as it appeared. He remembered that he had seen their tracks. *There*, he'd thought, as his flashlight illuminated an American boot print on top of Youssef's Iraqi boot. That meant the other two had been behind him. *An odd way to guard prisoners*, it occurred to him now. He would request that Captain Kasim have Youssef interrogated along with the Americans, but only when the time was right.

Their convoy set off toward Kuwait City, driving in and out of the protective oil smoke. With coalition aircraft watching the regular roads, they traveled on a bumpy trail used in peacetime by oil crews and Bedouins. Iraqi communications had already been so degraded that Kasim could not be certain that his division was still headquartered in the occupied capital, but he had no other means of finding out but to go there.

⤞—⤞—⤞

Twenty minutes after the downed aircraft rescue team was reactivated, it was on the scene. The tracks in the sand told the whole story. What body parts they could see were Iraqi. There were no American items or shreds of uniforms noticeable. They discovered the same tracks in the sand as around the Hummer. These were their people, and they were irrefutably in hostile control. Evidently the Iraqis had captured the three Americans and loaded them into an enemy vehicle. One of them was wearing jungle boots. The coalition had not heard any radio traffic from the front concerning a missing pilot. That was about to change.

Finding a radio channel that was not jammed or scrambled, Kasim informed his headquarters of the capture of an American officer and two enlisted men. Kasim was told to keep all the prisoners alive if possible. He also learned that his headquarters was in tactical retreat, and he was given coordinates to rendezvous with them.

Unknown to Kasim or his superiors, there was a reason he had found the channel open: Coalition communications experts were listening in on the supposedly secure broadcast via an electronic eavesdropping satellite capable of simultaneously monitoring hundreds of radio messages over a wide range of wavelengths. The signal was relayed for processing to Arizona where intel troops analyzed it. It took a while for the message to get unwound and sent to Saudi, but when it did, it confirmed the command's worst fears: The Iraqis held Colonel Washington, and the threat represented by his capture had to be neutralized immediately...

Chapter 32

HIGHWAY OF DEATH

As Kasim's troops neared Kuwait City, they were astounded to see thousands of vehicles blocking both the north and southbound lanes in the road. This was the same road the Iraqis had used when they had *blitzkreiged* Kuwait six months before. Now they were heading back to Iraq, but they had waited too long to leave. They had not been given safe passage out of the war zone. They had not "broken their swords" or "stacked their muskets" in capitulation, and this mass exit was not surrender but a tactical redeployment of their troops back across the border.

Saddam had said publicly that he would "sooner eat mud" than have his army surrender, and it was their intention to return to Iraq with their plundered spoils of war. So far, smoke from the oil fires had covered his army's withdrawal. But the wind shifted directions, and the previously blinded satellites and spotter planes could suddenly see the massive Iraqi column in all its naked vulnerability.

There were thousands of vehicles of every description lined up bumper to bumper, including tanks and other armored vehicles driving up the median strip, crushing road signs and vegetation and anything in their path. All were heading north on Highway 8, once called the "Sixth Ring

Road" from the days when it was an unpaved caravan path, and now a modern four-lane thoroughfare going from Kuwait City north to the Iraqi city of Basra.

Construction trucks, commercial buses, privately owned cars, vans, and pickups were packed with the plunder from Kuwait City and so loaded with stolen loot that their back ends dragged like low riders. Soldiers by the thousands filled every sort of vehicle on which they could make rooms for themselves amid the plunder. "No camels allowed" signs were posted on the entrance to the freeway in Arabic and in English. Mostly Bedouins, for whom it was dangerous to ride camels near the road, used the trail alongside the highway. Even that was full of vehicles trying to make it back to Iraq. There would be no quick run to headquarters for Captain Kasim and his men, who could not know that their parent unit was farther north along the seven-mile column, virtually immobilized in the road jam.

For the first time, Youssef saw Kasim unsure of what to do; then the Iraqi officer made a bold decision. There being no way to push through on the main road, he would go around the traffic jam via a desert path that he knew about.

Kasim radioed another message, but still no news from his superiors could be received. Coalition listening satellites and overhead communication-surveillance aircraft, however, picked up this second transmission, which put them closer to locating Kasim's patrol from its electronic signature. They knew the message originated from one of the vehicles in the evacuation of Kuwait City near the town of Al Jarah.

><><><

The entire road between Al Jarah and Basra, ever after to be known as the "Highway of Death," was about to become the scene of a giant turkey shoot—"a target-rich environment," as pilots say. But the air force and navy had been given word that one vehicle especially, and its occupants in particular, should under no circumstances be allowed to escape the coming fire storm.

An electronic surveillance plane, returning from a mission deep in Iraq, was the first to spot the Iraqi column when the pilot saw headlights through a break in the smoke. Jet fighters raced to the location and confirmed the observation. Ten minutes later, an air force fighter-bomber jet had located the head of the improvised parade, and set the stage for a rain of ruin from above. Just ahead of the lead element was a bridge spanning a deep gorge. The bomber pilot radioed back and got permission to cut off the Iraqi line of retreat. A few bombs later, the bridge span was broken, and several vehicles full of Saddam's soldiers fell to their death in the gorge. Unaware of why their progress had suddenly slowed from a crawl to a full stop, the drivers behind them slammed on their brakes and were subsequently slammed from behind by other vehicles. Drivers honked their horns, and officers ordered inferiors "out of the way," but there was nowhere to go.

Coalition warplanes began to bomb, rocket, and strafe the hapless procession, taking out the hard-skin tanks and armored vehicles first, as they possessed the best means of self-defense. A-10 Warthogs turned the close-packed tanks into Swiss cheese with 30-mm depleted uranium rounds. Tanks exploded from the inside when their fuel and ammo were ignited.

The same nimble fingers of the boys who had vanquished Atari and Nintendo enemies in the comfort of their living rooms and video arcades were now taking out real, live enemies with similar dexterity. There were no greater electronic warriors on earth. It was a natural step to go from the couch to the aircraft console, and then from doing homework in the military academy to doing night work on the Iraqis.

Wave after wave of fighter-bombers swooped down and loosed their lethal cargoes. Close-packed vehicles exploded or were reduced to inoperability by cluster bomblets, machine-gun bullets, and canon shells. The cluster bombs popped far overhead and spread a deadly blanket of submunitions that engulfed the traffic jam. Some Iraqis tried vainly to fire at the passing aircraft, but were killed by the following wave of warplanes. Explosion after explosion echoed through the desert air. Men screamed in fear and pain, but the roar of jet engines drowned their voices. Soldiers ran into the desert, and when there was a sufficient accumulation of them to attract the pilot's notice, were decimated by machine-gun fire. Other enemies tried to conceal and protect themselves under mattresses pulled from the vehicles. Here and there, fleeing men were shot in the back by Iraqi officers who themselves perished in the carnage moments later.

The jets were horrifyingly efficient. After two hours of air attack, the highway was reduced to a seven-mile-long junkyard and graveyard. Weaponry, clothing, bathroom fixtures, and all the paraphernalia and trappings of a formerly luxurious life were strewn about the bloody asphalt, as if a tornado had struck a shopping mall.

Tanks were still blowing up from internal, secondary explosions. Soldiers were lying about everywhere, wounded, or dead. Automobiles were burning; flaming corpses still held the steering wheels of their stolen vehicles. The impact of near-misses blew out windows and windshields. The glass shattered and ripped into the occupants' faces and bodies. The place had a strange fragrance, imparted by stolen, expensive perfume being sprayed about the carnage by concussive blasts. Huge craters were excavated into the asphalt by the bombs. Machine-gun bullets shot through vehicles, ricocheted off the pavement, and pierced other vehicles in front of them.

The injured called out for help, but there was none to be had. Dazed, shell-shocked soldiers wandered around wailing or in a wordless zombie-like trance while exploding bombs caused the ground and asphalt under their feet to shudder like the death spasms of some great, stricken beast.

Overhead, some coalition aircraft narrowly missed flying into each other on their bombing and strafing runs before speeding back to their carriers and land bases for rapid reload. Moments after they alighted, teams of enlisted personnel on flight decks and airstrip aprons worked feverishly, like NASCAR pit crews, to rearm and refuel the warbirds for return to the slaughter.

It was pandemonium and organized destruction, leaving tens of thousands of Iraqis dead and many more wounded. By the time it ended, there would not have been enough ambulances or hospitals in the entire Middle East to treat or care for them. They were left to slowly die because there was no help coming for them.

❊——❊——❊

All along the dirt trails, the Iraqis had constructed dugouts—vehicular shelters to hide their convoys from spy satellites and anticipated air attacks. Captain Kasim knew where a number of these were located, and, keeping a cool head amid the panic and devastation swirling around him, he led his three-vehicle patrol into a U-shaped earthen tunnel dug into the bank of the dirt road. The tunnel was virtually impossible to see from the air, and all three vehicles managed to get inside. From their protected site, about a half-kilometer from the road, the Iraqi soldiers watched out the tunnel openings while whole divisions of their army were being destroyed before their unbelieving eyes.

Kasim and his prisoners inside in the armored vehicle could hear and feel the vibrations from the blasts, but could only infer what was going on. Suddenly, the earthen cocoon in which Kasim had up to that moment felt his men and prisoners to be safe, was jolted by a skull-rattling blast that sent ripples of shock through the sand and clay.

The concussion rocked the three vehicles violently back and forth on their springs for a few terrifying moments, until their convulsions were smothered by the tunnel's collapse. Inside the APC, dirt cascaded onto the heads of Kasim and his driver through the opened commander's hatch. The driver held up his hands in a futile effort to fend off the cataract of clods and fine earth, but was soon nearly buried alive in his metal seat. After a little while, he started choking and coughing, and began frantically clawing his way out of the dirt. When the trembling of the earth around them at last subsided, Kasim, the driver, the mechanic, Youssef, the corporal, and the three Americans sat for nearly two minutes in stupefied silence. There was not enough air for all of them to breath. The vehicle was still running, and the driver switched on the red night lights so the others could see.

At first, when the earth swallowed them alive, they were in shock. The clay had been so hard that the Iraqi engineers who had dug the shelter never imagined that it would need shoring; nor had they imagined that an American warplane, wagging its wings to jettison a hung-up bomb, would ever score an accidental near hit on the tunnel's unreinforced roof. Now the survivors of this improbable misfortune of war faced the prospect of slow suffocation. And the first impulse of Kasim's men was to panic.

The captain soon put a stop to this activity by pulling out his pistol and assuring everyone that the next one to open his mouth would get a bullet in his throat. It had a remarkably calming effect on the Iraqis, as disobeying Kasim was more frightening than being buried alive. Only Mizzi understood what was said but could not translate it under the circumstances. Young One and the colonel could tell by the tone of his voice to be quiet. The corporal who mistrusted Youssef wanted Kasim to shoot the Americans to save air.

But Youssef pleaded to him, "No captain, they are too great a prize," and Kasim decided against it...if only for the fear that the bullets might traverse the victims' skulls and ricochet around inside the cramped space.

Besides, he had to have something to show his superiors for the loss of so many men under his command. An American colonel would be good to take to his superiors. The enlisted soldiers were expendable. If air got short, he would kill Mizzi and Young One first. He gave a bayonet to Youssef with instructions that upon Kasim's command he was to stab the enlisted men in the hearts and to hold his hand over their mouths to suppress their screams. Mizzi heard the words and whispered the translations to Young One and the colonel.

The metal hatch cover was their only way out, and it was fortunate that Kasim had left it open. The driver was shouting and desperately clawing at the dirt. He was trying to scratch his way through to the surface.

Heedless of what Kasim's reaction would be, and horrified at the thought of using it for its lethal purpose, Youssef began hacking with the bayonet at the mound of dirt blocking the hatchway. Seconds later, in response to a gesture from their officer, the other Iraqis joined in the excavation. The work was strenuous and consumed extra oxygen, and soon they were all gasping for breath as dust filled the air and made everyone cough. The engine of the armored vehicle finally stalled, and the lights went out. With the soldiers momentarily frozen in place by their sudden blindness, silence echoed through the metal trap that held them captive.

Sensing opportunity, Youssef felt his way back to the place where the Americans were, as Baalira, the driver, the mechanic, and even Kasim resumed digging furiously in the total darkness. With the Americans' hands tied behind their backs, they could not even cover their mouths and noses, and sneezed and coughed uncontrollably as Youssef took the bayonet and quietly cut through the bonds binding their hands.

Kasim ordered his men to start "digging like the blind." Soon the vehicle was half full of dirt, further reducing the volume of available air. They were slowly suffocating from breathing in each other's warm, expired breath and the dead engine exhaust that was creeping into their stifling enclosure. The Iraqis kept digging away, coughing and wheezing from the dust.

Suddenly, the driver let out a howl as his hand hit the open air. His fingers wriggled around the hole, enlarging it as the sand rained down into the APC. First his arm went through, and, in a few minutes, he was able to stick his face up and catch a few gulps of clean air. Kasim soon elbowed him aside and went up for air himself.

After a while, the opening was made large enough to permit escape from the entombed vehicle. First the Iraqis crawled out, and then they dragged up the Americans, who stood on the edge of the hatch and allowed themselves to be manhandled, up through five feet of earth, not using their hands to assist in their ascent to prevent their captors from discovering that their bonds had been cut. After what seemed an eternity, the three prisoners found themselves above the ground once more tossed upon the sand to re-ventilate their aching, anoxic lungs, still clasping their hands behind their backs as though their wrists remained bound. Youssef went back into the vehicle to retrieve the pilot's one crutch, then he too collapsed on the ground in exhaustion.

For several minutes the entire party lay like panting fish on the sand, exhilarated to be breathing clean air, and briefly united in their common humanity by having narrowly escaped an uncommonly gruesome death...

Chapter 33

DEAD RUN

Things were looking good for Corporal Baalira. He had just been rescued from being buried alive, and would help take the prisoners to Baghdad and be a hero along with his officer. Perhaps Captain Kasim could get him an assignment to the Republican Guards. Then he would become an elite soldier and perhaps even make sergeant for helping capture the American spies.

The corporal had heard Youssef whispering to the Americans in a friendly tone when Captain Kasim was not paying attention. He didn't know what Youssef had said, but he recognized that it was in Arabic. *Perhaps the Americans are not his prisoners after all,* he thought. He'd keep his speculations to himself, but would continue to watch this Bedouin boy. He considered Bedouins to be liars and thieves—gypsies of the desert.

Kasim went around the mound of earth to where the entrance of the dugout had been, and stood in shocked disbelief. The bomb blast had totally collapsed the structure leaving the two trucks completely buried and his men presumably crushed to death in the cave-in. Off to the north he could still hear the thunder of bomb blasts, but they were clearly growing more distant.

Now his immediate command was reduced to Corporal Baalira and Youssef, along with two privates—a Turk and a Kurd. Kasim knew that neither of these two former Kuwaiti soldiers liked him or Saddam. Nonetheless, he had no choice but to leave them with Baalira to help guard the Americans while he went off in search of transportation.

No sooner had the captain departed than the Turk and the Kurd switched off the safeties on their AKs and turned their weapons on the corporal and Youssef. As the latter stood in stunned silence, Baalira muttered a savage oath at himself for having been caught off guard.

The two conscriptees ordered Youssef and the corporal to kneel on the ground, intending to shoot both of them and then flee with the Americans, in hopes of using them as a ticket out of the theater of war, and perhaps even to exchange them for a reward. Suddenly, Mizzi shouted in frantic Arabic, "No, no, do not shoot him. He helped us."

Both men understood Arabic and were amazed to hear it spoken by a woman. The Turk walked over to Mizzi and squeezed her breast to confirm her gender, then began to laugh humorlessly. They were all so surprised that they did not shoot anyone.

"I knew you were no good," Baalira hissed at Youssef. "You wild desert jackal, you have no loyalty. They take me at gunpoint, but you go willingly. If I get the chance, I will kill you." Then the Kurd hit him in the head with his rifle butt and Corporal Baalira fell forward onto the sand. The Kurd then spoke to Mizzi in Arabic, "We will help you to escape if you will get us through the American lines." Mizzi translated to the others. Afraid that Kasim would return shortly, they agreed.

Moments later, leaving the unconscious Baalira behind, the six set out in the direction of the bombed convoy. They all knew that at any moment they might encounter the returning Captain Kasim, but the chance of finding something to drive away in to make their escape made it worth the risk. Young One and Youssef assisted Mizzi, while the Iraqis helped the pilot.

It was almost totally dark, with only the flashes from distant bomb bursts casting strobe-like freeze-frames of lurid illumination onto the hellish scene. As they approached the highway, they seemed to go unnoticed by the frantic Iraqi soldiers, many of whom were clearly shell shocked. Without their distinctive helmets, and with their uniforms covered in oil, there was nothing to identify the Americans to the dazed Iraqis, as they walked among them in the dark. Youssef and the other two armed Iraqi soldiers gave their group a look of authority.

Vehicles were aflame and bodies of both alive and dead Iraqis were strewn about the smoking asphalt. As they walked along the edge of the road, they passed a man in the fetal position hunkered under a pile of clothing, apparently seeking concealment. Another man was shouting religious sayings at the aircraft in defiance and shooting at out-of-range jets with his AK. His bullets were arcing in the air and falling among the vehicles behind him. Madness had overtaken the Iraqi survivors' shattered minds, and the Americans and their armed escort passed unseen before their crazed eyes.

They finally found a four-by-four that was still running, a silver 1990 Toyota Land Cruiser. After removing the dead occupants and brushing the remains of the windshield and windows from the seats, the escapees set off, in the opposite direction from the one in which the Iraqis had been heading. The road was still blocked, but the surface was hard packed enough for the tires to take hold and allow them to proceed. As they pulled away, directly behind them several bunches of delayed-action cluster bombs exploded like deadly grapefruit.

The headlights had been smashed, but the light from the far-off explosions and burning vehicles allowed Young One to see well enough to drive. And though they did not know it, they were heading toward Kuwait City.

Kasim returned to the top of the earthen dugout where he had a few minutes before left the prisoners, to find only Baalira sitting on the ground. "What happened to the Americans?" he screamed. The corporal did not speak but merely pointed toward the junkyard in front of them. Instantly comprehending that the Americans had somehow escaped in the direction of the blasted convoy, Kasim spun around and began running frantically back toward the highway. Without thinking, he began running in futile pursuit until a minute later his breath gave out and he stumbled to a stop, gasping in frustration and rage.

Then a dark star shined on the desperate captain. Coming along the shoulder of the road behind him, an undamaged Iraqi scout car was heading back to Kuwait City, its demoralized occupants hoping to cheat death. Kasim stood in front of them and, seeing an Iraqi officer, they halted before him. Kasim shouted to them that he was commandeering their vehicle to follow escaped Western prisoners. The Iraqis in the vehicle allowed Kasim to take the wheel and awaited his further orders.

><del>—</del>><del>—</del>><del>—</del>

All along the road and out into the desert, Young One could see Iraqi soldiers begging for help and trying to escape. They were ignored. The four-by-four already held six passengers, and there was no time to take on board people who would kill them if they knew what they were up to. Young One floored the Toyota, and several Iraqis jumped aside just in time to avoid being struck, then stood shaking fists and screaming curses at the speeding vehicle. A moment later, the scout car that Kasim had commandeered slammed into their backs and rolled over them, in pursuit of the Americans, its driver paying them no more regard than if he had run over stray dogs. He was determined to recapture the infidels.

Occasionally, as Young One drove forward, the Iraqis in the pursuing scout car took pot shots at the fleeing Land Cruiser. Hearing a couple of stray bullets strike the four-by-four, he realized that they had to leave the road, or they would likely be killed. Young One steered the vehicle out into the trackless sands. With each press of the clutch he winced in pain from his burned legs. He drove them deeper and deeper into the desert, with Kasim less than a half mile behind. Although the taillights were blasted out, every time Young One hit the brakes, one of the still working brake lights pinpointed the Toyota's position to their relentless pursuer.

It took several whacks from his helmet for the shock to break the light bulbs, but the Turk finally managed, and had the Land Cruiser passed over a rut or a rock, he would have been spilled out into the path of Kasim's careening scout car. But at that moment, the desert was as flat as a football field under their tires.

Unbeknownst to the occupants of the vehicle ahead of him, and despite their success as extinguishing the brake light, Kasim's night-vision goggles were allowing him to follow the Toyota's course without difficulty. The machine gunner in the scout car began taking three-round pot shots at the Toyota, but they were too far away to be effective.

Now the distance had closed to where his gunner could work the machine gun to better effect, and its next burst passed much closer to the target than the earlier rounds. Kasim was furious to the point of insanity. Youssef had gone over to the enemy. The devil must have tainted his simple nomad's mind to help the Americans.

Seeing the line of green tracers whiz past his ear, the Kurd pointed to the rear and screamed at Young One to drive faster. Behind them, silhouetted in the bomb-lit night, like a demonic specter, the outline of the armored vehicle was clearly closing on them.

The Kurd and the Turk switched their AKs to full automatic and began returning fire. But the terrain had suddenly turned bumpy and between that and Young One's evasive swerving to avoid both the bullets and the bodies of dead Iraqi soldiers, the rounds from both sides were mostly missing their mark.

At that instant, the Kurd's head exploded like a ripe melon and splattered brain matter onto Young One's neck and right shoulder. Recovering from his momentary shock, the Turk rolled the dead Kurd out of the Toyota and into the path of the charging armored vehicle, hoping to make it screech to a halt, or even be overturned by impact with the body. Moments later, another burst of machine gun fire hit the Turk, who after a single, strangled grunt of surprise, toppled out the back of the speeding Land Cruiser and bounced heavily on the desert floor.

In maneuvering around the Turk's body, Kasim sent the scout car bouncing violently over a bomb crater that Young One barely missed. The Iraqi gunner's face was flattened against the armor plating by the jolting impact, and he slumped to the floor, spitting out two bloodied front teeth. This temporarily stopped the machine-gun fire.

The bomb-loosened hood of the Toyota kept banging and slamming with each bump they hit. It was hanging by only one hinge, and that was breaking away. Without warning, it flew up and slammed into where the windshield should have been. Blinded by the wall of sheet metal, Young One stuck his head out of the side window to see to drive. Though he didn't realize it, the gas tank had been pierced by an Iraqi bullet, and the Toyota would be sputtering on vapors much sooner than he had hoped when he'd first glanced at the gauge. The scout car continued its pursuit, and though the Toyota was out of range, the bleeding gunner had regained his feet and resumed intermittent firing.

One of two American F-16 pilots orbiting overhead saw the vehicles racing out in the desert. The rules of engagement allowed them to fire at will upon any suitable Iraqi target in their zone. After a quick radio consultation with his wingman, the leader rolled into a shallow dive and bore down on the pair of vehicles, the nearest of which was clearly military and could only be an enemy. Just as he was about to press the firing button, he noticed muzzle flashes coming from the trailing vehicle and realized that its occupants were shooting at the vehicle ahead, which he could now recognize as civilian. Assuming the later might be filled with Kuwaiti resistance fighters, the lead pilot alerted his wing mate to hold fire as both jets zoomed over the Land Cruiser and turned back for another pass in the opposite direction.

Through a break in the smoke, the lead jet unleashed rockets and the second jet slammed machine-gun fire into Kasim's scout vehicle. Both planes swung around for another pass to assess the damage, but it was evident that they should save their ammunition. The circle of life had been completed for Kasim. He left the world the same way he had entered it, and the way he had spent many of his hours on earth—screaming.

"Confirmed enemy kill," radioed the first pilot to the other.

"Roger that, I hope those civilians get home all right."

"You've got a most 'Rog' on that, good buddy."

The escapees in the Toyotas could see the explosions behind them and knew what had happened. They were afraid that they would be next, but the planes had already departed. With Kasim dead, everyone Youssef had previously known in the Iraqi Army was gone.

The flaming carnage behind them diminished in size through the broken rearview mirror, as they continued toward Kuwait City through the open desert. A few minutes later, the Toyota sputtered to a halt in the vast sands. Young One kept trying to restart it until he thought to recheck the gas gauge and realized what had occurred. Their brief adventure as a motorized unit was over. The water cans being too heavy to carry, they drank all they could swallow before filling the dead Iraqis' canteens. Now that they were back on foot and with the morning sun just a few hours over the horizon, thirst might soon become their next adversary.

They were not sure what to do. Should they remain with the Toyota until daylight, or set off into a desert full of escaping Iraqis who could wander upon them at any moment, and would be unlikely to try to take them alive? Young One had an idea. The Toyota hood was hanging from threads of metal, and it came loose after several minutes of exertion by him and Youssef.

From the cannibalized vehicle, they fashioned a crude sled with ignition wires twisted together to make a dragging rope. From the seat-belt straps, they fabricated waist harnesses by which to pull Mizzi. First they laid Mizzi on the hood and dragged her several hundred yards through the sand. Then they returned with the sled and repeated the same laborious process with the colonel. It was hard work, but easier than trying to carry the injured soldiers as they had done before being captured.

Sometimes standing, sometimes on their hands and knees, the small party inched their way painfully towards whatever fate awaited them in Kuwait City. Should they be lucky enough to make it that far...

Chapter 34

MYSTIC WINDS

They had dragged the injured upon the homemade sled only a half-mile when trouble was again stalking them. Dawn had broken, and the sun could be faintly seen through the smoky sky, but it really was not light yet. Armed and unarmed Iraqi stragglers and deserters were all around them. Many had abandoned their vehicles and had run off into the desert when the bombing of the highway began. Hungry, thirsty, and desperate, those in the immediate vicinity seemed oblivious to their surroundings as they wandered about alone or in pairs. But off to the south, a sizeable number had organized into some sort of ad hoc, rag-tag assemblage, and were following the tracks of the vehicle in hope of finding food, water, and a ride out. And they were moving in the direction of the four escapees.

Youssef and Young One could not run with Washington and Mizzi, and leaving them was out of the question. For weapons they had Youssef's AK and one of the dead Iraqis' guns, but only twenty-six rounds all together. The Kurd and the Turk had shot most of their ammunition at Kasim's scout car before being killed themselves.

Briefly, Young One felt tempted to stop to scavenge ammunition from the bodies of the nearby dead; but a look back over his shoulder convinced him that the mob of maddened survivors was now only a quarter of a mile behind them and appeared to be ransacking the wrecked vehicle for food, water, and loot. He knew there wasn't a moment to lose.

Meanwhile, despite his constant pain and intermittent periods of semi-delirium, Colonel Washington had revived sufficiently to be increasingly cognizant of the party's predicament and how much his injury was retarding their progress. Now, to Young One's great relief, he abruptly refused to be shuttled any further on the improvised sled and, wincing in agony, managed to regain his feet and resumed hobbling forward. Though this enabled them to double their still snail-like pace, Young One knew they could not outrun the enemy soldiers and there were too many to fight it out with, even with an ample supply of ammo.

Maybe it was the knock on the head or the fatigue of so much exertion, but his mind began moving through space and time until he imagined himself back home sitting in Grandfather's stone hut in the herd camp. In his mind's ear he heard Grandfather retelling him a story he had heard years before...

✠ ✠ ✠

"Many turns of the sun ago, beyond counting by a whole village, son of my son, our people were returning from a religious festival many days from home when their tracks were discovered by a band of ruthless enemies. There were whole families, including old ones who were carried upon human *travois*, dragged by their women and older children. This was long ago, even before the time of horses for our people. They had a young dog with them, but it was not large enough to pull, and he ran with the small children. Although the ancestors of our people were not expecting trouble, they anticipated it with each step, as was their way.

"The little children rubbed away their tracks with brush branches, but the drag litters left marks that were almost impossible to totally hide, and the wind was not blowing hard enough to cover them. Because of this, members of a hostile tribe had discovered their trail.

"The enemies had horses, stolen from the Outsiders, and they could move faster than our families. They found our peoples' track and were following them through the barren red sands. The enemy was hunting and stalking them as if they were animals. Before the bad ones could be seen, our people felt their presence. These were the Comanche, a feared enemy.

"Their faces were painted with the colors of a raiding party. Its purpose was to identify each other in the fight, as well as to give them a frightful appearance. Their naked bodies were painted white with clay from far away. Their horses were lean and had been ridden far. They, too, carried war paint upon their faces and flanks. These were hungry, desperate, and evil men who grew nothing themselves but lived on the fruits of the labor of others.

"Our people were in the middle of the great red earth sands. There were no mesas close enough for them to climb up and throw rocks down on the heads of their enemies. There were not enough young men to put up a fight. For as peaceful as our people are, we will pick up the war club or bow and arrow in defense if necessary.

"Most of their best men were out hunting for meat for the evening's meal. The old man who was their leader had a vision of what was going to happen and called the others near to tell them. They could not outrun the enemy or outfight a raiding party on horseback. This was also before the time of the gun for our people. They were caught in the open, barren sands, with nowhere to hide, and nowhere to run to.

"The enemy was two hills behind them, slowly following their partially rubbed-out tracks. They were stalking them like predators, taking their time, reading the trail. The painted warriors were looking forward to an afternoon of murder, rape, torture, mutilation, and other unspeakable acts.

"Our people had to use their mystical power to fool the enemy. That was the peoples' greatest weapon. The elder instructed the twenty or so people to dig shallow trenches in the sand. Next, he instructed them to cover themselves with blankets and shawls and to lie quietly.

"While his people were following his words, the elder opened his medicine bag and took out two small bundles made of special bird feathers. The wings of birds can move the air. They sometimes lose some of their power and a feather falls off. Wherever or whenever the shaman walks, he looks for these fallen feathers. They cannot come from dead birds. That is bad medicine. Dead bird feathers are allowed only for ceremonial garb, but not for incantations. They have to be molted feathers that fall off during flight and are found by the person who will use them. These are the ones with the power to move the air.

"Holding the feather bundles in his outstretched hands, he kneeled, facing the west, and began singing the song of the wind as he slowly raised and lowered his arms, simulating a bird's flight. There had been a slight breeze blowing all day. As the old one continued singing, the air became still. The people were still digging with their hands and with corn bowls into the soft sands. Some had finished and were helping hide and cover others. Everyone was frightened, as they knew how bloodthirsty their enemies could be.

"The Comanche were too far away to hear the song with their ears, but they sensed it with their spirits. They knew that a shaman was performing spells on them. They whipped their horses and rode faster to stop him. The only sound was the old man singing the chants of the wind ceremony.

"The young people were huddling under their blankets when some of them thought they should be running away. But the older, wiser ones knew running would do no good. They were too old to run, and it is better to die together, so no one is left behind crying for the others in the coming winters. Among the rocks, they may have had a chance, but here, out in the open, they did not have any protection from an enemy with bows and arrows and horses.

"The peaceful air began to move. Very faintly at first, then the sand began to stir. Soon, the winds regathered their strength as the elder sang his song louder. Children clung to their mothers and each other, the older ones whispered instructions to the younger ones to be quiet. As they lay there, the swirling forces of the air began to cover them in fine, windblown sand. Around the shaman, a tiny whirlwind formed. The wind blew harder and harder. The red sands screamed in the air. The whirlwind became a tornado and howled in rage as the enemy came up over the hill. Their horses were balking, as the fine red sand blew into their eyes and noses.

"Their enemy could see nothing in the sandstorm. All signs of the Red Earth Pueblo people were gone. They had been carried away upon the wind. The ponies began to rear up and snort. They wanted to turn around to find shelter. The leader of the war party, who was almost half-animal himself, also thought shelter should be sought. They went back down the sandy hill they had ridden up and waited for the weather to clear. The shaman buried himself in a shallow trench that had been dug for him. He had also covered himself in his blanket and waited with everyone else.

"After a short move of the sun in the sky, the winds died down, leaving a thick blanket of sand atop the homespun blankets of our people. Looking at the spot, one would never know anyone was hidden there. The winds covered every track with red sand, and every hint of their presence was erased. Everyone lay perfectly still for hours. No one was sure if the enemy was gone or not. It was terribly hot and difficult to breathe. No one could see or hear what was going on. Everyone was frightened. No one could relieve themselves of their wastes. So it was a blessing that it was so hot that, their sweat eliminated the liquid wastes from their trembling bodies.

"The still air brought the enemy raiding party back. They set off in the direction they were going in before the sandstorm, trying to find the track of our people. As they moved forward, a thin coating of red dust settled over them and covered their war paint. Even their horses were covered in red dust that stuck to their sweat. This made them very angry. Your ancestors hiding there knew the elder's medicine was strong, but if they were weak, the spell would be broken. They huddled in desperate fear. If they were found, the shallow depressions they lay in would become their graves.

"The older children silently cried, their trembling lips mutely reciting their ancient prayers. A baby began to cry. Its mother tried frantically to stop its fussing. Then it too fell silent, instinctively responding to everyone else's hushed terror at the enemy's now audible presence. A raider's horse almost stepped into their hole. Its hooves could crush a skull or collapse a chest or break a leg. Everyone expected to be stepped on at any instant. If one of them screamed in pain or fear, they all would be discovered.

"Their worst problem was the dog. It followed some of the children all the way from their village. After days of walking, it was still with them. Now there was fear that it would bark and alert their enemy. A young boy held it in his trembling grip, with one hand over its muzzle. With its sharp ears, it heard the hoof beats of walking horses on the sand near them, and it began to growl. The boy whispered in the dog's ear to be silent and tightened his grip on its face.

"The horses walked right over their hiding places, some almost stepping on them. The enemy trackers were searching the sands for sign of their lost prey. The dog clawed at the boy's stomach and chest, but the boy did not let it go. He was strong and brave. He did not cry out in pain, even though he had been deeply scratched and was bleeding. The dog, sensing the stillness of its human, finally also became silent.

"But it was too late. One of the enemies heard the dog's low growl and turned around to go toward where he thought the sound came from. When he was almost upon them, an old trickster came to their aid.

"A large male coyote had also been following our people and had also temporarily lost sight of them in the sandstorm. Coyotes often follow herd animals and groups of walking people. Keeping off to the side, they catch the rabbits and other animals flushed by them. It is one way they hunt.

"When the Comanche saw brother coyote, they thought it was he they had heard. The enemy leader raised his bow and the coyote raced off as the flying arrow struck the sand behind him. The Comanche saw no more of him once he leapt over a dune. When he went to retrieve his arrow, he noticed that the coyote's tracks went farther in the sand than his eyes could follow. He knew it did not have the time to do this.

"Although this was a fierce warrior to other human beings, he saw that what he faced now was Pueblo magic, and he could not fight spirits. He told the rest of the war party about the unending spirit tracks, and they decided to leave that place.

"One said to the others, 'The winds have carried the Pueblo people off.'

"Another said, 'No, they are farther ahead on the trail.'

"The Comanches set off in the direction they were formerly going in and were soon lost over the hills. They were glad to be away from that bewitched place and hoped to find our people's tracks again. Some tales later told that it was the elder who changed into a coyote to fool the enemy. But that did not happen, except in the minds of some.

"The people stayed in hiding for the rest of the day and that night. In the morning, they discovered two of the old ones had suffocated in the airless pits while they were hiding. The grandparents could have easily pulled back the cover for a breath of life-giving air, but would not give away their children to the enemy. They died a slow death in self-sacrifice to their young. Their bodies were left there in the sands for scavenging animals. They could not be carried farther. Their empty shells were of no use now. Their spirits were back in the earth to reemerge later in birth.

"Our people set off again to the north toward the mesas that could provide protection. Without the burden of the sick ones, they traveled surprisingly fast on foot. Their hearts were filled with regret for leaving behind their dead without a proper burial. Their belongings and meager possessions were carried away to be placed on the sacred hill in the pueblo. That way when their spirits returned on special nights, they could find their belongings.

"The next day, they were rejoined by the men, who had left to hunt game, and who had killed an antelope. The people made their way to the red rock hills, where it would be harder to track them on the hard stone. They made a fire among the rocks and ate for the first time in days. It was a much longer, but safer, way home. Besides, the stone hills would give them more places to hide than in the open. The horses of the enemy would be no good, and the men could ambush them from hiding. Several days later, they were safely home. That is the way it was."

><del>— ><del>— ><del>

Almost as quickly as it left, Young One's mind traveled back across oceans and continents to the perilous present in the Persian Gulf, with his return to the present impelled partly by a sickening stench that was beginning to pervade his nostrils. Having no time to ponder the source of the vile odor, he signaled to Youssef to take over the dragging of the sled holding Mizzi and trotted ahead a few paces until he was by the side of the limping colonel.

Until that moment, the young soldier had been so absorbed in guiding the battered foursome safely through the steady stream of near-disasters that he'd given little thought to how brazenly if necessarily he'd ignored the chain of command. But now Washington was clearly regaining his mental acuity, and Young One realized that having only minutes to attempt the bizarre gamble he had in mind, and being unable to carry it off without the pilot's help, he would need to turn to the tight-lipped colonel for leadership.

"Excuse me, colonel, sir. Permission to offer an urgent suggestion?"

Without slowing his staggering gait, Washington replied through clenched teeth, "Fire away, soldier. I'm all ears."

"Sir, the Iraqi stragglers will overtake us soon. We cannot go any faster dragging the injured, and I do not think we will have much chance in another fire fight."

"Save the situation briefing, son. What's your plan?"

Young One took a deep breath. "We need to hide... hide in plain sight. It may sound crazy, but my people are Pueblo Indians, and we have escaped and evaded for centuries in the desert. Also, sometimes we get visions, and I think the one I just had might save us."

Glancing back at the approaching stragglers, he stifled a gag at the fetid odor, which he now recognized as dried blood, burnt hair, and decayed flesh.

"We have to act fast, sir, and you need to trust me."

The pilot listened silently to Young One's hurried plan. He well knew what it was like to have to rely on men in positions of higher authority to accept the views of those whose ideas—and skin color—were different. And as the young enlisted man had said, there was no time to lose.

"We'll try your plan and pray it works; but we can't let those shell-shocked Iraqis see what we're up to."

He pointed his crutch at a long, knocked-out vehicle off to the side, its overturned trailer resting at an angle that would screen them from view.

"We'll dig in behind that."

"Yes, sir," said Young One, "but where is that smell coming from?"

"From the dead animals, but that might discourage the enemy from getting too curious."

Without waiting for Washington to possibly change his mind, Young One signaled to Youssef to follow, and then led the way to the opposite side of the wrecked rig, where he stopped and gasped involuntarily...not at the worsening smell but at the grotesque and grisly sight that met his eyes.

Spilled out onto the sand next to the overturned stake-bed trailer—encircled by huge pools of dark, encrusted blood—laid the rigid corpses of two zoo animals. Washington thought they were African wildebeests, but it was hard to tell for sure because of their bloated condition. A few yards away, suspended half inside and half outside the shattered window of the truck, was its dead driver.

"Let's move, people; time's wasting and we've got digging to do."

Presuming that she would unquestioningly comply with whatever plan of action the senior officer present had approved, Young One hadn't bothered to explain to Mizzi his reason for putting all four of them at work scooping out two shallow ditches with their feet and hands. But when he directed her to drop into one of the holes and told her what would happen next, she reacted in near-panic, blurting out that since childhood she'd had a fear of being buried alive.

Young One looked at Washington, who with what seemed under the circumstances to be an almost eerily calm and gentle manner, laid a hand on her shoulder and said softly, "It is all right. We'll be fine." Without knowing exactly why, Mizzi suddenly felt reassured. Young One motioned for Youssef to bring Mizzi and lie her down into the trench. She reluctantly obeyed as Youssef assured her in Arabic that everything would be alright. He was not sure he told her the truth or not.

Young One then motioned for Youssef to lie next to her and placed the Toyota hood over them. Young One took his military poncho, which was rolled up into a tight cylindrical bundle on his web belt. It was the one thing the Iraqis had not taken from them. Next, he and the pilot dropped into the other depression, after which he pulled the poncho over them to create a nylon roof. Now all that remained to be done was wait, and—as the colonel said—pray.

The Iraqis were almost upon them. Young One could hear some of them tearing apart the Toyota, looking for anything they could use. At least so far, the Iraqis were giving the foul-smelling trailer a wide berth.

Though he didn't dare move physically, in his mind Young One took the feathers from his medicine bag and began whisper-singing the song of the wind of his people. If from the strength of his ancestors he could tap the power to move the wind, it would cover them in sand as in Grandfather's story from the old days.

Over and over, he repeated the ancient singsong melody of his people's past. He was not sure he could remember it correctly, nor was he sure it would work here on the other side of the earth. Young One was also not sure if he really had the power to do it.

Once, a few years earlier, he had sung up a tiny dust devil, a miniature tornado-like swirling of the wind. His grandfather had both praised and berated him. The praise was for reaching deep into his inner being to get the spirit to move the wind, but he had called up the wrong wind. He was supposed to create straight wind—not a toy tornado. It was, nevertheless, strong spirit power for one still in his youth. Grandfather knew that he was powerful but not completely disciplined. It worried him because he knew that medicine out of control was worse than no mystical power at all.

He lay there with the pilot under the stifling poncho, essentially a nylon sheet with a head hole in it. The poncho wasn't new when it was issued to him, and Young One had never bothered to wash it. It smelled like the breath, sweat, and body funk of everyone who had ever worn it, amplified in the contained space. For Mizzi and Youssef the ventilation under the hood of the Toyota was somewhat better, but the young Iraqi was particularly ripe after a lifetime of unhygienic living, and it was hard for Mizzi to breathe while being choked by his body odor. And for all of them, the atmosphere was made immeasurably worse by the malodor of decaying animal flesh permeating the outside air.

Young One tried to concentrate on the song, but kept interrupting its recital in his mind's ear to question himself, *Can I remember the words and syllables correctly?*

The song had never been recorded, merely transferred from mind to mouth, to ear, to mind, by each generation. The songs were the one thing the Outsiders didn't know about and couldn't steal from Young One's people.

Then the wind began to pick up. Granules of sand, at first gently, then violently, rose to assail everything that stood above ground. Just as some members of the gang of Iraqis, apparently impervious to the reeking odor, were drawing near, the wind's intensity increased still further, and began driving sand into their eyes, mouths, ears, and nostrils.

Meanwhile, Young One and Washington heard the wind begin to howl, and the sound of sand peppering the surface of the poncho, even as Mizzi and Youssef listened to the thin metallic pinging of the tiny particles against the Toyota's hood.

By now the stench from the dead animals had been swept cleanly from the desert floor where the four refugees had gone to ground, but the enemy stragglers suddenly had a more formidable impediment to contend with: The choking dust was filling their lungs and making them cough and gasp for breath, while the lashing sand cruelly stung and lacerated their exposed flesh, including that of many who had suffered burns in the bombing. Some tried in vain to crawl away from the sandstorm's fury; others dropped into fetal balls and pleaded for the Almighty's intercession.

In silence, Young One and Washington listened to the enraged whistle of the Arabian winds, while gripping the corners of the poncho for dear life to keep it from being torn away. Similarly, a few feet away from them, Youssef and Mizzi struggled to prevent the truck hood from taking off like a large metal Frisbee with them still holding on. The sand hitting the hood sounded like frozen sleet striking a windowpane in a storm. Youssef was very frightened. This was the strangest thing he had ever experienced.

For half an hour, the winds swirled. Then the air became still, and a thick shower of sand fell on top of them, not only covering them almost completely, but also creating dunes not there before. The desert landscape had been transformed so that it did not even look like the same place.

After the ferocious sandstorm died away, the four waited a long time, not daring to move or make a sound. Finally, Young One and Washington pulled back the poncho and cautiously looked around. There was not another living thing in sight. There was no sign of tracks. Even the deep furrow left by the Land Cruiser's hood had been obliterated by the swirling sands. If any sandblasted Iraqi stragglers had survived, they were nowhere to be seen, but those who had perished from suffocation were everywhere, some coated so thoroughly that they looked like toppled statues carved from sandstone, others so nearly completely buried that only their boots or here and there an up-thrust arm protruded from a mound of sand.

Young One called to Mizzi, who didn't need to be summoned twice. She and Youssef instantly erupted from their gritty bunker and shook off the clinging sand. Then she collapsed again from the renewed pain of her injury. But the colonel had told her true: She had been buried alive, and had lived to tell the tale. With winds calmed, the sky had turned smoky and ominous. After collecting the canteens they resumed their torturous trek toward Kuwait City. When the sandstorm came, Youssef told Mizzi, "It is the hand of the merciful Almighty who throws sand in the enemies' eyes to make them unable to see and to stop fighting."

Normally the desert boy would have been frightened out of his wits, but Youssef had seen so many very frightening things recently that he soon began to regard the apparent miracle as a mere curiosity.

After stopping to allow Youssef to perform his prayers, the party continued on, dragging Mizzi on the truck hood, while Washington insisted on moving slowly and excruciatingly under his own power. It was laborious work, and their limited supply of water had to be closely rationed.

Following a short discussion in which everyone was given a say, the colonel decided that while traveling over the sand was much tougher, at least for the time being, they couldn't take the risk of moving back onto the road. There was no disagreement that keeping Kuwait City as their destination was the right call. They moved in a direction parallel to the distant highway to keep from getting lost in the sand.

The Iraqis had evacuated the city, and it was safer than going back across enemy lines. It wasn't the way home, but it was the only way for them to go if they were to survive. They also had to find more water, and fairly soon. Most importantly, they had to get the colonel and Mizzi to medical attention. For all those reasons, Kuwait City seemed like their best bet, and it lay only a few miles away. But no one expected those miles to be easy to cover.

Like two lame sled dogs, they slowly made their way along, dragging Mizzi on the improvised travois. Fortunately, they encountered no other Iraqi stragglers or deserters. The desert was devoid of all human life but theirs. There were plenty of tire tracks from patrol vehicles, but they were old ones. There were no screaming aircraft, no distant thunder of war. All was strangely silent. Only the soft wind filled their ears, carrying the oil smoke overhead in hypnotic swirls.

At midday, after small portions of water, they set out again and made several kilometers before taking their next break. The crude oil on their skin caused acne wherever it coated their bodies, as it clogged their pores. The rash it created itched and annoyed them further as the stiff uniforms sand-papered the bumps. To Young One and Youssef, the fabricated harness, made of seat belts and engine wires from the Toyota, began to feel like yokes attached to beasts of burden. They formed a human sled team that dragged Mizzi along, accompanied by the iron-willed colonel, toward the capital of the invaded nation...

><---><---><

The ferocity of the sandstorm took coalition military planners by surprise. One military meteorologist watching the phenomenon from the safety of a secure trailer remarked, "I've never seen anything like this."

Another meteorologist said, "It was a tornado in the desert. This is the most amazing thing I've ever seen. Usually these kinds of events are part of some overall weather system. This one happened in isolation and wasn't associated with other storms. It wasn't very large, but was extremely intense for its size. And it occurred without warning; also, it was unusual to have an early-day sandstorm."

In fact, he told his colleagues, "Such storms were virtually unheard of. Mostly, they occur in the afternoon, after the sun has heated the sands and gets the air swirling."

This one popped onto the weather screens just after dawn. Several possible explanations were proposed. They tried to find explanations, such as that the fragile hard-baked desert crust had been broken by vehicle tracks, dug-in emplacements, and bomb craters. With that much loose sand around, perhaps even very little wind could cause a blinding storm.

Other meteorologists, studying it later, explained the extreme force of the strange occurrence as winds created by the oil fires. Nature abhors a vacuum, and the rapidly rising hot air had to be replaced with fresh. Hence, the winds grew stronger as the fires burned brighter. It was also the time of the spring winds. No one was particularly shocked by a sudden sandstorm in the desert, but the meteorologists were surprised by its confined area. They all agreed that they must study the phenomenon further. No one suggested, however, that a mystical song from an ancient time and a distant land may have played a role...

Chapter 35

FAT FAROOK

As they struggled onward, they could see the faint outline of what looked like a city through the smoke. Even though it was daytime, the horizon was dark and gloomy. Colonel Washington assured them it was Kuwait City.

"What if the Iraqis are still there?" Young One inquired.

"They'll probably be mostly stragglers. It looks as if they were pulling out when the air force hit them. We'll have to chance it. We are out of water, food, and luck."

The winds shifted, and the smoke was blown away on the breeze, leaving the sun blazing overhead through a dirty sky. Young One took it as a very good omen, but Washington knew they could be spotted by coalition aircraft. But this could be a mixed blessing, as they could be mistaken for the enemy and fired upon rather than rescued.

They were sweating a lot and had great water loss, exacerbated by the escape of moisture through their exhaled breath. Ten minutes later, the wind changed directions yet again, and the cloak of oppressive oil smoke reclosed over them.

On they labored through the parched sands, across what had once been the floor of an ancient sea. At times, it was hard and crusty with gravel, almost like frozen dirt. At other places it was windblown, fine sand that they sank into up to their ankles, while dragging the injured Mizzi. The colonel was still limping along with his single crutch and helping out as best as he could.

At last they reached a rocky plain that they could not drag Mizzi through on the hood sled. Youssef and Young One had to carry the burned specialist and then go back and drag the empty hood across. The combined weight was too heavy to carry in one trip.

In the open, they had no chance for cover and concealment. Also, distances in the desert could be deceptive. What appeared to be a mile could actually be three or four. As they took one of their frequent rests, Youssef looked toward the horizon and spoke in Arabic.

"What did he say?" asked the pilot of Mizzi.

"It is an old desert saying. It means in English something like, 'The eyes see farther than the feet can walk.' I think it means, 'It is farther than it looks.' "

Soon after resuming their arduous journey, they reached an abandoned Iraqi defensive trench. It had not been bombed and was of good construction. The day before it had been filled with enemy soldiers, who had apparently taken everything of value with them. After a cautious and futile search for any food, water, or medical supplies that might have been left behind, the party made its way through the defensive emplacements and finally found themselves nearing the outskirts of the city.

During one of their frequent rests, Youssef stared at the hypnotic shifting sand. He saw near him an unbelievable sight. There were sand spider holes dug into the ground. Each had a spider at the entrance to the hole, guarding it. It protected its territory and its young below.

A solitary large desert wasp flew overhead, and, with remarkable precision, drove its venomous stinger into the heads of three spiders in rapid succession. After a moment, the arachnids began to convulse, and then fell back into their tunnels to die as the poison took effect.

Somehow, the small drama made Youssef remember the coalition air attacks, and he wondered whether the colonel was one of those pilots who had killed so many of his former colleagues. Even if that were the case, he thought he could not really feel resentment, but only a kind of weary sadness.

As the four companions inched their way into Kuwait City, they could see that the Iraqis had not completely left town. There were still enemy vehicles roving the streets, and Iraqi positions were still occupied. They could hear the sound of small-arms and machine-gun fire punctuated periodically with a grenade or mortar blast. The guerilla war was waging quietly but audibly in the city's heart. The bulk of the Iraqi Army lay in ruins on the highway, and the soldiers who were left were too near Kuwaiti civilians for coalition warplanes to bomb them. But after six months of brutal occupation, the Kuwaiti resistance fighters were more than willing to take up where the coalition planes had left off.

Under the oil smoke, the city lay eerily dark in the daylight as the exhausted foursome advanced. Having agreed to make for what appeared to be an abandoned building, Young One and Youssef realized that the racket made by the truck hood could draw unwanted attention. They stopped and lifted Mizzi between them and carried her the last dozen yards to an unlocked side door. The building smelled of grease and used motor oil, and looked as if it had been a garage or maintenance shed.

From the sound of the shooting, the Americans thought that the ground assault had begun and that the marines were entering Kuwait City, and so they decided to wait and see if friendly forces would overrun them. After a while, however, Washington recognized that the firing was too sporadic to be an invasion force. He thought that the Iraqis were executing prisoners or perhaps fighting among themselves. In any case, he told them that their best bet for the time being was to remain in the darkened shed and try to catch a few hours of badly needed sleep. Youssef was the first to wake up. A rat ran over his legs and startled him out of his rest. A minute later, awakened by a surge of pain, Mizzi moaned softly and rose to a sitting position. Scanning the dimly-lit room, Youssef noticed a five-gallon can of automotive grease and crawled over to pick it up. Moving to Mizzi's side, he wordlessly motioned his intention and lifted the stiffened cuffs of the pants covering her blistered legs. With a handful of grease scooped from the can, he began gently rubbing the raw flesh as the specialist winced in renewed pain; but her eyes conveyed her gratitude. She knew that insulating the burns from the surrounding air was the only form of first aid available, and after a moment she began to feel that the crude salve was actually affording her some relief.

Next, Youssef wiped out the can with a dirty rag and crept outside in search of water. All around him was destruction. Every building was riddled with bullet holes, yet it did not look like a battle had happened there. It looked like everything was shot up in vandalism. He cautiously limped around each building, searching for a faucet. It was dark and smoky, and he had to be careful about tripping or falling.

He heard and then saw something move off to his left. It was a cat that ran away at Youssef's approach. The cat had found water from a faucet that was still leaking and was drinking it when interrupted. Youssef leaned the grease can under it and collected water from the dripping spout. It took a long time for enough water to drip into the can to drink. While it was filling up, he looked around several of the buildings. Everything of value had been stolen or damaged beyond repair. There were no lights working, and the oil smoke blocked the sun. It was also very dark inside the buildings, and he had no matches or lighter to illuminate the darkness. There was nothing useful he could see in any of the other surrounding structures. Youssef retrieved the half-full can and returned to the others. Though tainted by motor grease, no water had ever tasted better. Young One sat Mizzi up and gave her the first drink. After everyone had slaked their thirst, they conferred and concurred on the need to explore more of the city. But how? They could not carry Mizzi, and dragging the noisy truck hood over the pavement was out of the question. If they could find food and more potable water, their current refuge might do as a place to hold out and await the coalition advance, but they did not know when that would be, or if the attack would bypass Kuwait City and force the Iraqi garrison to surrender under siege. Meanwhile, there was nothing in the desert or in the outskirts to sustain them while they waited.

Under cover of the oncoming night, Young One took the next reconnaissance. There were piles of rubble in the streets. Trash was strewn all about, and bullet holes were ubiquitous. This had been a commercial district on the edge of the growing town. The sporadic firing had subsided, and there did not seem to be anyone alive there but them. Young One crept surreptitiously among the deserted buildings until he suddenly froze in his tracks, hearing the unmistakable sound of a motorized patrol.

He ducked into the doorway of a former office, but it was too late. He had been spotted. The Iraqis were in a jeep-like vehicle, and they drove up fast with their lights on. There were three of them. Two privates, one the driver and the other on the machine gun in the back. There was also an Iraqi corporal in the front passenger seat. He held a rifle trained on Young One, whose hand instinctively tried the handle of the door behind him. It was locked. He was trapped. The driver was out and was taking aim from around the front hood with his automatic rifle. The machine gunner locked and loaded and swiveled the barrel towards Young One.

The corporal came menacingly forward and spoke in Arabic. "What are you doing here? Come out where I can see you."

Not understanding the words, Young One stood waiting to be shot. The Iraqi corporal raised his weapon. It was deadly quiet as the safety was taken off, and then, without warning, pandemonium broke loose.

The stillness of the moment was disturbed with the stutter of automatic weapons fire. The corporal and his two men were cut down like blades of grass before a weed-whacker. Young One could not believe the suddenness of what his eyes had just perceived. His assailants were there one moment, and lying dead on the ground the next. Very slowly, like a mirage in the particulate fog, a vehicle emerged out of the smoke.

It was a slate gray-colored stretch limousine full of Kuwaiti freedom fighters. As it rolled to a stop the doors on both sides flew open, and several partisans jumped out, one of whom trained a spotlight on the frozen figure of Young One, who immediately threw up his hands. Meanwhile, a man standing upright through the sunroof kept a tripod machine gun leveled at Young One's chest.

After a few moments during which the Kuwaitis took note of their captive's very dirty American uniform, a voice spoke in English from the open window on the driver's side.

"Bring him here. I want to talk to him."

Picking up Young One's rifle, a couple of freedom fighters led him around the jeep and over to the limo. Their companions, meanwhile, began stripping the dead Iraqis of weapons and ammunition.

Abruptly, the man behind the steering wheel reverted to Arabic, and began barking orders in an authoritative voice.

"Get their uniforms as well. Use their underwear to soak up the blood. Throw some sand on the stains. Take their bodies to the holes we have dug. You know where. This way, their officers will not know if their men have been killed or merely deserted. They will never know what happened to their men. But we will know." He laughed with wicked delight.

While the speaker was thus distracted, Young One had the opportunity to study the man's striking appearance. First, there was his bulk, which barely allowed his barrel-like belly to clear the steering wheel. But more compelling was his attire, consisting of an immaculate dove-gray vintage chauffeur's uniform, complete with double-breasted jacket buttoned to the throat and matching wide-hipped trousers along with black high-top boots. Shading his swarthy, bearded face was the bill of a gray chauffeur's cap, below which his bushy black eyebrows formed a nearly unbroken line above a pair of shrewd and piercing dark eyes.

When he was satisfied that his minions were going about their tasks, the fat man turned back to Young One. "You are in the American Army, I see. Somehow, I expected that the liberation forces would arrive in greater strength. Do you have companions close about?"

Not yet ready to give his bizarre rescuer a full measure of trust, Young One chose for the moment to ignore the question. "Yes, I am an American. And who are you?"

"Why, I am Fat Farook, the Moroccan," he answered in a surprised tone of voice, as if Young One should know him. "We are freedom fighters. Are you part of the liberation force?"

Realizing his hurt and hungry compatriots would not be served by him being overly cautious, Young One explained that he belonged to a group of four escaped prisoners of war trying to get back to coalition territory, and that two of his party were badly in need of medical attention.

"Come then, we will help you. Where are your friends?" Farook then shouted to one of his men to "get the tarpaulins from the trunk." He instructed him to spread them over the upholstery and carpeting. He then invited Young One into the limo, and summoned back two of the young men he'd assigned to the burial detail. Young One accepted the invitation into the limo. Minutes later, with the pair of armed body guards trotting alongside like secret service agents, the stretch Cadillac rolled to a stop in front of the maintenance shed. Young One called the others out. Cautiously, the three fugitives emerged and blinked in disbelief. There was Young One in a stretch limo with reinforcements.

Colonel Washington was first to speak, as he smiled from ear to ear like an opossum.

"You did real fine, son,"

They had hoped to find a cart or wheel barrow to carry Mizzi, but this was beyond all expectations. But the Kuwaitis stiffened when they saw the oil-soaked Iraqi uniform on Youssef.

"What is he doing here?" asked Farook, as his bodyguards and the rooftop machine gunner raised their weapons menacingly. Not pausing to speculate why the man in obvious authority was dressed as a chauffeur, the colonel quickly explained how Youssef had helped them escape.

"Welcome, then. We must leave." With surprising dexterity, Fat Farook stepped out of the vehicle and looked with displeasure at their oil-soaked and grit-covered uniforms. He did not want them to soil his beautiful automobile.

"I suppose there are too many of you to put into the trunk," he said. The Americans were unsure what to make of this statement. Was he a friend or foe after all? Or was he just trying to make a joke?

"I will help you, but there is one condition. You must not touch anything in the car until we can get you cleaned up. Is that acceptable?" They all grunted and nodded in the affirmative, after which Young One and Youssef helped Mizzi into one of the tarp-covered back seats and climbed in beside her. Befitting his rank, Washington took the front passenger seat.

Before stepping back inside, Fat Farook addressed the guard with the bipod machine gun standing in the open sun roof. "And you be careful. Do not scratch the top of my car."

The guard replied, "Yes, Father, I will be careful."

"That is Kareem, one of my sons," the fat man remarked with pride.

"Most of these boys are the sons of my friends and neighbors," Farook explained as he drove toward their next, as yet undisclosed destination. "Their parents are dead now, so I am their father as well. Two of them are my own sons, and all have good cause to despise the Iraqi invaders." Though his mood had darkened while saying this, he immediately returned to his jovial manner as he continued.

"This is probably the craziest thing any of you have ever seen in your lives. Yes? Well, it has been a crazy time for all of us." Not waiting for prompting from his grateful guests, Farook proceeded to address the questions on all of their minds.

"I was the best limousine driver in Kuwait City," he said boastfully. "I met all the best people, took them to all the best places. I could find the most fragrant smoke, the freshest chew, the prettiest women, and the fattest little boys for my customers." He laughed the belly laugh of the mad, as he remembered the days not too long before. The three Americans sat in the back and listened to his thickly Middle Eastern-accented English as he drove them deeper into the heart of the city.

"I came here in 1964 as an oil man. But, as fate would have it, I was not well suited for that type of work. I lost my job and took all my meager savings and bought an old car. It was a 1958 Oldsmobile with the Jane Mansfield front bumper." He held up two hands in a mock gesture of squeezing a large woman's breasts, alluding to the cone-like projections on the massive chromed bumper. "I made money picking up passengers from the airport. I had to wait until all of the regular taxis were gone, and I got what was left. Mostly foreign workers. Very poor tippers, but I worked hard, and soon I had my own clientele. I bought a newer car, and everyone came to know my name.

"Soon, I no longer had to wait for the other taxis to leave, and I got the special rides. Important people began to ask for me. Foreign dignitaries, oil executives. Anyone who wanted to move quickly and unseen called for Fat Farook the Moroccan. I married a fine Kuwaiti woman, and she gave me four sons. I worked hard and was happy. I finally saved enough money to buy this armored limousine and this fancy uniform. Both were especially made in America. It is a large-engine Cadillac. Very fast and powerful. It has bulletproof glass and tires, and armored sidewalls. I was a very proud man.

"Anyone who was anybody asked for Fat Farook at the airport or had reservations. I was sought out because I could keep my mouth shut about who and what I saw. You should know the famous people who have sat right where you are sitting. But that is all over now."

The tone of his voice turned to sadness again as he continued speaking. "The Iraqis took my wife and two youngest sons and shot them. My family and my business were my whole life. Now both are gone. Only my beautiful automobile and my oldest sons are left. My other son, Rasheed, is driving the commandeered Iraqi jeep behind us."

"How did you keep the limo out of the hands of the Iraqis?" asked the colonel.

The big man's large bearded face bore a weary smile as he explained that he had buried it in his back yard. With the help of a neighbor with a backhoe and his two eldest sons, they had dug a large trench behind his house. He continued to explain how they placed boards over the top of the subterranean garage and covered it with earth.

"Then, we covered the whole thing in garbage, and no one could tell it was there. Iraqi soldiers came and searched our home and took what they wanted from us. But they never found my car. Now we hunt Iraqis with it. Many have left, and there are just enough of them for us to fight. It used to be very noticeable, but, in the smoke, its gray color makes it almost camouflaged. But this is enough talk. There are many enemies around."

At the next turn of the corner, they ran into another Iraqi patrol. This one was an armored car. Fat Farook darted into a side street, while behind him, as if in planned syncopation, the commandeered jeep turned off in the opposite direction. The Iraqis followed the limousine. Fat Farook floored the gas pedal, and the chase was on. The large vehicle seemed to float in the smoky streets as it sped forward with the enemy armored car hot in pursuit.

"Okay now, get ready. You know what to do," he said to Kareem, who pulled the bipod-mounted machine gun down from the roof. The enemy was bearing down fast and signaling them to pull over. The eldest son, along with another boy, took two anti-tank rockets from the floor, and quickly armed them for firing. Fat Farook watched his rear view mirror intently. Fortunately, the Iraqis could not see what was going on behind the smoked glass of the limo windows.

"At the next corner," he told the boys. They knew what he meant. After they rounded the curve, Fat Farook abruptly pulled the limo over to the curb in the middle of the block. A split second later, both of the youths popped up from the sunroof and took hasty aim with the rocket launchers. The armored car rounded the corner in pursuit, and, just as it straightened out, they fired.

The first rocket went over the top of the vehicle, skidded off the ground, and exploded down the street. The second caught the Iraqi armored car dead center. It exploded and the vehicle jerked to a stop. Almost before it did so, Fat Farook's eldest son began rubbing the rockets' scorch marks from the top of the limo with spit-covered fingers, so his father would not know he had burned the paint.

Moments later, Farook's other son pulled up in the jeep, and after pouring several bursts through the armored car's gun ports to make sure there would be no witnesses, the gang of partisans began exuberantly looting the metal carcass for anything of worth. They collected some Iraqi combat rations and a lot of ammo, but afraid of overstaying their welcome, left the machine gun in the smoldering hulk. In a few minutes, they were back on the road again.

Farook said, "We must head for the center of the city. There are fewer Iraqi soldiers there. Most are on the coast waiting for the American armored columns. Since the bulk of the Iraqi army left yesterday, the center of the city is poorly defended. Now we get our revenge. But this is enough for today. We should not push the blessings we have."

"Are the Iraqis looking for you?" asked Washington.

"They are looking for everyone to shoot. No one is searching specifically for us, as we leave no one to tell the tale." The boys laughed at that remark. The colonel said no more for the rest of the ride. They drove to a downtown garage, formerly used to house a fleet of taxicabs. Now it was Fat Farook's hideout. The Iraqis would be looking for their lost patrols.

One of the boys got out and opened a garage door. Soon the limo and its occupants were safely off the streets.

"We must get medical attention for this woman," the colonel said.

"We will do what we can. There are no doctors. The Iraqis took them all away to Baghdad. There are no nurses or pharmacies. Everything is gone. But we will do what we can. We know of a woman who helps bring babies into the world. That is the closest to a doctor that we can find for now. We will send for her." They settled Mizzi on a stained and cigarette-burned back seat from an old car. It was braced up with cinder blocks, and the cabbies used to sit on it waiting for fares. About an hour later, the midwife came but had no real medical equipment or supplies. They tore rags to make bandages. As the Kuwaitis were pulling Mizzi's sandy tarpaper BDU britches off of her to treat her injuries, she protested. Fat Farook responded disarmingly.

"Our hearts seethe with revenge, not lust," he said in Arabic. "You are as safe as if you were the daughter of my sister. No harm will come to you without coming through me first." There was something about this large man's voice that said he spoke the truth. Besides, they were completely at his mercy.

Then he told his sons to go away, and then did so himself. The midwife winced noticeably when she saw Mizzi's legs and feet. They were masses of blisters and raw flesh, contaminated with oil and covered with grease. But Mizzi held up under the pain. The midwife built a small fire in the middle of the floor and boiled some olive oil in a kettle, into which she placed the torn up rags to be used for bandages.

After boiling the cloth strips for several minutes, the old woman removed them from the kettle and took them out to cool in the air. When the bandages cooled, they were tied to Mizzi's legs and feet. That, and supplying a few aspirin, was all she could do to relieve the pain. She then gave a handful of aspirin to the colonel to administer to Mizzi and the others later. For the moment, he and Mizzi each took three. The midwife next tended to the legs of Youssef and Young One, which were burned, but not as badly as Mizzi's, and treated the gash on Young One's forehead as well as she could. After that, the Kuwaitis shared their meager foodstuff with the Americans.

As they ate, Fat Farook pulled the colonel aside and inquired of him, "Are you sure about the Iraqi?" He meant, of course, Youssef. "He says he is not an Iraqi. He says he is a Bedouin, conscripted at gunpoint from his family." The colonel then described how Youssef helped them to escape from Kasim and his men.

"I will listen to his Arabic," said Fat Farook. "I will tell you where he is from. And what about the woman soldier? Is she okay? How did she learn to speak Arabic?"

"She said her grandparents were from Lebanon and she learned the language as a child. She has been very valuable to us as a translator."

Having finished their meal, the Americans and Youssef used mechanic's hand cleaner to remove the oil from their bodies. Fat Farook apologized for the lack of bath water, but the Iraqis had blown up the water plant as a last act of revenge. They needed what little water there was for cooking and drinking.

They were brought Arab clothing. As an attractive woman, Nirada Mizzi would be expected to hide her face from the eyes of the unclean, and was given the full, dark *abbaya* of the women. Washington, Youssef, and Young One were given male Bedouin clothing. The garments smelled like their previous occupants, but were vermin-free. Obliged to give up his filthy and encrusted pants, Young One felt like he was wearing a dress, and being a large man, Washington's Arab clothes were tight and ill-fitting. Farook apologized and explained that they were all they could find at short notice.

"You must leave here tomorrow," Fat Farook said all of a sudden. "The war is coming. It is not safe. There is uprising all over the city. The Iraqis are looking everywhere for freedom fighters. Whole households are being taken out and shot. Whole neighborhoods are vacant from executions. We must get you out before the bombing comes or you are discovered. I do not know how, but I will think of a way. Now you must rest if you can."

The four escapees were given a place to sleep, piled together on the floor. Fat Farook slept in the back of the limo while his soldiers took turns watching and listening all night. When the Americans awoke nearly twelve hours later, it was to confront renewed danger...

Chapter 36

THE LOST CITY

Fat Farook and his youngest son and two other young men they had not seen before burst into their sleeping quarters with loaded assault weapons in their hands. They obviously had been running hard. Struggling to regain his breath, Farook's son gasped out the news that another unrelated group of freedom fighters had botched an attempted ambush of an Iraqi patrol and was under fierce counterattack.

Farook quickly translated for the Americans, then added. "Now the butchers will come to every building in the neighborhood and kill everyone in retribution. That is how they do it. They will be here soon. We must go now before they arrive. There will be too many to fight."

There was urgency in his voice that told the Americans and Youssef that Farook's advice wasn't to be ignored. In response to his emphatic gesture, they gathered up Mizzi and hurried into the limo. They pulled out of the garage just as the sound of gunfire erupted behind them.

The Iraqi occupation of the richest city on earth had been particularly brutal and was designed to frighten the Kuwaitis into submission. There was no reason for the Americans to doubt Farook's assessment of the situation. Given any opportunity to do so, the Iraqis would kill every man outright and rape and torture any woman to death, before their expulsion by the American marines. And at that moment they were coming with as much force as they could still muster to crush the vengeful Kuwaiti resistance that had suddenly risen up to make their departure as difficult and costly as possible.

There was a lot of shooting going on, and normally Fat Farook and his troops would be in the middle of it. But now he must help the Americans to escape. He was still the best limo driver in Kuwait City, however, and consoled himself for missing the action by delivering a running commentary on his country's sad recent history in his most impassioned oratorical style.

"They have destroyed our beautiful city. Our wonderful home is gone. What you see now is the lost city." The Americans began to see how such a jolly man could have driven himself to the edge of madness in his armored limousine.

"There came a cessation of civilization in Kuwait. Iraqi soldiers commandeered vehicles at gunpoint, and whole neighborhoods were looted and their occupants tortured and killed. Stores and warehouses were emptied. Any protest was met with death. The botanical gardens were chopped down for firewood; the zoo animals were shot for sport and cooked for meat. The university was looted of its high-tech equipment and supplies. Babies were thrown from their incubators, and the infirm were starved to death.

"The male population of whole blocks was lined up and machine-gunned. Women and children were defiled. Others were taken for torture and mutilation in interrogation centers. They even used the amusement park for artillery target practice, and turned the skating rink into a huge morgue, they killed so many. They would pick up the members of families who came to retrieve their loved ones' bodies and interrogate them as well.

"Before the Iraqi invasion, we had the greatest lifestyle on Earth; now we have one of the worst. How quickly human beings can turn Heaven into Hell on Earth. Our money wouldn't save us; rather, it made us targets. We thought our wealth and oil would be our salvation. It was our destruction."

Even as he spoke, in the back of his mind Farook was planning his course of action. He would take the Americans to the Bedouin district in the western section of Kuwait City, where he had friends who could help. But the route he must follow would take him directly through an Iraqi checkpoint. Slowing as he approached the center of town, he pulled over and shouted something in Arabic. One of the boys jumped out and fetched two small Iraqi flags from the trunk, then affixed them to the front fender with little magnets. Moments after, the limo resumed its slow progress; a jeep full of Iraqi soldiers pulled up alongside of them. Washington recognized them as Farook's other men.

"Be careful. Do not let them see the bullet holes or blood," he said to his troops, referring to the Iraqi uniforms they had recently acquired. "That will spoil everything, you see," he explained with an ironic smile to the Americans. The jeep then slowed down to allow the limo to take the lead.

The long, sleek armored limousine drove slowly up to the main checkpoint, one of the last fixtures of organized military occupation the Iraqis still had in place. There were many soldiers there, and it was a dangerous place. Farook could not drive out the way the Americans had walked in because of the risk that out in the open, coalition planes would assume the limo was occupied by an escaping high-ranking Iraqis and shoot them. Besides, he would never think of driving his fine automobile through the desert.

Everyone knew the coalition would come soon, but if Fat Farook and his sons were caught with the Americans, there would be no Geneva Convention for them. They would be tied to the nearest telephone pole and shot.

Fat Farook asked of his troops, "Is everyone ready?" All four young Kuwaitis responded affirmatively, and readied their weapons. Fat Farook hid his old Smith and Wesson 357-magnum revolver under a map on the seat next to him. It had always been a loyal friend. Then he said to the Americans, "Get down on the floor, and do not get up until I tell you it is all right. Okay, let's go."

The Iraqi jeep gave the procession a look of authority. They drove cautiously, but authoritatively, up to the Iraqi checkpoint. There was a Soviet T-55 tank and two sandbagged emplacements with machine guns protruding from them. Off to the left was a plywood building.

The Iraqi private on duty saw the limousine approaching, noted the Iraqi flags, and concluded that it was carrying a high-ranking officer. Glancing in the mirror, Farook saw that the jeep had dropped back about three car lengths, and all of its occupants were sitting bolt upright in a posture of attention.

Responding to the young soldier's upraised hand, Farook rolled to a stop as the private called for the sergeant of the guard, and immediately the limo was surrounded by four Iraqis. Another four soldiers, two in each sandbagged, machine-gun emplacement, waited watchfully. The tank seemed to be empty, but the hatch was open.

The sunroof was opening as he rolled down his window for the guards. At the same instant, Kareem and Rashid stood up through the sunroof, and tossed grenades into each of the Iraqi machine-gun positions. Before the surprised guards could react, Farook grabbed his revolver and drilled a .357 magnum round into each of the foreheads of the three guards standing nearest to him. His youngest son got the fourth Iraqi with a spray of AK bullets as the grenades were exploding.

Farook then ordered one of his boy warriors to fetch a five-gallon can of gasoline from the jeep and pour its contents down the hatch of the empty tank. Then he took a book of matches, lit it, and tossed it inside. With a loud WHAWOOSH sound, flames erupted from the open turret like a volcano. The boy began to run off, leaving the five-gallon can behind.

"Get the can. It is borrowed," Fat Farook shouted to him.

"I must tell them everything," he said apologetically over his shoulder to the Americans. Without waiting for additional orders, Farook's young soldiers began looting the bodies. Iraqi soldiers came pouring out from another building and began firing at the limo. The Kuwaiti youth on the machine gun blazed away at them with devastating effect as the other Kuwaitis got back in the vehicles. The tank blew up behind them and continued erupting in secondary explosions as the limo and the jeep sped away. The tank explosion took out most, if not all, the nearby Iraqis.

A safe distance away, Fat Farook pulled over and looked at the side and back of his car. At the same time his eldest son was removing the Iraqi flags. There were bullet marks in its beautiful surface. Farook vowed that if they weren't already dead, he would really fix those Iraqis on his return. He then instructed his men in the jeep to remove their Iraqi uniforms and put their Kuwaiti clothing back on. Farook was concerned that they could be shot by other resistance fighters, believing them to be real Iraqis.

After this was done, they drove without further incident for ten minutes toward the western edge of Kuwait City. This was the old Bedouin district. As they turned a corner, two men dressed in desert garb jumped in front of the limo. As if by magic, their vehicle was surrounded with armed men of the desert. Fat Farook rolled down the window and spoke to the one who appeared to be their leader, his old friend Major Naqib, a Kuwaiti soldier and cousin to the royal family.

"Hello, my old friend," the Kuwaiti officer said to Farook in Arabic.

The pair spoke briefly, as Farook explained that he was shepherding escaped American POWs, two of whom were injured and could not walk. The desert-garbed man entered the limo and poked his head out of the sunroof. He shouted orders to his troops, who piled into an ancient Ford pickup parked next to an abandoned storefront.

Naqib had stayed behind and continued fighting when the Iraqis overran his country. But his men were too few and war supplies so scarce that they had spent most of the occupation running and hiding. Now they were running and hiding no more, but preparing to assist the coalition by attacking the supply lines and the rear of the enemy. The three vehicles proceeded for several blocks before Naqib gave Farook directions to turn down a side street.

Fat Farook braked to a stop and the two friends stepped out and walked to the back of the limo. Popping open the trunk, Farook took out several cartons of Egyptian cigarettes.

"These are for you and your men." Meanwhile, the Ford had pulled up behind them, and Naqib's men gathered around curiously, though at a respectful distance.

"This is wonderful," said the major. "All we have had to smoke have been the harsh Iraqi cigarettes we take from their pockets. These will make the men happy. Thank you very much."

From the moment they'd seen the cigarette cartons, Naqib's men had begun chattering among themselves in a language that, overhearing them, neither the Americans nor Youssef recognized. Seeing the puzzled looks on the faces of his new acquaintances as they listened and looked at the strange-sounding and dressed men, Naqib explained in good English, "They are *mujahideen* fighters from Afghanistan. They are speaking their language. Your government sent them here to help us prepare the resistance movement. They are experts at such things."

Naqib then turned to give an order to the Afghanis, upon which the group moved to the pick-up and began transferring armloads of weapons, ammo, and claymore mines to the trunk of the limo.

"What are these?" asked Farook, pointing to the claymores. Naqib did not answer, but handed his friend a plastic bag full of cut-up goat meat. Then he said, "They are claymore mines. I will send two of my men with you to show you how to work them." He then instructed two of his soldiers to accompany Fat Farook and his sons. He also gave him a big wad of U.S. currency, saying, "This is to procure supplies and fuel for you to fight. Any left over, pay your men with it."

Farook said he would. "And what is this?" he inquired about the bag.

"It is fresh meat. We have plenty, and you should eat it while it is still good. The Iraqis have destroyed the electric plant, so there is no refrigeration." They also gave him a big bag of rice and another full of lentils. "You will have to cook them the old way with a small fire."

Next, Farook and Naqib began conversing in rapid and animated Arabic. When they had finished, and after a pause, the major looked at Washington and addressed him in perfect English. "My friend says you have a wounded woman soldier here." The colonel responded in affirmation and added that they were all injured.

"We have medics and a doctor who can attend to your needs. Also, we have the means to help you get out of the city. But we must be on our way soon. So, it will now be necessary to give up the luxury of traveling in my friend's magnificent automobile and take the next steps of your journey on a very different sort of conveyance." Mizzi translated for Youssef, and they got out of the limo.

Fat Farook was about to get back into his car and drive away when he said in English to the colonel, "You stay here with these ones; they can help you get out of the city."

Washington, who had retained his pin-on colonel's insignia before his flight suit was burned by Farook's sons, presented them to the limo driver.

"Keep these as a souvenir."

Fat Farook was beside himself with pride. Here was a real American colonel who had given him his rank insignia.

"I am a colonel now?"

"You sure are." Washington said as he pinned the eagles onto the shoulders of Farook's chauffeur's jacket. He then stepped back, and leaning on his one crutch, saluted as best as he could under the circumstances. Farook then returned his salute.

Fat Farook could not contain his elation. "I am a colonel now. You must salute me," he said to his neighborhood troops. He then turned back to Washington and gestured expansively, to the entire party. "May the peace of the Almighty go with you always."

Farook then bade his sons and the two new Kuwaitis back into the vehicle. With a hearty laugh, and a waving arm out of the window, Fat Farook the Moroccan and his orphaned assassins vanished into the smoky twilight of day. The red glow of his taillights grew dimmer and soon disappeared into the distance as he drove off, still laughing.

Young One, knowing that Fat Farook's hiding place had been discovered, asked, "Where will they go?"

"Do not worry. The Iraqis have compromised only one of his hiding places. He knows the city better than anyone does. We will provide him with another safe place. He risked all to bring you to us, and he has great respect for you. But we must not stay here. Although many Iraqis have left the city, there are still several hundred combat troops left behind. We have sufficient arms and provisions to attack the enemy, guerilla style, but we do not have the forces to hold out against an all-out assault. Farook the Moroccan and his men, along with other freedom fighters, have done a good job on the other side of the city keeping the enemy distracted so we can prepare for military interdiction here. But this is enough talk. Come, we must go now."

>+-><-><+<

The colonel was grateful that Fat Farook did not mention Youssef having been an Iraqi soldier, and Major Naqib must have assumed all four were military. Though they were nearly inured to the unexpected, the Americans were suddenly startled by the sound of large animal grunts and the sight that next met their eyes. From around the corner of a building, walking at a sedate pace, there emerged a foursome of saddled camels, each led by a Kuwaiti resistance fighter.

Under the correct commands, the eight-foot-tall beasts kneeled down on all fours to accommodate their human cargo. After helping the Americans on, the Kuwaitis ordered the camels to stand up, and the Americans soon found themselves swaying down the smoky street. The major and the *mujahideen* followed on foot, while another group went to hide the old pick-up truck. Naqib explained that the truck was too noisy and could give their position away.

The little caravan came to a stop in front of a warehouse several blocks away. It was the major's urban fortress. All means of entrance and egress were protected by hidden guards, snipers, and claymore mines. There were even decoy patrols sent to other areas to keep the enemy busy elsewhere. Young men on bicycles acted as scouts to give advance warning of enemy approach. The four camels disappeared into the dark building through a doorway that formerly accommodated delivery trucks. Inside the building were many people. Soldiers, women, and even some children were sleeping or busy preparing another combat patrol to go out and ambush the Iraqis.

The camels again kneeled on command to allow the humans to dismount. The four were taken to what had formerly been the office area of the commercial building. It was their makeshift hospital that had been stocked with American medical supplies and equipment, but was less than a doctor's office by western standards. Major Naqib spoke. "I know it does not look like much, but it is the only working hospital in Kuwait City. The Iraqis have stripped the other hospitals of their equipment and supplies and kidnapped the doctors and nurses to work on their wounded and sick.

"We have a doctor, a very good woman doctor. Do not ask about her family; they have all been killed by the enemy. How she keeps working is one of Allah's miracles. Come, here she is now."

A tired-looking Kuwaiti woman entered and examined the pilot's hip. Washington took her to be anywhere between thirty and fifty years of age. Grief had aged her too much to make a closer guess. She said, "I speak English because I went to medical school in the United States."

"What school?" the colonel asked hopefully.

"Johns Hopkins University, on a Kuwaiti scholarship. Because America was good to me, I will be good to you. But I must tell you something. Since leaving my residency in America, I have not been allowed to have men as patients. Only women have been my patients. So my trauma-care skills are, how do you say—rusty. I always like that way of saying it. Men require more of that care than do women, except for automobile accidents. That is our way here. When I was an intern, I worked in the emergency room in a hospital for the poor in Baltimore in the early 1980s. I saw many stabbing victims, gunshot wounds, and traumatic injuries from accidents. I was frightened, and I hated it. I used to pray and ask, why? Now my prayers have been answered. That knowledge has been very useful here in the last six months."

Lack of modern equipment in their warehouse dispensary required that things be done the old way, and the doctor conducted the examination with great care. "I believe you have a posterior dislocation of the femur from the hip socket. There is no evidence of sciatic-nerve or blood-vessel damage. The head of the bone may be broken, but we have no X-ray or MRI machine to tell for sure. Your injury is more than a day old. Usually, the best time to reset a hip is within six hours, so it may go worse for you. We will do what we can. You may have also injured your back, but we cannot tell here; I do not think you have spinal cord damage. It is mostly soft-tissue injury and possibly some disc involvement."

At that moment, apparently from a room some distance away, Washington heard low moaning. He thought it must be a wounded resistance fighter in considerable pain. The doctor excused herself and explained that she had other patients.

A little later, a large *mujahideen* medic entered and spoke to Colonel Washington in broken English.

"The doctor does not think your hip is broken. It is merely dislocated," said the Afghani, encouragingly.

"We will need to reset the bones. It would have been better to do it sooner, but that is the past now. It is a common thing in our hilly country. There are many places to fall, and there are many dislocated hips."

He took a hypodermic needle and filled it with amber liquid from a brown medical ampoule.

"What is that?"

"Morphine sulfate, for the pain," the medic replied.

"It doesn't hurt that bad."

"It will."

The colonel pretended not to hear what he had just heard. After giving the narcotic injection, the medic left him to rest and to give the painkiller a chance to work. He returned a half-hour later with the doctor and three other big, bearded men. They picked him up as gently as possible and laid him atop a large wooden desk in the makeshift dispensary.

All four of them held the pilot down while the doctor rotated and positioned his leg in preparation for resetting the injured hip, two grasping his arms and legs and the third laying his weight across and wrapping Washington's good leg in his burly arms so the patient would not camel kick the doctor. The medic placed a rag gag across his mouth. The pilot tried to pull it away under protest. Through a muffled mouth, he asked why they were doing that.

"They bind your mouth so that you do not scream as we set your hip and give our position away to the enemy."

"I won't scream," the colonel said, with a macho tone in his voice.

"Everyone screams," the large Afghani replied.

Then the medic placed his arms around the colonel's lower leg as if it were a handle, and pushed his shoulder against the knee while pulling and twisting it back and forth. Once the doctor approved the positioning of the leg, the medic nodded to his assistants and told them to get ready.

They tightened their grip to keep him down. A split second later, the large man yanked with all his might on the colonel's leg. There was an audible pop, like the cracking of a giant knuckle as the femur and hip socket were reintroduced. As his eyes bulged in pain, the pilot gave a muffled scream, and at that instant felt grateful for the gag. The doctor checked and was satisfied with the result. As the pilot was still moaning in anguish, the medic said, "There, that should be better. Now, rest."

Even with the morphine shot, the procedure hurt so badly that Washington could not catch his breath and passed out soon afterwards. It was the first good sleep he had had in days. The doctor then went back to Mizzi. She had previously given her a shot to relieve the intense pain of debriding her burn wounds. Like an archaeologist removing a mummy's wrappings, the doctor unraveled the boiled rags that had served to bandage Nirada's legs. She had first- and second-degree burns that had become irritated by the oil and infected. Some of the petroleum had soaked into the flesh.

The doctor could not get it out and told her that she might have stained scars that would carry the color of the oil. The Kuwaiti woman working with the doctor gasped when she saw her legs. She had heard of this brave American soldier—an Arab woman from the Lebanese people who had shot Iraqis and saved a shot-down pilot—and she regarded her as a hero.

After the morphine shot kicked in, the doctor cleaned Mizzi's wounds of both the grease that Youssef had rubbed in them as well as the oil pollution. She then lanced her few remaining blisters and drained them of the pus-like fluid. Then the other woman poured on a liquid that burned worse than the oil itself: vinegar, the only solution available for cleaning and disinfecting burns. She also gave her a few days' worth of the very scarce supply of antibiotics. Infection was already setting in, and they would be needed.

The burns and injuries of the others were also treated. After Young One's feet and legs were salved and bandaged, he hobbled around the place.

The doctor was still looking at Youssef's burns. In the warehouse, there were freedom fighters in small groups. Some were cleaning weapons, or assembling booby traps for the Iraqis. Others merely sat together smoking cigarettes and drinking tea, talking quietly.

Before he collapsed into unconsciousness from the morphine, Colonel Washington asked to speak to Major Naqib, to tell him he needed to contact the coalition to inform them of his and the two other soldiers' status. "I'm sorry, colonel," Naqib explained. "We have no telephone available. We used to have a fax machine, but the Iraqis discovered it, and we cannot use a radio or the enemy will find us. But we do have one way left to send a message." He left and returned with another man who gently cradled a beautiful homing pigeon in his hands.

"This man and his cousin are famous pigeon racers. These birds are from their stock. Their home is in Saudi Arabia, and that is where they will fly when released. Very clever, no? We will write three notes and attach them to the tail feathers of three birds. We send three in case one or two get lost. We have used these to communicate since ancient times, before even the time of the prophet Mohammed, may his name be praised. Our enemies thought we were sorcerers or wizards because we could communicate so rapidly."

Young One had been standing nearby, and overhearing the major's words, drew nearer to listen.

"I notice that you are looking at the color of their legs," said Naqib to the American private. "There is an old story about the Great Flood and the pigeon. When Noah was floating on a boat upon the great waters, he released three birds after the rains stopped. The first bird was a sparrow, but was not a strong enough flier to find land. Next, he released a dove, and it flew far away and returned some time later with a branch from an olive tree. Noah was not sure if it had found land or merely plucked a branch from a floating tree where it had stopped to rest.

"Then he released his best flier, a homing pigeon. It was not seen again for several days and was taken for lost. But it did return, with red mud on its feet and legs. Noah knew it had found land, and he prayed to the Almighty to turn its legs red permanently so that everyone would remember the wondrous thing that had happened. That is why today, all our pigeons have red legs." He held out the bird to Young One. Its legs were indeed red. "They are still colored to this day with the mud from the original flood. Praise be to Allah. But enough stories—we have much work to do.

The notes were written in Arabic, and each was tightly rolled up and tied to the strongest feather in the bird's tail.

"We do not tie on the leg like the Europeans do," Naqib explained. "They fly better this way." The handler then took the three birds outside and released them. The first flew in widening, elevated circles, then headed off to the south. The second pigeon flew to the next building and settled there.

"The oil confuses her," said the handler in Arabic to Naqib. "She cannot get her bearings." The third pigeon flew around and around, then set off in a westerly direction.

"That one may yet get her bearings in the open air," the man said. With that, they hoped and waited...

Chapter 37

FREEDOM FIGHTERS

A little later, while Washington and Mizzi were in morphine-induced stupors, Naqib and his people showed Young One around their hideout. There was a metal ladder to the roof where guards ascended and descended. Young One looked around at all the people there. It was strange to look into their faces. One of the other Kuwaitis walked up to Young One and introduced himself.

"My name is Gemel. Welcome to our private part of Hell." His accent was distinctly British. Young One looked at the Kuwaiti man in Arab clothes, with a puzzled look on his face.

"Do my words offend you?"

"No, I am surprised by your accent."

"Sorry, chap. I was schooled in England, and before the war, I was a petroleum engineer. It was almost like magic to take oil from the ground and convert it into fuel, plastics, and asphalt. It was like a miracle from the Almighty. But now, I see how they fight and kill for it, and my heart becomes sad. Come, let us go up to the roof and talk."

They climbed the metal ladder, to the tar-and gravel-covered roof, and stood looking out over the city. The sound of gunshots rang out here and there in the distance. The sky was still smoky and ominous.

To Young One it was strange and disturbing to see the sun, the very light of God, occluded from that place. The city had been cast into eternal twilight. There were no lights, no cars, and no children playing in the streets. All was destroyed and desolate.

Gemel said, "We Kuwaiti people have enjoyed many benefits, but now are paying the price of having it too good. We trusted our army to the *Bidun*, which is Arabic for 'without.' Without Kuwaiti citizenship, that is. Now, we must fight for ourselves. I am not trained in this; I am an engineer. Now I am a soldier. Unless help comes soon, we will all be nothing."

They went back down the ladder and walked around for a while in silence.

"Look over there at those people. Do not stare. We can speak freely; they do not understand English. That man with the stern look on his face was a millionaire. But he lost all—his family, his business, his happy and contented life. They are all gone. Now he sleeps next to and fights alongside people who would not have been allowed in his store before the war. He was a famous diamond, pearl, and gold merchant. His business was one of the first in town hit by the Iraqis. They shot everyone in his family while he was preparing things at his home to escape. Now he is like everyone else. Each bullet he shoots into an Iraqi is more valuable to him than one of his precious pearls. Strange, yes?"

They continued to walk along, looking at the weary people around them. "You see that woman there?"

Young One nodded that he did.

"She has killed fifteen Iraqi soldiers herself. They murdered and tortured her family. She was a singer. She had a very beautiful voice. She was much sought after to sing because she knew all of the traditional songs of our people. She has not said a word since she came here. She has lost the gift of speech. They shot her children in front of her, and then hit her in the head with a rifle butt and raped her over and over, but she alone survived. Now she is not right." He tapped his head with his right index finger.

"The other men over there are Afghani mercenaries. They have killed many Russians in their homeland. They are specialists in this kind of house-to-house fighting. The coalition is coming soon. The whole place will be shot apart."

✳──✳──✳

When the Kuwaitis had first seen Young One, they could not figure out what his ethnicity or race was. He was not white, not Arab, and not black. They asked the colonel, who told them he was an American Indian, like in the cowboy movies. Subtitled American western movies had been very popular in pre-war Kuwait. Comprehending Washington's explanation, one of the fighters took his hand and made the woo-woo-woo sound by patting his fingertips rapidly to his lips. Then they all did it and laughed. Having never met an American Indian they were delighted to have the opportunity to do so and meant no disrespect. For some, it was the first smile or laugh their war-weary faces had enjoyed in months. The Americans were made welcome.

Young One became somewhat of a celebrity among the fighters. That night, they sat around a smoky fire of dried dung and cardboard boxes in a metal can. Everyone listened in rapt attention to the landmine and sniper stories, and the tale of Farook and his merry band. Major Naqib translated from English twice, once for the Kuwaitis in Arabic and again for the Afghanis, who spoke the *Pashto* language. Young One would relate a part of a story, then wait patiently until the translations were finished.

485

He told of how the retreating Iraqi Army was caught in the open by the coalition warplanes. He described the bombing and strafing and the terrible destruction. The freedom fighters were elated, hoping that many among the Iraqi dead had been their former tormentors. Some of the stolen belongings had been theirs. Even the most stoic of their lot could not conceal their joy. Stories were very important to these people, and Young One's was wondrous to hear.

One of the Kuwaiti women asked, "Please tell us of the American woman." Nirada was quite a celebrity to them. Young One told them about the landmine explosion, about her removing the injured pilot while the helicopter blades swung just above her head. They made noises with their breath as if they were watching the circus as he spoke. He told them about how a snake bit the face piece of Mizzi's gas mask but did not touch her, and they were awed. Finally, he told them how she saved the pilot by running through the burning oil as it burst into flames around her. That was how she got burned. She was an instant folk hero to them.

Some of the *mujahideen* men seemed a little upset about this militant feminist story. Perhaps Nirada represented their real enemy. Then Young One told them of their meeting Youssef, and of his having been an Iraqi soldier. Naqib stopped translating, and asked Young One to repeat what he'd said. A hush came over the room. Youssef had been taken for a simple Bedouin boy, not an Iraqi infantryman. Suddenly the suspicion arose that he could be a spy, or worse, a deserter. No one could trust him. Serious trouble was brewing for Youssef.

Young One asked their permission to finish his story. Major Naqib settled the crowd, after which Young One told of how Youssef had helped carry the colonel, and how he had cooperated in the ruse to protect the Americans from being killed by pretending to hold them prisoner. He also told them how they had escaped from Kasim's capture with Youssef's help, and how he had gone out alone and brought back water for them.

Everyone was silent for a while; it seemed that they were not sure what to think. Naqib had Youssef summoned. He had been sleeping, and they awoke him. They handed him a cup of tepid tea and asked him to tell them his story. Sensing the tension of the moment, but not yet realizing that his life was on the line, he gulped down his tea and began to speak.

The freedom fighters' hard, cold expressions of angry disbelief began to soften as Youssef related his tale. When he was finished, most seemed satisfied. His account was close enough to Young One's to convince them that he spoke the truth and his version of events was corroborated by the colonel and Mizzi. Later, when the danger of his circumstances began to dawn on him, he was afraid to sleep. The tea was a stimulant, and also helped keep him awake. Half an hour later the fireside gathering dispersed and Young One stretched out alongside him on the desert mats. There was much behind them to forget and much ahead of them to live through. Finally, they both fell off to sleep.

>+—>+—>+<

When they awoke, they were given cups of tea and wandered outside to relieve themselves in a trench behind the building. A few yards away, a small herd of goats and sheep along with the camels that had carried them to the hideout, had been haphazardly corralled. Clearly pleased, Youssef walked over to the animals and gestured for Young One to follow.

Although Young One could ride a horse and was used to being with them, he found the large animals intimidating at first, and the camels seemed to sense his unease. Then Youssef spoke and sang to them in

Arabic, and as they gradually grew more relaxed, Young One became more confident in their presence. After a while, the pair went back inside and ate a closely rationed breakfast of lentils and goat meat, but their interaction with the camels had not gone unnoticed.

Though Naqib had kept his thoughts on the matter mostly to himself so far, he was now ready to set in motion his plans for the departure of his American guests, and in preparation had assigned Gemel to translate and to keep an eye on Youssef. After their meal, Naqib summoned the three to join him at the enclosure, where the camels now stood saddled.

Youssef looked from one camel to the other. "There is something wrong here," he said. "These two are not well fitted." Then he swiftly and expertly removed, exchanged, and adjusted the saddles he'd referred to. Youssef did not know it, but on the major's orders, he had just been tested. If he really were a *Badawi*, he would possess just such knowledge. Naqib then addressed Young One in English. As he spoke, as if to punctuate his remarks, a series of loud explosions sounded in the near distance.

"Do you hear this? Claymore mines are going off. The Iraqis are approaching, and that is one of our patrols fighting them off." He paused to let Gemel translate for Youssef.

"We can slow them down, but we do not have the wherewithal to fight them in a pitched battle. If you Americans are found here, they will think they have discovered a spy network, and will torture our people for information they do not have. We have no helicopter or jeep to transport you. Your injured comrades need more medical attention than we can provide. Please do not be offended if I tell you that it is better for everyone if you go. Please explain this to your colonel."

The major next turned to Youssef and for a moment gazed gravely into his eyes.

"To show you my trust, I must ask you for a favor," he said in Arabic.

"What kind of favor?" Youssef asked.

"A dangerous favor. For whatever this may be worth to you, know that if I did not trust you I would hold you here until the Iraqis or the coalition forces arrive, and let your fate be in their hands. Meanwhile, I would protect you from those among my command who still suspect you as a spy, or simply wish to kill any Iraqis they see. But to be honest, I don't believe the Americans can escape without your help."

Gemel started to translate for Young One, but Naqib shook his head. "No one unfamiliar with these creatures can control them for long," he continued, "and besides, the other Americans are badly hurt. But you, as one of the desert, may be able to guide them to safety. I have watched you with the camels; you are at home with them, as it should be. That is why I knew you were a *Badawi*. I have also seen that this 'Indian' boy is quick to learn. Therefore, I desire that you and he should ride two of these camels and lead the woman and the black officer on the other two."

Youssef decided that he, too, would be honest, and express his fears to Naqib. He did not want to be found with another man's animals any more than he wanted to be found by the Iraqis, he confessed. Rustling was a crime punishable by horrible death in his part of the world. The owner and his family would be the judge and jury.

The major responded patiently. "No desert nomad would abandon his camels with their saddles on. Perhaps a sniper shot the owner; perhaps he stepped on a landmine. We will never know. We have heard that some coalition soldiers shoot Arabs from helicopters for sport. In any case, it is doubtful that you will run into any of his family between here and the coalition lines, but you must take your chances. As I said, I believe it is your friends' only hope."

Youssef pursed his lips and nodded his head, "All right. I will do it. But where did these camels come from?"

"They wandered in from the desert. This section of the city was a wayfaring point for the *Badawi* and their herds. These four must have been here before and remembered the place; but if they stay here, and the liberation does not come soon, they too will be eaten for our food. Better they should be used to carry you away, even if it means those under my command may go hungry. That is another reason for you to take them with you."

Not comprehending what the major was saying to Youssef, Young One stood silently pondering what he had been told. He had expected to stay hidden with the Kuwaiti fighters, but it seemed that was not an option now. Abruptly, the major turned back to him and resumed speaking in English. "Please inform your colonel of my decision and of my request that he and the other members of your party honor me with your presence at the midday meal this afternoon. Now, you must spend time learning to ride the camels from the desert boy. After that, you must depart."

To Young One's surprise, Colonel Washington merely grunted his acknowledgement and nodded emphatically upon hearing the message, almost as though the pilot had already reached the same conclusion. Over dinner, Major Naqib showed all of his guests, including Youssef, a great deal of formal respect, beginning with an apology to Washington for not conveying his decision to him directly. As they began to eat, Youssef discretely took Young One's left hand and moved it behind his back, not wishing him to embarrass himself with eating with what an Arab knows is a dirty left hand. For some reason, both Mizzi and the colonel seemed already aware of this custom.

With their right hands, they all scooped in globs of rice and lentils and chunks of roasted goat meat from a communal platter. Youssef and the major spoke in their language. The entertainment for their meal was gunshots in the distance.

After they had eaten, Naqib had gifts for them. He gave Youssef a knife; it was a kitchen knife wrapped in a homemade cardboard sheath. They had a full goatskin water bag and some cooked meat, rice, and lentils, all dumped together in a plastic garbage bag. It was all they had to give. He also had a military compass. He gave this to Young One. The pilot's had been taken by Kasim's men.

He also had a present for Colonel Washington. Because it would be hard to hide the black man, Naqib decided that it would be better if he were dressed as a woman. A special black *abbaya* had been made for him by several of the women. They sewed cloth cut from one to enlarge the other because of his size. Reluctantly, Washington agreed to put on the woman's clothes, but only when they were leaving. He already felt he looked ridiculous enough with ill-fitting Arab clothes and did not wish to be seen dressed as a woman by the resistance fighters.

Naqib then spoke to Washington with seriousness in his voice. He told him that the Iraqi lines were shaped in a crooked V. He held his fingertips together to form the shape of a wide and shallow V.

"Do you understand this?" he asked, making clear that the question was addressed to Young One as well. "After you leave here, the Iraqi front line runs in a westward direction several kilometers to the south. This part," he said, motioning with his head in the direction of his left arm, "is the more dangerous way." He meant the southward route.

"The last intelligence I received said the Iraqis are expecting a raid by the U.S. Marines from the coast and from the south along the coastal highway. Their numbers are believed to be greater there. It would be better to go to the west for a day before cutting south, as there should be fewer enemy troops there. But perhaps not. No one knows, including the Iraqis themselves.

"Nonetheless, you may be fortunate to find a safe place to cross the enemy lines again. This way I recommend is longer, but safer. All of the fishing fleet is gone or has been sunk by the Iraqis and is in the bottom of the gulf. There are no boats; there will be no escape by water. You must go out into the deep desert on camel. There you may have a chance. You must leave immediately in the daylight because there will be much trouble here soon."

The colonel was dumbfounded and asked, "How in the world do you know all of this? That is a more complete briefing than I'd expect from my own G2 folks." Naqib did not answer at first, then spoke carefully. "I'm told you overheard a somewhat violent outburst in our infirmary just before your hip was treated. Without going into unpleasant details, I will say that now and then we have been fortunate enough to capture some high-ranking Iraqi officers." He paused, and allowed a slight, chilling smile to play across his features.

"And to borrow what I understand is a well-worn phrase from old American movies, 'We have ways of making them talk.'" His expression instantly hardened as he added, "If you had seen their unspeakable cruelty to our people, you would not condemn us.

"Now I must ask a favor of you, colonel: that before leaving, you allow this young soldier to go out and stand guard duty so that my men can come in to pray and eat. It would be a great consideration, and I would not ask it of a guest if times were not desperate."

Naqib told Youssef to ready the camels. He was sorry, but he had no water to give the animals; they must find what they could in the desert.

>*<—>*<—>*<

In Saudi Arabia, the first pigeon released in Kuwait City had at last found its way home through the smoke-filled sky. Its flight took nine hours. The second pigeon came in coated in oil two days later, and the third one was not heard of again. The owner found the note a few hours later, while doing his coop chores. He untied the oil-stained paper and read its instructions to take the note straight to the Saudi authorities, who were then to take it to the United States Embassy.

The man immediately notified the police, who questioned him for some time before believing his story. The man himself knew it was true because the sender was his cousin, and it contained a prearranged authenticating code word in the cousin's handwriting. The police took the man to the Saudi Arabian Army, where intelligence officers again interrogated him for holes in his story. When they, too, were satisfied, they went to the U.S. Embassy, who in turn contacted the coalition commanders. The thumb-prints and service numbers were verified. The colonel and his valuable information were safe.

><-><-><

Young One went out with Naqib, and they relieved the guard. Alone, Young One leaned in the doorway of a brick building that served as the temporary guard post that commanded a view of the intersection of two streets. He peered intently through the smoky haze and heard the sounds of war getting closer and more intense. He could hear it before he could see it.

The noise sounded like a large construction site with heavy equipment moving about. The squealing of the wheels was unmistakable. Tanks! Through the haze he gradually made out their dark, ominous silhouettes approaching the long street in front of him, with infantrymen running alongside and behind the metal beasts. It was clear that the compound's perimeter defenders had been overrun. Young One ran back to the warehouse where the major's men had finished their meal but were still at prayer. Between panted breaths, he shouted for Naqib, who emerged from the building seconds later.

Naqib sighed and said, "We have been expecting this for some time. Everyone knows what to do. Hopefully, they do not have helicopters." He turned back inside and at the clap of his hands his people jumped into action.

Within minutes the freedom fighters had deployed in a thin line down the side street and disappeared into side doors of the buildings. The first two tanks, Soviet T-62s, were now only a block away, and were covered with Iraqi riflemen and surrounded by dismounted infantry. Unexpectedly, from the rooftops above them, came a storm of lead. Muzzle flashes and grenade blasts were interrupted by the WAM-WAM-WAM of claymore mines being command-detonated, which combined to sweep the backs and sides of the armored vehicles clear of the Iraqi soldiers. The lead pair of tanks stopped literally in their tracks. The commander of one, still standing upright in the open hatch of the turret, was missing everything above the shoulders. Both tanks began backing up, halting the forward progress of the third tank in line, while crunching the bodies of the dead and wounded behind them.

One of the *mujahideen* ran up, jumped on top of the first tank, and dropped a hand grenade down the hatch, past the commander. An instant later the Afghan tumbled from the back of the tank and onto the pavement, riddled by the coaxial machine gun of the tank behind him. Almost simultaneously the grenade went off, blowing the Iraqi commander's mangled remains out the top of the turret.

As the Iraqis fell back, there was shooting from the other side of the street as the survivors from the returning perimeter patrol opened up. During the lull that followed, their badly wounded leader staggered over breathlessly to inform Naqib that the Iraqis were attacking from two different directions, and the defenders would soon be caught in a pincers.

Naqib told Youssef to get the Americans on the camels, and Young One sprang to obey. The colonel began changing into the Arab woman's clothes. At Youssef's expert commands, the largest of the four knelt to take aboard the pilot, whose shattered hip caused him excruciating pain as he straddled the animal's humped back.

Next Youssef helped Mizzi and Young One mount their camels, then leapt onto the last one himself. Before returning to the renewed firefight that had erupted just up the street, Naqib bid them all a final goodbye. It was the last the four companions ever heard or saw of him. The sounds of the battle slowly receded in the distance as they headed into the open desert. An especially loud explosion behind them caused the startled camels to bolt forward, with everyone hanging on for dear life, except Youssef, who took the abrupt change of pace easily in stride. They continued riding northwest, following the compass given to them by Naqib, until the gunfire finally diminished to inaudibility, and the skyline of the lightless city was no longer visible on the horizon.

>—⋊—>

Back in Naqib's embattled compound, the pigeon racer was among the last men left alive. He ran back to his birds and freed all but one, his best remaining flyer. To it, he attached a second note to his cousin, asking him to inform his contact in Saudi Arabia that they had been overrun by the

Iraqis, but saying that the three Americans had gotten off safely, followed by a scrawled goodbye. Seconds after releasing the bird out the window, he was gunned down by the advancing Iraqis and fell to the warehouse floor, leaving a crimson stain on the cinderblock wall.

>—✕—✕—✕<

Across the lines of battle on the coalition side, an officer burst into the war room. "General, sir, I have some incredibly good news. We have received word from freedom fighters in Kuwait City that they have Colonel Washington and the two enlisted people."

"Outstanding. Has the radio message been authenticated?"

"It was not a radio message, sir, it was this." He handed the note to the general. "It was tied to the tail feathers of a homing pigeon, written in Arabic by the friend of a cousin of a Saudi Arabian man in Riyadh. He was or still is a major in the Kuwaiti Army. His unit was overrun, and he's been conducting military interdiction behind Iraqi lines since they invaded. He has been rather successful at it. He also commands the Afghanis we sent in there. The Saudi Arabian cousin is sure it is from them because he signed it with his nickname as a private authentication code. Both the Saudi police and their military intelligence have investigated, and they think it is true. We have verified the names and service numbers, as well as the thumbprints. They all match up."

The general expelled a long breath; if the news were true, it meant he had not unwittingly ordered the death of his own troops, one of them a fellow officer. The Americans were alive, and not in enemy hands, which meant that the damning intelligence carried in the brain of Colonel

Washington had not fallen into enemy hands. As soon as the weather cleared, the next strategic surprise that had been prepared for Saddam's army could proceed...

Chapter 38

THE RIDE HOME

Youssef and the Americans headed west, back toward the burning oil wells, the way Major Naqib had advised them to go. Youssef rode atop the lead camel and looked the part in his Bedouin clothing, a part written for a desert boy who had been raised on the backs of camels and had drunk their milk during his infancy. According to prior agreement, he would ride the lead animal and do all the talking if they ran into Iraqi patrols. Young One would pretend to be a deaf-mute, while Washington and Mizzi would pretend to be too sick to speak.

For Mizzi, drugged into unconsciousness with morphine and tied to the saddle to prevent her from falling off, no pretense would be necessary. As the little camel caravan rode out into the desert, a motorized Iraqi patrol overtook them. Everyone adjusted their costumes and hoped for the best.

The escapees reined in their mounts as the vehicle came to a stop and two Iraqi soldiers jumped out and approached them. The colonel, dressed as a Bedouin woman, was only partially conscious due to the morphine he'd been given for his own considerable pain. He did his best to hide his hands and conceal his face, and his moaning was unfeigned.

"Where do you think you are going?" one of the soldiers asked.

Another military vehicle full of Iraqis soldiers abruptly pulled up in a cloud of dust. Armed guards immediately surrounded them. The hungry Iraqi soldiers looked at the camels with covetous eyes. There was a lot of fresh meat there. They were old camels, but they could be boiled or roasted. An old, stringy camel is better than no meat at all.

"Well, well, what have we here?" one of them asked rhetorically in Arabic as he walked up with an automatic rifle at the ready. The soldiers saw the women and thought it would be a very nice thing to be with them, even the old one. The colonel slumped over behind the camel's back, hoping not to attract further notice.

"Where are you going?" the Iraqi asked of Youssef.

Youssef spoke in flawless Bedouin Arabic. "We are a *Badawi* family and have been banished from the city because of illness. Please do not come any closer. We do not want to visit upon you our pestilence."

"What kind of illness?"

"We have the plague." Youssef walked around the camel and, for an Arab, did the unthinkable. He unraveled the bandages from one of Nirada's feet. He showed the ankles of his sister to other Arab men. They looked wide-eyed and aghast at the swollen mass of flesh on the end of Mizzi's leg. Her foot was blistered, pus-filled, and red raw, and she was moaning audibly. Young One remained on the side of the camel, trying to be inconspicuous.

"What is wrong with her?"

"We are lepers," he said. "Come, I will show you my brother's face, if you dare to look into the eyes of a leper."

The guards stepped back in utter terror. They did not even look at Young One. They had never seen leprosy before, but they did not like what they were seeing at all. All thoughts of shooting the men, gang raping the women, and eating the camels disappeared. In their minds, leprosy was a worse thing to bring home than AIDS. They did not want leper blood in their area. Someone would have to dispose of the bodies. The soldiers were in true horror. Somehow, the camels did not look so tasty after all.

"We have been banished from the city," Youssef continued. "We were told to go out into the desert alone to die." It was almost as if the colonel, disguised as the mother, and Young One as the brother, had not even been seen. The Iraqis had seen all that was necessary.

"You have the plague. You lepers leave immediately!" screamed one of the Iraqi soldiers.

Youssef tried to speak, but the sergeant of the guard who had been observing the incident from afar interrupted his words. Normally, the patrol would at least strong-arm rob them or demand bribes. They did not want to even touch the filthy money of these nomads. The colonel and Mizzi were safe from gang rape.

The sergeant drew his pistol. "You plague-ridden people will leave immediately, and take your animals with you. If you even look back, I will put bullets in your diseased bodies. Go now! Die in the desert, away from here! Go now!"

None of the Iraqis had ever seen plague or leprosy, but Nirada's feet looked worse than both did. The camels moved forward with a trotting gait, as the frightened Iraqis hurried away.

⟩⊹⟨⊹⟩⊹⟨

Camels have a particular way of walking. They step with both legs on the same side at the same time. This gives them their characteristic side-to-side movement, like that of a boat, which inspired their "ship of the desert" nickname. Young One was quite good at horseback riding, but the camel was a different ride. Still, he felt exhilarated. He was glad not to have to drag the injured all the way back to friendly territory and was now concerned only about getting shot by some trigger-happy coalition soldier. Although he had never seen it himself, he had heard stories of soldiers shooting Bedouins on sight, believing them to be Iraqi spies.

A camel can travel up to forty miles in a day, but Youssef kept them walking slowly because they needed water badly. On and on, the camels plodded in the sands, while their human cargo rocked back and forth in seemingly endless motion. Washington was still in the grasp of the painkiller but was more conscious after several hours of riding.

To their west and south, there was no smoke. The air was clear. Then, like being reprieved from Hell, they finally rode out from under the smoke altogether. Off in the distance, in the direction they were traveling, a flock of vultures orbited in descending circles.

The colonel saw the vultures and remembered something his grandmother had said to him many years earlier when he was a boy: "Buzzards flying overhead, something's on the ground, lying dead."

As they got closer, Youssef turned his head to listen. Then he turned his whole body and stood up to see. His hearing was better than the others', as was the pilot's, who said, "Yeah, I hear it too." It was the sound of a dog barking in the distance. At first, they thought the Iraqis might have reconnaissance or tracking patrols with army dogs. But the bark was not as deep as a German shepherd's. It had more the sound of a smaller dog.

Young One and Youssef went ahead on their camels to investigate, unsure what to expect. They thought there might be wounded Iraqi soldiers there. They had no weapons save the knife Naqib had given them. If the Iraqis were there, they would have to allow Youssef to once again talk them out of trouble. But as they neared the scene that had attracted the scavenging birds, it became clear that no words would be needed.

Of all the conflict's profane follies, one of the smaller but no less heart-rending examples lay before them: a lost flock of sheep and goats, stranded and abandoned. Where the animals had come from and how they had gotten there was a mystery, like so many things in that war. The creatures probably had been stolen from some poor family and escaped before being eaten by the Iraqis. Perhaps they belonged to a dead or run-off shepherd. If it were a *Badawi*, he would be lying lifeless somewhere in the desert. No Bedouin Youssef ever met would abandon his only means of livelihood.

There were numerous animals standing, crawling, or lying about. Some were oil covered and some were wounded, perhaps by Iraqis trying to kill them for meat. One female sheep had its front leg blown off, presumably by stepping on a landmine. It must have limped along with the rest of the herd until it died from shock and blood loss and was surrounded by voracious vultures.

Youssef counted twenty-one in all, dead and alive, including lambs and kids. The dog was doing his best to keep the vultures away, but there were too many. He was tiring. He was all alone defending his animals. Alighting from their camels, Young One and Youssef threw stones at the feasting buzzards, several of which flew off puking chunks of sheep, their wings flapping furiously to gain altitude.

Noticing the newcomers, the dog barked furiously at the strange human beings coming upon its herd, feinted a charge and then backed off, still barking all the while. The barking became more frenzied as the humans got closer. It was obviously a herd dog, but not one like Young One had seen back on the rez. Without its master and unsure what to do, it seemed both relieved and distressed at the sight of the two-leggers.

It was a Bedouin dog, whose ancestors had supplied the breeding stock for all sorts of modern canines. It was about eighty-five pounds, brown, with sandy highlights in its fur. It looked fairly young, and it was, because not many Arab dogs survive to old age. They lead a very hard life.

Youssef spoke to it in Arabic and it calmed down. After discretely kneeling a few feet away, he twisted to one side, knowing that to show the animal his front or his back could be misinterpreted as an attack or as flight, either of which could bring a bite. A dog instinctively knows that a friend would do neither. Youssef then cautiously allowed the nervous cur to sniff the back of his extended hand. In a world where rabies is endemic and medical attention is sparse, a dog bite can be a fearful occurrence. Youssef was doing a very brave thing. The dog moved a little closer and allowed Youssef to pet him on his head.

The colonel and Mizzi had ridden up and remained mounted as Youssef next introduced the dog to Young One by taking his hand in a shake and allowing the dog to smell the back of it. This primordial practice assured that the dog knew who was who by their smell in the dark. It also allowed the four-legger to touch first. Thus, the fearful animal was more in control of the situation.

A dog can not only smell evil in a human being, it senses it as well. A two-legger not "screened" in this fashion would be kept suspect, and the dog would keep a special eye on that person. In fact, Young One recalled that in distant times, a dog that growled and balked at the hand of a stranger was likely to get the human murdered, as it was believed that a dog could smell a bad man or a coward. Youssef left Young One with the dog, who sensed his kind nature and allowed himself to be petted with increasing eagerness.

All this while, the displaced vultures had kept circling overhead, their shit falling like fetid bomblets onto the sand and dead animals below.

The humans quit the site and moved upwind, abandoning the carcasses to the airborne scavengers.

Although the surviving herd members were hardy creatures and used to want, they had never lived without human supervision, and if they did not drink water soon, they too would be carrion for the birds.

Anguished that he could not spare water for the famished beasts, Youssef spoke assuring expressions in Arabic; then he selected one badly injured goat, and slit its throat in the traditional style, with the knife that Naqib had given them. He then dug a shallow hole in the sand and built a small fire of shrub sticks. As his fellow travelers looked on in silence, he expertly butchered the emaciated body into small chunks, then began roasting it skewered as kabobs on sticks, over the glowing embers of the fire. It would be the first hot meal they had had since the previous afternoon.

The meat from the old goat was tough as an inner tube, but the juice-laden saliva nourished their weary bodies and lifted their spirits. The flavor from the resinous desert sticks also imparted an unsavory taste to the cuts, but it was all they had to eat except for the cooked rice and lentils that they consumed by the handfuls. Even the dog ate with them. At first, it was hesitant to take food directly from Youssef's hand, so he tossed chunks on the ground in front of it. Soon, the dog was eating from his hand.

They washed their tough repast down with mouthfuls of leather-tasting water from the animal skin that had been provided by Naqib. The bag was porous, and the slow evaporation cooled the water inside. Although it tasted bad, it was refreshing and was the only water they had. The herd animals bleated for water—though there was none to spare, Young One gave a quick drink to the dog to wash down the chunks of goat meat that it had been given. Youssef carefully buried the remains of the fire under the sand after it had died down to ashes.

The dog, who was glad to be in the company of humans again as well as to be moving finally, kept the forlorn survivors of the herd together as they moved out. Young One walked with his camel and the dog, while the sheep and goats limped along behind. All seemed to "feel" his goodness and sensed that they were safe with him. Somehow, it made him feel as if he were back home. His feet had not been burned, but the skin on his legs between the boot tops and his knees was scorched. His legs hurt also, but it felt better walking in Arab sandals than scraping his burns against the camel hide.

>———×———×———<

After several more hours of unvaried, repetitious, back-and-forth rocking aboard the ships of the desert, the four companions drew abreast a rocky outcropping that rose like an isolated island from the surrounding sea of sand. From its crevices, a voice, as imperious as it was unexpected, suddenly challenged them in Arabic.

"Halt! Where are you going? Come near so we can see you better!"

Improbable as it seemed, they had happened on an Iraqi forward observation post, still manned by a detachment too stubborn or uninformed to join their army's general withdrawal.

Youssef knew they were far from the area of operations of his former military unit and that there should be no soldiers there who could recognize him. There was nothing about his person that identified him as an Iraqi deserter. Though the foursome had been caught off guard, and there was no place to run and hide, they should be safe, he hoped.

He waved in the direction of the hidden soldiers and in the customary Arabic greeting shouted, "Peace be to you."

"And peace to you," came the correct response, instantly filling him with relief and cautious confidence. Youssef got down from his camel and went up to speak to their challenger, leaving the others at a distance, as the enemy soldiers could recognize them as non-Arabs. As he approached the stony redoubt, three unkempt Iraqi regulars popped up from behind a pair of huge boulders. Looking over his shoulder, one of them asked about the women in the party.

"They are members of my family, sir. We have become lost from our tribe and are searching for them."

"And those animals?" asked the same man, pointedly licking his parched lips. "They represent our humble livelihood, sir, but the infidel warplanes strafed our camp purely for the cruel sport of it two days ago. Many were killed or lamed and had to be left behind." He paused, and looked at their haggard faces. "But of course, I would be honored to share our meager provisions with you." Youssef took a few steps toward his tensely waiting companions as the three enemy soldiers began to follow at his heels. Hoping they wouldn't notice the fresh beads of perspiration on his forehead, or the smell of fear rising from his sweat-soaked clothes, he stopped, turned again and raised a hand. "Please consider the modesty of my women, and allow me to bring back to you what food we can spare."

With surprising, almost formal courtesy, the Iraqis nodded, then stopped and waited as Youssef advanced to his resting camel, untied a haunch of goat on which he'd left the skin to keep off the flies, and returned with his offering, asking as he did so whether the soldiers had seen any other *Badawi*.

"We have seen no one for days, not even our own men," one of them replied. They asked him in turn if he had seen any coalition tanks or vehicles. Youssef just shook his head. He told them that he had seen nobody besides them. The sentries then warned him that his "family" was walking toward coalition landmines ahead, airdropped by a helicopter two days before. They advised walking toward the west, while pointing out the direction.

Now feeling sure his ruse had succeeded, and sensing the essential decency in these particular enemy soldiers (seemingly confirmed by the dog's placidity throughout the encounter), Youssef asked if they had water to spare, and was handed a nearly full goatskin bag.

After bidding the stranded soldiers farewell per Arab custom, Youssef returned to the others and, with Mizzi translating, explained what had transpired. They heeded the enemy soldier's instructions and headed in a westerly direction until they were out of visual and rifle range of the outpost. Then they cut directly south toward the coalition line. Unless they ran across a roving patrol or a band of deserted soldiers making their way to Saudi Arabia, they should be safe the rest of the way. And thanks to the generosity of the marooned Iraqi sentries, the thirsty animals had finally received enough water to improve the odds that they, too, might make it out alive.

><—><—><

As they approached coalition lines, they were in more danger, rather than less. With so many armies in the field, the greatest threat to straggling troops could be friendly fire; there was a real danger they would not be recognized and assumed to be hostile.

As he rode atop the camel, his hip racked in agony, the colonel was the first to hear it. It was the unmistakable whap-whap-whap of an American Black Hawk helicopter, coming fast from the south, right toward them.

Everyone was cheering and waving and screaming in elation. They were about to be rescued. But the chopper was in a hurry going somewhere else. It maintained its path, which took it slightly off to the left. Nonetheless, the starboard-door gunner had spotted them, and without warning, started shooting at them.

A line of machine bullets tore a furrow in the ground near them, the steel-jacketed missiles drilling their way into the sand and throwing up clods of clay. The goats and sheep scattered in terror, as the dog tried to circle them to keep them together. The camels bolted, and their injured passengers received a painful ride at full gallop. Somehow, Mizzi and Colonel Washington managed to cling to their panicked animals until they finally came to a stop.

Overhead, the door gunner was enjoying the pandemonium he'd caused.

"Man, I scared the shit out of those ragheads," he said with a laugh. "I'll bet they wish they used toilet paper now."

"At ease with that bullshit, soldier," said the pilot. "You have no authority to fire on the indigenous personnel. Do you understand that, troop?"

"Sorry, sir," he said, suppressing a sadistic chuckle. "I was just clearing the guns, didn't see anyone down there." The pilot knew it was a lie, and he told the copilot to turn around and head back to see if anyone had been hit. If so, he would have to file an incident report and prefer charges on the door gunner. That was entirely too much paperwork. The helicopter did a 180-degree turn, and the pilot surveyed the scene below. There was no blood in the sand or dead animals. The survivors, thinking they were about to be rescued for a second time, waved and shouted furiously at the approaching chopper.

The copilot said, "Look, they're waving."

"They all wave," the pilot said and reset his course back to their original mission.

Then he said over the on-board intercom, "You're real lucky today, Rogers. Had you hit any of the locals, your ass would be in Leavenworth. Do you understand me, troop? You're just lucky. Those are clearly non-combatants."

"Yes, sir."

"You know the rules of engagement. Don't make me read them to you during an Article Fifteen proceeding."

"No, sir."

Below, the four watched in disbelief as the helicopter grew smaller and smaller as it disappeared from view. Their native disguise had fooled their friends as well as their enemies. Had they been dressed in American desert cammies and wearing their helmets, they may have been recognized as coalition soldiers and rescued. Instead, they were almost collateral damage, victims of "non-accidental fratricide."

Back on the ground, the colonel was livid, the testosterone veritably bubbling out of his veins. Somebody was going to "get it sincerely" for this one. He had noted the helicopter's markings, and knew what division they were from. "I'll bring charges against those guys if it is the last thing I ever do," he said aloud.

They listened in disappointed shock as the sound of the helicopter disappeared in the distance. There would be no rescue for them. They would have to get themselves home...

Chapter 39

TORRENTS OF ARABIA

The camels kept walking toward the faint orange glow of the western setting sun. It was becoming evening on the third day. They had to find water soon; all that they could spare for the animals from what they'd been given by the Iraqis was now gone, and once again the sheep and goats were on the verge of collapse. Youssef noticed birds flying overhead, and he told Mizzi that they should follow them. She translated this to the others between painful gasps.

They could see that the birds were flying toward a rock formation farther to the west. Youssef explained that desert birds often drink at sunset, and, if they followed them, they might find water. But when they finally reached the place where the birds landed, they found only a nesting rookery at the base of a rocky outcrop. The birds were coming back from their afternoon drink, not going to it. Young One and Youssef dug into the sand at the base of the rocks, but to no avail. It had been too long since the last rain.

Just before dark, their path crossed an old camel trail. Youssef was hesitant to travel on it because they might run into Iraqis or Bedouin who might recognize the camels or other animals. But unless the trail was landmined, it would be safer than walking through the open desert at night. The sky had clouded over, and the air had a moist smell. The camels could sense the coming rain, and one even licked at the sky in hopes of getting a taste of it.

In the waning light, they sighted what looked like another pile of rocks protruding from the sand. As they got closer, they could see that it was the remains of an ancient structure, a fort of some long ago era, now abandoned. It was at a crossing of two faintly visible trails, and long-forgotten men must have once collected taxes from travelers through the area, or sent guards out from there to protect the caravans.

Colonel Washington guessed that it could have been of Mesopotamian, Greek, Persian, or Roman origin, and that if there had been a garrison stationed there, there must be a water well nearby. There were tire tracks around the area, suggesting it had been visited by soldiers recently. Whether they were coalition or Iraqi vehicles was impossible to tell.

The winds were picking up, and this place was the only shelter from a sandstorm, yet Youssef felt uneasy about staying there.

"Be careful for snakes and scorpions," he cautioned the others through Mizzi. "They like to hide among the rocks." She did not recognize the Arabic word for scorpion and the best explanation he could offer her was "insects with poison backsides." Washington surmised he meant scorpions and informed the others. While Youssef fettered the camels' legs so they could not run away in the night, the others looked around.

The walls of several small buildings were still standing, although the roofs had long ago fallen in and their wood had been burned for fires by passing Bedouins and bandits. Realizing, as had Washington, that the site might provide a source of water, Youssef pointed to a circle of rocks marking the location of an abandoned well. He hoped that someone in the past had placed a rock over the opening, but it appeared that that had not happened. The well was full of sand, possibly poured into it by the garrison's enemies after slaughtering the soldiers, to make sure no one else came back.

Youssef and Young One brought Mizzi and the colonel into one of the roofless structural remains of the long-forgotten outpost. They wished they could build a campfire in the center of the floor, but they had nothing with which to make a fire, and it would be too dangerous to try to pick up firewood in the dark. Groping for sticks on the ground, it would be too easy to grasp a snake, be bitten by a spider, or be stung by a scorpion. What's more, a fire might attract an Iraqi patrol or invite a coalition air or artillery strike.

There were no signs of other Iraqis, as they were so far into No Man's Land that only a roving patrol was likely to spot them. They sat in the darkness as the wind continued to rise, and took what rest they could among the haunting ruins.

A few hours later, Youssef and the Americans were awoken from their restless sleep by a strange whooshing sound in the distance, like large firework skyrockets being set off. Young One could see what may have been the firing of many rockets simultaneously. They shot forward in a line of illuminated streaks in the dark sky. Far behind them, they could hear the dull thud of distant munitions striking their targets.

"What's that?" gasped Young One.

"It's a multiple rocket launcher laying down suppression fire," said the colonel.

"They are scooting and shooting. They drive up, set up for fire. They shoot, and the next thing you know, they're gone. There must be occupied enemy positions behind us."

All four now wide-awake refugees watched and listened for more shooting, but there was none. Youssef was studying the night sky for another reason. A strange weather front was moving in. There was something he did not like in the clouds and the cool breeze. The moist wind was refreshing, but chilling. He said to Mizzi in Arabic, "The *Khamsin* is coming."

Her quizzical look told Youssef that the meaning of that expression was lost to her. He explained that it was a *Badawi* term for the rainy season that lasts almost invariably for fifty days in the Arabian desert: from late winter to early spring. During that period the dry *wadis* would once again be awash in ferocious rainwater. The dark, rain-laden clouds were preparing to empty themselves on the parched earth. With thunderous lightning strokes, it began.

At first, one drop was heard, then more and more. This was a hard-driving, large-drop rain, spilling torrents of run-off onto the desert's baked-clay floor. Soon, everything was wet, and the water kept coming. The party's garments were soon soaked through like the dirty rags they were, their dampness bringing out the body odor of the clothing's previous occupants. The ground surrounding the outpost was hardpan clay, and the water rolled off it as if it were raining on pavement. Very little percolated into the ground, and what did, did so very slowly and made everything muddy. Meanwhile, lightning and thunder blasts continued to tear apart the flashing sky.

After a while, the frightened camels knelt back down and trembled in the terrible storm. The sheep and goats took what shelter they could by crouching together beside a ruined wall outside the structure that blocked the fury of the storm.

The wind blew loudly, and the rain pelted everything. There was no roof to get under. The foursome just rolled up in their clothes and shivered under the lash of the rain and the cold, wet wind. Periodically, the lightning illuminated both earth and sky like a giant strobe light, flaring temporarily in the water-swollen sky, followed by huge blasts of thunder that brought the memory of the artillery barrage they had witnessed a few days before.

Near dawn, the furious rain let up and finally stopped. The thunder rolled off into the distance, and the sky began to clear. While the other humans were still sleeping after the terrible night, Mizzi was half-awake and becoming semi-delirious. There was nothing to replace her wet bandages with and infectious agents would surely soak into her wounds.

One of the camels was wandering around and nuzzled Youssef to get up, defecating among the humans as it did so. One steaming deposit plopped on the ground next to Colonel Washington, just missing his head and splashing nasty water onto his face. Startled from his sleep, the pilot opened his eyes just in time to see the camel's anus flex shut. Youssef had seen what happened and began to laugh. The commotion woke Young One, who wanted to know what was going on, and joined in the laughter when told. A moment later the offended colonel and even the pain-wracked Mizzi broke down too. It was the first light moment the four had shared since their adventure began.

The pilot got to his feet surprisingly quickly for an injured man. He felt his sore hip and winced in pain, but supporting himself on his crutch, he turned to the camels and barked an order to stand at attention. To his surprise, his commanding attitude and the unfamiliar English words brought the beasts to a state of alertness that seemed to simulate obedience, prolonging the hilarity and providing a welcome moment of analgesic relief to the injured Americans.

Sharing the bar of soap the doctor had given them, the group washed some of the oil and grime from their bodies and clothing, taking advantage of the larger puddles before they could evaporate or be absorbed into the ground. Young One found a hole big enough to permit him to take a shallow bath, discretely obstructed from Mizzi's line of sight.

His teeth chattered, as the rain water was chilly. He took the bandage from his forehead and let the wound get some sunshine upon it. Sunlight is good for healing. Lying in the water and looking up at the parting clouds, he could see the sun begin to shine through. The sun warmed his wet skin, and he dried off in the wind. It was the best he had felt in a long time, to be partly clean after being so thoroughly dirty.

He had little pimples all over his body from being plugged with oil residue. They itched much less now, but he knew enough not to scratch them. The colonel and Youssef also managed to wash themselves as best as they could in their own private puddles. Afterward, Young One and Youssef helped Mizzi to the clearest pool they could find and washed her face and hair clean of the oil. She managed a weary smile in response to their kindness. She was not doing well. They gave her the last of the antibiotics, but saved the last morphine shot until she had to travel again. Even the dog seemed happier with its stomach full of water, having found its own puddle in which to roll around and give itself an invigorating bath.

After the puddles began to dry up and soak into the earth, the ground became muddy and slippery to walk on, even for the animals. But that was also good, as no vehicles could drive up on them, as they had feared during the night, and their own tracks had now been completely washed away. If anyone was following them, they had lost them during the storm.

They rested all morning, trying to dry their wet clothing in the gradually warming sun. Youssef made a fire of desert sticks that were resin-rich and would burn even when wet. It was risky, but they needed the additional heat source and to cook some meat.

Toward the afternoon, Washington advised them that they must get going or Specialist Mizzi would die. They had no more antibiotics, and she was slipping fast. They could either go back to the Iraqis and turn themselves in, or continue ahead in hopes of running into coalition lines. Youssef knew that to the west, there were sand dunes where the camels could walk. The baked plain they had been on was now the consistency of moist modeling clay. It would make for rough walking for the camels. It would have been better to rest another day and allow the ground to dry out, but they had to get the injured to medical attention.

It was afternoon by the time they set out, but they immediately found themselves slogging through mud. Youssef had to stop often and scrape the thick snowshoe-like build-up from the hooves of the camels. The mud would make them go lame if it were left to stick. Each step was very heavy and could hurt their knee joints, analogous to a human wearing deep-sea diving boots on a forced march. Mizzi relapsed into delirium and shock as they progressed. The infection was finding its way into her blood stream.

After an hour and a half of walking and scraping hooves, they came upon a cobble-strewn plain. Beyond it were massive sand dunes disappearing into the horizon. The camels could get a better grip in the wet sand than in the plastic clay. But they stumbled frequently on the rough ground, much to the discomfort of the injured.

Scorpions sunning themselves atop some of the rocks turned their tails the dangerous way and acted menacingly as the little caravan passed. Scorpion stings are always worst after the rains that force them from their hiding places, when they are most active. It was late afternoon, and the sun was falling from the sky off to their right by the time the procession had traversed the rocky plain and moved into the dunes. The walking was now easier for the animals, but the humans soon became disoriented as they began winding their way through the labyrinth of shadow-dappled granular hills, with only the setting sun to guide them. Their spirits were sustained only by the hope that they were moving away from, and not closer to, further danger...

Chapter 40

THE BITTER END OF IT

The mud making the trails impassable, they moved among the sand dunes, and rounding one of them nearly collided with a light infantry vehicle. At the same moment, they heard the bolt of a machine gun slide into action and orders shouted in Arabic. Youssef and Young One instantly raised their hands, while the colonel and Mizzi remained slumped over their camels. As the Arab soldiers approached with upraised rifles, Youssef suddenly motioned to Young One with several sideward twists of his head. After taking a moment to decipher the signal, Young One lowered his arms and slowly removed the concealing headdress to show he was not a Bedouin. The Arab officer walked over to Washington and began questioning him in Arabic.

"I do not speak your language," Washington replied.

Then the officer looked him over and began speaking to him in broken English.

"What is your name?"

"Washington, John A. Colonel one-nine-two..."

"You are American!" the Arab interrupted, then added with a laugh. "We are not your enemy, Colonel Washington, so you needn't follow

Geneva Convention protocols. But please forgive my skepticism; you are clearly out of uniform and I must verify your identity." While his men stood watching with weapons at the ready, the officer walked back to the vehicle and reached for the radio.

A few minutes later, he returned. "My apologies, colonel, you are indeed who you say you are. I am Captain Ammon of the Egyptian Army. My scout unit has been assigned to screen for the main coalition assault forces. I must say that your countrymen seem most gratified to know of your whereabouts and are dispatching a medevac helicopter for you and your injured companions."

"Thank you, captain. Does this mean the ground assault has begun?"

"It started the day before yesterday, but the rains held us back in this sector until now. The ground is dry enough and the whole coalition is moving forward to destroy Saddam. Kuwait City has been retaken. I cannot tell you more for security reasons. I am sure you understand."

As the captain was talking, two of his men wrestled Youssef to the ground and began binding his hands behind his back.

The colonel said quickly, "Don't take him prisoner. He is a Bedouin boy who helped us escape from Saddam's troops. Allow him to return to his family."

He knew that revealing that Youssef had been a private in the Iraqi Army might seal his fate, and he hoped that the reference to his youth might suggest that he was harmless. Captain Ammon paused, then issued several commands, after which the soldiers continued to hold Youssef, though they handled him more gently. Other members of the detachment, meanwhile, helped the colonel and Nirada down from their camels.

"What are you going to do with these animals?" Washington asked, hoping that the Egyptians were well fed.

The foreign officer paused again. His unit had to keep up with the main assault force, and herding this bedraggled flock was out of the question.

"Go and take them with you," he said to Youssef, then ordered his men to give the young Arab a few full canteens of water and a small allotment of combat rations, some of which Youssef promptly tried to feed the hungry dog. Seeing the scrawny animal sniff at the morsels and then back away barking, all the Egyptians, including Captain Ammon, burst into laughter. "Even the dogs won't eat our wretched chow," said one soldier, and everyone seemed to relax a bit.

Colonel Washington called Youssef over to thank him and wished him a safe journey back to his people. Then he handed him the blood chit and told him it could help him if he were stopped by other coalition forces.

After bidding goodbye to Mizzi and Young One with a mixture of sadness and relief, the Bedouin boy rode off into the desert on the best camel, while leading the three other camels in a cargo-less caravan, with the dog trailing behind, barking commands at the herd animals.

He was unarmed and if stopped there was nothing on his person to suggest that he had been in the Iraqi Army. He was enjoying the prospect of being away from soldiers from whatever nation and, once reunited with his family, of adding these beasts to their family herd. By the standards of the local economy, they would allow him to live as a wealthy young man.

⋇⋇⋇

The Egyptians waited with the Americans until the helicopter landed, then helped the medics lift them aboard as Young One, Mizzi, and the colonel found themselves surrounded once more by the familiar uniforms of U.S. troops. Soon they were off in a cloud of dust, and as the air cleared, could look out through the chopper's open doors back at the empty desert they had traversed and ahead at the greatest convoy of military vehicles assembled since World War II, driving northward into Kuwait. Young One had never flown in a helicopter, and after all he'd been through, he found it a highly satisfactory form of travel that was allowing him to see history being made before his eyes.

All the vehicles that had previously clogged the roads were now headed into the action of Desert Storm in numbers beyond counting: tanks, armored vehicles, tanker trucks hauling fuel and water, personnel carriers transporting soldiers, and still more trucks full of food and ammunition. The land war had started with a spectacle that neither Young One nor anyone else who witnessed it would ever forget. And though he didn't know it, he was seeing only the tail end of the convoy. The vanguard was miles ahead, where the coalition forward forces had already breached the Iraqi berm and were pouring through the opening into Kuwait, moving inexorably toward victory.

After twenty minutes of flight, the medevac set down on a landing pad next to the hospital in the Emerald City. Young One had never seen such a place before. As the three Americans in Bedouin dress were unloaded and brought into the emergency room, onlookers buzzed in whispered speculation that they must be special ops troops who'd been inserted far behind enemy lines. Whatever the reason, they were treated like war heroes.

The colonel had been luckier than he'd thought. A thorough examination showed he'd suffered a dislocated hip, a cracked vertebra, and two crushed spinal discs in the crash, but had no damaged organs, and his head injury had only been a concussion. He would need time to heal, and he would soon get plenty of that in civilian life.

Young One spent a week in the Saudi Arabian hospital. For a day and a half, he slept under the influence of sedatives, then for the next thirty-six hours devoured several trays of food at each meal. After that, he was sick of hospital fare and ate sparingly. The doctors told him that unless he had plastic surgery back in the states, he would always have a deep, noticeable scar on his forehead, and that his leg burns would qualify him for VA benefits.

His time in the hospital was divided between sleeping, debriefing, giving statements to military police, watching appropriate Arabic-dubbed American and European shows, and seeing the reaction to the coalition *blitzkrieg* by the Middle Eastern news media. Though he couldn't speak the language, he could mostly grasp what was going on, and it was clear that the recent military action was making a powerful impression in a part of the world where power was respected above all else.

Due to the extraordinary circumstances of his arrival, everyone suspected that he was some sort of spy. They started to take the Bedouin clothes away to burn them, but he asked that that they be cleaned and returned to him as a souvenir. Normally such a request would have been denied, but the top of the chain of command rattled down the links and he got everything he wanted.

The main thing he wanted was to tell his grandfather that he was alive and well. He got his wish. On the day he placed the call, his people gathered around the trading-post telephone back in New Mexico to hear what had happened to their native son. This time he spoke only in English while his cousin translated for Grandfather at the other end.

In as much detail as time allowed, he proudly related that he was in a Saudi hospital after having been captured by the Iraqis and escaping, that he'd help save an Outsider colonel and a woman soldier, and was to receive the Purple Heart for being wounded, and the Silver Star medal for bravery in combat. He then spoke directly to his grandfather in their Pueblo tongue. Grandfather told him he'd had another dream about him: He would ride into their village a great hero to his people, he would have many children to honor his memory, and he'd be hailed as a protector of the Pueblo people.

><--><--><

Because Colonel Washington had been admitted to an officer's wing of the hospital, Young One needed official permission to visit him. Each time, his request was denied, with the explanation that the colonel was resting after his ordeal. The truth was that he was being kept pretty "doped-up" with painkillers to allow his injuries to heal without further aggravating them with movement.

As soon as Washington had sufficiently rested, he was vigorously debriefed. Assorted military and civilian interrogators interviewed him and the other escapees again and again, to make sure their individual accounts lined up. Finally everyone seemed satisfied that no serious breach of military security had occurred. Still, the top of the flagpole did not want the media to know anything about the incident. They wanted it kept quiet.

><--><--><

While the three recuperated, the ground war raged. Kuwait City was restored to civilization, and Saddam's best infantry and armored units were badly beaten, but not obliterated. He continued holding power and lying to his people about the triumphs over the armies of the West, and none of his opponents were ever entirely sure when the first Gulf War ended. It just stopped without fanfare. The ground assault went flawlessly, and in less than a hundred clock hours, Saddam was beaten and his military capability severely curtailed, but not enough to prevent him from fighting another day.

After four days, a Saudi orderly informed Young One that the colonel was well enough to speak to him, and escorted him to the officer's side of the hospital. Washington was glad to see him and thanked him for saving his life. In the days that followed, Young One was allowed to visit him as much as he liked, and on each trip, he noticed that most of the beds in the hospital were empty. It had been a war where the spin-doctors had done more operating on the media than the surgeons had done on wound victims. Young One was glad to learn that coalition casualties had been fairly light, and that Saddam's infamous weapons of mass destruction, if they existed, had apparently not been deployed.

>|—>|<—>|<

The day after being admitted to the hospital, Mizzi awoke to find herself handcuffed to the bed and told she was under arrest for going AWOL. Thereafter, between medical treatments, she was grilled by military-intelligence specialists on the tiniest details of her version of what had happened during the escape and evasion. But for her, the determination that no military secrets had been compromised brought no relief from her ordeal at the hands of "military justice." Soon after discharge from the hospital she was rolled in a wheel chair before an Army Board of Inquiry, facing possible court martial proceedings.

Young One and Washington were called to appear and testified to her bravery, toughness, and dedication to duty, and inwardly, every officer on the board admired the daring young woman who had risked all on an ill-fated joy ride that in her own testimony she described as having been motivated by a desire to make a statement about female equality. But the fact was that she'd abandoned her post in time of war and had belonged somewhere else, performing the military task she had been assigned. In short, she'd committed a court martial offense that in earlier days would have meant summary execution for a man and for her could mean a long stint in a federal prison for females.

In the end, however, recognizing the public relations disaster that would ensue by letting her become a poster child for the army's treatment of women in combat, the board reached a decision so swiftly that Nirada was still in her wheelchair, "sitting at attention," while a stern-faced female lieutenant colonel announced her fate: She had been charged with absence without official leave, dereliction of duty, and "failure to repair." But in light of her help with the rescue of an important, high-ranking officer, and other special circumstances, all charges would be dropped, provided she never divulged information about any aspect of the entire affair, which they said had been classified. Should she reveal such information to anyone, in or out of the service, she would be recalled to active duty and recharged with the crimes.

She was further informed that her medical records would be amended to reflect a motor pool accident in which she had been burned, so she could receive VA benefits. Finally, she was told that although she could remain in the Reserve, if she planned to make a career of the service, she was advised to reconsider. This incident would secretly follow her for the rest of her military life.

When her nightmare finally ended with a curt, "Dismissed, specialist!"

Mizzi saluted, waited for it to be returned, and did an about face in her wheel chair, wishing only to leave the horrors of war and military politics far behind and get back to her husband and family. She was free to go, and over the next few weeks she was pleased to find the system actually cooperated to expedite her departure.

She finished off her obligation with the army and never looked back, moving on with one part of her being broken and shattered and the other part seasoned and toughened by reality. Back home, she confided the details of her adventure only to her mother and husband, who swore themselves to secrecy. The rest of her family never knew exactly what had happened, other than she'd gotten herself into some deep trouble "over there" that no one talked about.

More than ever before, she wanted to help others as she had been helped, but for years she bore the bitter thorns of disappointment at the core of her being: She had been there, but had been denied her due. On the other hand, she had escaped the iron grasp of military law and had acquired a whole new way of looking at life. She was a survivor in the real game. She got her dream of finishing nursing school.

>―――×――>―<

After his honorable discharge, the colonel never flew a helicopter again. In truth, he had been forced to retire for his "free flight" in the chopper. He, too, could have faced court martial for serious military offences, but in consideration of his previously exemplary record, and with an eye on the political fallout that might accompany bringing charges against such a highly decorated minority senior officer, the brass gave him a "gentleman's out" and made him a civilian for the first time in twenty-seven years.

Madjack Washington never dreamed his career would end with the army quietly ushering him out the side door, expelled into civilian society without even a retirement party. In later years any sense of having been a "real" colonel came to him just once a month, when he marched to the mailbox for his pension check. It hurt to go out like that, and in his one overt gesture of resentment, he refused to use the appellation of colonel by which he was entitled to be addressed. He blocked bitter thoughts from his mind as best as he could and tried to remember that at least he'd lived to retire—something many with whom he'd served hadn't been lucky enough to do.

Young One was reassigned to light duty and went home with his unit. As Grandfather had foretold, he received a hero's welcome. He remained in the Reserve and made staff sergeant and still had time to spend in the herd camps with his grandfather. Over the years he heard nothing about Youssef, but he thought of him often, hoping he had found his family. He periodically wrote to Nirada and Washington. The war was over for all of them, yet it lingered in the backs of their minds, ready to spring forward when triggered by the sight and smell of a cloud of smoke or the whup-whup of a distant helicopter. Everyone went his or her own separate way, to walk the steps along the paths of their individual lives. But in their quiet moments when they sat in peace, they often wondered what had happened to each other...

THE END

ABOUT THE AUTHOR

Jerome (Jake) Joyce, Ph.D., is a former Green Beret sergeant. He is also an honorably retired commissioned officer from the U.S. Public Health Service with the rank of commander. He currently resides in Kansas City with his wife, Wendy. *Different Deserts, Same Stars* is his first novel.

www.ingramcontent.com/pod-product-compliance
Lightning Source LLC
Chambersburg PA
CBHW052347020726
47503CB00001B/149